The Last Roman

Book One in the Ongoing
Praetorian **Series**

Edward Crichton

Copyright 2012

This book is licensed for your enjoyment only and is not to be shared, reproduced, resold, or altered in any way. The author thanks you for respecting his intellectual property.

Acknowledgments

This novel is dedicated to those who helped make it what it is today; Alex, Amanda, Anita, George, & Taras. In particular, I would like to thank my wife, Michelle, whose devotion to making my story the best it could be ensured my characters became real people. Thanks, love.

Books by Edward Crichton

The Praetorian Series
The Last Roman (Book I)
To Crown a Caesar (Book II)
A Hunter and His Legion (Book III)

Starfarer
Rendezvous with Destiny

Table of Contents

Prologue
I – Hunter
II – Praetorians
III – Preparation
IV – War
V – Rome
VI – Caligula
VII – Claudius
VIII – Betrayal
IX – Legion
X – Agrippina
XI – Siege
XII – Endgame
Epilogue
Coming Soon
About the Author

Prologue

Rome, Italy
September, 37 A.D.

    All who traverse the streets of Rome by night should tread with great care, for criminals of many ilk prowl the city's narrow thoroughfares and dwell within its tenebrous alleyways during those nocturnal hours. The eternal city is home to many who would beg or thieve for their daily allowances, but there are also individuals far worse than mere vagabonds and bandits hoping for prey to stumble into their shadowy realm. Yet, despite the warnings known to all but the most dimwitted of Rome's residents, these thoughts were far from the mind of young Marcus Varus, because all he could focus on was how brazenly stupid the learned men of Rome actually were.

    It was *this* thought that dominated his mind as he approached the Palatine Hill and the great Temple of Lupercal located beneath. Now the home of the Caesars, legend told that this unassuming mound of earth was where the divine founders, Romulus and Remus, were raised by their adoptive she-wolf nearly eight hundred years ago. It was the place of Lupercalia, one of Rome's most sacred rituals, and where Varus had come to lay down his life in its defense be it needed.

Where are they? This is where the manuscript said to go.

    Varus, old at the age of twenty eight, was a scribe of the highest caliber. He was the personal documentarian, historian, linguist, and advisor to the Caesar himself, Caligula; but most importantly, he was proud that Caligula also considered him a friend. As he entered the temple, however, Varus began to resent their friendship, as his most recent assignment to research a point of interest for the Caesar had led him to the precarious position in which he now found himself.

    Documents of a very strange origin had been discovered deep beneath the Palatine Hill, buried in a hidden chamber that was found during Caligula's most recent renovation project of the *Domus Augusti*. They were wrapped around a perfectly round orb the size of a melon and were composed in a shaky hand, as though transcribed moments before death's cold grip seized hold of the author. They were written in an antiquated dialect of Etruscan, a civilization that had once resided north of Rome centuries ago.

When news of the discovery had reached the *Curia Julia*, ambitious senators had immediately sent word for both the object and the documents to be brought to the Senate building for inspection. But Varus had been overseeing the renovation project during the initial discovery, and was the first man to analyze both. In the short time he'd had with them, he'd held the sphere and attempted to translate the documents for himself, but it wasn't long before the Senate's sycophants forced them from his possession.

Varus later learned that their linguists had transcribed a message that spoke of a treasure Remus had hidden away beneath the Palatine upon hearing of his brother's treacherous plan to execute him. Riches were expected that far exceeded anything Rome currently held in its coffers, effectively guaranteeing its fiscal stability for decades to come. The Senate had dispatched its lackeys to secure this treasure immediately, a plan that would help fund a private coup against the great leader of Rome, a plot Varus had suspected for months but had only just now confirmed.

But the Senate had been wrong. Horribly wrong.

Upon learning of this treachery from Varus, Caligula had sent him to reanalyze the documents and discover their true contents. What he had found hidden in the nearly dead Etruscan language was a message that told of something far more powerful than a simple cache of lost treasure. Where the Senate had read of a treasure in the form of gold, silver, and gems, its true potential was something entirely different.

It hinted at Remus' association with the Druids who, while currently simple priests, were once rumored to have possessed great power and mystical abilities. Although any magic they may have wielded in the past was long considered extinct and forgotten, the fact remained that those lost powers were still feared by many. If they could indeed summon aid from realms unknown to Rome's wisest leaders, the empire's very survival could be in question. Varus only hoped he was in time to stop the traitors from unleashing whatever untold evils the document hinted at.

Finally, with the short run from the *Curia Julia* completed, Varus entered the temple, bowing in reverence to the sacred tombs ensconced on either side of the small dome, the final resting places of both Romulus and Remus. Early each calendar year, all of Rome would gather outside the small temple to participate in the rituals of Lupercalia, an event meant to promote fertility for young men and women. He thought back to his teenage years, running around the walls of Rome, whipping young girls with bloody goat skins, full of energy and vigor with nothing in front of him but the future.

Varus felt sad that all that was left of those innocent days were distant and fading memories, but forced himself to focus on his duty.

Creeping forward as quietly as he could, Varus found a small hole dug in the center of the magnificent structure's marbled floor. Grabbing hold of a rope, he slowly descended several meters into the dark abyss before making contact with the floor. He then followed a narrow tunnel before emerging onto a slight ledge overlooking a vast chamber. It was large enough to contain the entire senate floor and Varus marveled at how it had remained undiscovered for so long.

Then he discovered the object of his quest.

Six men stood around two others, all of whom were facing a lone object at the far end of the chamber, their faces glistening in the dim flicker of their torches. It was too dark for Varus to identify any of them, but two wore togas with a broad, purple hem running along the seams, likely identifying them as augurs, Rome's priests and seers. Their skills at interpreting and analyzing omens made them crucial for directing the future, and decisions were never made unless these omens were read favorably. Varus had never put much stock in their mystical abilities, instead trusting hard work and determination to drive his own fate.

As Varus crept through the shadows, he noticed that the rushed dig project had resulted in weak bracings holding back the tons of dirt above the freshly dug tunnel. His eyes were panning the walls and ceiling, looking for any way to bring down the hill and crush his adversaries, when the two augurs approached the simply adorned and seemingly harmless altar at the back of the room. They were carrying the orb-like object that had been found with the documents – which now exuded a dim greenish-blue glow.

Those below knew little about the object, except that it was adorned with incomprehensible markings, but Varus knew better. His translation associating Remus with the Druids convinced him that the object was the key to unlocking whatever evil secrets the document described.

Sorcery... Nonsense! If the Druids could utilize such powerful magic, how is it that they no longer possess such power?

It was with this thought that Varus realized the Druids' destruction perhaps had less to do with the overpowering might of the Roman war machine, and more with their own tampering in such dark realms.

By the time Varus found a cross beam he was certain would collapse the makeshift cavern, the object's glow suddenly flared into a brilliant blue. His eyes turned toward the incandescent glow, and he found himself unable to turn away from the alluringly beautiful object, for he had never before witnessed such a glorious sight.

How could something so beautiful be used for such evils?

As Varus stood there deep in thought, a magnificent blast of light and sound emanated from the object as it shone brighter than the sun itself, accompanied by a sound louder than the battle cry of a thousand legions. The force of the eruption was enough to knock Varus back against the wall and he knew he was too late.

When his vision cleared, he realized he was right. Emerging from the mist left over from the explosion were gigantic figures, rivals to the Titans of legend. He knew his last moments were upon him as he gazed upon the monsters, and when he closed his eyes, waiting calmly for his journey to Elysium, his last thoughts were of Caligula, and how he had failed him.

Part One

I
Hunter

C-130J Super Hercules(II), Over the Mediterranean Sea
July, 2021 AD

    C-130J Super Hercules(II) aircraft have often been lauded as the smoothest ride in the sky. First deployed only a year ago, the Super Hercules(II) was the most advanced military aircraft on the planet, and after only a few months of active service, were practically considered luxury liners by those who flew in them.
    Unfortunately, the hurricane type conditions currently surrounding my particular C-130J didn't care what people thought of them, and proceeded to toss and bounce my plane around like any other aircraft. Even prior to the storm, the ride was no smoother than my first HALO combat drop out of an old C-130 over Palestine three years ago, or the countless times since. I'd long ago concluded that people who named these things really should fly in one every once in a while.
    Perspective was a wonderful thing, after all.
    I smirked at my wayward musings; my constant companions for years. They'd become a relentless presence in my life, a simple way to pass the time when nerves became most acute. While five years in the US Navy, the last three of which I'd spent as an elite Navy SEAL, had extinguished any ability I may have once had to feel fear over something as mundane as a flight through a thunderstorm, that didn't mean I was completely steadfast. I could feel nervous before a mission and even anxious during them, but I was never totally afraid. Fear can compromise an operator's initiative or lock him up in the heat of battle, and that can get people killed. The one thing that always hits a nerve, however, was the loss of control, like the fact that I knew I couldn't do anything if something happened to the aircraft. I didn't possess the skill set required to help, and that made me feel helpless, hence the wandering thoughts.
    Being in control has always been important to me, ever since I was a kid, which is what brought me on this trip in the first place. I was a fourth generation Navy man, following in the illustrious footsteps of men who had served in Desert Storm, Vietnam, Korea,

World War II, and World War I. But my career hadn't started as early as it could have. Annapolis had accepted my enrollment straight out of high school, but I'd turned them down. Instead, much to my father's intense disapproval, I chose to attend Dartmouth to pursue a life studying history and the classics. I'd never seen him more disappointed, and it wasn't until after I'd graduated that I had finally redeemed my honor in his eyes by joining the Navy. That was five years ago.

I was his favored son once again.

Until today.

After turning down the appointment to Annapolis, I'd once wondered if my father would disown me. He hadn't, but after the events of a few hours ago, I wasn't so sure he wouldn't now. To him, boarding this C-130J Super Hercules(II) aircraft was paramount to high treason.

I rubbed my eyes to cleanse the contentious thoughts from my mind. There was no sense in continuing to go over them in my head now. My decision was made and the plane wouldn't turn around anyway.

I leaned my head back and closed my eyes.

We would be in Rome soon.

***

"Commander Hunter? Do you copy?"

My eyes snapped open, but it took me a moment to realize who was actually being addressed through my earphones. I must have dozed off.

"Yes, Captain," I replied, addressing the aircraft's skipper. "I read you Lima Charlie."

"Good. We'll be reaching your drop off point soon. Keep yourself strapped in until we reach it. Turbulence is expected to continue."

"Copy. Wake me when we get there."

"Yes, sir," finished the Captain, clicking off the intercom.

Newly promoted to the rank of lieutenant commander, I couldn't help but smile, still not comfortable being addressed as "sir" by a captain. Navy captains were two ranks higher than lieutenant commanders, but Army captains were about the equivalent rank of a Navy lieutenant, which I had just been promoted *from* earlier today. I was barely used to hearing the formality from the men under my own command, let alone half the military.

It didn't matter. I wagered that when I joined my new unit, it would be back to "yes, sir" this, and "no, sir" that. I suppose I couldn't complain too much. Leading men into combat was always more stressful than being responsible only for yourself and the enemy in your gun sights.

***

Forty minutes later, the captain came over the radio again. "Sir, we're minutes from drop off. I suggest you get ready."

"Thank you, Captain. And thanks for the ride."

"No problem, sir. Good luck."

"Yeah right," I mumbled.

Stick jockeys always acted like they had brass balls, but I knew the only time they'd actually grow a pair and jump out of their own aircraft was when it was shot up, on fire, and dropping out of the sky like a flightless bird. And even then I questioned if they would. Jumping out of airplanes in the middle of the night during a bad storm was generally reserved for the certifiable. And people like me, of course.

The entire trip would have been far easier had I been allowed to land with the plane and walk off the ramp onto solid ground, but not today. America may have possessed military bases on the Italian peninsula that I could have used, but my trip required slightly more discretion than even your regular black op. My plane would remain on its scheduled route, but not before taking a slight detour toward my drop point.

I heard a sudden whirring noise, and looked to the rear of the plane, noticing the rear door begin to open, revealing a gaping maw into the dark void beyond.

I tried to repress the chill I felt trickling down my spine.

Getting to my feet, part of my parachute reassuringly bumping against my ass, I made my way to another member of the crew standing near a light mounted on the hull. It was currently illuminated in red, but when it turned green, I would jump.

High Altitude Low Opening jumps were nothing new. The first were performed by the Air Force way back in the sixties, but that didn't mean they were easy. Currently, we were traveling near our maximum altitude of around forty thousand feet. As a result, I had to carry my own oxygen supply with me on the way down. In fact, I had been sucking on a tank of one hundred percent pure oxygen for the past half hour to help ready my circulatory system for the quick transition to the surface.

Moving to the end of the craft, I bumped my head on the ceiling. Glaring at the low hull, I swore about my height for the millionth time since joining the military. I was just shy of six and a half feet, which left me feeling cramped in practically any aircraft and pretty much ensured I'd never be a fighter pilot.

I was still rubbing my head when I made it to the crewman at the tail of the plane who attached a carabineer to my belt, securing my small go-bag on a rope so that it wouldn't get in the way. He patted me on the shoulder and threw me an okay sign with his hand, indicating all was ready on his end. I returned the gesture with a thumbs up, and pulled on my helmet, brushing brown hair out of my eyes. Always the rebel, even as an officer, I kept my hair slightly longer than military regulations permitted.

I shifted my oxygen mask for a more comfortable fit and slid my helmet's visor into place, blinking a few times when a digital readout projected itself on its interior. The heads up display was just one of the fancy new Future Force Warriors items slowly being redeployed by the U.S. military. My HUD displayed numerous mission critical details in bright, blue lettering scattered around every inch of the display. It boasted items such as a clock, compass, altimeter, barometer, targeting information, GPS, and night vision capabilities. Satisfied each of its functions were working properly, I bent my legs and waited for the light.

It wasn't long before it turned green and the crewman shouted, "Go! Go!"

I leapt into the abyss.

Free falling, I quickly picked up speed. I let myself fall in a dive for a while before I allowed my arms and legs to spread out wide in a position that would allow my body to generate enough resistance against the wind to slow me down. I glanced at the upper right hand corner of my visor which displayed my altimeter. I watched as the meters quickly ticked away toward zero, waiting for it to indicate when I was low enough to open my chute, but still high enough to not end up as a red stain on the ground. Content I had plenty of time to burn, I tried to relax and allow myself the pleasure of enjoying the view. High enough to almost see the curve of the Earth, I used my time to watch as dawn slowly crept from the East toward the inhabitants below and the storm we had just passed through tried to meet it from the West.

It was moments like these when I really loved my job.

I couldn't let myself get too distracted sightseeing, however. I was already losing sight of the Mediterranean as my descent took me directly over land, alerting me that it was time to start paying attention to my altimeter. I would still have to wait until I was low enough to spot an infrared beacon before I could accurately locate my exact destination, somewhere north of Rome.

After a few more minutes of free fall, I pulled my chute open, bracing myself as I was jerked in my harness. As the parachute opened, I reached for the toggles dangling near my head, and it wasn't long before I was in complete control and safely making my way to the ground.

Activating my HUD's night vision, I glanced around in search of the beacon. Under normal eyesight, infrared was effectively invisible, but night vision had no trouble picking up the pulsating strobe that flashed brightly in the infrared spectrum. I spotted it with little trouble, about a mile to my left, and slowly began my turn and descent toward it.

Nearly dirt side, I relaxed my knees and exhaled before I hit the surface. Rolling twice, I came to a stop and punched down my billowing parachute before it could lift me back in the air. Securing the cord and fabric back in its pack, I took a moment to compose myself.

I shook my head to loosen my helmet's grip and leaned over to grab my go-bag which rested next to my feet. The small single shoulder-hoisted rucksack held only a few soldierly essentials: my American military ID, a small multi-tool, survival kit, SureFire flashlight, SIG Sauer P220 semi-automatic pistol with two extra magazines, digital camera, a roll of duct tape, toiletries, and an extra pair of socks. The rest of my gear and possessions had been shipped to my destination earlier to ensure I would be ready for duty as soon as possible.

Turning around, I spotted a compact black car parked next to a dirt road that snaked off into the mountains. Standing next to it was a robed man and a full bird American Army colonel.

My attaché to Rome, I presumed.

Reaching the car, I stopped and saluted crisply, "Lieutenant Commander Jacob Hunter reporting as ordered, Colonel."

"At ease," the man said, lazily returning my salute. "My name is Colonel Reynolds. I will be your liaison with the Vatican until you have formally transferred to your new unit. When that time comes, you'll be on your own."

I nodded. "Understood, Colonel. I was briefed by the President before I left Washington."

Reynolds returned the gesture. He knew as well as I did how unique our situation was; one that had required the highest clearance level available, and had also been overseen directly by the Commander in Chief. A request from the Pope was not to be taken lightly these days. He carried tremendous influence and political clout, and considering the current geopolitical situation, his title was just as influential as it had once been centuries ago.

***

As I stood before the two unfamiliar men, I couldn't help but think of my father again. He was about as much of a stranger now as they were. But even so, I found my mind wandering back to Thanksgiving Day five years ago. With massive amounts of turkey, potatoes, stuffing, and gravy consumed, my dad, grandfather, and I were sitting around the TV while my mother and sister finished cleaning up the mess. Grandpa had already passed out in a turkey-induced coma while my dad and I watched yet another Thanksgiving football game.

Halfway through the third quarter, a breaking news report interrupted the game to reveal that Russia had sent troops into Georgia. The grainy footage revealed civilians massacred as they tried to resist, and we sat there completely stunned for a long while. The scene was an extension of the events that had transpired during the 2008 Beijing Olympics and an escalation of what happened in the Ukraine not all that long ago.

"I told you," my dad whispered finally.

"I know you did," I replied just as quietly, my attention focused on the report.

Everyone had known it was only a matter of time, even if my then young and idealistic self didn't want to admit it. Russia had been getting stronger for years under its overzealous leaders, and that Thanksgiving set into motion a chain of events that would later lead to another world war. And my dad had been right.

"That's where you need to be, son," my father continued in a low voice. "You need to be there to stop them."

I remember rolling my eyes, like I always did when he brought up the fact I had chosen to forgo military service. It was all he ever talked about.

"It's too late now," I replied.

"It's never too late!" He shouted back, slamming his fists on his cushy chair's armrests. His sudden outburst caused my sister to come in from the kitchen to see what the problem was, but once she realized we were even just speaking to each other, she quickly fled the scene.

"It doesn't even matter," I muttered. "We're too weak to go to war. All we can do is sit on our asses and defend ourselves."

It was true. The government had been cutting back funding for the military at a precipitous rate for years by that point. By the time I finally joined the military, most of the equipment employed was based off technology from as far back as the early 2000s. The gear was new, but of old design. Funds for America's air supremacy program were halved, Navy equipment was decommissioned, and America's Future Force Warrior program – for grunts and Special Forces units – was practically abandoned, which was exactly why the only piece of fancy new gear I currently had was the flight helmet I had worn during my HALO jump. I was forced to leave the rest of my toys that had trickled into my unit over the years with the Navy, and Reynolds would probably take back my helmet as well. Innovation in the realm of warfare had basically come to a standstill. Many were worried that it put America's military superiority at risk, and if you asked me, it had. But the critics had argued that things had settled down; that we no longer needed such expenses. It hadn't been until 2020, with war raging around the world, when funds were finally reallocated to the military and we started receiving new gear.

With the military underfunded, underpopulated, and sitting on their asses stateside, the country hadn't been prepared for what was about to come. Neither was the rest of the world for that matter, and it wasn't long before Russia began gobbling up lost territory, some nations coming willingly, others through military force, and it was years before America intervened.

Just as the news report came to an end, with an uneasy silence lingering in the room after my last statement, my father slowly got to his feet and made for the kitchen. Just before he left, he paused by the door and placed his hand on my shoulder.

"It's never too late, Jacob," my father repeated. "It's your responsibility to protect those unable to protect themselves. It's in your blood."

And with that, he left to tell my mom and sister what had happened. I remember sinking deep into my favorite chair, my chin resting on my fist as the guilt started to sink in. It was the beginning of the end for my civilian life, just as the European bloodbath of that Thanksgiving was the catalyst for the beginning of the end of everything else.

Months later, as the guilt had finally destroyed my pride and I applied for Officer Candidate School, Iran came through on a promise it had made decades earlier: to wipe Israel off the map, which they attempted to do with a deadly biological attack on Jerusalem and other neighboring cities. Millions were killed. Willing to sacrifice Muslim lives despite years of funding Palestinian efforts against Israel, Iran decided it was time to establish Islamic independence in the region by destroying the Jewish state. As have many wars over the ages, it started over religion, but soon it escalated into a political debacle the likes of which the world had never seen.

Because of America's connection with Israel, the U.S. military intervened on their behalf. At least we did our best. War between the U.S. and Iran had been brewing for years, but with the war in Iraq wrapped up, America wasn't prepared logistically for another major offensive in the region. Slowly and reluctantly, U.S. forces trickled into Iraq once again in preparation for a ground assault into Iran.

But everything began to unravel when it was discovered that Iran had been funded and supervised by Russian militants the Kremlin claimed they knew nothing about. They claimed it had been yet another splinter cell that remained from the dregs of what was left of old Soviet patriots. Although the public was still unsure of the truth, the net result was the ignition of yet another Cold War, worse than ever before. With Russia and Iran formally allied against the West, it was only a matter of time before the stakes escalated.

All of this had happened sometime before the later portion of my SEAL training, when I was stuck in Survival, Evasion, Resistance, and Escape – SERE. Most of my fellow trainees and I had bitched about the fact that the world wasn't quite crazy enough for us. We hadn't thought anything of Russia or Iran's newfound aggression. No one expected the two countries to become the threats they eventually became, and nobody had anticipated what was about to happen next.

We'd quickly come to regret our flippant words.

***

I pinched my nose again, reminding myself that the past was exactly that. I had to focus on where I was now and what I was doing. Nothing else mattered. I returned my attention to Reynolds, who nodded.

"Very good," he said before gesturing to the other man. "This is Father Vincent. He will take us to Rome and will escort you personally once we reach the Vatican."

I shook the priest's hand. His face was shaped like a pear, with a square jaw, strong features, and the weathered look of a man who had spent too much time in the sun, but not without a hint of handsomeness.

Combined with his age, I would describe him as "grizzled."

"A pleasure to meet you, Father," I greeted.

"And I you, young man. His Holiness will be most happy to meet you."

"I'm looking forward to it. It's not every day that you get the opportunity to meet the Pope, let alone work for him."

Opening the driver's side door, Father Vincent replied, "These are dark days, my son. Enjoy your opportunity while you can, but remember, there is work to do."

"I understand, Father."

With his ominous tone floating through my mind, I took a seat in the back of the car, closed my eyes, and couldn't help but allow my mind to reminisce about just how stupid we had been back in SERE.

***

Participating in SERE, completely cut off from the world and getting my ass handed to me by my trainers – or, I should say, my captors – the world reached the point of no return. When the Pope was targeted next, by the same extremists who were involved in the massacre of Jerusalem, the entire world erupted in conflict.

Early one Sunday morning, as faithful Catholics gathered in St. Peter's Square to hear Mass from the Pope, suicide bombers disguised as worshipers detonated charges strapped to their chests. Non-explosive in nature, these bombs emitted an invisible and odorless gas overwhelming everyone before they even knew what had happened.

It was hardly surprising that the Pope's elite Swiss Guard had been able to eliminate the targets and move him inside to safety, but despite their best efforts, only a few worshipers in attendance made it inside as well. Perhaps by an act of God, the strong winds which usually swept through the region were unusually calm that day, containing the gas to the area around the Vatican, so few of Rome's other inhabitants were effected.

Equipped with state of the art technology cleverly concealed by its classic façade, the Vatican was quickly sealed off, and all those inside were safe.

Those outside were not.

Any consideration that the Vatican would be the next target had escaped every western intelligence agency's radar. Iran's rhetoric had never indicated such a move was on the table. Lacking long range missiles and the ability to penetrate America's very competent domestic security agencies, staging a bold attack on the Vatican had served as the most grievous of statements. The West was on notice.

Thousands of Catholics were violently murdered, and with a mass of decaying corpses littering St. Peter's Square, a call to action was demanded.

In an age where secularism was at the height of its popularity, and church attendance across faith based institutions at an all-time low, many wondered what kind of reaction, if any, would come about from the horrific attack. No one had any idea that almost overnight, sects of Christianity, from Anglicans to Charismatics, and many forms of Protestantism in between, were in support of their Catholic brothers and sisters. The situation did not progress as far as uniting all Christians under a single religious banner – as it would be a cold day in Hell, ironically enough, before that happened – but the Pope began influencing the decisions of many individuals again, not just Roman Catholics.

Compounding matters was that Russia's involvement was no longer in question. The West could do little more than watch as Russia infringed on its eastern neighbors' sovereignty, resulting in an outbreak of hostilities in Eastern Europe and the Balkans between Russia and member nations of the European Union. After four years, places like Poland, Hungary, Slovakia, Romania, and Macedonia were war zones. Their cities were devastated and destroyed, and were littered with dug out trench systems reminiscent of those used in World War I, ones that never seemed to shift or move, only run deeper with blood.

Things continued to get worse in other parts of the world as well.

The conflict simmering for decades between Pakistan and India finally boiled over. The large populations of Muslims and Christians in both nations only fueled the fire, turning neighbors upon one another in a multitude of bloody conflicts. It became a trend the world over. Wars flared up all over the world, neighbors finally finding the excuses they needed to pick up arms against one another, and most didn't even need religion to justify their action.

By the end of the decade, the Americas became yet another victim. North America's southern border with Mexico became a war zone when Mexico was overrun by guerilla forces led by communists and warlords who had been slowly building their armies for years, mostly thanks to Russian benefactors. Russia had finally succeeded where the Germans had failed during WWI by opening up a second front against The United States of America. As a result, Canadian and American forces were posted all along the expansive border, constantly engaging in skirmishes and pitched battles.

North Korea crossed the thirty eighth parallel quite early in the conflict and invaded South Korea. With the bulk of American forces tied up all over the world, there was little the troops garrisoned behind the demilitarized zone could do. North Korean tank divisions rolled south with little impediment to their progress and their Navy blockaded the peninsula. For the past five years, South Korea steadfastly held the southern tip of the small nation, guarding against both the land and sea invasions that were sure to come.

Their fate looked grim.

And then there was Africa. Their part in the conflict was, for once, not to fight exclusively among themselves, but to somehow put aside most of their differences and wage war against anyone who got in their way. African warlords had cut a swath across the entire continent, fighting each other and together in equal parts. It hadn't been long before isolated coalitions had moved north toward Europe and East toward Saudi Arabia. The entire southern coast of Europe was on high alert and Spain was under constant threat, a situation which had the potential to become a horrible mess.

The one factor missing from the global war was the use of nuclear weapons. It was interesting how the threat of nukes had always had the citizens of the world on edge, always wondering if the end was just around the corner. Everybody knew that it would take only a small percentage of even one nation's nuclear supply to bring about the end the world. Yet, nukes had been a nonfactor since the beginning of World War III, not once being employed on the battlefield.

The world's unofficial "no-nukes" policy was hardly surprising, at least to me. Every finger poised over nuclear launch buttons around the world knew that as soon as they allowed gravity to overcome the strength of their fingers, every other button of mass destruction would likewise be depressed. No one wanted to be responsible for wiping mankind off the face of the planet. Even so, life was just as tense as it was in the 1950's, and sooner or later, someone was bound to get antsy and initiate a chain reaction that would lead to nothing short of the end of time.

As far as I was concerned, total destruction was inevitable.

***

    My two companions were dourly silent as we drove through the lush Italian countryside, so I had little to do besides look off into the distance and admire the view as my mind roiled with thoughts of our broken world. The land here was so rich with history that every hill had a story and every road a tale to tell. I'd been studying Italian and Roman history ever since my mom had made me take Latin back in high school, so I knew many of those stories.

    I'd enjoyed the subject so much that I'd continued my studies during college and had even begun work on a Master's Degree in Classical Studies before being pulled into the Navy. I was never sure why I'd grown so passionate about the subject, and had never really sat down to determine what kind of career I'd make out of it. It had been a serious point of contention in my family, especially since my darling sister had had her future perfectly mapped out since middle school.

    By the time we reached the outskirts of Rome, I retrieved my camera from my bag and started taking pictures of whatever caught my eye. A semester of photography in college and years of field recon ops gave me a solid eye for picking out ideal shots. Most of Rome was left unscathed by the countless battles that plagued Eastern Europe, but it had still caught some flak over the years and a few burnt buildings scattered at random reflected the sad reality of the age we lived in.

    It wasn't long before Reynolds noticed my interest.

    "Sightseeing, Lieutenant Commander?"

    "Yes sir," I answered immediately. "I've always wanted to visit Rome. I only wish it was under different circumstances."

    Reynolds nodded but said nothing, and the car continued to roll through the sprawling ancient city, driving slowly through the narrow, cobbled streets of both modern and old form. I was busy photographing the remains of the *Circus Maximus* when Father Vincent abruptly pulled into a seemingly random building. A few meters inside, the floor began to slope drastically downward, plunging us into darkness.

    "Where exactly are we going?" I asked suspiciously.

"You are a student of history," Father Vincent replied, his eyes locked on the dimly illuminated road. "What lies beneath most cities the age of Rome?"

I knew that over time, cities as old as Rome simply built over existing parts of the original city. When new buildings were constructed, old ones would simply be filled in with dirt and built over, one of the main reasons why new discoveries in ancient cities were constantly being discovered.

"You've discovered some ancient ruins beneath the city and have renovated them to provide an underground tunnel system."

"You are correct. Vast areas of the ancient city beneath and around the Vatican were uncovered ages ago. Most were left alone, but some have been converted into subterranean roads we now use to gain unnoticed access in and out of the Vatican. Very few know of their existence."

Not a bad idea, and not that surprising, to tell the truth. It wasn't like we were going to drive our secret car traveling on a secret mission through the front door. Governments always had secret lairs few knew about, and being the smallest sovereign governing body on the planet, the Vatican would be missing a prime opportunity to expand if they didn't.

Even with what I assumed was a vast network of secret tunnels, it wasn't long before the dark, narrow corridor came to an abrupt end. We emerged into a larger room shaped like a cul-de-sac, with an elevator opposite the entrance. Parking the car, Father Vincent stepped out and started toward the elevator. I grabbed my bag and followed.

"You coming, sir?" I asked Reynolds, noticing he was staying with the car.

"This is the end of the road for me, son. My orders were to escort you here and report back to the President that your transfer was completed. Hell, I'm not even Catholic. I'm not sure I'm even allowed to be down here. Anyway, you take care of yourself, Commander. You're representing your county on this one. Don't let us down."

"I won't, sir," I replied, snapping a crisp salute. "Thank you."

"You'll be fine," replied Reynolds, returning the salute. "Just keep your head down and do us proud."

"Come," Father Vincent said quietly from the elevator. "His Holiness is waiting."

I nodded, slowly turning toward the waiting elevator. With one last glance over my shoulder at the retreating black car, I knew things were never going to be the same again.

***

Not long after the assassination attempt, the Pope, in a strange bout of fury, had all but called for a crusade against the attackers. The public was furious, Catholic and Christian alike, and the militaries comprised of such people had no trouble filling their personnel quotas. Even an elite unit like my SEALs had grown to unprecedented numbers to help fight anyone we could throw our strength against.

Which is what brings me to Rome.

The Pope also commissioned a new military unit to help in the war effort. Officially, it was a branch of the Swiss Guard meant to protect his person; unofficially, it was a Special Forces outfit meant to seek out and destroy any potential threat he may face. At least, that's what the whispers around the water coolers were saying.

Little was known about the organization, including its name. Originally, members were selected specifically from a pool of veteran Swiss Guardsmen, but recently, in an attempt to further solidify friendships amongst Christian nations, the Pope had called for volunteers from the best they could offer. It was rumored that members from Britain, France, and Germany had already transferred service, but the entire process had been done behind closed doors. There were rumors of the first American from Delta transferring only a few days ago, but was again unconfirmed.

It hadn't been long after I'd heard these rumors that a young man dressed in a well-tailored business suit knocked on the door of my off-base home while I was on leave in Hawaii. The man spoke with a thick Italian accent, but in impeccable English. He'd explained to me the reality behind the Pope's Swiss Guard and that a spot was available to me for a two year stint.

Now, my mother was a devout Catholic, but my father never put much stock in religion. He was born Protestant, but non-practicing throughout his adult life. While I'd never known him to be a pious man, he had always been supportive of my mother, and had honored her wish that he convert to Catholicism and marry in a Roman Catholic Church. Afterward, Dad had no qualms about her raising my younger sister Diana and me Catholic, but he attended church only to support his wife. It was only thanks to my mom that I attended Jesuit schools and had a perfect Sunday church attendance record. That is, until I went off to college.

Nor had it deterred the fact that I had been quite the kleptomaniac as a teenager, had a few drinks while underage, and my first sexual experience was well before marriage. Outwardly, I acted the way every other teenager or young adult would, so when the well-dressed Italian man came to my door, the only thing I could think of was why in the world they would want me. As far as I was concerned, it was a position I didn't deserve, but when I voiced my concerns, the man's response had simply been that the people he represented had performed thorough research and that they knew the man beneath.

It was at that point that I'd faced a dilemma, and had needed a few days to think over. The man agreed and said he would return to receive an answer. I'd spent the entirety of the next two days wandering the beautiful Hawaiian beaches considering my options.

I knew that on one hand, I was completely happy with my current posting. I had joined the military at twenty three, shortly before the first bombing in Jerusalem, and thanks to my college education, had gone to Officer Candidate School, graduated near the top of my class, and placed a request for immediate transfer to the SEALs. I'd gotten very lucky. Fresh officers rarely had the opportunity to go to BUD/S right off the bat, but thanks to my record and the dire global circumstances looming, I was quickly off to Coronado Island near San Diego. Within a month I was getting my ass kicked with the other officers and regular enlisted men in Basic Underwater Demolition/SEAL training, BUD/S. I roughed it out, went through SEAL Qualification Training, jump school, sniper school, and so on. After more than two years of training and some field experience, and with the global war worsening, I was given my own platoon.

I had been more than lucky.

I'd gone on to establish close bonds with my fellow SEAL teammates over the tours, and didn't want to leave them feeling as if

I'd betrayed them. Life in the Teams was all about companionship and teamwork. We were as closely knit as any family, even if it had been extraordinarily difficult at first conforming to the community. I'd often felt like the black sheep of the family, having often been considered too much of a thinker for the vicious lifestyle of a SEAL, but I'd managed to secure my place regardless. On the other hand, the only reason I'd enlisted in the first place was to make my father happy, not knowing there would be a full-fledged global war on the horizon. We were a military family, and it had been my duty. But if I took the Italian's offer, I thought maybe I could continue fighting the war in a more meaningful way. I knew my father would be disappointed, but when the man returned two days later, I agreed to the transfer, taking solace in the fact that I'd be back with my SEALs in a few years.

The next day, at 0800, a naval lieutenant and two ensigns came to my door with my orders. I was to gather a few essentials and head to the airfield immediately. The ensigns would pack my personal belongings, as they had already done with my military gear back at the barracks, and ship them directly to Rome.

Grabbing my already packed go-bag, I was on my way to Washington, D.C. to meet with the President. After several hours and more time zones than I could count, I was standing in the Oval Office awaiting his arrival. Thanks to the growing religious hysteria and increasing hostility everywhere on the planet, a retired Army general was now the Commander in Chief. With him came increased funding for the military, combat experience, and a new direction for the war effort, but, sadly, at least from this sailor's point of view, still no hope for an end to it.

Staring down at the Presidential seal emblazoned into the carpet, I wondered if I was doing the right thing. Trying to push aside my doubt, I shifted my gaze toward the president's desk where I spotted a crucifix hanging from the wall behind his chair, and realized I wasn't abandoning my country – not really – but continuing the fight by answering a higher calling. Abandoning the war effort was out of the question, even with little hope for the planet's continued survival, but at least this way I would be doing it for my own reasons.

My meeting with the President was short and to the point, but also comforting. He assured me that I had made the right decision and that I was now, indeed, answering to a higher authority. He seemed almost jealous of my position, perhaps wishing he was a few years younger and that his tool of destruction was a rifle again, instead of a pen. Documents were produced within minutes, and with a few signatures, I was promoted and transferred to my new posting.

Within the hour, I was back at the airfield, waiting for my ride and my father. He had been informed of my transfer and was told he could see me off. Since no one had any idea when I'd be returning, this would be our only chance to say goodbye. But, as I'd watched the C-130J taxing down the runway, he was nowhere to be found.

Hoping to catch him approaching from some unknown direction, I'd scanned the tarmac three times, finding nothing every time. Only the fumes from countless aircraft and the ominous early morning mist swirling at the beck and call of powerful engines were there to greet me. Frustrated, I'd ducked my head as the wind from the C-130J slammed into my face, and felt my hands ball themselves into fists.

So, it was going to be like that then.

I'd suspected he wouldn't understand. In my father's eyes, there was no explanation for what I was doing. I'd hoped to explain that I was doing the right thing, that I'd be back in a few years and that I would still be fighting to defend my home and to protect my country.

I'd been willing to beg for his acceptance.

But he hadn't showed.

I'd shaken my head, already knowing why he hadn't been there. He'd never forgiven me for Mom.

She had died three years ago. Cancer. I had been in the field when she'd passed on and had missed her funeral. My father had never forgiven me.

I'd never forgiven myself.

Maybe I was doing this for her.

I hadn't spoken to my father since. Three years was a long time, and knowing I had to leave now with our issues still unresolved pained me. Our relationship had been strained since I was twelve years old, but I'd hoped to put some of that behind us.

No father should despise his son, and no son should hate his father.

I'd hissed through my teeth and glanced up just in time to see an air traffic controller beckoning me toward the rear access ramp of the C-130J. I'd waved at him to let him know he had my attention, and picked up my go-bag with an audible sigh of frustration. Step by step, I'd made my way up the ramp, each and every footfall a nail in the coffin of my former life.

As soon as I had passed into the body of the aircraft, the ramp began to close behind me. In a last cry for hope, I'd turned to look out over the runway, but again found nothing to greet me except the darkness. As the ramp continued to retract, genuine sadness crept over me, but the loud metal on metal grinding sound of the ramp completing its retraction had quickly snapped me out of it.

As the rear of the ship cut me off from my past, my head had dropped just slightly before I'd turned and walked into the belly of the beast. With a final sigh, I'd secured my gear beneath my bench in preparation for the flight, leaned my head back, and closed my eyes.

***

As the elevator doors opened, I noticed it was connected to the Vatican's normal elevator system and was accessible to the general public. I assumed that only someone with their thumbprint or other security measure cleared by the Vatican could reach the level we had just left. Father Vincent and I emerged on the first floor near St. Peter's Basilica, exiting quickly before a swarm of eager tourists entered the cab. I had to jump to the side when a small boy rushed passed me, dragging his young mother behind him as he feverishly sought out the random object of interest that must have caught his eye. She gave me an apologetic smile, but quickly moved on, trying to keep up with her son.

"That was odd," I commented, smiling in their direction, thinking about how nice it was that people could still enjoy the comfort of Vatican City despite the war.

Father Vincent smirked. "To this day, I still find it strange emerging into the public after having just returned from a secret rendezvous through an elevator that doesn't exist."

I looked at him, recollecting my earlier thoughts of secrets within secrets. "I take it this isn't the first time you've escorted someone in this manner?"

"Of course not. You are not the first to come to us. In fact, with your arrival, we have completed recruitment for the time being."

"And I suppose more information on that will have to wait?"

"You assume correctly. Do not worry. We are almost there."

***

A brisk walk later, we arrived at a large doorway ornately decorated with religious motifs. The doors had to have been centuries old, but I was hardly an expert in such matters. Before I could think much more on the subject, Father Vincent knocked gently, sparing a single glance in my direction to offer me a curt nod.

I understood.

This was it, time to meet the new boss, and I couldn't be more nervous. A quiet "enter" came from inside. Father Vincent opened the doors and led the way in. I spotted two individuals inside. The first man was in his golden years, although aging quite gracefully. He wore white robes and a skull cap, and had a rosary around his neck. He was sitting behind a desk situated in the center of a richly decorated room with religious paintings scattered throughout.

The second individual was standing rigidly straight behind the first man's chair and had the look of a career military man. His dark brown hair was cut short and he sported a thick mustache which, along with his slightly graying temples, prominent jaw line and nose and hawkish blue eyes, gave him the look of a dignified statesman. The man wore olive drab Battle Dress Uniform cargo pants, and a Woolly Pully combat sweater of the same color. If I had to guess, I'd peg him as a member of Britain's SAS – as members of the Special Air Service itself had developed the Wooly Pully during World War II.

I'd worked with members of that illustrious group before, and had nothing but positive memories of how they operated. So far, I was impressed.

I looked at the perfectly groomed and dressed man, and immediately felt horribly underdressed. His BDU pants and Woolly Pully were formal enough wear, but were also combat ready in a time of need. I, on the other hand, wore tan boots of a civilian brand, military style khaki cargo pants and a Hawaiian shirt obnoxiously colored in bright yellow and blue. To complete the ensemble, I had even left my shirt open, revealing the sleeveless undershirt I wore beneath.

Part of my orders had been to appear at the Vatican in civilian dress, and since I had lived in Hawaii for the past few years, I had little else in my closet but Hawaiian shirts. It wasn't until I emerged from the elevator into the swarm of tourists a few minutes ago that I understood the reason for the orders. As I came to a halt a few paces away from the desk and snapped a salute, I felt ridiculous doing so in the garishly patterned shirt.

"Lieutenant Commander Jacob Hunter reporting as ordered, sir."

The old man sitting behind the desk smiled and kept me holding the salute for a few seconds before waving me off.

"I can understand your instinct to salute, my son," the man said in clear but accented English, "but I am not your commander. At ease, or whatever it is you military types say."

I lowered my arm slowly, easing myself into a more comfortable standing position, but remained razor straight.

"Thank you, sir. I wasn't sure whether to salute, or kneel, or what. I'm a little out of my element."

The man continued to smile at me as he stood up and rounded the desk to stand within arm's reach. As he came to a stop, he held out his right hand, which held a rather large ring. I understood and knelt before him, kissing the ring before rising again to my feet. Straightening, I was surprised to see the man's smile was larger than before, and he seemed to have settled into a completely relaxed and informal manner.

"Sit, sit," he said. "We have little to discuss, but it is important that you continue your journey as quickly as possible."

I took my seat, noticing that Father Vincent had vanished. Sneaky.

The old man sat down carefully, faintly showing his age. Folding his hands on the desk in front of him, he stared directly into my eyes. He wasn't so intimidating that he made me feel uncomfortable, but his look was enough to ensure that I knew who was in charge.

"So," he began, opening his hands. "It is my understanding that you have been left completely in the dark concerning why you are here. You know that we are in the middle of not only a crusade, but World War III, that my life has been directly threatened, and that terrorists were very nearly successful at taking it. Finally, you know that I have created an off-shoot of my Swiss Guard, the members of which I have recruited from the best of all Christendom, adding additional security and protection to my person. Have I left anything out?"

"No, sir. That just about covers it." I kept my responses short. We were both busy men. No reason to delay our meeting with frivolous pleasantries or endearing platitudes.

Perhaps sensing my directness, he smiled again and quickly shifted topics. "We know all about your upbringing and have been watching you for quite some time. Do not be alarmed. We just wanted to make sure we knew everything we needed to about our potential candidates. But, as you are finally here, it is time to send you on your way."

I leaned forward, in order to hear as clearly as I could.

"You are here to join an elite group of soldiers whose sole purpose is to seek out and eliminate any potential threat to the wellbeing of myself or the ground on which you stand. My Swiss Guard is fully capable of defending this establishment from many threats, including an all-out siege, but it is the small, indirect kinds of warfare that a guard cannot defend against. Nuclear and biological attacks must be stopped at the source, and that is where your team comes in." He paused to look at me questioningly. "Is this acceptable to you, Mr. Hunter?"

I nodded, suspecting such an assignment. That suited me just fine.

"Desperate times," I said.

He returned my nod. "Indeed. I do not relish the need for such a force, but the dangers of today sometimes dictate preemptive action." He paused again, his body language indicating he wasn't quite finished, but it wasn't long before his composure returned. "Now, do you have any questions?"

"Just one: who are we?"

The man smiled once again. "You have no official unit designation, but to me, you are known as Praetorians. Do you know who they were?"

"They were once the elite bodyguard of the Caesars during the days of the Roman Empire."

"I thought you would know. You have inquisitive eyes, always open to learning new things. You are correct. You are Praetorians, a tribute to the men of antiquity who once protected the leaders of this great city. Now, since you have no further questions, allow me to introduce you to Major Dillon McDougal, formally of His Majesty's SAS. He will be your commanding officer. King William was kind enough to lend him to our efforts."

McDougal nodded, which I returned in kind.

"Now, my son, this is where we must part ways," the man said, standing and raising his ringed hand once again.

I rose to kiss his ring, but was once again surprised, in this day of surprises, as the man rotated his hand to offer a handshake instead. Tentatively, I gripped his hand, surprised at the strength he possessed, and shook firmly.

"Thank you. It will be an honor to serve as so many have before me."

"The honor is all mine, young man," Pope Gregory XXI replied. "You also have my thanks and my prayers."

I nodded and released his grip. McDougal started for the door and I quickly fell into step behind him.

On my way out I heard Pope Gregory quietly whisper under his breath, "God be with you, my son, and God speed."

Following behind McDougal, I asked, "Where to, Major?"

"Where else?" He replied. "To meet your squad."

II
Praetorians

Rome, Italy
July, 2021 AD

    McDougal led the way toward the elevator I had just arrived from. Once inside, he pressed his thumb against a pad on the elevator panel, activating the car to descend rapidly into the bowels of the Vatican. The ride didn't last long, and soon the doors opened to a long white hallway, not the tunnels I expected. We must have arrived on another subterranean level. The hallway was well lit and had the metallic sheen and sterility normally associated with military or medical complexes.
    New ones.
    At the first door, McDougal again pressed his thumb against a pad and the door slid open. As I followed him inside, I took in my surroundings in a glance, focusing briefly on as many details as I could. The immediate area consisted of a few benches and lockers, and doors to a shower facility. To my right was a complete weight room facility equipped with free weights, cardiovascular machines and a boxing ring. To my left was a mess hall and recreation area. Directly ahead was a small arms firing range and an obstacle course fit for training with weapons and gear.
    I was definitely impressed.
    Most training facilities possessed all of the present amenities, but never in such a vast, single area, obviously specialized to serve two purposes. First, to conserve space, as an underground facility would need to be as compact as possible. Second, to produce a more familial atmosphere where everyone present can interact with one another regardless of what they were doing. It was the perfect environment for assimilating a team of strangers who did not have the luxury of going through a rigorous and lengthy training process meant to build bonds of friendship and trust.
    I spotted five figures scattered throughout the facility. The first two were easily found as they were prominently displayed sparring in the boxing ring. One man outweighed me by at least seventy five pounds and had a few inches on me as well, while the other man was

short, ripped, and wiry. He reminded me of Bruce Lee. A third man was using a bench press machine behind the boxing ring, but only his calves and feet were visible.

The fourth figure I noticed was a woman. She was facing away from me and all I could see was black hair, tied up in a short pony tail that didn't quite reach the nape of her neck, and a lithe body covered by a tight tank top and BDU pants. She was at the other end of the facility, sitting at the long range rifle section of the shooting range, her eye buried in the lens of scope.

The final figure was sitting at the mess hall drinking a vanilla smoothie through a straw, leaning back in a chair with his legs crossed atop the table, one of his boots lying on the ground next to his chair – a relaxed demeanor that surprised me. Most soldiers, even when off duty, portrayed slightly more poise and discipline while on station, but what really shocked me was that I knew this guy, and his lackadaisical attitude immediately made sense.

"Well, well, well..." I called out cheerfully with a smile on my face. "If it isn't the sexiest man this side of the Air Force. Johnny Santino."

The man turned, nearly falling out of his chair in surprise.

"Jacob? Is that you? Good God, it's been forever," he said, pulling me into a friendly bear hug and lifting me off the ground. "Like what? A year? Since that op over North Korea?"

I rolled my eyes. He knew damn well it hadn't been that long. "You mean the time when you and your little ninja buddies couldn't make the extraction because your little tootsies got all cut up, and my SEALs had to come bail you out?"

Santino must have been that member of Delta who had transferred earlier. He'd started his Special Forces career as a Green Beret, a clandestine team that specialized in tactical instruction. Back in Vietnam, they were so sneaky that many theorized they executed their missions barefoot, making them targets of both easy jibs and respect simultaneously. "I see you're still putting your feet at risk," I joked, pointing at his bootless foot after he finally put me down.

"I take it you two know each other," McDougal said as he approached quietly.

"That's correct, sir. Although, I am a bit surprised to see his pretty face here at all."

Santino sneered at me. During basic training he took some shrapnel from a grenade accident, leaving him with a rather nasty web of scars on the right side of his face. It wasn't that bad really, and it gave him a dashing, heroic look that the ladies always seemed to slobber over.

"We're both Catholic, Jacob. I guess they just wanted another Italian around here, and called me in first."

"When I first heard they had recruited from Delta, I had my suspicion it was you, but I figured your patriotism would outweigh your faith. Guess I was wrong."

He put a hand on my shoulder. "I'm not sure how I feel about you thinking so much about me, Jake, kinda creepy, but it'll be good to work together again. This time on a more permanent basis. And, hey, I hear you've been promoted. McDougal told me the new guy was a Lieutenant Commander in the Navy. Looks like I'll have to start saluting you from now on." Before removing his hand from my shoulder, he pinched at my Hawaiian shirt and pulled on it slightly. "Nice shirt, by the way," he commented.

I smiled. "Thanks, and don't worry about saluting, the only thing I care about is the bigger pension."

His smile faltered and he cupped his chin between thumb and forefinger in thought. "I wonder why I wasn't promoted…"

"I hate to break up the reunion, but now would be a good time to clear up a few things," McDougal interrupted, looking at me. "First of all, 'Captain' Santino is no longer a captain as you understand it, but a lieutenant once more."

"Sir? He was demoted?"

"No, not demoted per se, but merely realigned into a new chain of command. In fact, *you* are now a lieutenant as well."

Go Figure. I knew it would only last a few days before I was at the bottom of the food chain again, but at least my bank account would still reflect my old rank. I sighed, feigning disappointment with a lazy shrug while McDougal continued.

"We did not want to strip any member of the team of their rank, but we needed to consolidate our system so as to avoid confusion. The chain of command is simple and you would most likely recognize it from your American Army. I'm team leader and highest ranking officer as a major. My second in command is a captain, and the rest of you are of equal rank as lieutenants. Any questions?"

"No, sir," I responded. "Sounds straightforward to me."

"Glad I was able to clear that up, mate. Now, would you like to meet the rest of your squad?"

"Of course, sir."

"Follow me."

Leaving Santino to finish his smoothie, we started toward the boxing ring when I heard the distinct *crack, crack, crack* of a high powered rifle firing in rapid succession. I glanced over at the young woman sitting at the shooting range as she summoned her paper target from far down range. Considering the amount of time it took for the target to reach her, I estimated that it had begun its journey from pretty far out. When the woman pulled off the target sheet and held it to the light, I noticed a neat smiley face made from bullet holes in the target's head.

The woman was a fantastic shot, and the smug smile at the corner of her mouth indicated she knew it.

It figured.

Snipers always were hot heads.

Meanwhile, the two men in the ring continued to pound on one another with distinctively different styles. The bigger man, wearing blue trunks, was clearly a brawler who'd participated in one too many bar fights over the years. His lunges and long swings were meant to inflict major punishment at the expense of finesse, mobility and his hit count.

The second man, in red trunks, fought like an experienced martial artist, well-schooled in hand to hand combat. He utilized jabs, chops, kicks, counters, and stayed extremely mobile, dancing in and out and side to side. With his fluid grace and obvious fighting superiority, he simply shrugged off his opponent's blows while he searched for the right time to strike.

After about five minutes of constant fighting, with both men sweating profusely, the man in red trunks finally found his opening. As the man in blue threw a powerful right hook toward his opponent's face, the smaller man easily spun to his attacker's right side, twirling beneath his upraised arm. Now at the man's back, it was easy to pull off a spinning leg sweep that took the big man to the mat and the smaller man's elbow to his neck.

A few heartbeats passed as the pair stared at one another before the big man started laughing and allowed the other to help him up.

"I thought I had you there with that last hook, but you are too damn quick, *mon ami*. How many shots did I actually land in that fight? Three? And those barely connected, as if you knew they were coming. How do you do that?"

"I've been studying martial arts since I was able to crawl," the smaller man replied. "It's not just about fighting, but learning how to anticipate your opponent. Read them. But don't worry, you're doing better. I'll make a warrior out of you yet."

The two continued to chat when McDougal cleared his throat.

"If the two of you are finished, I'd like to introduce you to our final member. This is Lieutenant Jacob Hunter. Hunter, let me introduce Lieutenant James Wang," he said indicating the smaller man, before turning to the larger one, "and this rather large brute is Lieutenant Jeanne Bordeaux."

My head snapped to the side in sudden confusion. "Sir? *Jeanne* Bordeaux?"

McDougal shook his head at me in a silencing manner, and the look turned on me by the large Frenchman gave me immediate pause. I'd thought Jeanne was a French girl's name, but I certainly wasn't going to question either of them at the moment. Instead, I cleared my throat and nodded at them.

"Nice to meet you both," I said, covering my flub quite well.

Bordeaux offered me the flick of his hand as he hung on the ropes, while Wang bowed slightly and offered a very British, possibly Welsh, "*ello*."

To say Bordeaux was a large man was an understatement. His legs were the size of tree trunks and his arms like honey baked hams, while his shirtless upper body was just as intimidating. In all my time in the military, I couldn't remember many men who matched him in size. Yet, despite his massive frame, his features were oddly gentle. He had a thin face, with a chiseled jaw and cheeks, and a slightly pointy nose. Sandy brown hair and scruffy facial hair gave me the impression he was pretty successful at picking up women at night clubs.

His boxing partner, Wang, was his polar opposite. Only five and a half feet tall, I estimated even the woman at the sniper range was taller than he was. Not only was he small in height, but also thin in girth. That said, even if Bordeaux hadn't known what kind of fighter he was, he probably would have thought twice about getting into a fight with him. His thin body was ripped with muscles in places I didn't even know the human body could have them. It wouldn't have surprised me a bit to learn he could out-bench me.

He had a round face and narrow eyes that appealed to his surname's ethnicity but his nose and his mouth had a distinctly western quality to them.

I was about to inquire into their backgrounds when the man previously using the bench press came into view. The man, wearing shorts and a sleeveless undershirt, was well muscled, and bore a striking resemblance to Father Vincent from my car ride in. It wasn't until he came around the last corner to face me, that I realized it was Father Vincent.

"Father Vincent," I stammered. "What are you doing here?"

The priest smiled, "I'm part of the team, Hunter. Indeed, I am a man of the cloth, but prior to taking my vows, I served in the Swiss Guard, and before that, the Swiss military."

"Really?" I asked skeptically

He rolled his eyes. "I was a soldier before you were even in primary school, but when my term of service was up with the Guard, I discovered a higher calling. I was ordained and came to serve here at the Vatican, where until recently I served as both priest and Pope Gregory's personal bodyguard, cleverly hidden as a fellow servant of God. Currently, I serve as the team's liaison with His Holiness, but don't worry; I still know how to handle myself in a fight."

I was still trying to process this new information when he continued.

"When I'm on duty, you may refer to me as Vincent, or Vince, I suppose, as my mother used to call me. I don't want my position to add any undue stress or distance between us, but while I wear my collar or preside over the team, I am once again Father Vincent."

I glanced at McDougal, who confirmed Vincent's story with a nod. "Captain Vincent's story is all true, lad. He's been a soldier longer than I have and will serve as my XO and take command should he need to. You'll receive more details at the briefing, but let's introduce you to our final member first and have you perform a quick inspection of your gear as well."

That sounded like a reasonable plan to me. I was not only looking forward to meeting the last member of the team, but also to having the familiar grip of my beloved rifle in my hands once again.

With a quick nod to Vincent, and with Bordeaux and Wang once again sparring in the ring, we made our way to the range where the woman was retrieving a second target. The large sheet of paper had but a single small hole, dead center-mass. Upon closer inspection, I noticed the hole was really the culmination of multiple shots all fired almost directly upon one another. It was an impressive feat, even if the distance between shooter and target had not been as great as before.

She spent a few seconds studying the target as we approached, but her head jerked in our direction when we got close. I wasn't entirely surprised she'd noticed us, but many snipers were notorious for severe tunnel vision due to the constant use of their scopes. I knew this because it was something I suffered from slightly myself. It was a good indicator of what to expect out of her, but I didn't really have long to think about it. When the woman completed her turn and I finally had the chance to get a good look at her, all I could focus on were light green eyes, so bright and piercing that they bordered on a color meant only for those deemed clinically insane.

Yet, it wasn't the way her eyes lit up the room that caught my attention, but how they widened in surprise upon meeting my own. Her expression suggested that she knew me but I couldn't imagine from where, as I was sure I'd remember a face like hers. Attractive, she had sharp features that suggested a traditional European ancestry, but her deeply tanned skin and jet black hair suggested a more diverse background.

Her eyes shifted to McDougal as he stopped beside her, but returned quickly to my own as he started to speak, only narrower now, distrustful.

"Lieutenant Strauss, meet Lieutenant Jacob Hunter, our final member. Hunter, this is Lieutenant Helena Strauss."

"A pleasure to meet you, Lieutenant," I said as I took a step forward to shake her hand.

Her eyes didn't waver, and neither did her hand. It stayed firmly by her side as she held her rifle with the other, leaving me to stand before her with my hand held out, looking like quite the idiot. Her eyes flicked down to my hand, making it clear that she didn't intend to shake it, so I brought it back to my side as I heard chuckles emanating from behind me.

McDougal covered his mouth with a hand and cleared his throat before continuing. "Lieutenant Strauss, if you would be so kind as to show Hunter here the armory so he can inspect his gear. Report to the briefing room in one hour."

"Yes sir," she responded with a salute.

Without another glance or word, she turned on her heel and marched through a doorway off to the side of the range. I glanced at McDougal whose stone hard expression twitched ever so slightly. I continued staring at him as I passed by, still wondering if there was something he knew that I didn't. Reaching the door, I glanced out at the complex and noticed that every member of the team, save McDougal, had gathered near Santino, watching me expectantly. It wasn't until I passed through the armory door that I heard the soft drone of laughter.

And I had no idea why.

***

The armory was an impressive sight.

The rows of gun shelves were lined with numerous weapons from all sorts of countries and manufacturing companies. At the end of the racks were explosives and other more destructive types of weaponry. Beyond were ten lockers, wide enough to hold a single soldier's plethora of gear. Most operators had multiple sets of gear, swapping out mission essential items, only using what was appropriate for individual missions. Despite the weapon porn on display in such extravagance, I couldn't help but notice my companion, bent at the waist as she cleaned her rifle, her rather supple backside presented for my full inspection.

I couldn't help but stare, my head lolling to the side. I tried to quickly glance away and cover my mistake when she turned to show me my locker, but I wasn't quick enough. She settled with giving me another cold look and hooking her thumb behind her shoulder to direct my attention toward the only other open locker. Fate, having a sick sense of humor it seemed, decided to take it upon itself to place our lockers across from one another. Crossing to the bench, I sat upon it and accidentally brushed my back up against hers. I flinched automatically at the contact but she didn't react. All she did was turn her head to glance in my direction, a slight smile tugging at her mouth.

I shook my head with a smirk of my own, but forced myself to clear my head with a crack of my neck to work the kinks out, and began a cursory inspection of my gear. With a task so familiar and enjoyable, it was almost easy to put the woman out of my head and focus.

Everything seemed to be in order. All of my camouflage uniforms were present, as well as two pairs of boots, one black, the other coyote tan. My Navy dress uniform hung neatly to one side of the locker with my wet suit opposite it. All of my other gear was present and accounted for as well, placed neatly on racks, shelves, or hooks. Helmet with camera and optics eyepiece, rifle magazines, radio and throat microphone, night vision goggles, mobile PC, combat knife, medical kit, glow sticks, zip ties, combat notebook, pen, Escape & Evasion kit, and a plethora of other tools. Last but not least, placed on top of my foot locker was my MOLLE combat rig.

Besides my rifle, my rig was the most important piece of gear I had. MOLLE, or Modular Lightweight Load-carrying Equipment, was a system for attaching compatible pieces of equipment together via webbing and snaps. Without it, I would be unable to carry the heavy amounts of gear essential for a successful mission. The vest was festooned with numerous pockets and pouches scattered around the stomach area, chest, sides, and back.

The back of my rig held a small computer cleverly tucked away near my CamelBak hydration pack to keep it out of the way and cool. It was wirelessly connected to an eyepiece that hung in front of my left eye. The eyepiece, which was no more than a thin, translucent lens, operated as a GPS device, a screen to view videos, a compass, and a rudimentary targeting reticle amongst other things. The computer was synced to my teammates', so I could intercept data updates such as grid coordinates and targeting data.

In order to send and receive these updates, a long, thin touch screen interface would be attached to my left forearm. It was covered by a protective sheath, which could be pulled off at its Velcro seams so I could view and interact with the screen. It had a small joystick with two buttons, much like a pilot's flight stick, which acted like a computer mouse. I could extend the joystick into my left hand with a quick flick of my wrist, making the entire set-up fully functional with my left arm alone. Complete with Blue Force Tracking Tech III software, updated only a year ago, I could upload troop positions on a map with a simple touch of the interface, overlay my own map over satellite imagery, or call in airstrikes with a single tap of the finger. The possibilities were almost endless. It was a handy tool, but not one a good soldier relied upon in combat.

My last piece of equipment lay alongside the back of the locker, entombed in a solid protective case. As I placed it on the bench next to me, I accidentally bumped into my companion again. I was about to apologize when I realized she ignored my mistake completely and continued cleaning her own weapon.

I opened the case and pulled out my closest ally and true love, my HK416 Gen II assault rifle, Penelope, as I had named her. Despite being decades old in design, thanks to the veritable hold on military R&D, mine was manufactured only two years ago, with many new bells and whistles to show for it.

Penelope had been the loyal wife of Odysseus in Homer's *The Odyssey*, my favorite classical epic. Despite her husband's absence for twenty years, and dozens of hopeful suitors hoping to take his place on the throne, she remained faithful, waiting patiently until he finally returned. I was a sucker for a good love story, and I hoped that like the woman of myth, my weapon would remain just as loyal.

I reached for a cloth and rubbed its exterior, wiping away the subtlest pieces of dust and lint. "It's been a while Penelope," I said to the rifle, "I hope you've kept yourself out of trouble while I've been away."

I only hoped Strauss didn't overhear me. My theory was if you love and respect your equipment like you do a friend, it will in turn treat you with the proper respect and never let you down. Some assumed this kind of thinking meant you were a crazy person, although I had no idea why.

After field stripping and cleaning the rifle, as well as inspecting the ACOG-II Scope, SureFire flashlight/laser, and bi-pod, I finished wiping down the exterior and gently put it back in its case. "Goodnight," I said quietly, hoping my companion didn't hear me. "Sleep tight."

I placed the case back in the locker, gave the entire enclosure another look, tossed my Hawaiian shirt inside, nodded in satisfaction, and shut the cage.

Donning a more appropriate duty jacket from my locker, I announced, "I'm done here. Everything checks out. I'm ready to go when you are."

Her reply was to barely even glance in my direction as she continued cleaning her rifle's barrel with a long pipe cleaner brush.

I sighed, unsure what even I could have done to spark such annoyance in her already. Unfortunately, tact was rarely my first option when dealing with pigheaded individuals.

"Excuse me," I asked, "but are we going to have a problem here? You've barely grunted a word in the fifteen minutes we've known one another and I'm starting to get the feeling you don't like me, which, you know…" I gave her a Hollywood, teeth sparkling smile, "…is kind of hard to believe."

She continued to ignore me.

"Look, sweetheart, I've had just about as much trouble as I can stand with pretty girls who think they…"

I never got the chance to finish. She was on her feet like a cheetah and staring green-tinted icicles upwards into my skull.

I gulped. It was the only thing I could do as I returned her stare, gazing into her face that was frighteningly more beautiful when displaying such anger.

"So?" I asked, trying to stay brave. "Got something to sa…"

The words were barely out of my mouth when her fist connected with my right eye socket, pitching me backward and into my locker. Stars flashed in my vision and the rest of the world went black when my head slammed against the metal surface. My hand was already flinging upward to my face as my head cleared in the sad hope of staving off the inevitable swelling and darkening.

Speechless, I just stared at her, completely confused and taken aback by her assault. I wanted to yell at her and hit her right back, but it was probably a good thing that I kept my mouth shut and my hands to myself. She might have killed me.

I checked my hand to make sure my face wasn't bleeding. Thankfully, it came back clean. Risking one last look at my attacker, I turned for the door and beat my retreat from the crazed woman who had hit me for seemingly no reason. She was already back at work cleaning her gun, oblivious to our encounter.

Despite the pain, I couldn't help but smile.

***

The multiplex was eerily silent when I returned to the common area. Everyone, save McDougal, had gathered in the mess area and was in the midst of socializing and chow. Noticing my approach, they all stopped what they were doing mid motion and turned to look at me. Santino had a glop of noodles hanging from his mouth, while Bordeaux had paused as he sipped a steaming drink.

I stopped in front of their table, hands on my hips, and looked each man in the eye. Each wore a passive expression and for a few moments, the five of us did nothing but stare at each other before, all of a sudden, the four men at the table burst out in playful laughter. In the midst of their laughter, I couldn't help but noticed Wang pass a few Euros to Vincent.

"Something I should know, gentlemen?"

Santino was the first to stop laughing, but he had to catch his breath before explaining the situation.

"Jake, man, it's nothing personal, but before you got here, all of us, including Little Miss Strauss," he said the name, emphasizing it in a haughty and disrespectful manner, "had lunch. Chit-chatting. She told us how she had just broken up with some longtime boyfriend of hers or something because he'd cheated on her when her time in the service kept them apart. Sad, right? Well, here's the funny part. She said she'd kill the next guy she saw that even remotely pissed her off. I guess it doesn't help that you kinda look like how she described him. Tall, wavy brown hair, broad shoulders, dashing good looks, whatever, as soon as I saw you I knew there would be trouble."

I continued to stare at him stoically.

"Vinnie over there won the bet."

I glanced over at the aging priest with narrow eyes. He simply smiled, raised his fork in a salute, and continued to eat.

"He said she'd throw a punch. I said she'd knee you in the balls, and the boxing twins over there thought she'd go easy on you, but I knew you'd do something stupid to get her all worked up. So what happened? Strike out swinging?"

My response was delayed as the group noticed our female comrade exit the armory and head directly toward another set of doors, opposite the ones she emerged. She spared a single, distant look in our direction, glowering.

"Didn't even make it to the on-deck circle," I reported as we all watched her leave.

Santino stood up, placing a hand sympathetically on my shoulder while some of the other guys snickered at me.

"Don't worry, my friend. Maybe it's still pre-season."

***

Grabbing a tray of food consisting of Salisbury steak, tater tots, and an unknown gelatinous substance, I joined the rest of the team at their table. Needless to say, I was famished. I hadn't eaten a proper meal since I had left for Washington at least twenty four hours ago. I continued receiving jeers from my teammates, but took them in stride, knowing that the "Strauss" situation had been a good ice breaker.

The guys were conversing as I ate my meal, but I started growing restless not knowing a thing about them. Popping a few tater tots in my mouth, I decided my stomach was full enough to start a conversation.

"So, Wang," I started, mumbling with my mouth full. "What's your story? How long has your family been in England?"

Wang waited until he finished chewing his food before answering, perhaps wondering if he too should hit me for what some might consider an insensitive question, but I suspected he wouldn't. Mouth clear, Wang leaned back in his chair and spoke in what I could now confirm was a Welsh accent.

"My grandparents fled China's Great Cultural Revolution in 1966 and made their way to England with my father. My grandfather ran a martial arts school in a quiet countryside, but when local Red Guard members came to the area, he knew it was time to leave. My grandparent's life was a quiet one, and they despised the Communists and their hope of wiping any memory of old China from the history books, so they took up residence in Cardiff, Wales and opened a kung fu academy. My father took over when my grandfather died a few years back." He paused and took a quick drink from his mug. "And, aye, before you ask, my father married a local lass and I was but a wee product of both worlds." He smiled. "And a jolly good product at that."

I chuckled at his intentionally overdone accent, quickly determining that I liked Wang. He seemed level headed and dedicated, but a little cocky – typical for elite operators – good man to have at your back.

I glanced over at the large Frenchman. "What about you, big guy? Any interesting stories?"

Bordeaux put a hand over his chest in a sarcastic gesture. "*Moi*? But, of course. I have many stories. Besides McDougal and Vincent here," he said pointing at the aging priest who was sipping a cup of tea, "I almost have more years on me than any two of you combined, with plenty of stories to go with them."

I inspected the man's face, but couldn't find any evidence to prove he was any older than thirty five. Remembering what he looked like with his shirt off, if he was as old as he claimed to be, he must be immune to aging. Hopefully, he wouldn't mind sharing his secret.

"But what about you, *mon ami*?" He continued. "We've all had some time to get to know one another, but we know nothing of you."

"Me?" I asked, as I realized pathetically that there wasn't much to tell. "I'm just a country boy, I guess. Born in the Midwest and raised by hardworking parents, I enjoy very bad movies, long walks on the beach, and love good 80's music."

The guys smiled at the lame and cliché attempt at humor.

Wang coughed politely into a fist. "I hate to break it to you, Hunter, but there's no such thing as 'good 80s music', as you call it."

Santino leaned back in his chair and pointed at me like a child. "See, Jacob, even the Brits don't like it. I've been telling you that since I've known you." He turned back to Wang. "He even likes Duran Duran…"

Wang turned to look at me and shook his head very slowly and completely deadpanned, before saying, "Jesus, Hunter… Duran Duran? What year were you born in?"

I smiled knowingly. "None of your business, but I think it's fair to admit that my soul is perpetually stuck in the 80s."

Santino rolled his eyes and laughed to himself.

"I'm certainly familiar with Duran Duran," Vincent commented, "but I'm more partial to the Beach Boys myself."

"Really?" Santino asked skeptically.

Vincent looked hurt. "And what's wrong with that? Can't an old man enjoy quality music as well?"

Santino smirked. The Beach Boys were about as classic as music came in his opinion. I always enjoyed them too though.

"Of course, sir," Santino replied as he held up his hands near his shoulders, and raised and lowered them like a scale. "It's just that when I add together European and Priest, the Beach Boys isn't exactly the answer I get."

It was my turn to smirk. Santino generally came off as dimwitted as a donkey, usually in one of his ridiculous attempts at humor, but I knew better. The guy was Delta, the most hardcore of them all, next to my SEALs, of course.

They were trained not just to infiltrate, but to completely immerse themselves in a society, blend in, and systematically take it apart from the inside. You wouldn't know it by looking at him, or especially speaking to him, but Santino was one of the smartest guys I knew.

He spoke Russian, Arabic and Spanish fluently, and I knew he had been in the process of learning Mandarin Chinese in preparation for possible future operations in the area. The guy was a ghost, able to slip through borders on a whim, mingle amongst the natives, get the job done, get home safely, and make it all look easy.

"I just thought," Santino continued, "a guy like you would stick to Mozart or Beethoven."

Vincent leaned back in his chair, and grinned. "Ah yes, I enjoy them as well, although Vivaldi is my personal favorite."

"The *Four Seasons* is one of my favorite classical pieces," I offered, nodding appreciatively.

Vincent smiled at my recognition of his favorite composer's most well-known piece while Santino dropped his head and shook it. Wang and Bordeaux chuckled at the interchange and the conversation quickly broke down into banter and debate about an assortment of topics. I followed passively as I finished my meal.

I was working on my so-called dessert when Vincent checked his watch.

"Okay, briefing room in five. Hunter, eat it or leave it."

"Yes, sir," I mumbled around the goo in my mouth.

***

The briefing room was small enough that creature comfort was at a minimum, forcing everyone gathered to sit shoulder to shoulder in six chairs which were arrayed three across and two deep. In front was a podium and a flat screen monitor. McDougal was at the podium checking his notes and the rest of the team was already seated. Santino, Wang, and Vincent were in the first row and Bordeaux and Strauss were in the back, with an empty seat between them. Bordeaux turned and smiled, patting the seat next to him. The rest of the guys turned and tried not to laugh while Strauss sat, arms folded, completely focused on the chair in front of her.

Making my way to my seat, McDougal did a double take when he noticed my swollen eye and looked at me with severe disproval. I tried to ignore his stare as I took my seat, and made doubly sure I didn't so much as glance at Strauss, deciding two could play her little game.

McDougal cleared his throat and began his briefing.

"Welcome to His Holiness' Service. Hence forth, you are now a part of the Swiss Guard, specifically the Pope's Praetorians as he likes to call us, and all allegiance to your former commands have been transferred here. As you know, you have come here in an effort to not only protect the Pope, but to also help end any threat facing Christendom and its allies. Each of you have brought unique combat experiences and skill sets, so get used to teaching one another and learning from each other as well.

"All right, since most of you have already gotten a chance to get to know each other, we'll run through introductions quickly. My name is Dillon McDougal, Major, Special Air Service. I've been in His Majesty's service for thirteen years and have commanded troops in Afghanistan, Iraq, North Korea, Russia, and Iran.

"You all know Captain Vincent. He's our liaison with the Pope as well as our Chaplain. Prior to joining the military, he studied political science and classical studies, speaks numerous languages throughout Europe and the Middle East, and is literate in ancient Greek and Latin as well."

My interest perked up. I hadn't been aware of Vincent's educational background. I'd have to pick his brain later about his knowledge of Ancient History.

"Next up is Lieutenant James Wang. Wang has served with me for over five years in the SAS and is extremely proficient in hand to hand as well as small arms combat. He's also team medic.

"Lieutenant John Santino was a member of America's 1st Special Forces Operational Detachment-Delta, and has spent considerable time with the Green Berets. He specializes in stealth infiltration, reconnaissance, and believe it or not, is our cultural expert, having spent years of service behind enemy lines in Romania, Ukraine, Lebanon, and Brazil."

There were a few mock gasps of surprise from the audience in response to Santino's status as "cultural expert," while the man himself stood and offered an obnoxious wave and bow.

"Are you through, Lieutenant?" McDougal asked.

Santino merely smiled and I smiled with him. It was easy to see why we had always gotten along so well. We were both notorious jokesters. While Santino was more of a prankster and standup comedian, I was just a smartass with a penchant for his sense of humor.

McDougal continued his briefing, waving a hand toward the large Frenchmen.

"Lieutenant Jeanne Bordeaux was a member of the National Gendarmerie Intervention Group. He's worked mainly in Africa subverting terrorist activity before it reached Europe, and played an integral part in planning Operation Raven Claw, stopping the only major African offensive at Gibraltar in 2019. He's our demo man.

"Lieutenant Helena Strauss is our sniper. She's only been shooting in Germany's KSK for a few months, but prior to joining, won gold in multiple shooting events at the Olympics. In the short time that she has served in the military, her kill count is quite impressive, so gentlemen, please try not to end up in her crosshairs."

Santino tossed his head back and laughed, and I shifted in my seat.

"Finally, our newest arrival is Lieutenant Jacob Hunter. A U.S. Navy SEAL, Hunter is our water insertion specialist. Our location on the Tiber River is ideal for covert departures and arrivals back here to base. To do so, we'll be utilizing underground sewers that require us to swim out to a tunnel system constructed by the Vatican and fed by the Tiber, before continuing out to the Tyrrhenian Sea where a sub will pick us up and take us where we need to go. Each of you has done at least some water insertion training, but if you feel you need some extra help, see Hunter after the briefing. He is also cross trained in underwater explosives, Bordeaux you may want to get in touch with him in regard to that. Finally, he is also a qualified sniper. You're quite the Renaissance man, Hunter. With that, swim buddy assignments."

My stomach churned, knowing exactly where this was going.

"Our combat operation doctrine is that of two-man elements working in tandem. Santino, you're paired with Vincent. Bordeaux, you're with Wang, and I'll tag along with you two when we're in the water. That leaves Strauss and Hunter. Hunter, you'll act as her spotter, and since she's the least experienced in the water, you two couldn't have been a more perfect match."

This time it wasn't just Santino who couldn't help himself, but the rest of the guys mimicked his laughter as well. I even saw Vincent's shoulders bobbing in silent amusement.

Grudgingly, I finally looked over at the one person on the team I would soon have to become closest to. I saw her turn and catch my eye with equally deliberate slowness.

I smiled, keeping it completely platonic.

Strauss let out a small sigh, resigning herself to the situation and offered the first sign of affection since we met – a nod – and that was enough for me.

"All right lady and gentlemen. We've been granted leave for seventy two hours starting now. I understand Lieutenant Hunter has been in transit from the States for over a day, so go get some sleep. The rest of you, hit the gym or the range, but don't leave the base, not that it's bloody likely you could find your way out. In sixteen hours, we'll start running through combat and arms drills. You're all professionals, so it shouldn't be long before we're operating like a well-oiled machine. Dismissed."

The Praetorians stood and saluted smartly before filing out of the room.

I headed straight for the rack, having to ask Vincent where it was first.

It had been a long and tiring day, full of interesting surprises and developments.

After finally finding my bunk, I thought of my lovely new swim buddy as I kicked off my boots and collapsed onto the bed. My final thoughts as my head hit the pillow were of soft knuckles and piercing green eyes.

III
Preparation

Vatican Undergrounds, Rome
July, 2021 AD

I awoke after ten hours of uninterrupted sleep, having dreamt of nothing but floating green eyes.

When I was a child, sleeping had been a tumultuous affair. Even after nine hours of restful sleep, I still awoke every morning drowsy and my fatigue would continue throughout the day. Thankfully, years of military service easily kicked that habit. I was still a light sleeper, but as soon as my head hit the pillow these days, I was out like a rock and rarely remembered what I had dreamt about.

Glancing at the wall clock, I noticed it was only six in the morning, but as for what day of the week it was, I had no idea. After hours in transit, jet lag, more time zones than I could count, and extended sleep deprivation; I had no clue what week it was, let alone what day. Pulling myself out of bed, I felt the calling of a long, hot shower, a shave, and a fresh change of clothes.

I found the shower almost immediately, noticing it was "male-only" and wondered where the ladies room was. I gave up wondering as soon as the steaming water began to scald my face, and twenty minutes later, I felt fresh, rejuvenated, and ready to start the day.

Before leaving, I synchronized my watch with the wall clock and decided to head to the mess. On the way out, I noticed four sleeping bodies in the racks and figured the last was busy in the large multiplex outside. McDougal or Vincent could be anywhere. I also noticed another dozen or so empty racks and immediately wondered if we shared this facility with the first Praetorian team, and also wondered when we'd cross paths. It seemed like I'd find out sooner or later, so I pushed it from my mind and left the barracks. It wasn't long before I wandered my way into the large training facility and started my way toward the food.

A few steps in, I heard the *crack, crack, crack* sound of the same high powered rifle I had heard before. A quick glance toward the shooting range revealed my lovely swim buddy carefully firing down range once again. Five full magazines stood in a neat row on the table next to her, awaiting their chance to fire.

I decided it was probably a good idea to ignore her for the time being as I understood the Zen-like peace snipers experienced when shooting. I knew I hated it when someone disturbed me while I was shooting, and considering her obvious temper, I made sure to give her a wide berth as I passed by.

Instead, I followed my nose.

Not that there was an actual aroma wafting from the cafeteria so early in the morning of course. In most modern training facilities, at least the ones that housed the kind of Special Forces units that required around the clock feeding due to their erratic schedules, traditional cooks and cooking facilities were no longer up to snuff. Instead, new technology was developed that took orders, processed them, and finally, cooked the meals before delivering them to a serving tray. They were quite expensive, but the casual food consumer could hardly tell the difference from a flesh and blood cook and an automatic food processor.

I stepped up to the machine and punched up an order of bacon, scrambled eggs, wheat toast, a bowl of cereal that looked like fruit loops, and hot tea, and waited while the machine worked its magic. A few minutes later, it dispensed a sectionalized tray that held extremely generous portions of my selection. Armies were run on their stomachs after all, as Napoleon's disaster in Russia had proved, so the machines were designed to serve more than double of a normal serving, a detail I definitely approved of.

Even so, I called up an extra order of bacon.

Sitting with my back to the ever diligent Lieutenant Strauss, I put spoon to mouth and dove into my breakfast. I ate slowly, listening to the meticulous sounds of rifle discharges behind me. I'd barely made it through my first serving of bacon when the shooting abruptly stopped. Out of the corner of my eye, I noticed Strauss gather her rifle and spent magazines and carry them to the armory, emerging minutes later empty handed, undoing her tight pony tail.

I watched as she continued to ignore me, making her way to the automatic food dispenser. A few minutes later, tray in hand, she turned and walked straight toward my table, seating herself directly opposite me.

I put down my spoon, loaded with circular, fruity goodness, folded my hands on the table, and waited. Unsurprisingly, I found myself staring once again into those lovely green eyes.

"You know," I said, breaking the silence. "We've got to stop meeting like this. I'm beginning to think that you actually like me, what with the way you keep staring and all."

After what seemed like an eternity, she finally broke her gaze, shook her head, and spoke.

"To begin with," she began, apologetically enough, "I would like to apologize for hitting you yesterday. I let my anger get the best of me. I'm sorry."

Her voice was just as lovely as her face, with a crisp German accent behind it that made me think of my childhood crush on Heidi Klum rather than, say, Hitler. I was less than happy, however, with the reminder of her punch. I touched my eye socket and grimaced as the pressure caused a fair amount of pain.

"Yeah," I said. "That one hurt more than just the pride."

Her mouth tightened upward, but just slightly. "Again, I am sorry. As I'm sure you're well aware of by now, my... situation..." she sighed, "...well I had my reasons for what I did, but I suppose they were the wrong ones. I shouldn't have punched you."

Instead of pressing her for clarification on her 'reasons', I decided to move on.

"I'm just glad Santino didn't win the bet."

"Why?" She asked curiously.

"Never mind," I added, quickly glancing down at my tray, trying to push the thought from my mind. "Look, I accept your apology wholeheartedly and want to reassure you that I didn't take it personally. In fact, I'm glad we were able to push through this. It isn't every day you meet someone as attractive and deadly with a sniper rifle as you seem to be. How'd you manage such a combination?"

"Seem?" She pointed her fork at me threateningly. "That was a pretty risky statement... especially from someone like you."

"Like me?" I joked. "Whatever do you mean?

She smirked at me. "You're just lucky we've been assigned as swim buddies or else I'd have to finish what I started with your face."

I shrugged. "I'm told my curiosity gets me into trouble."

"Well, you seem harmless enough. Fine. I was born outside of Regensburg, Germany where my family has been for generations. My ancestors were wealthy merchants who dealt mostly in Eastern goods with Turkish traders, so much so that some of them married their Turkish counterparts, which is probably where I get some of my features, and it has been a business my family has been in ever since.

"But I have no doubt that you will be more interested in the fact that the very first thing my father ever taught me was how to shoot a rifle. It was a tradition so that I could accompany him on his many outlandish hunting trips. And I loved it. I practiced with my father whenever I could during school vacations and qualified for the Olympics as soon as I was eligible. I've even medaled in the Biathlon, a rather difficult event."

"The biathlon, huh?" I smirked, always considering the event something of a joke. "Ever think of becoming a Bond villain?"

"A Bond villain?"

"Never mind."

She gave me a wry look. "I'd just graduated from Oxford, leading our marksmanship team to an international championship, when I decided to spend a year in America to further my education – a very interesting country, by the way."

I shrugged. "We try."

"Well, when I returned to Germany after the war started, I debated joining the military, but it wasn't until just a year ago that I decided to finally do just that. Papa was not happy, but I signed up despite his disapproval. He lives in a fantasy world with no idea what is going on outside his estate. He wasn't even afraid for my life, just upset at my decision. I didn't care. My life was without direction and I wanted to do something important. The war was just getting worse and worse, and I needed to do something.

She leaned away and crossed her arms as she looked away, the gesture implying she was frustrated by what she was going to say next. "My shooting scores propelled me into sniper school. I worked alone, never given a spotter, probably because they wanted me to wash out, but I still graduated at the top of my class. I'm a great shot, so your job should be pretty easy." She turned back to me and offered me a sly look. "But I'm sure I'll appreciate the company, at least."

"Well, it's my pleasure," I said honestly, even if there was something to her story that didn't add up. "I've done plenty of shooting over the years, and killed my fair share. I have no problems spotting."

"Perhaps we could arrange a little friendly competition later?"

I held up a hand. "Yeah, I don't think so. My competitive streak ended a long time ago. I have no desire for showmanship or impressing anyone. I'll shoot with you, but I'd rather not turn it into a competition."

She gave me another odd look. "You are a curious man, Lieutenant Hunter. You don't meet very many men, let alone snipers, who aren't interested in seeing whose is bigger." She leaned back and smiled, and she suddenly looked better than ever. "And, please, call me Helena. Such formalities are unnecessary considering our partnership."

I smiled, wondering at the ambiguity of her word choice. "You know what? We've never been properly introduced." I held out a hand. "My name is Lieutenant Jacob Hunter, but my friends call me Jacob."

She smiled and lightly gripped my hand, hers not being nearly as soft as I thought it would be. It was heavily callused from years of shooting, more so than even mine. "It's nice to meet you, Jacob."

I smiled back, "It's nice to meet you too, Helena."

As we sat there, smiling at one another, hand in hand, Santino emerged from the barracks. He grabbed a cup of coffee and came to sit at our table.

"So?" He pondered, as he glanced at our clasped hands. "You two married yet?"

Just as he was about to take a seat next to me, I responded by kicking his chair out from beneath him. He fell hard on his ass with a loud thump and he glared up at me, rubbing his rear.

I crammed an overloaded spoonful of fruit loops into my mouth and looked down at him.

"Nope."

***

Helena and I were lounging on our stomachs, lying very close, drenched in sweat, contemplating our next move. It was an hour after our reconciliation and we had decided to take our relationship to the next level.

The obvious thing to do was to get out the rifles and hit the range.

Helena lay to my left, rifle at the ready, while I held a pair of high powered binoculars to my eyes, acting as her spotter. I was situated just behind her, with the left side of my body resting up against her right leg. Our close proximity allowed for the perspectives seen through our individual scopes to sync up more precisely than if I was resting beside her. I rested my binoculars on my gear bag to stabilize my view while her rifle's bipod kept her aim steady.

"Wind... six clicks left," I told her.

We were shooting at long range, so Helena had traded in her standard rifle for a German version of the Barrett M107 Special Application Scoped Rifle, the G82. The weapon was a beast, sometimes referred to as an anti-material weapon, a name that carried serious weight behind it. The "Light Fifty" fired a .50 caliber round, the newest versions of which allowed the Barrett to shoot farther than ever. Its unique design reduced the recoil of such a powerful weapon to a manageable level, and I was about to find out if my female friend could handle it.

Our target was just shy of two kilometers down field, which wasn't the furthest a modern sniper could shoot at, but it was a challenging range. I had no idea how the Vatican had dug out so much territory to create the range, accommodating for bullet drop and everything, but the compass on my watch indicated we were facing northeast. Ancient Rome hadn't extended that far in that direction, so I assumed the range was simply carved out of dirt. The flight time of a bullet at this range was so long the shooter could basically recite the alphabet before the round hit its target.

To make the simulation even more difficult, the base's ventilation system was set to imitate various weather patterns and wind speeds. I had no idea what the system was set at, relying instead on calculations I performed in my head based on the fluttering of shrubbery off in the distance. To further enhance the simulation, we pumped up the heat on our end of the room to mimic the harsh environments of the Middle Eastern region we would most likely be operating in.

It was currently hotter than Hell, and I wondered if Santino had messed with the temperature control just to screw with us.

These variables were of utmost importance to a sniper, as even something as minute as a slight shift in air moisture could affect a bullet's trajectory. Snipers have to take every detail into account and excessive care went into preparing for each and every pull of the trigger. These days, technology calculated most of these variables for us, but any sniper worth his weight in salt did it himself first.

Helena adjusted her scope appropriately while sweat beaded its way down her brow, relying on her spotter, me, to relay the relevant information needed to make the perfect shot.

Peering through my binoculars, I tapped a button on the bottom of the optical device and the range finder function displayed itself in the upper right hand corner of the view. With the Earth's natural curve and gravity's pull on the bullet, elevation adjustments were needed to ensure the most accurate shot. Years ago, spotters would have to determine ranges with the naked eye, but technology now calculated the distance for us. However, every sniper was still trained to gauge ranges with their eyes only as technology couldn't always be relied on.

I predicted the range was nearly two kilometers.

"Range... 1.86 kilometers. Elevation, seven clicks."

Making matters worse, Helena was performing what was known as a cold bore shot, meaning it was her first shot in a cold barrel, with no set up shots to help guide her true shot. Firing from a cold barrel not only affected the trajectory of a fired round, but was also a psychological hurdle to overcome. This was the hardest shot for a sniper to make and consisted of the exact same shot used in the kill missions snipers were used for. Not that I'd ever "assassinated" anyone before. At least that's what the CIA kept telling me.

The rest of the team had assembled in the cafeteria, paying close attention to the meticulous effort of the sniper pair, binoculars at the ready.

Just another distraction to deal with.

Luckily, snipers were masters of the self.

Stamina. Endurance. Patience. Precision. These were the tools of a sniper. Tools we knew better than anyone else. Snipers took great pride in simply being better than everyone else. It was a job most could never dream of doing. It made us lords of the hunt, a stalker in the jungle. We were expected to track, locate, and wait out a target for days and days if need be before taking a cold bore shot in one hundred degree weather during a hurricane, all the while the rest of the world sat at home watching Animal Planet. It may very well be the toughest job ever, and it makes us immensely proud that the majority of mankind wouldn't make it five minutes in our world.

While we didn't need to seek out and wait for the best shot on our current target, it still took us around twenty minutes to prepare for the shot. Another few minutes and four impatient operators later, we were finally ready for the moment of truth.

"Target established," I reported. "Fire for effect. Fire. Fire. Fire."

With my affirmation that our checklist was complete, Helena had the go ahead to shoot. I heard her take three slow, deep breaths, holding it on the third. A half second later, she squeezed the trigger, handling the weapon masterfully. I had wondered if the recoil of the shot would be too much for the woman to handle, but it seemed as though she possessed a hidden strength few could mimic.

It took a few seconds for the projectile to reach its mark, which it finally did successfully in an explosion of watermelon. Our audience cheered, thankful their sniper was more than fully competent. I even saw Bordeaux wipe a hand across his forehead in mock relief before he turned back to the others as their conversations resumed.

I was impressed as well.

I'd taken that shot many times as a SEAL, but even for the best snipers, it was never guaranteed one hundred percent of the time.

I rolled off Helena's leg and onto my back, stretching as many muscles as I could. Doing so relieved the stresses accumulated while lying completely immobile since I'd gotten on the mat.

"A fine shot, Lieutenant," I said. "You definitely deserve to be here."

"Thanks," she replied as she rolled onto her back as well. "To be honest, I haven't made very many cold bore shots with the fifty, but every successful one I perform makes me feel that much better."

She shifted onto her side and used her left hand to knead some feeling back into the shoulder that her rifle had rested against for the last hour. "And I have to admit, having you spot for me was refreshing." She paused. "It calmed my nerves. Doing it in a controlled environment is one thing, but in the field is totally different. If I have trouble here, what's to say things won't be worse when it matters?"

I rubbed my eyes before I turned to look at her, for once not finding anger and annoyance in her expression. Why was she doubting herself? She may have been the least experienced operator here, but her mere presence automatically made her one of the best.

"Helena, you're a fine sniper. You just proved that. You can handle anything out there, trust me. And don't worry. I'll be by your side whenever you need me."

She smiled. "Thank you, Jacob. I'm not used to having someone to rely on, and frankly, it's a bit overwhelming. It's almost like being in a..."

I frowned. I knew where she was going with that thought as she trailed off. It's exactly like being in a relationship or a family. Most sniper pairs were men, and therefore, brothers. Trust had to pass equally and unequivocally between them, because each relied on the other for everything. A business company may do team building exercises where individuals fall backwards off a ladder in the blind hopes of being caught by their peers. They did this to build trust and cooperation to create a more efficient work environment. The equivalent exercise for a sniper pair was to perform such an exercise while blindfolded in a monsoon, during an artillery barrage, with a nuke going off in the background, and zombies closing in on all sides.

Would Joe Blow from human resources stick around and catch you during all that?

I doubted it.

Helena and I needed to trust each other. She needed to be my partner. My sister. I had to know she wasn't going to buckle under pressure and run away when I needed her support, and I couldn't have her lying to me. I couldn't trust her if she did. Santino had said she'd just ended a relationship so serious she threatened to kill the next guy who even looked like the shmuck, yet here she was talking like she didn't even know what the word *relationship* meant.

"Helena, do you mind if I ask you a personal question?"

She hesitated, but nodded. "We need to be honest with each other, of course."

My thoughts exactly.

"Your experience not having a spotter is understandable, but the way you speak of not having someone to rely on, well, sniper pairs utilize the same kind of trust as relationships do. You should know that. Yet you say you've never had anyone to rely on almost like you've never had anyone at all, but that's not the story I got from the guys..."

I let my last statement trail off, hoping the point would sink in before things got more awkward than they already were. Her silence only confirmed my suspicions that the story I got from Santino wasn't the whole one. I decided to go easy on her.

"Look. I'll understand if you don't tell me right now what's going on. We have plenty of time to get to know each other more before..."

She rolled onto her back again and took a deep breath. "No, you're right. You've obviously heard the story from one of the other guys about why I reacted to your arrival, but what I told them wasn't completely true. I was betrothed, actually, but it wasn't out of love. It was an arranged marriage agreed upon before I was even born, forced upon me by my father, as my fiancé's father did upon him."

As far as I was concerned, arranged marriages were all but extinct, but I did know in some societies they were still common. I had no idea the Germans still practiced it, but in the high class society I assumed Helena was from, it was probably more prevalent than most thought.

She took another deep breath before continuing.

"He was nice," she continued, a small smile tugging at her lips before it just as quickly vanished, "and as children we were rather close, but there was never anything between us deeper than friendship. I was trapped by an agreement, and Papa watched me like a hawk. We tried being intimate with each other but it didn't work. It just didn't feel right. It felt forced and unnatural. It's why I eventually joined the military. I thought that I could just run away from my problems without ever having to face them."

She paused, but I didn't interrupt.

"He was killed in a car accident not too long ago. He was drinking and hadn't been paying attention when he ran off the Autobahn and collided with a tree. He and his passenger were killed instantly." She sniffled, before her voice rose angrily. "He was with another woman! Meanwhile, there I was, a perfect little angel, while he was off doing whatever the fuck he wanted while no one said a thing about it!"

I noticed her eyes were moistening with tears of sadness and rage, and I could feel the anger in her voice.

"If you two were so distant, why are you so sad and angry, and why did you tell the guys that story about being cheated on, and nothing more?"

She stayed silent as she pondered her answer, and I thought she was about to clam up completely. I suddenly felt like an ass for pressuring her to tell me something that I guess wasn't exactly relevant to our professional relationship. It was something we would need to talk about sooner or later, but I shouldn't have pushed her.

I put a hand on her shoulder reassuringly.

"Helena, you can trust me, but I'll understand if you need some time."

"Damn it, Hunter, I've known you all of an hour and it's scary that I'm telling you anything. Trust me. I'm not used to that."

I looked at her with a neutral expression. I didn't want to offer her a reason to give up more than she was ready for, but I didn't want her to stop either.

She took another breath and continued, releasing years of pent up frustration. "He didn't deserve to die, and we were still, if anything, friends. He may have been cheating on our relationship, but it wasn't much of one anyway. I told the guys the story about being cheated on because I wanted to fit in. I'd already figured I would have to do something to establish myself here, something to prove I belonged, so imagine my surprise when I saw you. What were the chances that you would look even remotely like him?"

"Pretty good I guess."

"Yeah, pretty good."

"I am sorry for that."

She sighed. "It's okay."

"So, do I really remind you that much of him?"

She looked away before answering. "Yes and no. I was so focused on shooting that when I saw you, I didn't even think. I just saw a tall man with brown hair and I immediately thought of him. I thought of what he represented. A lie. A life of loneliness and years of anger, frustration and pain. He represented the life I had but didn't want. One I shouldn't have had. A life wasted. It was all I could think about while we were in the armory, and your asinine comment did not help."

I felt a small smile tug at my lips. "Sorry."

"I said it was okay. I suppose I still need some time to put my life in order, but I'm fine. I guess I should be thankful that I actually like the military."

I nodded in agreement and waited for her to make eye contact again. "You know I'm not him, right? You don't have to be reminded of him when you see me anymore."

"I know," she said. "Thank you."

I gave her a reassuring smile. "No problem. Besides, I'm sure I'm way better…"

I was cut off as a shadow loomed over us. Together, we looked up to see Santino standing there. He hesitated before saying anything, probably deciding whether to tell a joke or not as he remembered the last time he tried to say something funny. Deciding on tact over humor, he held out his hands to help us off the ground. Each of us gripping a hand, he hauled us to our feet.

"Briefing," was all he needed to say.

***

The team assembled in the small briefing room for the second time since our inception. This time, Helena and I were the first to arrive and took the same seats we'd originally occupied. McDougal noticed our newfound friendship and looked back down at his notes. I saw him shake his head, obviously relieved that the kids were able to settle down and play nice. It wasn't long before the rest of the team filed into the room and took their seats. Once everyone was comfortable, McDougal started his presentation.

"I know we haven't had much time together, none really, but you're all highly trained operatives, elite, familiar with confusing situations, and it's time to get to work. American intelligence has information confirming a direct threat against the Pope. Some kind of biological concoction cooked up and readied for use."

He paused, taking a deep breath before continuing.

"This is the kind of threat we were designed to handle, mates. Most of our allies' special operations teams are otherwise engaged in other theaters around the globe, and we are being called on to take action. The first Praetorian team is already in the field, so our deployment time has been advanced. Any questions?"

There were none.

"Righto. Our target is a small fishing town off the Mediterranean coast of Syria. Population is around two thousand indigenous residents known to have harbored terrorists in the past. Intel has informed us of a cave just outside of town where satellite imagery has shown mass transit and large amounts of cargo transported in and out. We suspect these cargo containers are what we're looking for."

He turned on the monitor and called up some photos of the town, the cave, the cargo containers, and a bearded man, wearing aviator sunglasses and a long, leather trench coat.

"A joint CIA and SIS task force has been searching for known terrorist Mushin Abdullah for years, but has been unsuccessful. He's a bioengineer whose resume begins in the eighties with his work for the Russians, and we know he was the man who created the weapons used against both Israel and the Vatican."

Bordeaux fidgeted next to me in reaction to McDougal's words, but he didn't say anything.

I wondered what that was about.

"An analysis of the bodies found at both sites produced a list of necessary compounds he will require to make more of the agent. Intelligence compiled the list and cross referenced it with shipping manifests scattered throughout the Middle East. The man is not an idiot. His list went through a number of intermediaries with numerous phony IDs and falsified bank accounts. What got him was a slip up in logistics, resulting in most of his purchases ending up at the same place at the same time. We can probably thank some middle management lackey for that mistake. Either way, we have an opportunity to take out the one man capable of making this rubbish, as well as one of the primary coordinators behind both attacks."

McDougal paused, looking at each of us in turn, letting the impact of his words sink in. Satisfied he had our attention, he continued.

"Everything he needs has collected in those containers. We know they will be imported from a dockyard on the Mediterranean and moved by vehicle to the cave. Our assumption is that he's hiding out there. Our plan is to sneak into a few of these containers and infiltrate the facility right under his nose."

He clicked a stylus and the multitude of images shifted to satellite imagery of the port and immediate area.

"Here's the plan. We infiltrate the cargo ship after hitching a ride on the HMS Triumph, one of Britain's nuclear submarines in the area. We'll rendezvous with them in the Tyrrhenian Sea where they will take us the rest of the way. Once aboard the cargo ship, we'll locate these containers and stuff ourselves into as few as possible. Then, we take a ride."

He utilized his stylus again, enlarging the image to encompass the port and town, highlighting the predicted route in red. He then shifted the image to show just the town and the location of the cave.

"Once the trucks reach this position," he pointed to an area just before the edge of town, "Lieutenant Strauss will disembark and take position within the town to provide sniper support. You up for this, Strauss?"

"Yes, sir," she replied with a sidelong glance at me.

"Brilliant. Hunter, you're with the team. We'll need more shooters inside for this one."

"Yes, sir."

"Now, our primary objective is to recover the high value target: Mushin Abdullah. When we see him, we try and take him, but if he turns out to be too much to handle, we take him out. Wang, you're on hostage transportation. Keep him quiet, but keep him mobile, we may need to cut and run. If I give the order, take him out."

"Not a problem, sir," Wang said.

"Okay. Bordeaux, once we're out, we blow the entire place, Abdullah or no. Bring enough C-4 to bring down the house."

"It's what I do best, sir."

"Cheers. Finally, we'll have a little extra backup on this one. Two days ago, the CIA was gracious enough to store some extra equipment we may need in a safe house inside the town. They've also made contact with the local resistance. If things get hairy and we need to hole up and wait for extraction, that's where we'll regroup."

Odd. I couldn't remember a time when an operation was gifted with additional supplies for a simple smash and grab mission. The logistics of even arranging such a thing were unimaginable. In a worst case scenario we'd have to hump it back to the docks on foot, but that shouldn't take more than a few hours, even if we had to shoot our way out.

I continued pondering until McDougal continued.

"Our contact's name is Omar. He'll be watching the docks upon our arrival and will signal us when he's ready for our insertion. Again, if things go bad, we'll have his local militia for backup, but we can't rely on them. We'll fall back to the equipment cache and call for extraction, but only as a last resort. Hopefully, we'll be able to get in, plant the charges, secure the high value target, sneak out, and wait for the place to blow on a timed delay. I'm not holding my breath on that one, so prepare for the worst. We'll be moving out at 1300. It's now 0900, so get your gear and get some rest. Any final questions?"

I raised my hand. "Sir, rules of engagement?"

"The townspeople are harboring known terrorists. If they get in the way, take them out. Let God sort out the rest. Anything else?"

He glanced around the room one final time. Everyone was silent.

"All right, dismissed."

***

A few hours later, the team assembled in the armory, the first time I had seen everyone congregated in the small room at one time. Each member of the team was going through their equipment and checking their weapons. Wang with his UMP submachine gun, McDougal with a G36C assault rifle, Bordeaux with the Mk 48 Mod 0 version of the M249 SAW light machine gun which fired the larger 7.62x51mm round, and Vincent had an M4 carbine. Santino had an HK416, similar to mine.

Strauss was preparing two weapons. A German made AMP Technical Services DSR-1 was her primary rifle. It was an efficient sniper rifle that fired the same large round as Bordeaux's SAW, but while not as handy in a large scale firefight, it was obviously far more accurate. McDougal had informed her that a M107 .50 caliber Barrett sniper rifle, similar to the one she and I had trained with earlier, was waiting at the weapons cache.

I again wondered at the purpose of such a cache, especially one containing such a powerful rifle…

Whatever. Out of sight, out of mind. At least hopefully.

Her second weapon was a Belgian engineered FN P90 personal defense weapon. Preferred by tank and helicopter operators, its compact bull pup design gave it more range than another weapon of comparable size, and its large magazine size and high velocity round made it ideal for personal protection.

As for me, I already had my rifle secure and my wetsuit on, and was just completing preparations on my re-breather gear well ahead of everyone else.

The Draeger Mk V breathing apparatus had been standard issue for SEALs for over thirty years, its design and function so effective. Instead of regular scuba gear, where a wearer breathes from an isolated oxygen source, the Mk V recycles the air breathed. With it, I could remain submerged beneath an enemy dock for the better part of a day, as long as I kept my breathing under control. The new Mk VI, developed only a few years ago, merely needed to have its internals cleaned as opposed to having them replaced, an operation one can do in the field.

As I waited, I made sure to avoid looking at Helena in her wetsuit, which was harder than it sounded. I was fairly certain we were friends at this point, but I didn't want to risk offending her again, as much as I wanted to in this case. The rest of the team was likewise averting their eyes. After all, women in the Special Forces were still a rather new concept, and one wearing a wetsuit was completely novel. I glanced at Santino beside me, who returned the look with a knowing smile.

Shaking my head, I completed my preparations by packing my MOLLE rig into a water tight bag and giving the locker a final look-over. Everything was secure and ready to go. My rifle was secure in its waterproof bag and the rest of my equipment was stored in another waterproof bag.

With a breath of satisfaction, I reached for the laces of my black waterproof boots, but my thoughts continued to stray toward that equipment cache. Something just did not click with this mission. In all the years I'd been in the field, I had never been provided with additional gear to help out if things got bad. Sure, I'd raided the enemy's supplies numerous times, but I'd never been given this kind of support.

Maybe working for the Pope had more advantages than I thought.

Tying off my second boot, I stood and turned to see if my lovely swim buddy needed a hand but was interrupted by McDougal's commanding voice. "All right everybody, we're leaving in ten. Get your gear and meet up at the airlock."

I shouldered my gear bag and hefted the rest of my gear, noticing Helena was already finished.

"Ready, Lieutenant?" she asked.

I waved a hand toward the door. "Lead the way, ma'am."

***

The airlock was little more than a room with a grated floor and a hatch such as one would find on a submarine. On the floor were seven underwater propulsion vehicles, or UPVs for short. They were little more than a thin bed to lay in with foot rests, dashboard with a windshield, a propulsion lever and a joystick. The dashboard had a night vision view of what was in front of the UPV, a GPS radar screen, fuel and power readouts, and a radio. The craft was powerful enough to carry one person, a reasonable amount of gear, and travel through the water at a respectable speed. It didn't possess a cockpit, so it forced a pilot to use his own breathing device. I was extremely familiar with the small craft, but the rest of the crew had rarely had the opportunity to even work with flippers, something every diver should be competent with anyway.

McDougal ordered me to give the team a quick briefing on the crafts since I was the most familiar with them. I went over the basics: throttle and directional controls, dashboard equipment, as well as to remind them that they should keep their legs firmly secured in the foot rests.

Only Santino had a question. "Phasers?"

I shook my head and tried not to laugh.

Any eight year old could control the small submersibles. The controls were designed like any video game controller and as long as the user stayed on the bed, feet secured, they wouldn't float away. Even if they did manage to separate from the sub, the controls had an automatic shut off if separated from the pilot. All it would take was a quick swim back.

After I finished my quick briefing, the team spread out amongst the UPVs, McDougal in the center flanked by Wang and Bordeaux, Santino and Vincent on the left, and Helena and myself on the right. After we were situated, the room automatically filled with water and the team was left floating within. I looked through my goggles to make sure Helena wasn't freaking out or anything, but thankfully she seemed fine. Noticing my inspection, she turned and gave me a thumbs up. Her face was masked by her goggles, and as we were unable to communicate via our radios, I couldn't tell if she was truly all right, but I suspected she was tough enough to handle it.

She'd be fine.

McDougal pressed a button on his dashboard and the double doors in front of us cracked open. Beyond them was nothing but blackness, no plant or aquatic life visible. I knew ancient sewer systems had been discovered by modern archeologists over the year and could be used as a means to navigate the ancient city beneath the modern one. They were also pretty disgusting, steeping for millennia, a breeding ground for hundreds of kinds of bacteria and diseases.

McDougal gunned his UPV and the team smoothly exited the room into the murky water. Our headlights only penetrated a few feet into the darkness, forcing us to rely on our GPS. It provided us with waypoints laid out on a rudimentary topographical map, connected by lines already programmed in the system. Our progress was slow going though not through any lack of skill on our part, but simply because we were new to the terrain.

About fifteen minutes into the trip, we came to a solid wall, but our waypoints clearly indicated we needed to go through the blockade. McDougal held up his fist, indicating for us to hold our position. He manipulated another switch on his dashboard, and I began to hear a steady whirring noise and could see the water clearing. I glanced behind me and noticed a wall was blocking the way we had just come through. McDougal must have activated some kind of system that filtered the water in the sewer.

A few seconds later, I saw the water clearing noticeably before the doors opened before us. McDougal motioned forward, and the team gunned their engines, making a quick right turn into a narrow passageway to follow the Vatican's artificial corridor straight to the Tyrrhenian Sea.

It took us another forty-five minutes before we left the coastline and came face to face with a lumbering, whale shaped behemoth that would become our ride.

My earpiece crackled to life as McDougal contacted the submarine using his radio's push-to-talk button to transmit a quick burst of Morse Code. The Navy still taught the archaic form of communication developed in the 1840s, and most Special Forces outfits learned it as well. Quickly squeezing a radio's PTT button transmits a sharp burst of static, which makes for a perfect way to send the code.

I heard a return transmission that indicated the sub was ready for our arrival, and saw McDougal point in my direction. I sent him an okay sign with my hand, and made my way to the gigantic vessel, Helena right behind me.

Boarding a submarine in nothing but a wetsuit wasn't a challenge for a seasoned Navy SEAL, but could be potentially lethal for an amateur. Had I been in a submarine of my own, and not alone in a wetsuit, a docking collar would be used to attach the two subs together. The collar would pressurize, and coming aboard would be as simple as opening both hatches and crossing the threshold.

To a achieve my task, however, I would need to turn the wheel on the hatch, climb down a ladder till I reach a second hatch, close the first one, wait for the water to recede in the little airlock, open the second hatch, and climb down into the submarine.

It sounded easy in principle, but it was far more complicated than it sounds.

The first step was to secure my UPV in one of the submarine's external storage lockers. I found it easily, already open, and astern of the hatch. Piloting it into the locker, I abandoned my small craft, secured my gear bags to a carabineer attached to my wetsuit, and approached the wheel I would need to turn in order to open the hatch. I signaled for Helena to hang back. There was no sense in risking a possible accident when I could easily perform the operation by myself and in my sleep.

I began by firmly grasping the wheel, and reciting the age old "lefty loosy, righty tighty" mantra everyone utters before turning something. Next, I planted my feet on the hull, squeezing the slight lip that juts up encasing the hatch. Slowly and surely, I turned the wheel to the left, thankful when it offered little resistance.

After a dozen or so turns, the hatch popped open with a slight sputter of bubbles. The small antechamber would have been filled upon our arrival to ensure the hatch didn't explosively decompress, probably killing me. I signaled for Helena to swim in first.

Following her in, I pulled my gear bags in behind me, and shut the hatch. The space in the cylindrical airlock was cramped and tight, forcing us to float chest to chest, inches apart. I grasped the ladder with my right hand and right foot, while Helena mirrored my position. With my left hand, I grabbed a crowbar from its resting place and pounded the inner hatch three times, and waited until the water started to slowly drain from the compartment.

As the water passed my face, I pulled back my hood and removed my goggles and breathing apparatus as Helena did the same.

"Tight squeeze," I said, adjusting my position, accidentally bumping my elbow against her breasts.

She glared and I looked around, trying to ignore her while also trying to find any way to make the water go faster. Failing, we endured a few more moments of uncomfortable silence before the inner hatch finally opened.

"After you," I offered.

Helena gave me a smirk before descending a few steps, lowering her gear to the deck, and dropping behind it. I followed quickly.

I landed in a crouch, stood and moved aside to let Helena close the inner hatch while I keyed my radio. In order to stay efficient and silent on the battlefield, instead of speaking into the radio to confirm orders, or signal an all clear, we simply clicked the PTT button twice in quick succession, an efficient way to indicate all was well on the other end of the radio. The double click could mean many things depending on the situation, but McDougal would understand that I had sent it as an all clear to send in the next pair.

After sending the transmission, I turned to face the two seamen emerging from the hatch to my left. The pair wore British naval uniforms, midshipmen according to their rank insignias, and had the look of men who spent way too much time under the water. Noticing my inspection, the pair halted and saluted.

"Welcome aboard the *H.M.S Triumph*, Lieutenant."

I returned the salute. "Thanks for the warm welcome."

After securing the hatch, Helena turned and stood next to me.

The pair's immediate reaction was to salute a second time, but with obvious hesitation. These men probably hadn't seen a woman in months, especially not one that looked like Helena, who was looking especially radiant with her damp hair and face.

"Welcome aboard the *Triumph*, Ma'am."

"Thank you," she replied.

"Our orders are to escort you to the briefing room after your team has had an opportunity to change out of your wetsuits and secure your gear. If you will just follow the corridor beyond the hatch we just came through, the second door on your right will be your staging area. You can head there now if you'd like."

"Thank you," I replied as I gestured to the hatch for Helena to go through first. "Lieutenant, after you."

She offered me a cynical smile and bumped me playfully on her way to the hatch. The two midshipmen watched, tilting their heads to watch as she bent at the waist to fit through. I had to chuckle as I watched as well, a slight feeling of possessive pride passing over me. It reminded me of a time back in college when I attended a party with a foreign exchange student from France. She had been beautiful, and every guy there hated my guts because of it.

My arms crossed against my chest, I glanced over at the two seamen who looked at me with jealousy in their eyes, the silent one of the two arching an eyebrow suggestively. I let out a quick laugh before placing a hand on the inquisitive man's shoulder.

"I wouldn't go there, my friend," I told him, pointing at my black eye. "Trust me."

Whether he thought I was threatening him or merely reaffirming his fears that he had no chance, his shoulders slumped in defeat.

Releasing his shoulder, I followed after Helena.

Halfway through, I heard the inner hatch open and two men drop to the floor.

"Welcome aboard the…"

The man didn't get a chance to continue before Santino cut him off. "Yeah, yeah, now where's this 'tea' I've heard so much about?"

***

It took fifteen minutes for the last of the team to cycle through the airlock, and another twenty before we had our gear in lockers, had our wetsuits hung up, and had changed into duty gear the crew had provided for us.

Gathered in the small briefing room, the team chatted while we waited for our briefing to begin. Joining the team was the sub's skipper, Captain Billings, whose physicality could have in no way better fit the role of a sub commander. He was short in stature and thin like a runner, a perfect build for the cramped confines of a submarine. His square jaw and perpetual five o'clock shadow gave him a roguish look that the ladies probably loved. I couldn't help but notice Helena's interest, which was probably more annoying than it should have been.

Don't be jealous, Jacob, she'll probably never see him again.

Jealous? What the hell was wrong with me?

I tried to distract myself by probing my damaged eye, which was still black and hurt like hell. I'm sure at least Santino would find something funny out of all this.

The thought of my troublesome friend brought my eyes across the aisle, where I found him already looking at me, flicking his eyes in Billings' direction, then over at Helena, giving me another one of his annoying smiles.

There were times when I wondered why we were friends at all.

Still, despite his antics, I appreciated his attention. It reminded me that I *had* a friend, someone I could rely on… even if he was an arrogant jackass. So, I did what any good friend would do: took a rubber band from my briefing packet and loaded it around my fingers. Taking careful aim, I fired, nailing him right between the eyes. One of his hands reactively flung to his forehead to ease the sting, and he gave me the same glare he'd offered earlier when I'd kicked his chair out from beneath him.

I couldn't help but chuckle.

"Something funny, Hunter?"

I glanced over at Helena, feigning innocence. "Hmm? Oh, nothing. Just Santino being Santino."

She leaned forward to see him rubbing his struck forehead, mumbling.

"You two have a history don't you?"

"Oh, yeah," I sighed. "We certainly do."

"Oooh, I feel a story coming," she replied excitedly, clutching her hands together between her thighs and shrugging her head between her shoulders, giving me an uncharacteristically childish smile that made her look annoyingly cute.

I sighed again, realizing I owed her a story, but was doubly annoyed because I knew I couldn't just end this one with Santino. It was about more than just him.

"The abridged version then…" I began before taking a long breath. "Over a year ago, his Delta squad was cut off from extraction while on an op in North Korea. We were assigned as their standby unit and were sent in to pull their asses out if they got in trouble. They did, and my team was ambushed in the process of rescuing them and we were cut off from Santino and his men. Through a stroke of pure luck, our two positions ran into one other. The momentary confusion on the enemy's part gave us the time we needed to get the hell out of there. But on our way out, I was shot in the leg. Twice. In the same damn leg. The wounds were pretty bad and I was losing a lot of blood. Possible arterial bleeding. I never knew and never asked afterward, but I'd known that I was done for when a bad guy blundered onto me as I lay there dying."

I had to pause and close my eyes as the flashback forced me to recall one of the most horrible memories I had. My hand instinctually moved to my thigh to massage the area where I'd been hit. The scars on that leg remained, and were not pretty.

"He pointed his gun at my face and started to taunt me, laughing all the while. I'd lost my rifle after hitting the ground, and my pistol was inaccessible. A few seconds later, he shot me in the arm." My hand now moved to massage the area just above the elbow on my left arm. "Just for the hell of it, I guess. It was at that point I knew I was going to die. Even thought I saw some angels. But, the next thing I know, Santino was there, ramming his knife through the back of the man's throat, severing his spinal column. Guy died instantly. That's where he does his best work, you know, up close. Santino's as quiet as a ghost and even scarier than one with a knife."

Helena nodded, waiting for me to continue.

"Anyway, we didn't really know each other yet. We'd only met once during a cross training operation a few months back. We were barely acquaintances. Even so, he came back for me. He slapped on a few field bandages, picked me up, and pulled my fat out of the fire. He even found my rifle for me."

"For such a free spirited asshole, he seems like a good man to have your back."

"He's the best," I said wholeheartedly. "I spent three months in the hospital where we ended up. Santino was assigned to a training detail on the base at the same time and he came to visit every day. I always wondered if he used some of that Delta pull to swing the training detail, but he'd never tell me if he did. We just sat there every chance we got playing cards and video games, cracking jokes at lame daytime soap operas and shooting the shit. We became instant friends. I'll never make a better one if I live a dozen lifetimes."

I smiled, remembering the days as Santino became one of my best friends, before sighing a third time, my mind wandering to the rest of the time I spent in the hospital. The time I'd spent in the company of someone else as well.

A few minutes ago, I'd thought about telling Helena the rest, but now, I wasn't so sure. The second half of the story began the day I awoke from my surgery, and was assigned a nurse to take care of me. It was a story I hadn't told anyone before, and even Santino didn't know the full extent of it. That nurse had changed the way I looked at my life.

After a few sessions of rehab where we had to work very closely together, it was obvious the nurse was interested, and so was I. After a few weeks, our time together transcended the typical patient/caregiver relationship and bloomed into something more. During my recuperation, we would go on long walks and spend hours in the gym together rehabbing my injury. I remembered how every day, when she came to my room, Santino would just sit there as she completely ignored him while tending to my every need.

I sighed to myself while Helena waited patiently for me to continue.

I'd never grown closer to a woman than I did during those few months. Relationships had never been my strong suit, but somehow she and I had just clicked. I fell hard for her. I was completely unfazed by the fact that I knew we'd probably never see each other again after I returned to active duty. The war had just barely begun and the average life expectancy of service men and women deployed in the field shortened every day.

After I was finally discharged, I knew it was over.

When she and Santino carted me out in a wheelchair, the nurse helped me out while Santino went to pack the taxi. Neither one of us had known what to say. We just stood there looking at each other, but after a few seconds, still not knowing what to say, she threw herself into my arms and gave me a kiss that held us there for minutes. When she pulled away, she told me she hoped to see me again, but I knew even she didn't believe her own words. I said goodbye as strongly as I could, which only managed to be little more than a whisper. She put on a brave face, but as I watched her retreat back to the hospital, I noticed a trail of tears tracing her steps like fat rain drops on the pavement.

It had all been like a fairy tale.

Thinking about those happy, but inevitably painful few months did little to lighten my mood now. Those days could have been better. It's why I hated the story about Santino and me meeting. It was like one of those dreams where everything was so perfect, and you felt so happy, only to wake up and realize that it was all just a dream and your life was everything but.

I had to live that dream.

As I played the story over in my head, I found myself staring at the back of the chair in front of me, but my mind was interrupted by Helena waving a hand in front of my face.

"Hello... Jacob..." she said. "Anybody home?"

I jerked my head in response and turned to look at her.

"What?" I asked.

"I believe you were about to finish your story. You and Santino were in a hospital?"

I turned away and took a deep breath, letting it out slowly.

No. I couldn't tell her quite yet.

"Sorry, Helena," I said, looking back at her, "but the rest of that story can wait for another time."

Her eyebrows narrowed in confusion, probably wondering what could be so personal that I couldn't tell her after she'd so readily offered her own story. She opened her mouth to inquire further, but she never got a chance to finish her question before Billings began his briefing.

"All right, mates," his voice, from an American's perspective, was a typical British drawl, "I'll try and keep this short. I know you've already been briefed on your specific mission parameters, so I'll key you in on the operational position of my sub."

Billings pulled up a map of the Mediterranean Sea on a monitor, and zoomed in on the Eastern coast where we would be making our insertion. The map looked similar to the one McDougal had presented earlier.

"We'll be dropping you off here," he said, indicating a point on the map with a laser pointer, "a few miles off the shore line. Once you disembark, you'll be on your own. Our presence here is completely off the grid. We're not even supposed to be in the Mediterranean."

He manipulated the map to show the satellite imagery of the port we were going to hit. The image showed a shabby town, looking typical for the impoverished area. The port had numerous ships docked, cargo ships mostly, but no military gear.

"This image was downloaded ten minutes ago from an Argos II Surveillance Satellite that will remain in geosynchronous orbit throughout the duration of the mission. The port has little to no military presence that we can see, and both intelligence and satellite imagery confirm there won't be any guards in the area. Your target ship just docked, but unloading isn't scheduled until later tonight. Your contact in town is part of the crew, so our information should be accurate."

He shifted the image again, zooming out and eastward toward the town.

"As you can see, the town is quite the opposite of the port and is crawling with armed guards, patrols, and picket points. Intel suggests this activity is normal for the area, so expect plenty of resistance should it come to a firefight. When it's time to leave, you will need to get back to the port so we can pick you up. We'll have a team waiting to bring you back to the *Triumph*. Chopper extraction is out of the question as resources in the area are negligible and the risk of RPG attacks is too high."

That last part caused me to wince. Even if things go completely by the book, and we accomplish our mission goals without alerting anyone, extraction will still be the most difficult part. Commandeering a vehicle will be difficult without alerting any guards, especially if that image was right, and the bad guys had check points set up. Picking up Helena would only complicate matters, but if we had to come out guns blazing, having her covering our asses would be invaluable.

"If there are no other questions, we're done here. We'll be arriving at our drop off point in thirty five hours. Until then, my ship is yours. Questions?"

The Praetorians were silent

"Well then. Good luck, chaps."

IV
War

Mediterranean Sea, Syrian Coast
July, 2021

    The next day, we were once again in our wetsuits and awaiting the go ahead to get our feet wet, the past day having been relatively uneventful, a first for me these days. I spent the time chatting with Santino and my new teammates, exercising, resting, and making sure my gear was ready to go, all of which was once again safe in its waterproof bag.
    To get off the sub, we were going out the same way we came in. Helena and I were first out, and were well on our way to removing the CRRC from the sub's external equipment locker by the time Vincent and Santino pressurized the hatch for their use.
    The Combat Rubber Raiding Craft was simple in design and nature, and had a legacy almost as long as the SEALs themselves. Stored, it was the size of a small sofa, folded around its high powered engine. When we disengaged the mechanism keeping the sub's external storage area door closed, the CRRC shot out, inflating as it sped toward the surface.
    Helena stared up after it, prompting me to give her a quick nudge. When I had her attention, I pointed upwards and waggled my hand in a swimming motion, indicating she should head up after the boat. She nodded and went on her way.
    I waited a few seconds for the next group to come through the submarine's hatch. As soon as I saw Santino's head pop out, I began my ascension.
    After breaking the surface, it was a quick swim to the boat which was conveniently deployed and ready to go, and a simple exertion of muscle got me aboard. Helena was already there, removing her re-breather and donning her combat armor. She cut a pretty sexy figure in the moonlight, as her wetsuit glimmered tightly against the curves of her body and her damp black hair shimmered in the subtle light given off by the moon
    I couldn't help but smile as she covered her hair with a backward baseball cap and painted her face with a stick of black

camo chalk. She went light with the chalk in areas that produced natural shadows like her eye sockets, and darker in places that reflect light, like her cheeks and forehead. Good training, and I had to admit the hat was rather fetching on her.

"What?" She asked, noticing my attention. "Does it work?"

She started performing poses with the hat and made goofy facial expressions as she modeled it for me.

I laughed. "It looks good. You may pass for a sniper yet."

"Ha. You know, we never got around to finding out who's the better shot. When we get back. You and me. On the range. Maybe then you'll put your money where your mouth is."

Her banter was calming and the playful inflection took all the sting out of her comments as she handed me the chalk.

"You're on, sister," I shot back.

As I took off my re-breather gear, Santino surfaced just off the starboard side.

"Hey! Quit smooching and help me up."

***

Once the entire team was aboard and our combat gear was ready to go, Bordeaux activated the engine and we sped away quietly.

It was only during these few minutes before things got interesting that I started to worry. It wasn't that I was afraid, just that I thought too much. People do it all the time. I can remember nights before a big test back in college where I would spend hours awake, trying to process my accumulated knowledge, only to end up confusing myself even more by morning. The same concept applied here, only if I second guess myself now, I could not only get myself, but my entire team killed.

I glanced up at the moon and wondered why I really transferred my service. I'd just settled into my command as a SEAL team leader, and was working with some of the finest operators on the planet. My team and I had been deployed to Iran, Mexico, Siberia, Pakistan, North Korea, Africa, Azerbaijan and countless other countries, and each time I had made it out alive and relatively unscathed… except for Korea, of course. I'd had some of the most highly qualified men at my side to thank for that, and I remembered too many close calls that could have ended in my death if not for them. So why, only a few months later, am I sitting in this boat with two Brits, an aging priest, a beautiful Ice-Queen, a Frenchman, and of all people, Santino?

I'd always lived by the tenants of God, country and family, only I'd never known what order to put them in. Up until the war, I'd always considered myself Catholic because that's how my mother raised me. Granted, I understood the faith, believed in it and appreciated the values, but I'd never really felt like it meant that much to me. While I went to church when I could and tried to lead as pious and noble a life as I could, up until maybe four years ago I didn't really care that much.

This goddamned war put things in perspective.

It was Muslims versus Christians again, but the lines were nowhere near as clear as they used to be. We had excommunicated Russians, South American extremists, African rebels, Hindu Indians, Pakistanis, expansionist Mexicans, Chinese, Japanese, Europeans, Koreans, and Americans, all involved in one way or another.

When word came out concerning Russia's involvement in the biological attacks on Jerusalem, China started mobilizing. They didn't care much about Jerusalem, or any other Western interest, but there had been growing tension with Russia for years over natural resources, territorial expansion, and aiding terrorism. Within weeks of the attack, China closed its borders permanently. The only thing they continued was trade with the West, especially America, but even that was in question thanks to tension mounting over China's near stranglehold on rare earth elements. Their Eastern front was another matter. Armed to the teeth and defensively entrenched, China was ready for anything. As a result of their military buildup, the first hostilities were over border contention near Kazakhstan. Blood was spilt on both sides, but it also set a precedent for years to come between the two nations of mere skirmishes, with no gains for either side.

While China and Russia were at a stalemate, Pakistan and India continued to wage a bloodthirsty land war. Europe and Islamic forces in the Middle East were still fighting over the same "promised land" fought over for a thousand years. African warlords slaughtered anyone they could get their hands on. South America warred within itself and Mexico fought against both neighboring continents. There wasn't a day that went by without hostilities.

Cities on nearly every continent lay in ruin, the North American one included. Cultures were devastated; maybe two billion souls lost already.

Nope, the world was pretty much fucked. The war had no end in sight, and my two year stint away from the Teams wasn't going to hurt anyone... as long as I survived long enough to go back.

"You all right, Jacob?" Helena asked cautiously.

"I'm fine. Just reminiscing." It was probably best she got my attention when she did. I hadn't had a chance to think about my father yet, and all the bullshit that came with that stream of consciousness.

"Well, wake up. The shore's in sight. We should reach the ship in ten."

I gave her a quick thumbs up and got to work.

***

A short distance from the giant cargo ship, Bordeaux cut the engine, allowing the small boat to drift idly toward its target. The rest of us were crouched low in the boat, weapons at the ready. Making contact with the ship, Wang attached a small, but powerful, magnet to the hull, securing a rope between it and the CRRC and anchoring them together. Next, Santino took an old fashioned grappling hook, a device left relatively unchanged in design since the Romans, and flung it over the edge of the railing. Giving it a quick tug, making sure it caught, he turned toward McDougal and smiled.

McDougal nodded and pointed up. Santino returned the nod and started his ascent, Vincent not far behind him, ready to take point. A few agonizing minutes later, Santino transmitted the all clear double click over the radio.

Wang, Bordeaux and McDougal followed. Once their feet cleared the railing, Helena started up after them, leaving me to deal with our little boat.

Making sure I had a firm grip on the rope, I pulled out a stopper holding the air within the inflated ring around the boat, allowing water to flow aboard. Within seconds, the boat started to sink, engine and all. Normally, SEALs would take their CRRC ashore and hide it, but our mission parameters made that difficult. When it was almost fully submerged, I detached the line attached to the magnet and pocketed the anchor.

Quickly pulling myself up the rope, I reached the railing, swung my feet over the edge and dropped quietly to the deck. I pulled up the rope, collapsed the grappling hook, and handed it off to Santino, who efficiently reattached it to the appropriate spot on the back of his rig. As the team's lead scout, he traveled light. His rig was more of a harness than a vest and was lightly burdened, with only magazines, a few tools, the grappling hook and rope, and a rather nasty looking knife that belonged in a Rambo movie. He had a small pack attached to his back, containing his computer hooked up to his eyepiece, and as our scout, he was in control of a small aerial drone that Vincent carried on his back.

The UAV was basically a small helicopter, its circumference no more than that of large dinner plate. It consisted of three helicopter blades that jutted out from the circular chassis to create a three points of a triangle. It was extremely quiet, almost invisible, and very effective. It carried high resolution cameras outfitted with night vision and thermal lenses for use in the dark and could climb a thousand feet in the air. It was solar charged, had an effective radius of two miles, and had the shelf life of a Twinkie.

As soon as Santino secured his grappling hook to his rig, he crept forward while Vincent kept pace with him. Santino could tip toe over broken light bulbs to sneak up on a prowling panther if he had to, so I wondered if Vincent would have trouble keeping up, but the man was a veteran and knew what he was doing. He'd keep up. Besides, Santino could easily peel off on his own if McDougal thought it necessary. He probably preferred going lone wolf anyway, with nothing but a knife in his teeth and streaks of blood on his cheeks.

As he crept forward, the rest of us followed at a safe distance. I was rearguard in the formation, checking our six constantly to keep our rear secure. Thankfully, everyone must have been asleep as we didn't run across a soul. After a quick stroll over the deck of the ship, we came across the stacked cargo containers.

Santino pulled down his night vision goggles to scan the containers. According to intelligence, our local contact had tagged those going to the terrorists' stronghold with infrared paint, invisible to the naked eye, but brilliantly luminescent under night vision.

Santino pointed to three containers, the first of which we inspected was conveniently only half full, but still a tight squeeze for any swim pair. It was a good thing I wasn't paired with Bordeaux, since we were the two biggest guys on the team. He was with Wang, who was the smallest, but McDougal would be with them too, making for a tight fit.

Granted, being in such close proximity to Helena probably wouldn't be the most comfortable thing either – only for far different reasons.

I made sure not to look at Santino, who I knew would never give up an opportunity to screw with me. I was saved from my embarrassment when I saw him move to the side of the ship to look for an infrared beacon that would point out our contact's position. When he located it, he would send a return signal to alert the local resistance to our presence.

McDougal pointed to Vincent and then a container, then Helena and a container. They nodded and headed toward their assignments while I followed Helena. She opened our container and we peered inside, noticing it was even less spacious than the last. Looking at each other, I gave her a shrug.

"After you, ma'am," I whispered.

She gave me an indignant look, but went inside all the same. She studied the layout, but after a few seconds, decided the best position that kept her close to the exit and comfortable was for me to go in first and have the two of us basically lie in a spooning position. I sighed as I climbed in, wishing I could have at least been on the inside of the position. With luck, I wouldn't need my tight wet suit to confine my dignity. As Helena tucked in beside me, I tried to focus on things other than my lovely swim buddy, but a quick memory of her leaning over in her wetsuit earlier distracted me.

I shook my head. Get your mind out of the gutter, Hunter.

There was nothing I could do to avoid the awkwardness but take the initiative and make the first smart ass comment. "Keep your hands to yourself, Strauss, we're on a mission."

She couldn't turn to look at me as she shut the door, securing it from the inside, but I knew she must have been fuming. "Don't get any funny ideas, Lieutenant. Remember, I'm supposed to be covering your ass on this mission."

Ouch, the innuendo was killing me.

"Well, just don't take a nap, you're going to need some fancy moves to get out of this thing."

"Is that a hint of concern I hear in your voice, Lieutenant?"

"Well, umm, no," I stuttered. "Just offering unsolicited advice. I'm sure you love that."

"Funny. But don't worry," she consoled. "This isn't the first time I've had to jump out of a moving vehicle."

That sounded like an interesting story, but it seemed best to just shut up at this point, no sense rising to the bait.

"Listen." She whispered before I could come up with a witty retort. "The crew is getting ready to put us in the truck."

I hadn't heard, but after she mentioned it, I craned my neck and did in fact notice the obvious clanking sound of machinery.

She had good ears, I had to give her that. Having good eyes wasn't everything for a sniper, ears were important too, especially when people snuck up on you. She probably carried a myriad of motion sensors and fisheye cameras that she could hook up to doors, ladders, or any other entry to guard her back, as well. If the sensors were tripped, a 3D map of her location would be displayed on her eyepiece to show where her sensor was triggered, then fisheye cams would give her visual confirmation.

Clever little gadgets.

I knew she also had a few claymores as well, which she could set up as a last line of defense. These she could set for either proximity detonation, when someone tripped the lasers, or for manual detonation.

But even with all those toys, it always helped to have sharp ears.

As our containers were loaded into the truck, Helena and I tossed and bumped into each other uncomfortably. Once our container was finally secured, the truck started to speed away down the road. I checked my watch and hoped the dock boss waited until later this morning before he started asking questions about why a half dozen containers were loaded at one in the morning and mysteriously transported away. I also hoped the guards around town didn't ask any questions either.

Currently, my eyepiece showed real time imagery from the Argos II Reconnaissance Satellite orbiting above us. Each member of the team had a wrist implant that we received from our respective militaries upon completion of basic training. They provided a few functions, but were currently used as locator beacons that showed up as pulsating dots on my screen. Seven of these dots were currently spread out in a line, pulsing green, indicating life signs were nominal. Another nice function of Santino's UAV was that it not only provided aerial imagery, but also updated the locator beacons' positions as well as our vital signs. It allowed for continuous data updates even if every single satellite somehow spontaneously went off line.

Manipulating the small joystick that extended from my wrist sheath, I zoomed out on the image to show our position and where we were heading. Using two small buttons, I traced a line from our position to the enemy cave, and had the computer calculate the distance. A half second later, the computer estimated we were about six miles from our target destination. Helena would be jumping off about a mile out, finding a good spot to cover us.

The map also showed a green square deep inside the city. I clicked on it only to realize it was probably our equipment cache. As a precaution, I had the computer calculate the fastest route from our target location to the cache, mapping it out with straight red lines, with blue flashing dots as waypoints. Once it showed up on my screen, I saved it and filed it away in case we needed it in the future.

I retracted the joystick on my wrist sheath and opened the protective flap away from my forearm with my other hand, awkwardly maneuvering it around Helena's form. It revealed a small touch screen about half the length of my forearm, a display peripheral for the computer stowed in my back pouch. I called up a simplified E-mail system, meant to send small packets of information that worked with Santino's UAV. The information we sent to one another was coded, and nearly impossible to crack. I quickly typed in **Cave -> Cache**, attached the file, and sent the data containing our escape route on its way.

"Nice thinking, Lieutenant," Helena said a few seconds later. "It'll be good to have this in a pinch if things get nasty."

"You being nice to me, Strauss?"

"No. Just keeping you honest."

"Right. So, you ready to jump? Looks like we're almost there."

"Yeah. I just called up the info on my eyepiece. I'm ready to go."

"Good. Just, umm, well, you know… be careful."

She was silent. She knew I was serious. Combat was tough, both physically and mentally, no matter how experienced an operator you are.

"Thank you, Jacob," she said quietly. "To be honest, I'm a little nervous. I've been in the field many times before, but something just feels wrong about this one. Like there's something we're missing."

No kidding, but there was no sense telling her I felt the same way. I didn't want to add to her discomfort, so I stayed quiet, waiting for her to continue.

I felt her shift in her position. "But don't worry, I'll cover your back. We'll get through this with no problem, and be back in Rome in a few hours listening to Santino complain about something. Hey, maybe we'll get a little down time. What better place to be based out of than Rome?"

I felt the same way.

"You be careful too, Jacob," she said, finishing her thoughts. "I'm just starting to like you, and I'd hate to have to make Santino my new best friend on the team."

I had to laugh at that. She'd soon realize that, really, he could be as best a friend as they came.

"I will."

A few minutes later, she started shifting again, ready to disembark the vehicle.

"Well, Lieutenant, if you're quite done… what is it you Americans say… 'spooning me,' I'm ready to go."

I coughed but recovered quickly.

"Don't worry, Strauss. I've had better."

"Ooh, you'll pay for that one."

I laughed. "Just get out of here," I said with a gentle nudge.

"Good luck," she said, opening one of the double doors.

"You too."

Taking a deep breath, she clutched her rifle close and leapt out into the darkness. She hit the ground roughly, rolled twice, and came up on a knee. She immediately slung her rifle and pulled her P90 from its secure location on her back all in one fluid motion.

I spared a wide eyed look for just a moment. That had been damn impressive. I shut the door as quickly as I could, surrounding myself in darkness once again, this time alone. It was more nerve wracking than I thought it would be. I tried to comfort myself by slowly stretching myself out in the more expansive space I now had.

I kept close watch on my eyepiece, watching the green dot that was Helena slowly move off into the narrow alleyways of the town. She would be fine. I shouldn't dwell on her. It would only lead to distraction. I zoomed in the view on my eyepiece so it only encompassed the grouping of green dots surrounding my own, eliminating Helena's position from view. If something happened to her, the computer would let me know.

***

It wasn't long before my GPS tracker showed we were coming up on what I assumed was some kind of military checkpoint. The truck started to slow, confirming my suspicion, before coming to a complete stop.

This was it. If the driver, whoever he was, couldn't smooth talk his way through the guards, we were as good as dead.

Hearing muffled voices outside, I pulled out my Sig P220. It was equipped with a suppressor, so I could make silent work of any potential peeping Toms and hopefully turn a bad night into a slightly less shitty one.

I held my breath, hoping the additional silence would prompt the checkpoint guards to send us on our way. Three minutes in, I began to feel the need to breath, but knew I could hold it for another two minutes if I needed. SEALs spent considerable time training our lungs to withstand water pressures at slightly deeper depths than most people, and we could hold our breath well beyond the average minute and a half.

Just in case.

Thankfully, a few seconds after the fourth minute mark rolled around, the driver gunned the engine and I slowly exhaled under cover of the moving vehicle.

So far, so good. All we needed to do was make it through the guards at the entrance to the enemy's base and we could slip out of the containers in the unloading area. Hopefully, most of the base would be asleep and only a few drowsy guards would be milling around.

Thankfully, the rest of the trip was relatively uneventful. We slowed as we rolled up to the base's entrance, but the guard must have waved us through because we quickly sped up and moved inside. As we passed into the cave, my GPS stopped updating through the satellite, and instead our green dots were overlaid against a black background. Thanks to the UAV, stowed away but still active, we could at least keep track of where we were in relation to each other, but without all the terrain details.

The truck stopped and I heard two car doors open and shut quietly. Then came the sound of someone subtly tapping on the container. All clear. I waited a few minutes until I heard the double click over the radio, indicating it was time to move.

I opened the container door carefully, pistol aimed and ready. As the door swung open, I tracked the opening down my gun sights. It seemed clear so I carefully hopped out of the cramped container, finding myself in what looked like a large storage room. It was a domed cave the size of a small warehouse with a shit ton of boxes, crates, containers, and the like sloppily arranged throughout. There was no order to the chaos, just junk strewn about in as inefficient a manner as I could think of. It looked like my old dorm room. I guess mommy terrorists didn't make their spawn clean their rooms or make their beds as baby terrorists.

Holstering my Sig, I pulled out my HK416, checked the inserted magazine, flicked off the safety, and formed up with the rest of the team. With Helena playing sniper, I was teamed up with McDougal. He quietly started issuing orders.

"All right, mates. Nice and slow and quiet. Remember, don't pop the first thing you see. We're here for Abdullah. Santino, you're on point. Vincent, hang back a bit with the rest of us. Bordeaux, place the C4 at your discretion, but keep it subtle."

There was a chorus of affirmatives and a second later my eyepiece flashed. Quickly tapping through the sheath that covered the touchscreen, the most recent activity was brought up on my eyepiece. Helena had sent a data packet labeled "Strauss" which consisted of a single green dot with two adjacent green lines running out from the dot in the shape of a V. The area between the lines was shaded a light green, indicating Helena's field of fire. She also had a few, smaller, red V's, indicating areas where she'd placed her claymores. The red indicating they were set for manual detonation.

Thoughtful of her.

It looked like she had taken position on the roof of a building situated alongside the main road we'd recently traveled. Three red V's were situated along that road, intermittently placed, indicating three individual explosions to cover our escape. The map I had drawn earlier to the equipment cache ran right through the field of explosions. If we had to bug out quick, straight ahead was our best bet.

The cave complex was typical of the kind used by terrorist cells throughout the former Crescent Empire. It was a honeycomb of passageways and dead ends, and no two complexes were anything alike. The ceilings were low, forcing Bordeaux and me to continuously keep our heads down, and the tunnels were poorly lit, with a string of light bulbs hung sporadically along the way. There was a dank, old smell in the caverns, even though they may have only been dug out a few months ago. Santino, thankfully, was an expert at navigating through this type of terrain. He'd been in caves just like these before and had an innate ability to find whatever he was looking for. He was a born tracker.

He carefully made his way along the walls, never straying more than a few inches from them, pausing at each junction. Occasionally, he'd pause and drop his night vision for a clearer look, but never long enough to break up our rhythmic movement. We didn't run into a single soul for most of the trip. Not surprising, considering the unprofessional discipline of this particular bunch, as well as the late hour. Occasionally, Bordeaux would stop and place a brick of explosive along the ceiling, hiding it away inconspicuously in the shadows.

After ten minutes of wandering through the seemingly endless maze, we made it to a doorway guarded by two men leaning lazily against a wall, flanking a curtained entrance. Santino halted and held up a clenched fist. He then pointed to his eyes before holding up two fingers, indicating the count of bad guys. Turning his hand into an open palm, fingers spread apart, he indicated toward the bad guys' position.

McDougal understood and slashed a hand along his neck, indicating Santino dispatch the guards silently. Santino gave him a sinister smile, completely devoid of the jovial attitude he normally exuded. It was a smile filled with nothing but vehement professionalism, a trait that had once saved my life. He drew his nasty looking combat blade and doubled back along a side passage, coming up along the guards' flank.

Vincent moved up to the corner and pulled out a small mirror to keep watch in case he needed to help. A few seconds later, I heard a small clatter, which I assumed was Santino getting one of the guard's attention. Santino probably took him out the second he was out of his partner's vision. The second guard, confused as to what happened to his buddy, followed his partner's path. A few seconds later, Santino emerged from the corner, wiping his bloody blade clean on the shirt of one of his downed targets. We made our way to his position.

I glanced down at his handiwork. Both men had died by a single knife thrust through the back of the neck, their spinal columns severed in typical Santino style. Their deaths had been quick and relatively painless, at least as far as death by knives went.

"Nice job, buddy," I told him.

"Thanks," his friendly smile returning. "The second guy didn't walk directly into it like the first, but he went down just as clean."

I had to remind myself that he was just doing his job. Santino had always been able to simply "switch himself off" whenever he needed to. He could be a compassionate friend one moment and one of the deadliest killing machines ever made the next.

Vincent used his mirror to look through the curtain, making sure it was clear. After a few seconds, he sent a thumbs up our way. Slowly, we proceeded through into a conference room of some kind. There was a long table with chairs positioned along its sides. The walls were adorned with decorations, easily making it the nicest area we'd seen so far. There were still cups and the remains of a meal lying about, proving my earlier theory of poor parenting. Along the far wall was another door.

This time, Vincent pulled out a long, thin snake cam that connected to his eyepiece. He slipped it under the wooden door and scanned the room. Retrieving it, he nodded.

"He seems to be sleeping," Vincent reported. "He's lying on his side, facing the far wall."

"All right," McDougal ordered. "We go in slowly. Wang, you know what to do."

"Aye, sir," he whispered, already pulling out zip ties to handcuff the prisoner with.

McDougal stood primed beside the entryway, his mustached face a chiseled block of marble, his posture relaxed but poised. He took one last breath before whispering, "Go."

We breached the room with fluid grace. Despite not having worked together before and coming from different schools of learning, we flowed into the room with deadly efficiency. Quickly confirming the room was clear, easy due to its large size and sparse furnishings, Wang moved for Abdullah. Unfortunately, our target was far from sleeping. Facing the wall, he was mumbling incoherently while clutching an object about the size of a volleyball. It was giving off an eerie blue glow and was dimly illuminating his side of the room.

Our entrance didn't go completely unnoticed, and our target sluggishly moved into action. It was unfortunate for his wellbeing, however, that Wang was far quicker. As soon as the small Brit entered the room, he leapt at Abdullah as he lay on the bed, locking the man's arms behind his back before maneuvering him to the floor, slamming his face into the ground. Forcing his knee into the man's neck and placing the barrel of his rifle into his cheek, Wang effectively neutralized the target without a sound, but it didn't seem like Abdullah would come easily. He struggled ferociously, far more than expected, and his eyes flitted about in unfocused confusion.

"Wang, confirm ID on target," McDougal ordered.

Wang nodded, pulling the grainy image supplied by the CIA up on his eyepiece. The rest of us spread out amongst the room, covering the entrance we'd just entered.

"ID confirmed, sir. This bloke is definitely Mushin Abdullah."

"Good. Gag him, bag him, and prepare to move him out."

Wang responded by stuffing a piece of cloth in the man's mouth and taping it shut with duct tape, followed by applying two zip ties around his wrists. I recalled times in training when I played the bad guy and my buddies had to breach my position and secure me for transport. They were generally pretty nice about the zip ties, and left them relatively loose. Sometimes, however, they weren't so nice, and I remember one asshole who tied them so tight, I lost all sensitivity to my hands for hours. I only hope Wang did just as thorough a job.

Once Wang had him secured, he hauled Abdullah to his feet and poked his gun into the captive's back. Abdullah started moaning through the gag, so Santino shut him up with a simple cross-check to the man's jaw with the butt of his rifle.

I looked at the man as he struggled, noticing foam seeping through the tape on his mouth, and eyes that didn't seem to focus on anything. He didn't look like the bioengineer and terrorist mastermind I had pictured. He just looked insane.

Shaking my head, I glanced at Santino as he walked over to Abdullah's bed. His eyes squinted at something on the floor and I saw him lean over and pick up the weird glowing ball Abdullah had been clutching earlier. Santino turned it over in his hands a few times before shrugging and placing it in a bag.

McDougal twirled a pointer finger over his head in a circular motion and indicated toward the door. We filed out the way we came in, pausing only for a second so Bordeaux could plant one of his charges. This one, a C-4 satchel charge, was the largest bomb he had. It had enough force to demolish a small office building. The room's location near the center of the cave complex made it the best spot for the bomb.

Santino led us back the way we came, again stopping at each intersection, making sure the coast was clear. Things were going well until we were about halfway to where we left the trucks.

That's when the shit hit the fan.

Rounding a corner, Santino ran into a trio of bad buys turning from an adjacent corner down the hall. The three men hesitated. Santino and Vincent did not. Santino shot the man in the middle with a quick three round burst to his chest while Vincent surgically placed a single bullet in the second man's skull.

The third man was the lucky one... for the moment. Santino quickly adjusted his aim and shot him in a similar fashion as the first, only those few seconds were all the other man needed to pull the trigger. Our rifles were equipped with suppressors, effectively muffling their noise to a soft cough, but the third man's weapon was not. Thankfully, all the dying man managed to hit as he fell to the ground were the walls and ceiling, but the sound of the rifle aimlessly discharging echoed throughout the tunnels.

So close.

"Bollocks," McDougal whispered. "Double time it."

He didn't need to tell me twice, and I started to pick up speed to catch up with the rest of the team. Only a dozen steps past the fallen men, I heard the familiar non-stop firing of a M249 as Bordeaux opened up on a group of bad guys coming up on our rear. SAWs were notorious for their ability to put an amazing amount of rounds down range in a hurry, and Bordeaux's bulky frame and the cave's narrow corridors made his line of fire a death trap for anyone who ventured down the hall. Within seconds, a dozen bodies hit the floor, twitching in a final act of protest as their nervous systems shut down.

We continued down the perilous corridors, mainly relying on Bordeaux's cover fire toward the rear to survive. Only four other men got in our way, and they were quickly gunned down by precision fire from our lead pair.

Reaching the warehouse cavern, we quickly found a 4x4 pickup truck and piled in. Wang and his hostage moved inside the cab while Bordeaux, Santino, Vincent, and McDougal jumped into the flat bed.

"Hunter! You're driving," McDougal ordered.

I didn't have time to answer. In true Dukes of Hazzard fashion, I dove through the window feet first and into the driver's seat before frantically searching for the keys.

Visor. Cup holders. Under the seat. Where?

They were in the ignition.

Leave it to the terrorists to be either that smart, or that stupid.

Before I started the engine, I noticed Abdullah struggling against his restraints. Wang, having none of it, threw an elbow into the side of his head, and the terrorist leader slumped unconscious.

Wang leaned over him and smiled. "Bloody good fun, eh, Hunter?"

"Yeah..." I replied, noticing a bad guy emerge from the hallway we had just come through. Before he could bring his AK-47 to bear, I stuck the muzzle of my rifle through my window and triggered a three round burst into his face. If not for the shemagh wrapped around his head, I would have been rewarded with the sight of a disgustingly mutilated face. "... real fun."

I felt nothing at his death. I didn't care about the nameless terrorist he had been, or his father who had just lost a son or his son who had just lost a father, and I wouldn't feel any different later. It had been me or him, and I shot first. I didn't like it, but that wouldn't stop me from doing my job.

Ignoring my first kill of the night, I quickly floored the clutch, threw the truck into first gear, and gunned the engine, fishtailing through a one hundred and eighty degree turn.

I heard a loud crack against the rear window, and I saw blood on it.

"Jesus!" Santino shouted, holding his head with one hand, shooting his rifle with the other. "Where the fuck did you learn to drive, Hunter?"

I laughed. Serves him right for all those smartass remarks. And I was all the happier for the chance to put all that reckless street racing time as a kid to good use. With a smile on my face, I slammed on the gas.

We accelerated quickly, but not quickly enough to dissuade two guys with guns from jumping out in front of us, firing their AK-47s wildly.

"Down!" I shouted.

Everyone ducked as bullets passed through the area where our heads had just been, riddling the front windshield, making it impossible to see through. Wang kicked it out.

It didn't stop bullets anyway.

The guys in back made short work of the shooters as we passed by.

But we weren't out of the woods yet. My rear view mirror revealed no less than six other trucks turning on their head lights and revving up their engines for what I could only imagine would be a rather fantastic chase scene.

Communication silence no longer necessary, I radioed Helena.

"Strauss. We're outbound from the cave complex. Under fire and pursued. Prepare to offer cover fire and get ready for extraction in a black pickup. We're the ones getting shot at."

All I got in response was the telltale double click of static.

It wasn't long before I saw the end of the tunnel we were racing through, the light from the night sky never looking so good. My passengers were keeping the trucks in pursuit honest, making them think twice before gaining any ground on us. One lucky shot took the lead driver in the head, causing him to turn directly into the wall. The truck careened off of it at high speed and at an angle that caused it to roll over and over, ending up on its side. The other trucks slowed down, managing to avoid the crash.

"Sir, I suggest Bordeaux blow his charges in five seconds," I yelled over my shoulder at McDougal.

That would just about give us enough time to squeeze out of the entrance before the tunnel collapsed behind us and the debris cloud obscured my vision completely.

"Do it, Bordeaux," McDougal ordered. "Three, two, one. Hit it!"

The shock waves hit us in succession, one for each charge, the truck bucking after each detonation.

Too soon. The trucks behind us would make it out as well.

My apprehension was quelled a bit when we arrived at the cave entrance where I saw six bodies crumpled on the ground, blood oozing from shots to their chests.

That's my girl.

About the same time, I also noticed the lights strung along the tunnel behind us going out, the dust cloud chasing after us as the cave collapsed. Maybe I could lose them in the cloud if I wasn't caught in it as well. Just as the cloud reached the last truck, I blew through the entrance and never looked back.

Outside the narrow tunnel, I immediately swerved the truck violently, hoping to throw off the incoming heavy fire. The enemy trucks that had managed to escape spread out in a long line and fired on us simultaneously. My passengers in back were now at a disadvantage, and were reduced to keeping their heads down and hanging on for dear life.

I couldn't see Helena, but I saw an update on my eyepiece, which I called up with one hand on the wheel. It showed a solid green dot on a side street, with a timer running steadily toward zero. She'd be ready at that position in twenty seconds.

Within that time, I noticed two of the trucks behind us swerve out of control with one neat little hole apiece through each windshield. These trucks didn't receive the punishment from the gunners in my truck, so it must have been Helena.

And she didn't think she could handle it.

"That girlfriend of yours can really shoot, Jacob," Santino commented from the flat bed.

"Shut it," I replied, swerving the truck through a wicked turn down the side street Helena indicated would be her pickup location.

Slowing as I approached the waypoint, I saw Helena bolt from a side alley and leap into the back of the truck with the same grace she had shown exiting the cargo container earlier.

"She's aboard," McDougal yelled, his rifle ablaze. "Move!"

I gunned the truck once again, following Helena's map through the field of claymores, our pursuers gaining quickly.

"Those claymore would really come in handy now, Strauss," I heard Santino yell.

"Give me a second!" She snapped back.

My map showed we had just crossed the middle claymore when Helena blew the first one, then the middle one a few seconds later, and finally the last one when we were well beyond the kill box. But each one going off in succession was enough to shake the town awake. We'd taken care of the trucks in pursuit, but seconds later, the town's civilian population apparently decided now was a good time to file out of their homes and into the streets, probably wondering what was happening so early in the goddamn morning.

Then I saw him. A man. No more than thirty years old standing in the middle of the street. I know McDougal had said civilians were to be considered expendable, but this man had a baby cradled in his arms.

In the seconds it took to close the gap between us, our eyes met, and I instantly knew I couldn't run him down. His face was awash in sheer terror and with my eyes widening, I tried to swerve down another side street, managing instead to do the worst possible thing.

I flipped the truck, and we started to roll. By the time our truck rolled three times, my vision had already flashed brightly behind my eyes before going completely black when my forehead smashed into the steering wheel.

***

Pain induced hallucinations were a bitch. They were the ones that hit deeply, stung like hell, and were just subtle enough that they left you questioning the entire experience. Then the pain smashed into you like a boulder falling on your head. My particular hallucination this time was of my father's disapproving eyes, staring deep into the recesses of my lost soul, before combusting into flames.

Yeah. Real subtle.

Just as my head started to clear and my vision returned, I felt immense pressure building inside my skull. It took me a moment to realize we had flipped upside down and that I was hanging in my seat, suspended by my seatbelt. Looking over, I could see Wang similarly dangling but still unconscious. Abdullah was slumped on the roof, bleeding from a gash across his temple. His chest rose and fell, so at least he was still alive.

Placing one hand against the roof of the truck, I unbuckled my seatbelt and roughly tumbled to the ground. I shook Wang awake, and indicated that he get Abdullah out of the truck. He responded groggily, mumbling something about how he thought Duran Duran really wasn't that bad after all. It took him a few more seconds to come around but when he did, I saw him take out his frustration and pain on Abdullah as he roughly tried to eject the unconscious terrorist from the truck.

Crawling out of where the windshield had been, I hoped everyone in back had managed to jump away before we'd begun to roll. The first troops I saw were Santino and Vincent running toward my position as I crawled to my feet. They seemed fine.

"Are you all right?" Santino asked.

"Yeah," I replied, smacking my head to clear it. "Help Wang with Abdullah. Where's everyone else?"

That's when I noticed Bordeaux hurrying over with a slight limp. It wasn't until he reached the light given off by the overturned truck's headlights that I noticed he was carrying McDougal over his shoulders.

"He's hurt badly." Bordeaux said. "He's unconscious and from what I can tell has some broken bones and is bleeding from numerous wounds. We need Wang."

I nodded, turned around, and knelt to look inside the cab. I saw Wang hauling Abdullah forcibly out the passenger side window. He handed him off to Vincent and Santino and immediately went to work on McDougal.

I looked around, surveying the damage, waiting for Helena to arrive.

"Where's Strauss?" Wang asked as he started checking McDougal's vital signs and shining a small flashlight in his eyes.

Everyone looked around, but each shook their head in turn, unable to locate her.

"Stay here with McDougal," I said. "I'll find her."

I tried to determine her position via her GPS locator beacon, but where it indicated she should be, she wasn't. It wasn't until I saw a leg, clad in the rubbery material of a dive suit hanging out of a window that I found her.

I ran to the window praying to God I hadn't killed her. Fearing the worst, I found her sprawled on a wooden table, the leg dangling from the window thankfully still attached. She must have been thrown from the truck like the rest, but hadn't been able to control her direction. Luckily she hadn't hit the wall, not to mention the fact that the window didn't have any glass.

Lucky or not, she was still bleeding from a head wound and had an extremely nasty gash on the leg sticking out the window. The wound started a third of the way up her thigh, wrapping its way from the side of her leg to her hamstring, appearing to end just below her left glute, but at least it didn't seem too deep. Looking back to call for Wang, I saw he was still working on McDougal.

We didn't have time for this. We needed to get the hell out of here.

Our best bet was to get to that equipment cache and regroup.

Moans from inside drew my attention back to Helena. She was regaining consciousness and started mumbling a name. I couldn't make it out, but it sounded distinctly masculine. I put my hand behind her neck, propping her head up, and snapped my fingers in front of her face.

"Helena. Wake up. We've got to get out of here," I offered before lightly smacking her cheek, again to little affect. "Wake up."

She wasn't responding, which was probably a good thing considering what I was about to do to her leg. Pulling out my knife, I tore open more of her wetsuit around the wound to make room for a battle dressing. I retrieved a packet of QuikClot from my pack, a powder-like substance that helped open wounds clot so that the patient wouldn't bleed out. She'd have a scar, but at least she wouldn't bleed to death, and Wang could stitch it properly later.

Unfortunately for her, the stuff stung like hell.

I paused and rolled her onto her side just before dumping it on the wound.

"I'm sorry, Helena," I said to her unknowing form, "but this is going to hurt. A lot."

Her reaction was as expected. The jolt of pain snapped her awake like she was just struck by lightning. Her body snapped into a sitting position and she threw her arms around my neck, shaking uncontrollably.

"It's okay," I told her while pulling out a bandage. It's just a scratch. Just hang on while I dress the wound.

"Th-thank you, Jacob."

"Hey. Rescuing damsels in distress is part of the job."

I thought I felt her slug me in the arm, but I couldn't be sure. If she hadn't, it wasn't a good sign.

I attached a few butterfly bandages to keep the wound closed despite the QuikClot and wrapped gauze around her leg several times, tying it off as tightly as I could. She cried out in pain again and buried her head in my neck, trying to force away the pain

"Sorry, but it's got to be tight. Now hang on."

She clasped her hands around my shoulders and pulled herself in close, keeping her head against my neck. Determined she was secure, I wrapped my left arm around her waist, my other under her legs, staying clear of the wound, and gently extracted her from the window. With my adrenaline pumping, she felt as light as a feather.

Helena in my arms, I made my way to the truck.

"Put me down, Jacob. I can manage."

I did as I was told, only to have her stumble under her own weight. I had to scoop her back up into my arms before she put any more pressure on her cut leg. She must have hurt her other ankle as well.

She smiled up at me, her head lolling. "Never mind. You're doing a great job."

"Just don't get too comfortable. You're not as light as you look."

I waited for her head to turn and glare at me, but it only slumped against my shoulder instead.

Definitely not a good sign.

Back at the truck, Santino and Vincent had set up a perimeter at the end of the alley and were already trading fire with enemy combatants. It was still dark, so we had the cover of night and the advantage of our night vision at least, but we couldn't hold out forever, especially since a third of our squad was combat ineffective.

"How's he doing, James?" I asked Wang.

He looked up and shook his head. "Not well. I've stabilized him, but his neck is very nearly broken and he's bleeding internally. We have to get him some place safe so that I can perform more extensive repairs."

Wang didn't have anything as complete as a field hospital in his backpack, but his very large bag did have many new features of modern medicine that would allow him to perform much more complete first aid than the combat medics of even a decade ago. All he needed was time.

"Fine," I said, laying Helena on the ground. "She needs a shot of morphine and a bandage on her head. Bordeaux?"

"I'm okay. Just a sprained ankle."

I nodded. A sprained ankle could wait.

"Vincent!" I yelled. "We need to get the hell out of here!"

I saw him look over at me from down the alley and nod. He patted Santino on the shoulder and indicated with the flick of a hand for him to hold the line. He came running over.

"What's our status?"

"Strauss is immobile, but should be fine. McDougal is in really bad shape. Abdullah is unconscious. Bordeaux has a sprained ankle, and Wang and I seem to be okay except for a few cuts and bruises," I summed.

"All right," he said, rubbing his rough chin. "Bordeaux, you take McDougal. Hunter, you grab Strauss. Wang, don't forget Abdullah. Santino will be on point, and I'll be on crowd control in the rear. Let's move out."

We gathered up our charges as gently as possible, except for Wang who had the hardest time with Abdullah. Once we were organized, we set out deeper into the alley and followed our map to the safe house. We needed some place to lay low and tend to our wounded.

Santino was the first to head out as he hauled ass to the front of our rag tag line and scouted out ahead of us, leaving stealth as a mere afterthought. We managed to sneak around pretty quickly and efficiently despite our loads, but we were lucky that most of the people we encountered ran back inside immediately after they saw us. We kept to the shadows as much as possible anyway, avoiding main throughways and homes with their lights on.

Along the way, Helena drifted in and out of consciousness, muttering gibberish. Only once did she open her eyes to look at me, brushing my cheek with a hand. I could only imagine what was going through her dazed and confused mind as she uttered my name. Her eyes rolled back inside her head and she slumped into my arms, unconscious once again.

Hallucinations were a bitch.

Fifteen minutes later, we reached the building we were looking for. Only a few bad guys stumbled on our position along the way and they were easily dispatched by Vincent. Santino opened the door to the house and waved everyone inside. Last in, he shut the door quietly behind him.

The house was barren, lacking any kind of furnishing. Its walls were bare, its windowsills dusty, and it didn't appear as though anyone had lived here for years. It was only a single story, so we headed down to the basement, the only other place left to go.

The dark, musty, scary basement.

Wonderful.

The last to descend into the dark cavern, I noticed the basement door was conveniently equipped with a large wooden plank to secure it. How thoughtful of the homeowners. That would only hold off the invading horde for about twenty seconds.

Once below, we found a few light bulbs dangling from the ceiling. Their illumination revealed a very plain room as completely barren as the rooms above except for a few cots and a half dozen metal containers about the size of queen beds stacked along the wall. I gave the containers an annoyed look before heading over to one of the cots.

I lowered Helena gently onto the soft fabric, afraid that even the slightest impact might break her in half. She looked peaceful in her drugged state, but I knew she had to be suffering. I stayed only long enough to check her pulse and brush some stray locks of hair away from her face. Giving her shoulder a quick squeeze, I stood to survey my surroundings.

There wasn't much to see, only a mostly empty basement, but Santino seem perplexed at what he was seeing.

"What the fuck?" I heard him yell from the rear wall. "Jacob, get over here."

My eyebrows creased in suspicion, but I did as I was told. I passed by Wang along the way who was still working on McDougal. He had a scalpel out and looked ready to perform an incision and Vincent was there to assist in any way he could. Not knowing much about medicine, and always rather squeamish during medical TV shows, I averted my attention. Bordeaux, meanwhile, was charged with the dual tasks of watching Abdullah and the door.

I found Santino rummaging through one of the containers, already having opened three others.

"What's up?" I asked. "Did they forget your blankie?"

He glared. He must be getting used to it these days.

"Funny. Look at this," he said, opening another one. "These are filled with enough supplies to last us years. That first one has nothing but MREs, enough to last each of us for months. There are explosives, replacement parts, ammunition out the wazoo, extra magazines, and even a few rifles, not to mention clothing, cooking equipment, bottled water, filters, toiletries, survival gear… and I've only opened half of them. Why would they give us enough supplies to set us up as an independent mercenary force?"

I had no idea.

"Have you tried your radio yet?" I asked, hoping for some good news.

"Yeah, but all I get is static. These fucking Ragheads are probably jamming the signal."

I smirked. Cultural expert indeed.

I gave him a doubtful look. "That doesn't seem very likely considering what we've seen from these guys so far."

He shrugged. "We know the Russians have been supplying terrorist cells with some of their fancy new equipment. It wouldn't surprise me if they could block our satellite uplinks."

I didn't have much time to think on it when the door leading upstairs began to shake.

So much for our "safe" house. I glanced at Santino who rolled his eyes, retrieved his HK416, and helped me pile the containers for use as barricades. We stacked them three high and two wide, enough for about ten feet in length and five feet high of coverage. We piled them around McDougal's inert form, and I dragged Helena next to him. Those of us who still could, took up positions behind the containers and trained our guns on the narrow door.

And we waited.

I had to give these terrorist bastards some credit they were patient and had themselves some style. Instead of merely beating down the door, they used a directional explosive to direct the force of the blast toward us, but we were ready for them. We had decent cover and the additional protection of our electronic ear buds. The little devices allowed ambient noise to flow through the eardrum, but as soon as they detected any sudden deafening noise, would activate to block it from entering the ear. The end result was a few seconds of slight deafness until the filters allowed sound to flow through them again, but alleviated any symptoms of distortion that would occur from an explosion.

When the bad guys finally blew their charge, we shrugged it off as though nothing had happened. Then they started to pour through. One after the other, they came through the door only to get mowed down by my precision shooting and hails of gunfire from Bordeaux's big ass gun. Ammo wasn't an issue anymore. Theoretically, we had enough to kill a million of them if we wanted to.

Hopefully, we wouldn't have to.

There were lulls in the battle when either Bordeaux or Vincent would chuck a grenade through the door and force the bad guys to either run or be killed. We timed it so that we had fresh magazines in place before they came back for more. Occasionally, the enemy would lob their own grenades, but our containers were bullet proof and could easily handle shrapnel from second hand grenades. Especially ones that probably began their lives in some shady Russian manufacturing plant. I was surprised none of them went off in their hands, but so many had been exchanged by that point, maybe I'd missed one that had.

Most landed in front of the containers and the rest fell harmlessly enough that we just kicked them away, but I still managed to get nicked in the leg with a glancing piece of shrapnel when I covered Helena from a grenade that went off on top of our barricade. Most of the team took a piece of something here and there. But we were holding. Hopefully not for much longer, because we had to counterattack and get the hell out of there fast.

Twenty minutes into the firefight, it got to the point where their dead provided extra coverage in front of our barricade. Their bodies also littered the stairs and blocked the doorway. We were just about to try the radio again when our prisoner decided to wake up. It must have taken him a while to fully regain consciousness, but all of us were too distracted to notice. Still tied, he got up and made his way to the bag Santino had put his glowing ball in. It wasn't until he took the ball out, and the blue light illuminated the room, that I noticed him.

Ball in hands, he lifted it high over his head, staring right at me.

"With this device, the servants of Allah will finally…"

A stray bullet from the enemy upstairs nailed him between the eyes. He fell to his knees, eyes rolling into the back of his head, dead before he hit the floor.

I caught Santino's eye and he smiled at me.

As Abdullah's body crumpled to the floor, the sphere fell from his hands and rolled in my direction. I was immediately enticed by its glow as I watched it roll closer and its allure only grew as it thudded against my boot. Staring down at it, I saw clouds swirl within it like the epicenter of a hurricane, revealing a cavern filled with men dressed in white robes kneeling reverently. An additional lone figure stood in the background, clearly not a part of the group.

Unable to contain my desire to reach for the orb, I bent over and picked it up in my gloved left hand. I barely noticed the bullets whizzing their way around my head as I peered ever closer. I couldn't discern any details from the images within, nor were they overly interesting. They appeared as a still photo would and were grainier than a photograph from the 1940s, yet I couldn't take my eyes off them. Like the blaze of a fire or the steady drip of a leaky faucet, for some reason I was entranced by what I was seeing.

With my right index finger, the only finger not covered by my gloves, I poked at the sphere. My hand moved without thought, without conviction, but it moved all the same. The globe felt soft, despite its apparently hard façade, made out of a material completely foreign to me. I felt my finger begin to push through the surface. At this point I was completely oblivious to the sounds of battle raging on around me. All I could think about was the silky surface of the sphere and how I knew I had to probe deeper. Buried to the second knuckle, my finger suddenly felt resistance, then, a tugging sensation. It was gentle at first, but soon became very persistent, steadily pulling my finger inside. It wasn't long before my entire hand was submerged in the sphere.

That's when I started to panic.

I didn't feel any pain at first, but when the tugging stopped, my eyes widened in terror at what I somehow knew was coming. It was the calm before the storm. In a single moment, all the insanity occurring around me became nothing, before becoming something again. The globe instantaneously sucked the entire room inside out in one fell swoop, taking everything with it in a brilliant blue explosion. The dead bodies, my friends, the containers, even the staircase. It was the single most nauseating experience of my life. More so than the roller coasters as a kid, the weekend drinking binges during college, or the life threatening rolling truck little more than an hour ago. It was the same with the pain. Unlike anything I've ever felt, or dreamed I could have felt, it was if my very soul was being ripped from my body only to be stitched back together, piece by piece.

I fell to the floor and felt my muscles automatically clench in the vain hope of staving off the pain. My body tried too little, too late. My eyes stung, my mouth parched, my brain fried, my stomach churned, my bowels threatened to do something I'd soon regret, and every shred of my being seemed to be on fire.

But, as quickly as the pain began, which seemed like a million years ago, it just as quickly ended. It was gone. In the blink of an eye, the most unimaginable pain I'd ever experienced receded to nothing and even the memory of what it had felt like quickly faded.

I blinked my eyes.

We were in a cavern, a big one, with dead bodies littered all over the place. Before I could take in more of my surroundings, the stair case behind me collapsed and fell to pieces. My first thought was to make sure Helena was all right. I struggled to my knees and felt her neck for a pulse. It was steady, and her breathing was normal, but even though she was drugged before the transition, the painful reentry had jarred her awake. Her eyes fluttered open and slowly focused on me.

"What happened?" she asked weakly, before going under again.

"I have no idea," I responded to myself.

Santino was already on his feet, eyes darting back and forth, looking for a way out. He noticed I was also conscious and helped me up to survey the area with him. I was looking at the pile of corpses in front of us when he poked me in the arm. I turned to see him staring in the other direction.

"What…" I started to say just as I noticed what he was looking at. What I saw couldn't be real. I was looking at the same group of toga wearing men I had seen through the orb. They were in the same semicircle I saw before, all kneeling in our direction. And they all seemed just as surprised as we were.

Santino and I exchanged glances, but it wasn't long before he couldn't help but say something.

"Togas?" He asked, peering at the men. "So, where's the keg?"

Part Two

V
Rome

Location: Unknown
Date: Unknown

"So. Jacob." Santino said offhandedly a few seconds later. "Want to fill me in on what the fuck you just did?"

I looked at him, his expression a reflection of my own.

Neither one of us had any idea what was going on.

The faces of the men arrayed before us were likewise confused. They seemed more shocked than frightened, but where I knew we could take them in a fight, they didn't seem so sure. Not surprising considering these men were no taller than five and a half feet, and were wearing what looked like togas, compared to us in our body armor. Even Wang stood above the men, and he was the smallest of us all. He was still working on McDougal and Helena as Bordeaux and Vincent joined Santino and me.

"Who are they?" Bordeaux asked.

"I can't even begin to guess," Vincent said, squinting carefully at the men, "but, as odd as this may sound, they're dressed like ancient Romans."

They were wearing togas, just like the ones worn by thousands of college students every year at the ever popular toga parties. But these were different somehow, more genuine, used, and worn in. There was a thick stretch of purple, about three inches wide, running down the main opening seam on two men's togas. If these people really were Romans, even though I knew they couldn't possibly be, that could signify a number of things. Certain kinds of magistrates, I couldn't remember which, or maybe augurs, ridiculous sight seers who determined a man's fate based on whether or not it was an eagle or a crow that took a shit on you.

I shook my head. Roman fashion hadn't been my forte. Besides, this wasn't really happening. We couldn't possibly be standing in the presence of ancient Romans. There had to be a perfectly reasonable explanation for this. There always was.

Right?

Maybe... maybe Santino was right, and we somehow happened into a college toga party in the middle of Syria. What other explanation could there be? I knew I couldn't be dreaming. If I were, I'm pretty damn sure ancient Romans wouldn't be here, or Santino, and Helena would either be naked or wearing something slutty and certainly wouldn't be unconscious.

I tried to think.

I did touch that glowing ball thing, whatever that was. But how could that have caused all this? I could barely remember what it had even done at this point, even though I remember that I should be remembering something. Even if I believed it somehow had something to do with this, that meant we had just found a glowing, blue time machine.

As stupid as that sounds.

Only one way to find out. Plan B. If it failed, at least we'll be able to pick up a beer pong game or two.

"Vincent, I'm going to try something, back me up."

"What are you...?"

I unslung my rifle and handed it to Bordeaux, whose jaw hung limp in its sockets. Cautiously, I approached the men with my hands up. Thinking back to my old Latin classes, I did the best I could.

"*Meus animus et summus pacis.*"

Yeesh. Was I really that rusty?"

I believe I said, "Me friend and we are peace." I always got tripped up on those damn endings. Hopefully, it was close enough to get the message across. Sure, it relied on these guys actually being Romans, or at least a classically oriented fraternity, neither of which seemed overly plausible, but what else could I do?

The "Romans/frat boys" looked at each other, perhaps wondering who this barbarian was butchering their language, perhaps wondering where the nearest bikinis-only jello fight was. I wouldn't blame them on the language issue. Speaking Latin is harder than it seems. It's a dead language for a reason, and while it may be used daily in medical and law professions, and probably at the Vatican, its conversational usage went extinct centuries before I was born.

I just hope I got the point across.

One of the men stood up, and after glancing at his partners, said, "*Salve.*"

"Hello."

My jaw dropped.

"Speak English?" I asked hopefully, to no response.

"*Parlez-vous Français?*" Bordeaux offered, to even more blank expressions.

Damn. They *were* Romans. Or maybe a Latin club? I shook my head and looked over at Vincent, his expression likewise in shock. I caught his eye, still not believing my own ears. "I guess you're going to have to talk to them, Vincent. My Latin is beyond rusty. I'll see how the Major is."

"I'll do my best," he said awkwardly, still not completely buying it that these guys were Romans either, "but you know as well as I that nobody really speaks Latin anymore."

"Seems they do now," Santino mumbled.

I ignored him. "Write it down and..." I paused, forcing myself to believe my own words, "show it to them or something, just make sure they know we mean them no harm. Maybe they really are just a bunch of Roman cosplayers."

He nodded shakily, and I wondered if he understood what I was talking about.

I wasn't even sure if *I* understood what I was talking about.

My mind was whirling, but Romans or no, time travel or no, alien abduction or...

Stop it.

We still had wounded. With no idea what to think, I made my way to their position. Both had their eyes closed, but I knew McDougal was in far worse shape. It wasn't until I was close enough to use my flashlight that I saw Wang pressing a defibrillator against McDougal's chest. The transportation effect must have been too much for him.

As I arrived, Wang's shoulders were slumped in defeat, and he dropped the paddles to the floor.

I knelt beside him and put a hand on his shoulder.

He choked back tears as he glanced up at me. "He was a great man, Hunter. I served with him for years, and he never let me down. He pulled me out of a burning helicopter once and carried me all the way home. But I couldn't help him now. I couldn't save him."

I looked over at McDougal's mustached face, before slowly pulling the blanket from the cot over his head.

"It's not your fault, James. If anything, it's mine. If I hadn't flipped that truck, he may still be alive. Hell, we may be back on the *Triumph* by now."

"No. I was in front with you. I saw what you did. To hell with the ROE, you swerved to miss that man and his child. You did the right thing." He paused. "Look, I need to clean up here. Go make sure Strauss is all right. She should be awake by now."

"Okay."

No point in telling him it might have been my fault that we arrived here as well, I turned away from him. Wang had enough on his mind.

I shifted positions so that I was facing Helena. She seemed fine, her breathing was regular, and her skin color was normal. I put a hand on her forehead, noting it likewise felt fine, before I whispered for her to wake up.

Her eyelids fluttered open.

"I was dreaming," she said, shifting her eyes toward mine. "I dreamt of men with red capes and swords. It was… weird."

I smirked. "How are you feeling? Can you move? We may need to get out of here in a hurry."

"I think so, but you're going to need to help me up."

"Don't worry. I'm here."

I helped her straighten into a sitting position, but she was able to swing her legs over the side of the cot on her own. She rested her elbows on her knees and supported her head in her hands for a few seconds. She tilted her head up to look at me as she kneaded her temples.

"I think I have the worst headache I've ever had. There is no way you're driving next time."

"Somehow…" I said, gesturing to our surroundings. "I don't think that's going to be a problem anymore."

"What do you mean?"

"Well I'm not sure exactly, but I think – and this is going to sound really odd – we somehow traveled back in time to the days of Ancient Rome."

She stared at me, probably considering whether to punch me or shoot me. Probably deciding both required more effort than she could summon at the moment, instead, she decided to threaten me.

"Hunter, I swear to God, if you don't tell me what's really going on in the next ten seconds, I promise, I will kill you."

I chuckled. That would be a fun fight.

"I'm not kidding." I paused. "McDougal didn't make it."

Her hands sprang up to cover her mouth as she looked at the cot next to her, noticing the covered corpse.

"What happened?"

"I told you. Whatever happened, the trip wasn't easy. It was the single most painful experience I have ever endured. You were drugged up, so it probably didn't register as badly, but McDougal was just barely hanging in there. The transition was too stressful on him, and it killed him. Wang did what he could, but it wasn't enough."

Helena looked over to where Wang knelt next to the body of his long time commander, still cleaning his medical supplies. His face was a mess, a reflection of his failure and guilt. Helena's glance lingered respectfully, before turning back to me.

"Say I believe you. What do we do now?"

"Again, I'm not sure, but Vincent is talking to these people. We think they're Roman because they're speaking Latin and wearing togas. Not a lot to go on, I know, but..." I waited, trying to rationalize everything, "...oh fuck it. Let's go see what Vincent's got." I stood. "Need a hand?"

I offered her my hand, which she lightly grasped. Gently, I helped her up until we both realized she needed way more help than what was already being offered. I had to swing one of her arms over my shoulder, and wrap my own arm around her waist, supporting her entire frame against my own to keep her from collapsing under her own weight.

I grunted slightly with the effort. She was heavier than she looked. "Gee, Strauss, lay off the desserts next time, will ya?"

"I'm not kidding this time. I will kill you."

I didn't laugh. "Come on."

We approached Vincent and the men in togas conversing when I noticed another man, clearly not part of the group, slinking toward the only exit. He noticed my attention and quickened his pace, his face ablaze in terror. He was gone before I could say anything.

I guessed we'd have a welcoming party when we got out of here.

Vincent clasped a fist over his chest, indicating the conversation was over.

He turned, and everyone, save Wang, gathered to try and make some sense of it all.

"So?" I asked.

"Well…" Vincent started. "It turns out we have in fact traveled to the days of ancient Rome, and from what I can gather, during the time of Caligula," he paused. "Simply amazing."

"You have got to be kidding me," Santino commented, offering his usual, helpful two cents.

"But how is that possible?" Bordeaux asked, his French accent thickening from the stress of the moment. "What possibly could have done such a thing?"

"They didn't say," was the only thing Vincent could report, shrugging.

The last thing I remembered was that glowing ball, and knew it had something do with our predicament.

"I know," I said. "At least, I think I do. That sphere Santino picked up from Abdullah's room had to have done it. During the firefight, I picked it up, and saw this exact room and those men within it. Then, when I touched it, I felt it pull me through, I guess taking everything in the room with me. I don't know why it didn't activate when Abdullah held it."

Everyone just stared at me. They had no idea how to respond. They didn't cover time travel back in basic, in any of our countries' boot camps, but we were faced with the dilemma nonetheless. I considered myself a bright guy, and had taken plenty of philosophy classes in my time, and realized we were faced with two viable realities right now: either we'd traveled back in time or this was all an elaborate setup by our enemy, one meant to confuse and then inevitably destroy us.

Unbelievably, illogically, and insanely, when trying to determine which conclusion reflected actual reality, the only one that made any sense to me was the one that involved time travel.

"You realize we're all dreaming right now, right?" Santino said a few moments later. "I mean, we're standing in the middle of an impossibly paradoxical situation right now. In fact, I'm just about to wake up with Strauss rubbing my feet and Hunter feeding me a smoothie. Bordeaux, pinch me, will ya?"

Bordeaux pinched his arm, shrugging sadly when nothing happened. Never one to give up so easily, Santino slapped his face, but the result was the same.

"Shut up, Santino." Helena growled at him.

"He is right, though," I added, nodding at Santino. "And he did use the word 'paradoxical' properly. I'm impressed."

I tossed Santino a thumbs up, and he grinned stupidly, loving Helena's scowling expression.

"The point is, wherever we are..." Helena informed us, splitting her attention between each of us, "...there's nothing we can do about it right now. We need to focus on getting out of this cave."

"She's right," Vincent replied, all business. "We need to secure our gear, and see to our dead and wounded." He lingered on that last part, the impact of command finally sinking in. "And then we should contact the local leadership, and see if we can figure out where to go from there."

It was good to see he was taking to command so smoothly. We were going to need some form of leadership if we were going to get out of here...

Get out of here?

What happens when we do get out of here?

If we had been sent to Ancient Rome – and I wasn't exactly ready to admit that we had – then that meant we were two thousand years in the past. Having studied no actual precedent for time travel, I had no idea how such a phenomenon worked, but I did have decades of television to at least give me something to work with. I'd seen enough to know we were in an extremely dangerous position, not to mention totally uncharted waters. Everyone's seen the movies where people travel backward into the past and fuck up the future. Could that happen to us? Had we already messed something up with our mere presence alone?

I still couldn't believe the fact we actually traveled into the past hadn't really hit me yet.

"There's another thing," I added.

"Go ahead," Vincent ordered.

"We can't tell these people anything about who we are."

"Why not?" Bordeaux asked.

"Well. We're in the past, right? Our past. I'm no expert, and I'm sure Vincent can back me up on this, but in Roman history there is absolutely no mention of soldiers that fit our descriptions. That can mean one of two things. First, no one wrote it down because we either die real soon, or we don't make any kind of impression on anyone, which is kinda hard to believe. Or, simply, we were never here, and what we do here and now, can potentially alter the future. Our mere presence may have already been enough to change something. We have to be very careful. We could accidentally kill our own ancestors just by forcing them to avoid walking into us, and then I have no idea what would happen."

Again, they all just looked at me.

"You have got to be kidding me," Santino repeated incredulously.

"Come on, Santino. You watch TV. As far as I know, we're the first time travelers in recorded history. I have no idea how this shit works, but from what I think I know, I believe we have to be very careful. We can't mention people, places, terms, dates, anything. It can completely change history."

Before my words could completely sink in, the room started to shake.

Violently.

Cross beams and bracings started to drop and rocks began to fall from the ceiling. The room was about to collapse.

"Remember what I said about dying really quick?" I asked, twirling Helena away from a falling rock.

"You have got to be kidding me," Santino said for a third time, maybe hoping his final repetition and the clicking of his combat boots might whisk us away from this nightmare version of Oz.

The Romans were already rushing out of the room, quick on their feet.

Vincent took control. "Quick! Bordeaux, help me grab one of the containers. You too, Santino."

Wang came running over. "What about McDougal?"

"Don't worry about him. He isn't going anywhere."

"But..."

"Shut up, Wang," Vincent yelled. "We're going to need those supplies."

Helena and I were already limping our way out of the room. Santino, Bordeaux and Vincent had one of the containers hefted and out the door when Wang came rushing by us. With a last look at the crumbling room, we waited while Bordeaux and Vincent pushed the container up a hole while Santino dragged it out of the way. Next went Wang and Vincent, followed by Bordeaux and then me. I pulled Helena up through the hole just as the ceiling collapsed in on itself, with a plume of dust and dirt following behind her.

We exited a small domed structure, emerging into the night sky on top of a rather high hill, surrounded by a familiar, sprawling city. I couldn't quite place exactly where we were, but the city was beautiful and majestic. If I had to guess, I'd say we were back in Rome.

But that was impossible.

Right?

So, not only were we transplanted into the past, but also transported half way across the Mediterranean?

"Well, that figures," I said, still in disbelief.

"What?" Helena asked, from my shoulder.

"We're back in Rome."

Her only response was to look out confusingly over the huge city.

"Damn, that really kills my frequent flyer miles," Santino said.

I would have punched him had Helena not been on my arm, but my attention was drawn down the street anyway. I saw the men from inside kneeling before a dozen armed men, wearing plain white togas and wielding swords and shields, torches illuminating their stone cold expressions. The sneaky man from the cavern was standing beside them, finger pointing accusingly in our direction.

This time, I couldn't help having the last word.

"Aw, shit."

***

The two sides did little except wait, stare, and see who would make the first move. The Romans were a hard looking group, short and lean, with stern faces and cold eyes. They looked bulky in their togas which, combined with their weapons, probably meant these guys were real Praetorians.

Army legions were not permitted in Rome, and only under a few historical circumstances had they ever entered the city. Such times were normally reserved for civil wars, such as the ones between

Marius and Sulla, and more famously, Julius Caesar and Magnus Pompey. If we were indeed in the days of Caligula, the military would definitely not be in the city.

That left the personal bodyguard established under Augustus, the only military unit stationed in the city. Contrary to the way modern film portrayed them, with flashy black armor and billowing purple cloaks, these men wore simple white togas, and there wasn't a stitch of purple on them. Only a few people other than the emperor were allowed to wear imperial purple, and Praetorians certainly were not some of them. They probably wore the typical *lorica segmentata* armor worn by most legionaries of this era beneath their togas.

One of the men, a centurion I would guess by his helmet, which possessed a plume that ran from ear to ear, the only helmeted man in the group, stepped forward, and extended an arm, palm upwards. Then, in a voice that would not accept "no" for an answer, I think I heard him say something about our weapons.

"What did he say?" I asked.

"Well," Vincent answered, "these Romans speak so fast, it's hard to keep up, but I think he said he wants our weapons."

"What do you think?"

"We could take them out before they had any idea what was happening, but if what you said is true, these men may play integral roles in the future. We can't just kill them."

"I'm glad someone was paying attention."

"Hey, I heard you," Santino said. "I just think you're nuts."

"In any case," Vincent said, ignoring him. "I say diplomacy is our priority. Everyone, put your rifles on safe and unload your mags, and don't forget the chambered round. We don't need these guys accidentally shooting each other."

We all complied, securing our ammo, before laying our rifles on the stone road. The Romans gave our rifles a dubious look, and then at each other, before gathering them up. One man picked up Helena's curiously designed P90, trying to figure out if it was actually a weapon or a piece of art. Knowing they had no idea what exactly our weapons looked like, or did, we kept our side arms at the ready.

I noticed the man I had seen creeping in the sphere out of the corner of my eye. He seemed completely out of place. I couldn't help but wonder what role he was playing here, and whether he could help us. The way his eyes panned over us suggested he was more interested than anything. They continuously focused on small details concerning our clothing and gear. Even when his attention focused on Helena, he only examined her gear and weapons, as well as her bandaged wound, and moved on.

That, in and of itself, was impressive.

The Roman Praetorians, satisfied that we had relinquished our weapons, or at least anything we could hit them with, formed into a square around us, and started moving. I glanced at my watch, its compass indicating we were heading northeast.

"What do you think they're going to do with us?" Helena asked.

"Well, hopefully they don't crucify us," I replied, only half joking. "Romans made the process famous after all."

"That's a wonderful image. Thanks."

"Anything I can do to help."

"But seriously. What are we going to do here? If everything that's happened in the past twenty minutes isn't actually a dream, and we can't risk changing the future by actually doing anything here, how are we supposed to find our way home? We're going to have to interact with something or someone if we're going to figure this out."

"That's a good point. But again," I said with a shake of my head, "I don't know. Honestly, I think I would like it here, but we can't stay. The longer we do, the bigger the chance we screw something up.

"Don't you think meeting the emperor of Rome might change something?"

"What do you know about Caligula, anyway?"

"All Europeans aren't history scholars, you know," she said indignantly. "All I know is that he was crazy."

"I guess that's more or less true, but he wasn't always crazy. In fact, when he was young, he was a very inspired and hopeful young man. His uncle and foster father, Tiberius, emperor at the time, would bring him along on campaign when he was barely a teenager. He spent much of his youth learning the ways of war first hand. In fact, the legionaries loved him so much, they called him "little boots," which is where his nickname, Caligula, comes from. The

Roman word *caligae*, which means shoes, or sandals, or boots, or whatever."

"So what happened?"

"Well, that's the thing with history. Since so much has been lost, we're not exactly sure. Little information contemporaneous with his life exists, except for the works of a few historians, most of whom wrote after his death. Suetonius, for example, wrote extensively on the Caesars from Julius to Domitian. However, as a source of historical fact, he's not so helpful. He's great at describing the drama and debaucheries of the crass imperial families, but I can't remember a single date offered in his writings. It reads more like gossip. A soap opera. He's not considered a very reliable source, but he's still one of the main providers of information we have on the time period. People like Claudius wrote extensively on many subjects, including his family tree, but unfortunately, none of his work survived. Suetonius quotes it at least once, but has the nerve to describe it as tasteless. Claudius is Caligula's uncle and the next emperor, by the way. I'd actually love to meet him."

"Thanks for the history lesson, but what about Caligula?"

"Well, when Tiberius died, Rome was very excited. Tiberius went down in the history books as a rather mundane ruler, but in reality, he was a very successful military commander, and while his time as emperor was uneventful, Rome hardly suffered from it. So when Caligula took the reins, big changes were expected. All for the better."

"Any reason why it's taking you so long to get to the point?"

"I'm just trying to provide context," I sighed. "Yeesh. It's always the pretty ones. Anyway, Tiberius introduced Caligula to more than just warfare during his formative years. On his island retreat of Capri, Tiberius immersed Caligula in debaucheries that made the ones in Rome seem like tea parties. Ever see the movie *Caligula*?"

"No," she answered.

I grimaced. "Probably for the best. It's one of those movies you have to see to believe, and while probably more farfetched than reality actually was, it definitely portrayed Tiberius as the sick bastard he, again, very probably was, and Caligula was raised around all this sex and degeneration and violence. Many historians credit this upbringing as the cause of his eventual insanity, but it wasn't until he became very sick that his mind was finally warped. Supposedly, he started doing things like appointing his horse as Consul, Rome's highest elected position, and having an incestuous affair with his sisters. All three of them. Historians are conflicted on the matter, though. They're conflicted on everything.

"One of the earliest writings about Caligula claims he went insane as a direct result of his illness. There are many historians, though, who feel that too much emphasis is put on the illness, and shouldn't be taken seriously. Either way, he rose pretty high on everyone's shit list, including his own Praetorians. It wasn't long before they assassinated him, and proclaimed Claudius emperor. The way things were going, it was definitely for the best. Claudius did a good job, and despite the hiccup with Nero, Rome prospered for quite a while before beginning its inevitable decline."

"So..." she said, her voice dripping with impatience.

"So..." I mimicked, her impatience beginning to irritate me, "that's about the gist of it. If we got here too late, chances are we're fucked. Better expect to suffer a painful, painful death in some gruesome, grotesque manner. Hey, I once learned about a Roman execution method where they would have you stand on a platform above a ramp with a revolving buzz saw running down the center. Then, they would slice your Achilles tendons, causing you to fall off the platform because, you know... pushing would be too nice. So, you'd fall from the platform down onto the ramp and slowly slide your way into the saw, slicing you in half. Right down the middle. There. Happy?"

Her stare was blank and I wondered if she was thinking about the execution method I'd just detailed or whether or not I really was crazy, like Santino suggested.

"So were you some kind of high school history teacher before joining the military?

I smiled, forgetting my tirade. "No, but I did go to college, and had to major in something. Double majored in history and classical studies. Mom was proud. I always figured I'd spend my life as a history teacher, not in the military. Hopefully, meet a nice, saucy Spanish teacher and settle down."

"You really are a strange man, Jacob."

"Hey. A guy can dream, right?"

She rolled her eyes.

"I was even working on my Masters when I was forced into the Navy," I provided proudly, "and hoping for a PhD one day."

"Why would you need a PhD to teach children?"

"Why not?" I asked with a look that suggested her question should have had an obvious answer.

She ignored the sarcasm, but I saw she had a small smile on her face. "So, why were you forced into the Navy then?"

"For a girl who couldn't take a little history lesson a few minutes ago, you sure do ask a lot of questions. But again, sorry. Let's leave that story for another time."

That was another annoying story, and I wasn't about to let it ruin the fantastic dream I must be having right now. Here I was, strolling through Rome with a beautiful woman on my arm, taking in the sights like a couple on vacation. It was something I'd always wanted to do, but had never actually had the luxury.

I must be dreaming.

Granted, the woman was half unconscious, came close to losing a leg, we were under armed guard, and while we may be in Rome, we were somehow in a time when gladiator tournaments were still popular…

Even so, I couldn't help but admire the view.

The landscape was almost completely unrecognizable from the city I had just driven through. St. Peter's Basilica was gone, and many of the ancient ruins were either in perfect condition or not even built yet. A good portion of Rome's landscape was due for a series of major renovations in the coming years, and most of what I was seeing now would be gone in two thousand years. Nero would build his magnificent golden palace, along with a pool the size of a football field just a ways down the road to my right. It wouldn't last long though, as Vespasian would later build the Flavian Amphitheatre, better known as the Colosseum, on the same spot. Later, Trajan would move half of a mountain to build his own forum, just because he needed more room.

But none of that was here at this point, and I found myself saddened that we weren't transported to a time when Rome's more lasting structures existed. Sure that sounded superficial, but all the fun times of social and civil wars occurred well before we got here and the wonderful building projects were probably out of my life span, even if I had to stay here. I even missed Augustus, my favorite emperor, probably one of the top five most influential figures in all of western civilization. At least as far as I was concerned.

Oh, well. It looked like we were about to meet another influential figure in history. I just hoped we were sent back early enough. After all, he was only emperor a few months before he got sick.

***

Twenty minutes, a few drunken witnesses, and a number of reproachful charlatans later, we made our way to the *Curia*, Rome's senate chamber. As we passed through the *Forum Romanum*, I couldn't help but feel overwhelmed. I was walking through Rome's political epicenter, the place where most of its major decisions were made. A thousand years of governance and policy were debated right here. Everything so was saturated in history, I felt drenched just thinking about it. Every debate settled by the men of this city affected the world in ways few truly appreciated. Without these walls and the men who filled them, my world would have been far different.

I saw the *Curia*, an unremarkable building, with its plain, brick façade, as well as the *Rostra*, on the other side of the forum. There was the source of it all.

"Take a look over there," I told Helena, nodding off to our right. "That's the *Rostra*, a speaker's platform. Back during the Second Triumvirate, one of the greatest writers and orators of all time, Cicero, had spread some rather nasty propaganda about Marc Antony. It had something to do with how Antony should have been killed along with Julius Caesar on the Ides of March or something like that. Anyway, Antony, being the spoiled little shit that he was, had Cicero killed, and had his head and hands cut off. He then had them placed on those poles to further insult him as if killing the most learned man of his time wasn't enough. Those poles are actually called *rostra*, by the way, the Roman word for a ship's prow, which is where the title for the platform came from."

"Always the history lesson with you."

"There's just so much of it here. I'm overwhelmed. How can you be so disinterested?"

"I'm not 'disinterested.' I'm just a bit queasy and I could really use some sleep."

"Oh, sorry. Well, perk up. A few more months with me and you'll be an expert in no time."

"Fantastic."

"Heads up, people," Vincent announced. "Looks like we've arrived."

Making our way to the building, the enormous outer wall blocking the moonlight, we were ordered to stop by one of our guards. He, along with three others, made their way inside, while the rest of us were directed toward a few stone benches just outside the *Curia*.

Dragging Helena all this way was tough work. I had been ready to pass out the moment we entered the *Forum*, and by the time we made it to the benches, Helena was practically moving under her own power, receiving little help from me. I heard her moan in pain when she took a particularly heavy step on her bandaged leg, but we managed to make it to the bench before either one of us collapsed completely.

I swung her onto the bench, and sat beside her, resting my head on her shoulder. "Next time, you're carrying me."

She pushed my head away. "Yeah right, Lieutenant."

Santino plopped down next to me on the ground, while Bordeaux and Wang sat next to him. Vincent took up station by the entrance, waiting to go inside. Bordeaux and Santino stretched out to lie on their backs, probably just as exhausted as I was, while Wang had his head between his knees, still unsettled by the loss of his long time commander. Helena was leaning against a pillar, and seemed out cold. Rejuvenated by my few seconds of respite and with no one to talk to, I rose to my feet and joined Vincent with the remaining guards.

He noticed my approach. "So what do you think, Hunter?"

"Well, sir. It's the opinion of this sailor that we could have picked a more interesting time to find ourselves in. I, for one, would have loved to meet Augustus."

He smiled. "I would have preferred Marcus Aurelius or Constantine, but I see where you're coming from. Still... while there is certainly something exciting about all this, we can't stay here."

"I couldn't agree more, sir. I'm not sure if I can live without my TV."

"Well, Lieutenant, in that case, we definitely need to get out of here."

"Right, and remember, whenever we meet Caligula, or whoever we're here to talk to, we can't mention anything about who we are and where we came from."

"What if he asks?"

"I guess we can tell him we're observers from far away, but no specifics. If we tell him that I'm from America, a place beyond the Pillars of Hercules, or whatever… who knows? They might just go there and colonize the place, a millennium before Columbus, or even before the Vikings poked around. Just keep the details vague, and tell him we have no idea how we got here. They seemed to know that blue ball thing would do something, or else they wouldn't have been ritualizing it, so we'll just play the hapless bystander card and hope they bite."

"All right. We also need to see about digging our way into that cavern to secure our gear, and make sure we can get McDougal out. We need to give him a proper burial."

"That might be harder than it sounds. We'll have to find a way to impress these guys just to get our weapons back, let alone ask for them to dig out a cave."

"That shouldn't be a problem."

I flinched at his last comment, but nodded all the same. I turned back toward the cityscape, ending the conversation. It certainly wouldn't be a problem to impress these people. All we needed to do was show them a lighter, or give them a demonstration of our weapons, but that would be a bad idea.

I heard the clicking of Roman style boots against marble, and turned to see one of the Praetorians emerging from the *Curia*. *Caligae* were constructed with hobnails imbedded in their soles, offering cleat-like characteristics. Like soccer players who used them for traction during matches, the Romans' application was the same for the battlefield. The centurion spoke quickly to Vincent, who held up his hands while replying. The Roman looked at me, his eyes cold as ice. He looked back at Vincent, and nodded rapidly, saying, "*celere*."

Basically, "make it quick."

Vincent tilted his head in thanks, and made his way toward his wary soldiers.

"Wake up people, break's over."

Years of training kicked in, and while only Wang stood, everyone else was back on task and paying close attention.

"It seems these Romans have been gracious enough to grant us an audience with the Caesar, but they will only allow me and one other to see him. Hunter, you're with me. I may need your ridiculous ability to comprehend this… sci-fi stuff."

I smiled. "My mom always told me I watched too much TV."

"Your mom's a smart woman," Santino said.

"The rest of you will be taken to a holding area," Vincent informed. "They know of your injuries, so they've agreed to keep you together. Bordeaux, get your ankle taken care of, and I'm sure Strauss can use another look at that leg. Santino, make sure nothing happens to them."

Santino nodded, completely serious.

"All right, Hunter. Let's get this over with."

VI
Caligula

Rome, Italy
October, 36-41 AD

    I fell into step behind Vincent as we followed the Roman Praetorians through the *Curia*, which in and of itself, was remarkable. Augustus had found Rome a city of stone, and left it a city of marble, or so he'd famously boasted. Judging from what I'd seen so far, he hadn't been kidding. Absent were the decaying and rundown buildings historians indicated were here merely a few decades earlier. Instead the area was opulent, radiant and, well… shiny, is a good way to describe it. The floor and walls glistened in the moonlight, and everything seemed in pristine condition, a clear indication of Rome's majesty.
    A few turns later, we arrived in the Senate chamber. While it wasn't all that big, the sheer scope of decisions debated in this room was enough to make it seem much bigger. It was circular in design, with elevated rows of long benches, illuminated by small fire pots hanging sporadically around the room. They cast off a spooky atmosphere throughout the room, with many areas cast in shadow while the remaining area flickered intermittently. So many elected officials, emperors, despots, and tyrants had ruled from this room, but there was currently only one on my mind.
    The one who sat center stage in the only independent seat in the house.
    The man was nothing like I imagined he would be. He was tall, blond, well-muscled, but rather unattractive. His eyes were small, his nose had a bump on it, and the tips of his ears flared out noticeably, but the way he looked at us indicated an inquisitive intelligence. He measured us up in a quick glance, no hint of intimidation or fear in his eyes. Instead, he seemed completely unimpressed by what he saw, as though men who looked like us passed by him every day.
    What was missing was the air of arrogance and godliness, traits reportedly common of the man. Not to mention insanity.
    We must have gotten lucky.

The man stood and circled us like a panther, continuing his inspection. At one point, he opened one of my pouches equipped with Velcro, which he merely accepted with a curious face and his mouth pursed approvingly. Everyone else appeared as though they had just seen magic. Two Praetorians jumped away from me in shock.

He stopped after two revolutions, and spoke his first words to Vincent. I tried to follow along as best I could, but mostly had to wait for Vincent's translations.

"Who are you?" Caligula asked.

"My name is Vincent, and this is Jacob Hunter."

"That is all very well and good, but where are you from and what is the meaning behind your appearance in my city?"

Vincent glanced at me before answering. "Where we are from, I cannot say."

"And why is that?"

"It may prove harmful to the future of your great empire."

Well. So far, so good. I guess this conversation could have been weirder.

"I am not sure how that could be so," Caligula continued, "but judging by your appearance, I would assume you are not from this area, nor any other part of my domain. So where? Deep in Africa or perhaps Asia? We've seen many strange things from these lands, but I must admit, none more so than you."

"I can confirm that we are not from any of these places, but little else. I will assure you, however, that we mean no harm to either you or your people. We are not here by choice. We find ourselves just as surprised as you are concerning our presence here."

"So you will not tell me where you are from, or who you are," he continued, tapping his chin with a finger, "nor will you tell me how it is you found your way into the city and beneath one of our most sacred temples, because... you don't know?" He asked, his expression indicating he clearly didn't believe us. "Of course."

"All of what you said is true, Caesar." Vincent paused, seeing Caligula's skeptical expression. "I feel the need to reassure you that we have no intention of acting against the will of Rome."

That was smart. 21st century technology or not, we wouldn't survive long with Rome as an enemy.

Caligula lifted his chin slightly, now giving us more of a suspicious, rather than skeptical, look. "How is it that you speak *my* language?"

Vincent paused for a second and glanced at me again. I didn't dare move. That *was* a good question.

"I've spoken Latin for most of my life," Vincent responded with a shrug.

Good answer.

"From where, I have no idea," Caligula continued. "Your accent is most bizarre."

Vincent shrugged again.

Caligula's suspicious glance lingered as he held out his arm toward one of his Praetorians, indicating for one of our rifles. The man brought Vincent's M4 for Caligula's inspection.

"What manner of weapon is this?" He asked. "I would not have thought it one had my guards not informed me these were what you surrendered to them. It is not of balanced weight, or design, nor is it sharp in any place. It also seems too fragile for a bludgeoning weapon, so what does it do?"

"It is a projectile weapon, similar to a bow and arrow, only slightly more sophisticated. Currently, it is not loaded, so you will be unable to fire it."

"And what is this device?" He asked, indicating the flashlight attached to the barrel, which had conveniently slid free from its mount. Caligula was fiddling with it while Vincent answered.

"It is an illum…"

Caligula accidentally pressed the activation button, projecting a brilliant beam of light that collected on the ceiling. The guardsmen gasped in horror, while Caligula dropped the flashlight and skipped away, perhaps fearing it was possessed.

"It's as though the rays of Apollo are contained within." One of the guards commented, moving away from the rolling light, probably thinking he might spontaneously combust should it touch him.

I bent down and retrieved the small tool.

"We call it a flashlight." Vincent informed, using the American term, retrieving his light. Manipulating it, he lit up areas of the room otherwise in the dark. The Romans seemed thoroughly impressed after composing most of their dignity.

"As you can see, it creates light in a nonflammable way, focusing it tightly for increased efficiency."

"How does such a device operate?" Caligula asked, retaking his U shaped seat, appearing only slightly startled.

"To be honest, the specifics of its function are slightly beyond me, but just like your catapults, it has been constructed from earthly materials, by human hands. No divine inspiration was required."

"Such a device," Caligula mumbled, shaking his head at the floor. "Its abilities are far beyond that of a simple torch. If your weapons are just as advanced when compared to our own, I am becoming more and more reluctant to trust you."

"Caesar, we are willing to perform any test needed to prove our honesty. If it would please you, we are prepared to offer a demonstration of our abilities at your convenience."

Caligula spent a few minutes considering, occasionally glancing at his guards, and then back at us. A few minutes later, he stood up and moved closer to us.

"I have been given word that some of your people have sustained injury. Again, how, I know not. It is for that reason that I have let them stay together and why I will now allow you to rejoin them. However, I will require your demonstration tomorrow evening. It is very late, rest as much as you need. Food will be provided when you wish, but be ready."

"Your kindness is greatly appreciated, Caesar. However, I have but one request."

"Speak."

Vincent took a step closer. "In our rush to escape the collapsing cave beneath your temple, we left one of our people behind. He was already dead upon our arrival."

I guess now wasn't the best time to mention the large amount of gear buried along with him. That wouldn't really help our case much.

"Where we come from we have a practice of not leaving fellow soldiers behind, as well as burial rituals for the dead. If it is at all possible, we ask that we be allowed to retrieve him, and give him the proper respects."

Of all the conquerors and empires throughout the ages, Rome, surprisingly, was probably one of the most tolerant. That is, until us poor Christians came on the scene. Prior to the advent of

Christianity, they could care less about who you worshiped or what gods you prayed to, as long as you paid tribute to the emperor. Additionally, Romans took their own burial preparations very seriously. They had important rituals, imported mostly from the Greeks, which would help prepare the dead for their journey to the afterlife.

Caligula looked thoughtful for a second, understanding our desire to lay our dead to rest.

"Tomorrow evening you will perform your demonstration, as planned," he answered. "Afterwards, should I feel it prudent, I will order the retrieval of your lost friend. However, if all goes well for you, I will require a more thorough test of your loyalty at a later date."

"Thank you, Caesar." Vincent bowed, and I followed suit.

"Now go. The hour is late. I hope all goes well tomorrow. For your sake."

***

We left the senate chamber in silence, our guards close at hand. I thought the discussion had gone well enough, although I wasn't sure a demonstration of our weapons was the most intelligent course of action. The fact that these Romans now know of flashlights alone might be enough to change the course of history. They say that a butterfly fluttering in Ohio can produce a hurricane in China, but the question is, when does he know to flutter? We simply had no idea what action we performed, no matter how small, could result in a change in global history.

I was a little worried that just by arriving here we had already changed something. I still didn't understand why, in all my research, I had never once heard of us being here.

And here's where things got confusing.

In our present, in 2021, our history books include no account of beings fitting our description. If we gave our demonstration tomorrow, which seemed very likely at this point, we were going to leave a mark on someone smart enough to write it down. While writers such as Plutarch, who wrote extensively on important individuals and events, hadn't even been born yet, his work centered on earlier figures, and ones who made a real difference. If Caligula could harness our abilities, he would have certainly been one of them, which he wasn't. Even if Plutarch didn't write about it, surely one of the many historians still to come would have. The kind of spectacle we could put on seems right up Suetonius' alley, but again, he includes no mention of us. Pliny the Elder, Tacitus, Seneca, the list goes on, and yet there was still no mention of us.

It may have seemed odd to think in such terms, but there was a basic theoretical approach dealing with how and why we could already have been here. However, the only answer I had left to go on at this point was that we simply weren't here, and that the blue sphere opened some kind of inter-dimensional, time bending, "flux capacitor" type portal that transported us here. If that was the case, then it only confirmed my theory that whatever we did here could impact the future. If there had been some indication that we were here in our histories, all we would have had to do was act naturally, knowing that things turned out in 2021 the way they did, despite our presence.

By the time we reached the entrance, I'd just about had enough of the subject. I'd always found the concept interesting. Whenever a special on the subject was on TV, I made a point to catch it. The formulas and science behind it went well over my head, but the concepts and fundamentals always lined up pretty easily. I always did enjoy those cheesy sci-fi movies as well.

My sister had always been the real brains in the family. Younger by only eighteen months, she had become more successful than me the day she entered college. An aerospace engineer, she had been one of the driving brains behind the new ion propulsion engines NASA used to ferry equipment to the moon. The new US-EU Joint Operation Moon Base, which she had helped establish as the first woman to step foot on the moon, and one of the first to go back since the last Apollo mission, could now receive supplies from Earth in forty eight hours, as opposed to the seven days it took Neil Armstrong, Buzz Aldrin, and Michael Collins in 1969.

Like I said, she was the successful one. I remembered when she started getting her feet wet in the business, and tried to explain the concept of the new engines to me. By the time she used words like magnetoplasmadynamics, everything had gone way over my head, and she had to settle with describing it as, "Star Wars stuff." That at least made some sense. The time travel stuff came up occasionally but usually she'd just roll her eyes and tell me to get my head out of the clouds.

I hadn't seen her in person since my graduation day from BUD/S a little more than three years ago, my time in the service and her time in space kept us apart.

Thinking about her sparked the first real revelation that I might never actually return home. Beside my SEALs, there were very few people left in my life I was close to, my father not even included. My sister was one of the few real friends I had, and the thought of never seeing her again had finally hit me.

We really were stuck in ancient Rome.

I tried to push the frightening thought from my mind as we exited the building. The first thing I noticed was that our group was gone, and that our escort continued ushering us through the Forum, hopefully to meet up with them. It would probably be best to voice my concerns to Vincent before we regrouped.

"You did a good job with your Latin back there, sir. You really fell into it."

"You're not the only one schooled in the subject, Hunter. At the Vatican, I had many friends who were quite proficient in Latin, and we enjoyed conversing in it. We weren't perfect, and we weren't sure exactly how certain words sounded, but we did our best. Listening to it here has allowed me to fill in the gaps, making it easy to pick up."

"Well, I'm pretty rusty, and I was barely following the conversation. I guess we'll all have to figure it out pretty quickly. I feel bad for Helena, she'll probably have the hardest time of us all, with German being so different. Then again, she's probably had a Latin lesson or two considering her education."

"Probably, but I have a feeling you have something else on your mind besides linguistics."

The man was sharp, that's for sure.

"Yes, sir. It's just that I don't think a weapons demonstration is a good idea. In fact, it could be devastating."

"We need these people to trust us. We may need their help to get home."

"I know," I replied, hoping this conversation wasn't automatically going to go unheard by him, "but I'm positive it may change too much. The Romans will get too many ideas. You know how clever they are. They'll probably have primitive muskets in the next decade."

"They'd need gun powder for that," he pointed out.

"The Chinese have had it for centuries at this point, and the Romans aren't unaware of their existence. All they'd need to do is kill us and analyze our equipment, not to mention all of the supplies buried with McDougal. I have no idea what those people were doing in there, but if they were looking for a treasure, I'd say they found one."

"So what are you saying?" He asked, giving the guards a paranoid glance, who for the time being seemed to be ignoring us. "We should get our people and run?"

"Doing that would be fruitless at this point. They don't need us anymore. We've already shown them too much. That flashlight was just the tip of the iceberg. They know we have someone buried beneath the temple. All they need to do is go down there and discover our gear. These people are very smart. They'll figure it out."

"Then what should we do?"

"I have no fucking clue," I said, my voice rising slightly. One of the Praetorians looked at me suspiciously, but I tried to ignore him. "I'm as in the dark here as you are. But I'll tell you this, I'm beginning to wonder if we'll even be able to get home."

That caused Vincent to hesitate. "Care to explain that one?"

"Look, as I've said, I'm no expert, but what I do know is that through technological means, many scientists theorize that it's impossible to go back in time. For many reasons. Ever heard of the Grandfather Paradox."

"Passingly."

"Well, say I was to go back in time and kill my grandfather before he spawned my father, therefore eliminating my chances in the gene pool."

"Okay," he said hesitantly.

"Well, the deal is, if I killed him, how is it that I existed in the first place to go back in time to kill him? I shouldn't exist."

"So, if you don't exist, then you can't go back in time to kill your grandfather?"

"Right. That's why it's a paradox. It simply can't happen. It goes against the laws of time."

"'The laws of time'?"

"Yeah, well, that's another problem. It's called a paradox because it goes against the 'laws of time', but the word 'law' is hardly appropriate. No one's ever been able to prove anything, so the term is actually horribly misleading," I said, chuckling at my own ridiculousness.

"But you just said this grandfather paradox doesn't even exist, because we have no idea how these so-called 'laws of time' work."

"Well... kind of. It's just one theory out of many. The point is, from what scientists think they know, these paradoxes do exist. Basically, physics and these so- called "laws of time" add up to to one universal fact: time travel is impossible, because anything done in the past, from an entity that does not belong in the past, has the potential to change the past, which is impossible."

I took a deep breath, that mouthful of an explanation taking a lot out of me. If only we had a DeLorean and a suitcase full of plutonium, none of this would be an issue. I just wish I'd spent more time talking with my genius sister about this stuff. Maybe then we'd be a step closer to figuring this out.

"Then again," I continued cautiously, "Einstein's general theory of relativity does allow for time travel. His math states that it is possible, but again, no one really knows anything. There's no proven math with all the variables in the universe involving time travel; and inevitably, that's what you need to do it, and math was never my best subject. Nor am I an omniscient being with all the knowledge of the universe.

"Then there are those others who say that even if you could travel back in time, it would be impossible to change anything. Their theory revolves around the idea that fate's grip on reality is too strong, and that one way or another, things will level out in the end, and nothing will change."

"Destiny?"

"Call it what you like," I said.

Whether it be fate, destiny, God's will, or the "laws of time," what's done in the past is done, and cannot be changed. Yet, here we were, stuck in the past and in a timeline in which we didn't belong in, probably already changing history as we lived and breathed.

"So what about traveling forward in time?" Vincent asked, keeping me focused. "Getting home?"

"Going into the future is a completely different concept all together. Traveling forward in time is completely possible. The means are extremely plausible, only not that easy to replicate. The trick is speed."

"Go on."

"Well, the closer to the speed of light one travels, the slower time moves around that person, relative to those on planet Earth. In theory, if we took a ship and set a course to orbit our solar system, continuously picking up speed toward the speed of light, by the time a month was spent traveling in that orbit, hundreds of years would have passed on Earth. I don't know the exact numbers, but that's the gist of it. However, finding a way to travel that fast, let alone survive it, is way beyond modern technology."

He waited for a few seconds, letting everything sink in, before offering me a skeptical look.

"You learned all this from watching TV?"

I nodded. "Pretty much. I used to read a lot of science fiction as a kid as well. I suggest checking out *The Future War*. It should be available at your local library."

Vincent snorted in amusement. "And they said the youth of America was doomed generations ago. All right, pretend I understand half of what you are saying. Why do you think we can't go back, besides not being able to travel fast enough?"

"Well, think about it. If it's impossible to time travel by any known technological means, the only other way I can think of this happening is through... well... magic."

"Be serious."

"I am serious... I think. Tell me, how does a glowing blue ball cause a temporal shift like the one we experienced? It has to be magical. The way the ball felt in my hands... it didn't feel natural. Here's another thing. When I first gazed through the ball, I noticed there was a similar one in the hands of the men we met in the cave. When we were transported, the ball I held came with us. Did you notice if the men had one of their own?"

"One of them did have one, yes."

"I thought so. If technology is the culprit, how could one of these balls exist during the days of the Roman Empire?"

"I'm completely lost." He said with a scratch of his head

I sighed. "Me too. I'm starting to confuse myself. There is one thing I don't get, though. How come when Abdullah held the ball nothing happened, but when I touched it with my finger, something happened?"

"Good question, but immaterial to our problem. The question should be whether any more of these balls exist at all."

"There very well may be a dozen of the damn things in the future, but the one we used certainly isn't where it was anymore. If we tried to connect with any other sphere out there, we could end up wherever and whenever that sphere is, not 2021. We could end up anywhere in time. That's what makes me think there are only the two. If there were more, why did we connect to this one? Why not all of them? Why did I only see images from this time, and not images from 1453 or 2543 as well? Who knows when another sphere, or this sphere, would have been found along the timeline."

"Hunter, you are thoroughly confusing me."

I laughed. "I get that a lot. Here's another wrench to throw in the engine." I waited, giving Vincent a chance to catch up. "Are you ready for this? I think the ball we found is the same exact one the Romans have. I don't mean the same kind of object, but the same ball."

Vincent just stared at me as we continued to stroll through the city. I thought I saw anger brewing in his expression, but it was probably just utter confusion.

"I hate to sound like Santino here, but you're crazy."

"I'm sorry. You have no idea how much I hate sounding like a know-it-all, but I'm really just spit-balling here. Look. Clearly the ritual being performed in the cave before we got here happened in our history. We know that because we just dropped into it an hour ago... it being history and all. But if that be the case, from our perspective in 2021, we all should have been in those history books too, yet there is no record of us. Why not? Two possibilities. As I said earlier, maybe we were here, but we just died real quick. The cave may have collapsed killing all of us and nobody thought twice about it. Think *Terminator*, just without as much Arnold. We had to be here to fulfill some predetermined roll we played here, namely to die."

Vincent held up a hand. "Wait. What's a terminator?"

I looked at him whimsically. "Your favorite band is the Beach Boys, but you've never heard of *Terminator*?"

"Just get to the point, Hunter."

Man... he's no better than Helena.

"Fine," I continued. "In any case, that theory doesn't seem very likely though, because our gear would have been found eventually, leaving an obvious record. So my theory is that when the ritual originally took place an hour ago, the original time before we got here, nothing happened. The sphere was deemed useless. It was then packaged up as a pretty trinket, and lost to the annals of history. It wasn't until a hapless soul such as myself found it in the future and activated it, that it did what it was supposed to do."

"Which is what?"

"I'm not sure. Maybe it's enchanted... or whatever, to open a one way trip through time to a prearranged destination. I guess that would explain how we ended up in Rome. Not only does it transport you through time, but through space as well. Think of it this way. Imagine a rubber band. Now, grab it with both hands and slowly stretch it out. Over time, it gets longer. It's actually moving through both time and space. Now, let go of one end, and it will return to its original form. But instead of just moving through space, like the rubber band, it moves back through time as well, to when the stretching began."

He sighed. "So, you're saying that the sphere, like the rubber band, has its physical existence stretched through time, and when activated, will find a way back to when it was originally activated?"

"It's a theory. Although, I guess all this presupposes linear and not cyclical time..."

"Hunter! Focus. So this sphere would take everything in a room with it?" He asked skeptically.

I shrugged.

"But how is it activated?" He asked, moving past the things we couldn't immediately explain.

"Great question. Haven't figured that part out yet. But the rest makes sense. Sort of."

"Nothing makes sense at this point," Vincent mumbled. "So how is it that two exist now? How is that possible? Shouldn't they have joined to become one sphere?"

"That's another very good question. It seems as though we've created yet another fundamental paradox of some kind. How can the same object be in a different place at the same time? It's easy to say my boot exists here at five o'clock, and then in the same place at six o'clock, but for the same boot, to exist at the same time, in two different places, is seemingly impossible." I tapped a finger against my chin thoughtfully, before wagging it at Vincent. "On the bright side, we may have just discovered a way to replicate glowing, blue, time traveling balls at no expense. I bet we can market them for a good price back home."

"If this situation wasn't so insane, that might actually be funny. So I ask again, more confused than ever, what do we do now?"

"I'm sorry to say that I'm just as lost as I ever was. Who the hell knows? Honestly, I'm ready to just throw in with the Romans and join the legions."

Vincent didn't respond, and for some reason his silence bothered me. It was like he knew something I didn't, like he was hiding some important piece of information.

I shook my head and decided to drop it. I didn't want to think about it anymore, so I ignored the man and focused on the road. All I wanted right now was a hot shower and a fresh change of clothes. Luckily, Roman baths were way ahead of their time, and a hot dip was perfectly feasible. Another plus was that some were openly co-ed.

Maybe Helena would be up for it.
Nah.

***

We walked the last few blocks in silence, both of us too tired to think anymore.

My fatigue surprised me. I knew I had to be in better shape than ninety nine percent of humanity, but while the last few hours had been strenuous, I'd gone through way worse before, but I'd never felt this bad afterwards. Everyone else had to be feeling it as well. My only conclusion was that the trip through the orb taxed its travelers far more than the painful transition alone.

A few feet before I collapsed out of exhaustion, the Praetorians slowed, and made their way to a wooden doorway, which opened to a small and simple house. It didn't seem like a prison, but I assumed these kinds of clandestine operations were common practice in the backstabbing world of ancient Rome.

The two men guarding the entrance saluted in greeting before opening the door. As they waved us through, one of the guards told Vincent to ask his counterpart stationed out front in the morning for food. It seemed like that bath was going to have to wait, but I'd settle for a meal.

The guard shut the door behind us, and locked us inside with a wooden plank. The house was little more than a wooden shack, with four small rooms. A number of mattresses, made out of unknown materials, were scattered throughout. There were no windows or other exits, and a small fireplace was blazing away, with some additional wood nearby.

And then there were the Pope's Praetorians. Scattered, they looked the worse for wear. Beaten, demoralized, and completely cut off from the chain of command, not to mention home, a soldier couldn't find himself in a more compromising situation.

Wang was sleeping on one of the mats in the main room, while Bordeaux was out in the room opposite the entrance, only his lower half visible, and Santino was leaning against the door. I couldn't see Helena, so I assumed she was probably asleep in one of the other rooms off to our left.

Santino noticed our arrival and came to attention, managing to pull off a very weary salute in the process.

He smiled. "Sorry, sir. I'm pretty tired, but I wanted to wait until you got here before sacking out."

Vincent put a hand on his shoulder. "We appreciate it, son. Don't worry, you'll be able to rest soon enough, but first I need a sit rep."

"Yes, sir. Our guards escorted us here as soon as you were taken inside. They even let us bring our gear container. We weren't manhandled, but they were very persistent. When we arrived, we were given indigenous clothing and food. There's some bread over there if you'd like."

He pointed to a small table, toward which Vincent and I headed immediately while Santino continued.

"We're in a small, square building, with four equally sized square rooms within. There are no windows or other forms of escape, save the fireplace, and each room is connected, except the back two," he finished, pointing behind him toward Bordeaux, before shifting his attention to the room to our left.

"The container is filled with explosives and ammo. We've got enough to hold out for a long time, and I'm pretty sure Bordeaux could level the entire city if he wanted to. Probably does, the sick bastard. Anyway, we restocked our magazines just in case. Then Wang got to work on our wounded. He set Bordeaux's ankle, which as it turns out, wasn't just sprained but fractured in two places. He'll be out of commission for a few weeks.

He took a deep breath, his fatigue worsening by the second. "In addition to her leg, Strauss has a dozen or so minor gashes over her body, some needing stitches. Her wetsuit is completely trashed and unusable. Wang finished with her by reopening the main injury on her leg and stitched it back together properly. It was pretty nasty. He said Hunter couldn't have done a worse job setting the wound."

"Hey. We were in a bit of a rush."

"We know. He also said you saved her life. And don't worry. He took extra care with the stitches so your girlfriend's leg shouldn't be too scarred."

"You know…"

He cut me off with an upraised arm. "He also set her other ankle as well which has a minor sprain. Once Wang was finished, he cleaned his tools and passed out over here." He prodded Wang's body with his foot.

I looked down at the young Brit, who clutched his UMP to his chest like a small child would his teddy bear. I noticed the weapon was at least set on safe, but still had a magazine loaded into the magazine well. Kneeling beside Wang, I gently reached out and removed the magazine, releasing the loaded round through his rifle's ejection port as well. There was no sense risking the man shooting himself in the night by mistake. We were safe. For now.

"As for me, it turns out I have a concussion," Santino concluded, that fact quickly becoming more evident as he started swaying in place, forcing him to reach out and brace himself against the wall. "I must have hit my head when the truck flipped, so with your permission, I'm just gonna go ahead and pass out."

"Go ahea…"

Again, Santino didn't give Vincent a chance to finish before he collapsed onto the mattress, unconscious.

Vincent checked his vital signs, just to make sure he was still breathing. He gave me a questioning look.

I shrugged. "What can I say? He's a tough son of a bitch."

"Well, he's not the only one who could use some rest. I'll go check on Bordeaux and sack out in his room. Go check on Strauss and get some sleep."

"Yes, sir," I replied, heading through the door on the left.

"And, Hunter?"

"Sir?"

"Don't blame yourself for any of this. You did well."

Nodding, unsure how to respond, I made my way into the next room. It was empty save for the cargo container. No room to sleep, and no sign of Helena, I continued through into the last room. I found her sprawled out on her back, her left leg propped up on a number of pillows, wrapped in a bandage. I looked away, noticing both legs were bare to the waist, exposing her injuries, underwear, and perfectly bronze skin.

Turning my back to the near naked woman sheepishly, I searched for someplace to sleep. Vincent had probably taken the last mat in Bordeaux's room, leaving just the one here in hers'.

I probably couldn't haul the mattress out of her room at this point even if I wanted to.

Sighing, I removed my MOLLE rig before taking off the rest of my gear, placing it in the corner quietly. Once my shirt was off and I had my pants around my knees, I heard Helena shift behind me. Fearing the worst, I froze.

"Nice butt, Lieutenant."

I shut my eyes, wishing she really couldn't see me. My ability to make a complete fool out of myself on a consistent basis continued to amaze me.

"Says the half-naked woman," I replied, trying to make light of the moment.

"Aw, I couldn't resist. Especially with those smiley face boxers you're wearing."

Now I did blush. I liked these boxers.

Resigning to my humiliation, I took off my pants, and removed my undershirt, folding everything with military neatness. I crawled onto the mat next to Helena's and pulled an itchy blanket to my chin. A few sniffs later, I removed it completely. I looked over at Helena to find her gazing in my direction.

My voice lowered itself to a whisper, too tired to speak any louder. "So, how are you doing, Helena?"

"I'll live, but my leg really hurts."

"Looks fantastic to me."

"Cute, Lieutenant."

I smiled despite it all. "Well, rest up. Tomorrow's going to be a big day."

I closed my eyes, feeling sleep's hold creep up on me.

"Anything I should know about?" Helena asked.

"Not tonight," I whispered, rolling onto my side and a bit closer to the warm body beside me, "not tonight."

Helena was quiet for a minute.

"Hunter?"

"Hmm?"

"Don't get any ideas."

***

About five minutes later, I heard someone calling my name. It sounded distinctly feminine, but in my near deathlike state, I couldn't be sure. Peeking through my right eye, I noticed a blurry figure dangling long, thin, snake like protrusions in my face. They smelled wonderful. As my vision cleared, I realized it was Helena, her face dangerously close to mine, her hair tickling my cheeks and forehead.

I groaned. "Aw, mom, I don't wanna go to school this morning."

She cocked her head to the side and gave me a dubious look. "Mother?"

I lifted my head off the pillow but just as quickly lowered it before I could get a real look at what was underneath Helena's loose fitting shirt, forcing the inevitable image out of my head.

"Sigh," I said. "Fine. You win."

"That's what I thought. Now get up. They've given us some food so we'd better eat while we have the chance."

"Are you kidding me?" I asked, getting comfortable with my feather pillow again. "Wake me up for lunch. I just fell asleep."

"Jacob. As far as we can tell, it's well past midday. You've been asleep almost twelve hours. We all have."

I opened my right eye again and rolled it to look at her. "Damn, time flies when you're having fun."

"I bet" she said, offering me a hand. "Now get up."

"I take it back. You're worse than mom ever was."

"Just get up," she said, playful irritation in her voice.

Groaning, I took her hand, and hauled myself up under my own power, fully aware of her injuries. On my feet, I noticed her Roman style clothing slip down one of her shoulders scandalously.

She smiled as she fixed the slip and I couldn't help but give her a whimsical look.

This was going to be a long life in ancient Rome.

Sighing, I pulled her close, and wrapped her arm over my shoulder to help her limp out of the room.

We made our way to the main room to find the rest of the team seated on the floor eating bread, cheese, fruit, a bird of some kind, and a gloopy oatmeal type food. Helping Helena to the floor, she and I quickly devoured what we could. We were famished, and I tore into the random foul like a ravaged lion. The rest of the team quietly ate their food at a more reserved rate, having already had their first course. It seemed Vincent was already finished and I watched him take a few sips of his wine. He glanced at the cup approvingly and nodded.

In ancient Rome, fresh water was a scarcity, so most of the time wine was used as a perfectly acceptable substitute. Its alcohol content was extremely high, which worked well to fight off bacteria. Romans watered it down as much as possible, but ancient wine was still far more potent than the variety found in the 21st century. The wine also tended to be extremely dry, as opposed to sweet or fruity, making it a very acquired taste. I happened to like it, as apparently did Vincent, but I was sure it would take the rest a while to get used to, especially Bordeaux. I couldn't imagine any Frenchman liking excessively dry wine.

Washing my food down with my own glass, I too gave the wine an approving nod. I noticed Helena wince after she tried it.

"Don't like it?"

She placed a hand on her throat, as though she were parched. "It's so dry, I can barely swallow it."

"Get used to it. It's all they got."

"Great."

Vincent put his glass down and cleared his throat. "Last night, Hunter and I had the chance to speak to none other than Caligula himself. I'm not sure what you people know about him, but we were happily surprised. At some point early in his reign, he becomes rather insane, a result of a horrible fever, or so some think. Thankfully, we got here before that happened. Instead of murdering us outright, he agreed to let us live. He has also given us the opportunity to prove our worth to him, which will hopefully allow us to work with the Romans to find a way home."

"How?" Bordeaux asked.

"Well, Caligula accidentally turned on my flashlight last night, and needless to say, was thoroughly impressed. He also knows of our weapons, but has no idea how they work. Basically, he wants us to give him a demonstration."

"You realize," Santino started, "that if what Hunter rambled on about last night is true, if we do this, we will probably change the course of history?"

"Perhaps, but it's not like we are supplying the entire Roman army with firearms. What harm could occur from us just showing them what we can do? I suspect very little. However, there is more you should know. Hunter's done a little more, 'thinking,' I suppose you could put it, and he's got something you all should hear."

All eyes turned toward me expectantly.

Sighing, I retold my thoughts on time travel, and how in the end, everything I've said may mean nothing… everything about paradoxes, light speed, and duplicating, magical, time traveling spheres. I tried to spread things out a bit more, simplifying information and adding more detail. I wanted to make sure everyone was following, and that I limited confusion to a minimum. By the time I was finished, every face seemed deep in thought, except for Santino, who was never one for deep thought.

"You know, Jacob. I always thought you were just that shy guy who sat at the end of the bar and got all the ladies because they saw some deep, contemplative, brooding type fella, just looking for some love. Now, I've finally realized that you're just a big nerd."

His joke received the desired response. Everyone laughed and it snapped them from the looks of worry they all wore after having just heard how dire our situation actually was. Soon, the group was arguing among themselves about how we were going to get back, except for Wang, who still seemed wrapped in his own little world.

Vincent got to his feet, raising his hands for silence. "Whatever the case may be, we need to worry about our safety and survival. So we focus on the demonstration, if for nothing else, so that they'll agree to dig out McDougal and we can put him to rest. Bordeaux, do you still have any explosives?"

"*Oui*, I was not forced to use it all on the cavern. Besides, that container has plenty."

"Right. I forgot. Good. We'll use some of it in our demonstration. A small amount, however. We don't want to give too much away. Wang, leave your medical supplies here, but bring some pain relievers, maybe we can impress them with our medical knowledge as well. The rest of us will demonstrate rifle and small arms fire. Strauss, you are you able to field your DSR-1?"

"I should be," she replied, trying to stretch her injured leg, "as long as I can do it sitting down. I can't stand for long on my own and I don't think I could lay on my stomach with my leg."

"Fine. Hunter, back her up. We can't afford to botch this one. We need to impress them beyond a shadow of a doubt, so look sharp."

**

An hour later, we were joined by four Praetorians.

Leaving our wetsuits in the room, we wore navy blue BDUs Bordeaux found in the supply container, and donned our full complement of combat gear, sans headgear. The men who came for us had not been involved last night, so when they got a good look at us, they were humorously shocked. We had to have looked even more imposing than we did in the dim moonlight.

Hesitating, the centurion stuttered slightly when he spoke to Vincent, making him a little tough to understand. The message seemed to get across, however, and we soon found ourselves walking through the streets of Rome on a warm, late afternoon day.

As opposed to last night, where there had only been a few drunken miscreants about, there were now hundreds of people lining the streets going on about their daily lives. Men were gathered in small groups, discussing the day's events, while the women carried baskets, and bundles of clothing, going about the day's errands. As each noticed our arrival, their attention immediately shifted to us. A few women dropped their baskets, while plenty of jaws dropped all around. Some of the more confident children braved an attempt to touch us. They were rewarded with warm smiles, and maybe tousled hair, all in an attempt for us to show our friendliness.

Our march through Rome was short lived. We passed through a gate, beneath a large wall that must have stretched around the city. Since we had arrived in the days of Caligula, it must have been the Servian Wall, the original wall named for Rome's sixth king, Servius Tullius. The Romans weren't big on defensive walls, relying on their legions to defend them instead. It wasn't until the Aurelian Wall was erected that there was a defensive barrier around the entire city. The Servian Wall didn't even cross the Tiber River, and there were many buildings and structures outside its defenses such as the *Campus Martius* and the *Castra Praetoria*, near where I believe we had just spent the night.

I knew the layout of ancient Rome fairly well. I'd studied the city extensively in college, and knew that since we were heading southwest, and had passed through the walls, we had to have come from the barracks that housed the emperor's Praetorian cohorts, the *Castra Praetoria*. While we probably didn't actually go inside their fort, built by Tiberius at the prompting of his prefect Sejanus to house the entire force of Praetorians, we probably spent the night in a nearby house.

I felt a slight rush as we passed into the *pomerium*, the sacred city limits, thought to have been drawn by Romulus as he drove his plow around the Palatine Hill and surrounding area, hundreds of years ago. The 'line' wasn't real, but I estimated we were in the right place.

The *pomerium* was an interesting piece of history. Only the land within its imaginary border was considered to actually be "Rome," while everything outside was simply territory owned by Rome. Foreign sovereigns could not enter into it, weapons were not allowed and only Praetorians had permission to carry them as long as they were concealed by their togas, which was why you never saw them walking around in their armor.

Rounding a large hill, I saw what I could only assume was the *Circus Maximus*, just a few miles southwest of where we stayed the night. My eyes widened with awe as they were drawn to the enormous structure, still in the prime of its life. The stadium held various races, gladiatorial fights, and other spectacles and was the largest open-air stadium on the planet, a record which would still stand in 2021 were there more than just remnants of its foundation left. It was here that in the movie *Ben-Hur*, Charlton Heston raced his childhood friend-turned-enemy, an event which took place only a year or so ago from this point in history, during Tiberius' reign.

At least it had in the movie.

I felt a chill as we passed through the gates. I started thinking about just how many charioteers and gladiators never made the return trip home. I wondered if we would meet that same fate in this historical structure. Hopefully, all would go as planned, and we would leave with the key to the city instead.

We made our way through a maze of hallways before emerging onto the field. It reminded me of my old football field, with the track running along the perimeter, except this field was much larger, and had a large structure which ran through the middle. It was known as the *spina*, which acted very much like the vertebrae of the field. On the *spina* were roman idols and an Egyptian obelisk, put there by Augustus, captured in Egypt. That obelisk was moved by Pope Sixtus Something to the *Piazza del Popolo*, just outside of St. Peter's Basilica, and was still there the last time I checked. The stadium also sported bronze dolphins, which could pivot downwards to indicate how many laps had elapsed in a race.

Walking along the dusty track, we made our way to the imperial viewing stand, where I noticed Caligula and a number of other men and women were already present. The women sat in the back, quietly chit-chatting among themselves. There was one young woman in particular who was pregnant, and had a kind of beauty that was unrivaled amongst the group. Her blond hair and sharp nose gave her a sinister hotness found mostly in the movies. She looked familiar somehow, and when she winked at me, I almost dropped Helena. Last, but not least, I couldn't help but notice the small man

I had seen in the cavern the night before, who was very quickly beginning to annoy me.

Coming to a halt in front of the grandstand, I realized just how ragtag we looked, with Bordeaux limping along, and me practically carrying Helena. I hoped we didn't look so weak that Caligula would jump to the conclusion that we were of no worth to him after all.

No, he was aware of our wounded. The man knew combat, and would understand our situation. He'd wait until he saw what we could do before he made any kind of judgment.

Vincent, taking the initiative, snapped to attention and pounded his fist against his chest before extending his arm in a very Hitlerian type salute, used by the Romans long before that menace had slandered it's meaning, the only difference being that Vincent's hand was closed.

In as commanding a voice as he could manage, Vincent laid out our case for those present. "Hail, Caesar. My comrades and I are here to prove our loyalty through a demonstration of our skills and technology. Should we succeed in doing so, we would like the opportunity to retrieve our fallen leader, as we discussed, as well as some equipment left behind."

I froze for half a second. Vincent did a good job of surreptitiously adding the fact we had gear down there, but I hoped he hadn't overplayed his hand. We didn't need Caligula getting suspicious.

The Roman emperor approached a railing and lean over the edge on a forearm almost nonchalantly. "Should you meet my expectations, I will agree to your request. To help facilitate my decision, I have requested the presence of some of my closest advisors, friends, and family."

That sounded odd coming from an emperor with a reputation like Caligula's. Maybe historians got more wrong than they thought, but I had to remember to keep things in perspective. We knew little of his few sane months, but for all intents and purposes, he had been a promising young man.

"Gathered here are some of my generals, members of the senate and my uncle, Claudius," Caligula continued, sweeping his right arm behind him.

Claudius?

I looked among the gathered men, but could not spot anyone who fit his description. I wasn't sure what he looked like, but he was known to stutter and twitch, not to mention he was described as feeble and weak. Unfortunately, none of the men present displayed any of those qualities. One man was tall and blond, with the short hair reminiscent of Caesars, but was far from the feeble stutterer I imagined.

Claudius must have been in the back, out of sight somewhere, which wouldn't have been a surprise considering his reputation.

"With their help," he finished, "we will determine whether your existence shall continue, and whether you have a place amongst my people. Now, what will you require?"

Vincent answered immediately. "First, we need our weapons. With them, we will demonstrate their range, accuracy and lethality. In order to do so, we will need a dozen spare suits of armor set up to appear like men. We will also require a large piece of fruit, and a marble column as thick and strong as you can spare and move here."

Smiling, Caligula replied, "Is that all? Perhaps I should have the entire Gaulic war band present for you to defeat. Perhaps then," he said, the arrogance and depravity that was missing earlier now surfacing, "you would be able to do enough."

Vincent returned his smile. "I think we'll be all right."

***

Forty five minutes later, our column finally arrived. A simple stone cylinder, barely Doric in style, it was easily the width of a large oak tree, and twice as tall as Bordeaux. It would explode beautifully.

During that time, we were presented with our confiscated firearms, and had the opportunity to quickly inspect them and make sure they were ready for use. I had to admit, it felt good to have Penelope back in my hands, her reassuring weight doing wonders for my confidence. I pulled back the cocking mechanism and checked the ejection port for any kind of tampering or dirt buildup. It seemed clear, so I released the mechanism with a loud clank, resulting in murmurs spreading through the crowd. I turned to look at them, a nervous smile on my face, before returning my attention to my gear.

Caligula noticed our focused attention and returned to the railing. "While we are waiting," he said impatiently, "why don't you describe what these weapons do."

Vincent nodded, pulling a magazine from a chest pouch, and extracting a bullet. "Of course. This," he said, indicating his upheld M4, "is called a rifle. These are our primary weapons. Most of the ones we are using are of various designs and models, each having their own particular advantages and disadvantages. We all chose our particular rifles based on which one we felt suited us best. Each of our weapons fires a projectile, whose size is different depending on the rifle."

He held up one of the bullets and demonstrated how he loaded it into a magazine.

"This small object is a bullet," he said, always using the English terms to describe modern items. "We insert it into what we call a magazine, which holds multiple bullets. Then, to prime the weapon we insert the magazine thusly."

He finished by ramming the magazine into the magazine well and pulled the cocking lever, feeding a round into the chamber. "The rifle is now ready to fire."

"So, these... bullets," Caligula said, having trouble wrapping his mouth around the foreign word, "are like the lead pellets used in slings? I ask, because while slings have their place on the battlefield, they are not the most effective projectile weapons. Additionally, they are only effective in mass barrages. What use are these bullets with only the six of you?"

Vincent smiled. "Patience, Caesar. Things will become very clear, very soon."

Caligula mused over Vincent's paternal tone, clearly annoyed. "What is that shiny object on your leg?" He asked, indicating his side arm.

"This is a pistol. We refer to it as a sidearm or secondary weapon. It too fires bullets, but with reduced efficiency. We use them as backups."

"You carried that thing into my presence?"

"Yes, we did. Hopefully, the fact that we did not use them helps alleviate any fear or concern you may have toward us, for we could have at any time."

"So you say, but I have yet to observe anything that leads me to fear these so called, 'weapons'."

Caligula was demonstrating more curiosity, tact, and intelligence than I had ever given him credit for, but that imperial arrogance was getting irritating.

When the column and legionary armor were finally in place, I couldn't be more excited. Not because I thought this was a good idea, but because I really didn't want all of Rome's military might bearing down on us if we delayed too long.

Vincent walked over to the railing and held out his hands. "I suggest you wear these," he said, holding small, foam ear plugs. "These will help muffle the noise of our weapons. They will be extremely loud."

One of Caligula's military men stepped forward and accepted the small gifts, nodding in thanks.

"Just squeeze them until they are flat, insert them in your ear, and allow them to expand. You will experience a slight drop in hearing ability, but trust me, you will appreciate it later.

The men and women struggled to insert the 'foamies,' which was understandable, since none of them had ever used anything remotely like them.

They were in for one hell of a surprise.

One of the men, a burly, older fellow, refused to use them at all, dropping them to the ground with a haughty laugh.

Content the spectators were adequately protected, Vincent joined Santino, Wang, and me in a firing line twenty feet from our targets. Helena and Bordeaux sat off to the side, saving their particular skills for later. We three shooters glanced over at Vincent's position, waiting for the go ahead. Each of us made eye contact, acknowledging his unspoken question with smug looks.

Turning his head, he spoke to the grandstand. "With your permission?"

Caligula waved a hand dismissively.

Vincent offered a small smirk of his own. "All right. One magazine each. Don't worry too much about accuracy. Fire in controlled bursts, but do it quickly. Understood?"

There was a chorus of affirmatives.

"Open fire!" Vincent bellowed.

A half second later, we unleashed a hailstorm of fire that echoed throughout the city. We fired in controlled bursts, as ordered, but it seemed like one continuous stream of rifle fire with the four of us shooting in tandem. The suits of armor, set up on stands that we requested be anchored to the ground, were permeated with a hundred little holes and one even fell over.

The Romans' reaction was laughably predictable. Every single hand went directly to their ears, and the man who had thrown his earplugs on the ground went diving after them. Some of the men almost fled and most of the women did. Curiously, the extremely attractive blond did not, and instead sat there calmly with her hands lightly cupping her ears. Even Caligula had his hands to his ears, but did a pretty good job of maintaining his imperial demeanor.

Not twenty seconds later, with our magazines spent, we unloaded, put our guns on safe, and admired our handiwork. Not a bad clustering for a couple of Special Forces fellows. The dummies would have been dead a dozen times over. We gathered up the mutilated armor, and brought them before the Romans for their inspection.

Vincent described what it was they were seeing. "As you can see, our weapons are quite formidable, more so than a simple sling. Just one or two of these holes could kill a man. Additionally, we can carry at any given time at least three hundred rounds of ammunition each, and can easily wield more if necessary. The lethality of our weapons is also high at ranges far greater than those you just witnessed."

Caligula inspected one of the gaping holes with a probing finger. His jaw was slightly ajar, amazed at our rifles' stopping power. "What is the range of your weapons?"

"They can easily surpass the range of your arrows, which we will demonstrate next. If you will please, have someone place that large piece of fruit on the highest level of the arena, at the farthest end."

"Impossible. That distance is too far to hit such a small target."

"Are you sure?"

He thought about it for a second, glancing at the ruined sets of armor.

"No."

Ten minutes later, the piece of fruit high above the rest of us, Helena and I sat down to take aim. We ran through the calculations quickly, and while she wasn't using the Barrett, her DSR-1 was more than able to reach the mark. Another ten minutes later, the piece of fruit exploded in a shower of sticky fruitiness. This time, the Romans applauded. Even Caligula joined in.

Helena and I joined Vincent near the podium.

"An impossible shot! Miraculous. And from a woman! How is that a female has the same skills and status as a man in the realm of warfare among your people?"

"What did he say?" Helena whispered, clearly aware of his attention on her.

I wasn't exactly sure, but I got the gist of it. "You don't want to know."

"Where we come from, pure strength isn't the only prerequisite needed for war," Vincent informed. "Many more aptitudes are required, and while women comprise only a small minority in our militaries, their presence is still noticeable and appreciated."

Caligula thought this over for a few minutes before nodding. I wasn't sure if he simply understood or shared our sentiments, but considering what he just saw, he didn't need to.

"And what are you to conclude with?"

"You have seen our primary weapons at work, but to facilitate our needs, we can call on many other pieces of equipment to aid us in battle. One is an explosive device able to obliterate extremely large and durable objects."

"Are you referring to that small brick I saw your very large man place on the column?"

"Indeed, and if you would be so helpful," Vincent said, holding out the detonation device, nothing but a small box with a trigger, "when I say all is clear, squeeze the two pieces of this box together, and you shall see."

Caligula accepted the device, turning it over in his hand, before nodding to Vincent.

Vincent turned to Bordeaux. "Ready?"

"*Oui*, but I suggest we move everyone to the far end of the arena."

Once Vincent requested everyone do so, we were ready to go. Vincent gave the go ahead, and Caligula squeezed the detonator.

Across the arena, the column exploded in a plume of dust and debris. The explosion ballooned well above the walls of the arena, sending a shower of marble in all directions, and the sound was deafening. It seemed as though Bordeaux used a bit too much C-4, but I'm sure it was purposeful. He just wanted to make a big bang, something all demolition men took way too much pride in. I always figured they were overcompensating for something.

After the debris cloud settled, and a few of the Romans had returned from their hiding spots, some not returning at all, Vincent turned toward Caligula, a slight smile on his mouth.

"Well? Have we satisfied your interests, Caesar?"

Caligula continued to stare at the ruined column, barely recognizable after its explosive ending. For a second I thought he was going to declare us evil sorcerers and have us crucified, but soon his face softened.

His eyes met Vincent's, his look of superiority gone. "You have, indeed. I will order a team to recover your fallen comrade, and then we shall talk about how you may best serve the glory of Rome."

***

Three days later, we were still waiting for Caligula to come through on his end of the bargain. We were still locked up in the same building we had been thrown in the very first night, but there really wasn't much room for complaint. We were no longer treated as prisoners, at least not officially, and we were allowed to leave the building, a freedom we took advantage of twice a day to workout. Food was provided, we were given fresh clothes and bedding on a regular basis, and we had our very own private bathroom which was, thankfully, only a short walk away from our little house.

On the downside, however, we were always under the watchful eyes of Praetorian guardsmen, and our weapons were confiscated again, including our side arms. The Romans weren't going to let that trick fly twice. Occasionally, one or two particular Praetorians, their names not provided, would spend hours speaking to Vincent. He spoke in detail about our weapons, as well as modern combat tactics. The Romans were extremely interested in our methods of waging war, where the largest battlefields saw small, eight man squads engaging in endless skirmishes, as opposed to legions of thousands of men fighting one massive battle. He left out the parts about tanks, planes, ships, and nukes, at least for the time being.

I continued to voice my disapproval about telling them anything at all, reiterating the fact that we could still be in the process of altering future events. I even recounted to him a story about time traveling dinosaur hunters who accidentally killed a butterfly in the past and ended up changing their utopian government into a tyrannical regime, sixty five million years later. Granted, it was a fictional, extreme, unscientific opinion of what could happen, but I hoped it would be enough to change his mind.

It didn't, and I eventually realized there was nothing I could do to convince Vincent. For some reason, he was being particularly stubborn about his decisions.

Still, despite the tight spaces and endless boredom, the time helped the unit bond. As a team, we spent the time playing cards and chatting endlessly.

Generally, the games left me pretty frustrated, especially after I realized Wang and Helena were phenomenal poker players. I never knew poker was so popular amongst the English and Germans, but while I gained little from the games, I learned plenty about my teammates.

Bordeaux, for instance, spoke of his checkered youth, a life of crime and insolence that landed him in the foreign legion. He told us how his military life had changed him, how he had found God, and even a wife.

During a mission in Africa, his team had rescued a group of French peacekeepers, captured by a local guerrilla militia. After the successful rescue, one of the young women immediately fell in love with the bulky hero, and eventually married him. The story lacked a happy ending, however, as Bordeaux also told us how she had died in the Vatican terrorist attacks. The attack only sharpened his focus, and it had driven him to find his own way into the Praetorians, instead of being chosen like I was. I immediately connected his loss with the reason behind his unfocused attention during the briefing back in modern day Rome.

Wang continued to grieve, but his attitude quickly shifted when he realized his poker skills were far superior to the rest of ours. Poker soon boiled down to a deadly game of one on one between him and Helena.

I didn't mind. I wasn't very good at poker, anyway.

He seemed happiest, though, when he told stories of McDougal and his heroics. From what I learned, he couldn't have been a better commander, and I only wished I could have served with him longer.

Santino, meanwhile, had a story for everything. Whether it was about his first stealth kill in North Korea or the first vanilla smoothie he ever had in high school, he always had something to say. And while it may have seemed annoying, they were actually good stories, even the one about the smoothie, which he seriously told.

Helena and I held back our more personal stories with the group, both of us reluctant to delve into our personal lives. It was, however, a personality quirk that strengthened our own friendship. Since swim buddies were bunked together, we had plenty of alone time, and we often found ourselves talking about things we couldn't have told the others. She became someone I could really talk to.

Our stories tended to revolve around our repressive fathers, who always had the best intentions at heart, but at the expense of what their children wanted. Her father had taught her to hunt, and mine, to play baseball, but both led us in directions neither one of us really wanted to go. When she had pressed the issue of why I never finished my schooling, I told her it was because of the way my father forced me into the military. It was his opinion that school was unnecessary after achieving an undergraduate degree, and only because *that* degree was important in securing entry into Officer Candidate School.

It was a bad moment in the Hunter family saga. Dad spoke of cutting me off, severing my ties to the family if I didn't comply with the family tradition. The shouting matches had been epic. When I'd given up completely, figuring I'd have to settle for Christmas cards from mom only, she and my sister took up the cause and pleaded with him to let me make my own choices, but he was adamant. My sister stopped talking to him for a long while, but my mother was more diplomatic. She loved her husband and wanted to make him happy, so she relented and sat me down. Like any good mom could, she compromised, making me understand that military service would be good for me and my career, and that since the world was as peaceful as it had been in decades, it would be safe. So, wanting to make my mother happy, as she did my father, I signed up, and instead of taking the safe route by joining the intelligence sector, I decided to stick it to my father and do something he never could. I joined the SEALs, something he'd tried for back in the 80s, but couldn't hack.

We didn't hate our fathers, we just didn't understand them, like they didn't understand us. After my father had snubbed me back at the airport, though, hate wasn't that far off.

Our mothers, on the other hand, were startlingly similar, despite completely different backgrounds. Loving, guiding, and our primary care givers, we had both spent more time with them than our fathers and had loved every moment of it. After the way Helena spoke of her mother, I really hoped to meet her one day.

A duchess or baroness of some kind, Helena had described her as eternally loving and beautiful, far more so than even herself, reason enough to get home so I could meet her. She had been very hands-on with Helena, always a guiding presence, in spite of the cadre of maids, nurses, teachers, and other caregivers Helena had been surrounded by. My mother had been horribly pedestrian in comparison, but after I'd shown Helena a picture of her that I kept stashed in my go-bag, she commented that she must have been a wonderful lady, beautiful both inside and out.

She had been surprised at how close my mom and I had been, and had jokingly called me a "momma's boy" because of it. I told her to try my cooking and see if she still wanted to joke about it. She backed off immediately, admitting she could barely boil water herself.

I still held back my "nurse" story, figuring there'd be plenty of time to get into that one later.

The only one of us who seemed aloof was Vincent. Plagued by the duties of command, he knew better than to socialize with the rest of us in a casual atmosphere. Even so, we spent plenty of time in "Latin 101", as Santino dubbed it. A few times a day, we would learn the basics as best we could from Vincent's instruction. It took me six years to learn what I know now, and the rest of the time since then to forget it, so I sat in on the basic grammar and vocabulary lessons as well. By the third day, I began to wonder if Vincent had actually written the text book I used in high school, as he seemed to follow the lessons almost to the letter.

While the rest of the team struggled, and would probably continue to do so for the months to come, I started picking things up rather quickly. Listening in, as well as trying my own hand at conversation when the Romans came to chat, I found myself slowly reaching my old level of proficiency and beyond.

I always knew I was good at Latin, even though my professors would never admit it.

All in all, things were going well, if not boringly well, but by the end of the third day, our patience was rewarded with the news that the Romans had recovered McDougal's body, and our gear containers, thankfully locked from prying eyes.

The next morning, dressed in our BDUs, we met McDougal's corpse a few miles outside the walls of Rome, an area we estimated was clear of the city in our own time. Interestingly, Caligula was also there, indicating his wish to be present both to honor the dead, and to observe our burial rituals.

Father Vincent, back in priest mode I had originally seen him in, began with a prayer.

"*In nomi...*"

He paused. As with many masses spoken in the twenty first century, much of it was still spoken in Latin. Vincent looked me in the eye, realizing how odd it would sound to the Romans to hear their own language spoken in our prayers.

He covered with a cough before starting again. "In the name of the Father, the Son, and the Holy Spirit." He cleverly left out the "amen" what was originally a Latin word.

We continued as many funerals did, with the reading of a scripture passage from a Bible Vincent kept on his person, as well as a eulogy, delivered by Wang. His delivery was heartfelt, but strong, the discipline of a military man showing itself. Nearing the end, we all gathered some dirt, and sprinkled it over McDougal's body, already laid roughly six feet deep in the earth.

"Ashes to ashes, dust to dust. We commend this soul into your heavenly embrace, oh Father. Look upon him kindly."

With that, Vincent ended the funeral as it had begun.

The ceremony complete, we finished burying the body, staking a wooden cross in the ground at its head, wrapping one of McDougal's dog tags around it. Vincent kept the other half.

Noticing our ritual had ended, Caligula approached, respectfully. "You have my deepest sympathy and my thanks for your permission to attend the ceremony."

Vincent spoke up. "Who am I to deny the most powerful man in the world?"

Caligula smiled. "Who indeed? Still, I found it very interesting. Now, to discuss more important matters."

"Of course."

Caligula took a deep breath of the fresh, crisp fall air. "Such a beautiful day. Why don't we walk back to Rome together?"

Vincent nodded, gesturing for the rest of us to fall in behind them.

"You seem to know quite a bit about my little empire," Caligula began, strolling down the pristine Roman road. "Yet, I know almost nothing of you, except that you have capabilities far beyond anything I can muster. So, I ask you again, who are you, and where are you from?"

Vincent and Caligula walked side by side, with the rest of the team filed in behind them. Helena was limping on her own at this point, while Bordeaux had a cast around his ankle and a cane to help support him. Surrounding us were more of Caligula's Praetorians, hands on the hilts of their swords, ready to protect their emperor at moment's notice.

Vincent held out his arms, palms open, as innocently as possible. "I am sorry, but I cannot say. It may do more harm than good."

"Yes, you keep telling me that, but your words mean nothing to me. You speak in riddles. How am I to fully trust you if you will not answer my questions?"

"We are here to serve, Caesar."

Well, that was interesting, Vincent. Since when did we have plans to throw in with the Romans? I mean, really?

Caligula thought it over. "Very well. If that is truly the case, there is something you must do for me."

"Name it, Caesar."

"I mean to claim the northern island of Britannia into my domain. However, my plans are not yet ready and with the winter months approaching, will have to wait. However, with your abilities, you should be able to speed the matter up rather effectively."

Speed things up is right. Caligula never made an attempt to invade Britain for at least three more years, and things didn't go so well. Sources claim that he ordered his troops to gather seashells, and little else. It wasn't until his uncle Claudius that Rome made any progress in the area.

"What would you have us do?"

"The country is far from unified, or civil. It's nothing but a barbaric hinterland. But, that is our goal as Romans, to bring civilization to the far corners of the world. For your part, there is one particular war chieftain, Adminius is his name, who is quite troublesome. I would like you to eliminate him, and cause as much destruction to his camp as possible. We have word that he is keeping a large portion of his military strength close to him, but we don't know why. Additionally, we have learned that he has erected his winter quarters deep on the mainland, for peace talks amongst the Gauls. Probably not for any direct action against us now, but maybe to build up his strength for the future. We can't have that."

"I understand." Vincent considered for a minute. "Very well. I will send three of my people."

"Only three? Would not all be better?"

Vincent looked over his shoulder at us. "Two of my people could do it alone if I allowed it, but these are hardly normal circumstances, and I'd prefer only sending a small team."

"Surely the woman is not one of these two?"

"Actually, she is, and she will be one of the three that goes. I will also send the man who destroyed your column, and myself. However, the two of them will need time to heal. At least two weeks."

Caligula mulled that over. "That will do. It will allow me to send for a guide who is familiar with the area. Now, tell me how you plan to accomplish your task."

So he did.

Vincent went over every detail of what he planned meticulously, as if he had been planning it for weeks. The way things were going at this point, that wouldn't necessarily surprise me one bit. He spoke all the way to the gates of Rome, with Caligula venturing questions at random.

Vincent's plan called for a jungle creep, a term coined for any lengthy excursion through the wilderness. When they reached the camp, they would spend a day scouting the location and identifying the high value target, before using the cover of darkness to place demolition charges in key positions around the camp. Come morning, they would eliminate the HVT, blow the camp, and extract as quickly as possible. The team would have ample cover, not to mention at least a mile between their targets, so getting out wouldn't be a problem. In theory it seemed simple, and for once in my military career, I could honestly say that it really was.

In our own time, the same kind of mission was relatively straightforward as well. However, the enemy here would have no idea what hit them, and would more likely be prostrating themselves before their gods than looking for any mortal culprit.

It was a safe bet Caligula had already figured that out, and had planned exactly for it. We were a perfect way to inflict a crushing military blow against his enemies, with absolutely no expense to him, or fingers pointed at Rome. The man must have been planning this since the day we met him.

By the time we reached our little home away from home, Caligula seemed pleased with our plan, and told us he would call for us when our guide arrived. Until then, we were back to being his guests, under armed guard of course. We were stuck in our four bedroom apartment, allowed to leave only under the watchful eye of the Praetorians.

So, when we got back to the room, there was little more to do except pull out the cards and start playing.

It was going to be a long two weeks.

VII
Claudius

Rome, Italy
October, 37 AD

    In all honesty, the two weeks turned out to be one of the most relaxing fortnights of my life.

    The food provided was better, we were given cleaner and more comfortable sleeping accommodations, the Praetorians were much more casual around us, and we were invited to dine with Caligula himself on a few occasions. It was also the only time I could remember ever having a two week furlough without the risk of being spontaneously summoned by the Navy. The longest leave I'd ever had since the war began, the time recovering from my wounds notwithstanding, was five days, and that was to pay my respects after my mother's passing, and included travel time.

    The best part though, was that we were finally allowed full access to the entire city of Rome and at the start of every day, Helena and I would go for a morning jog. We took it easy at first, rehabilitating her leg and ankle with walks and light jogs. Helena still had a bit of a limp, even by the end of the second week, but she was getting stronger. By the end of the first week, while not quick, she was nimble enough that she and I could sneak away from our Praetorian escorts.

    Once away from their watchful eyes, we'd wander around the city for a few hours every morning, becoming as familiar with its narrow corridors and back alleys as its residents became with us. Wearing our combat boots, shorts that hung above the knees and loose shirts, we stood out like a sore thumb.

    Over the course of a few days, I noticed a few women gathering together on a street corner, giggling and pointing as I ran by. Their numbers grew as the days went on, and I always made sure to smile as goofy a smile I could and wave. Some of them were fairly attractive, and if not for my overly protective and combative swim buddy, I may have made a pass at one or two of them. As we made our way around their corner, Helena would always glare at me, quite the hypocrite since she didn't have a problem with any of the guys who ogled her, of which there were, of course, many.

Vanity aside, our runs were really just a good way to pass the time. With little else to do after our daily calisthenics, Helena and I would head to those public baths I'd been dreaming about earlier, but we always kept our distance from each other, hoping to avoid any inevitable awkwardness. After a scrub down with scented oils, and a quick dip in warm water followed by cool water, we'd rendezvous at the entrance and head back to our small building.

The rest of the team would be there, but not for long. We spent plenty of time in each other's company throughout the day, but everyone went out to explore the city at one point or another. Generally, we all made it a point to gather for lunch, dinner, and Latin 101, but other than that, the day was ours. After dinner, Helena and I would head out and admire the sights again, continuing our exploration. I always brought my camera along and took pictures that would have had historians back home drooling all over themselves.

Occasionally, Santino would join us - "chaperoning" as he put it.

The truth is, despite his antics, charm, and pleasing disposition, Santino didn't really fit in. Surprise, surprise. Most people could only take him in small doses, but I loved being around him. We jelled wonderfully.

Besides, Wang wasn't really in the mood for jokes yet, Vincent had to remain distant from the rest of us, and while Bordeaux had a good sense of humor, Santino didn't dare cross the big Frenchman. That left just Helena and me, which was fine by me.

Helena, on the other hand, was as uptight as they came around people like him, which only gave us the openings we needed to really piss her off. It didn't take her too long before she realized it was all in good fun, and began a practice of slugging me in the arm to deal with her annoyances. Girls always thought it was cute to punch guys in the arm, but I never understood what was so fun about it. I didn't mind too much, as long as she stayed away from my face.

Her childish antics notwithstanding, on the twelfth day of our vacation, I finally found the nerve to tell her my "nurse" story. I was starting to feel like I could truly trust her, and even though I'd been hesitant before, it was a story I'd been longing to get off my chest since the day it ended between the nurse and I. So, as we sat on the Capitoline Hill, with the Temple of Jupiter behind us and the Tiber River running south in front of us, I recounted my sad story.

With my first words, stating bluntly that the nurse who'd taken care of me happened to be very attractive, Helena rolled her eyes and turned away. We were seated on a low wall, with our feet dangling beneath us, a thirty foot drop below that. She used her position to kick my knee.

But not that hard.

"If this is going to be one of those 'wild romps in the nurses' ward' stories," she said in annoyance, "I'd rather not hear it. I've had enough of that from Santino."

"It isn't," I said quietly, but she folded her arms in doubt anyway.

When I began the story, her interest level seemed low, but as the story slowly developed, just as it had in my head back on the HMS Triumph, her attention started to grow. Her look of disinterest quickly softened, to be replaced by one of concern, and something else I couldn't quite place. She seemed surprised at how close I'd grown with the nurse, and almost shocked at the revelation that I'd thought about proposing.

As I completed the story, just as the nurse and I had failed to find words as we parted, Helena and I couldn't find any as well. But again, just like the nurse, it was Helena who spoke first.

"What was her name?"

It took me a moment to answer. "Cassandra."

Helena paused a moment, giving me a chance to recover from the very personal story. She took my hand in her own and gave it a slight squeeze. "If it's worth anything, Jacob, I think you handled the situation as well as anyone could have. It couldn't have been easy."

"Thanks," I managed softly.

"Sounds as if we both come from depressing love lives," she commented distractedly. She looked regretful for a moment before fixing her attention back on me. "I think it's good that you told me. Thanks."

"Want to know the worst part?" I asked with a frown.

"What's that?" She asked, genuine concern in her voice.

"She looked exactly like you."

She reeled back slightly, releasing my hand, and stared into the best puppy dog eyes I could muster. I almost felt bad using her memory that I resembled her late fiancé, but it was too good of an opportunity to pass up. My lips must have cracked a bit, because her eyes quickly narrowed, and she looked very angry.

"Wait a second," she started.

I started to chuckle. I had a horrible poker face. "I'm kidding. She looked nothing like you. She was blond, five and a half feet tall, and you get much cuter when you're angry."

It felt so good to have the story off my chest that I couldn't help but laugh. The rage in her eyes only made me laugh harder, but it faltered when I saw her eyes still ablaze in fury a minute later.

Settling down, I apologized. "Look, Helena, I'm sorry. It was a bad joke. I didn't mean to bring it up again."

Her mouth twitched, and her look softened, a smile spreading across her own face.

"You're so gullible, Lieutenant," she said slyly.

It took me a minute before I smiled as well. "Oh… oh, you're good."

After that night, the two of us never hesitated if either one of us needed to talk.

As for the team as a whole, we spent our nights going through our gear and cataloging it. Needless to say, there was a lot of it, much more than we originally thought. If the situation called for it, we could spend most of our lives working as a private mercenary group, and never need to pick up a shield and sword. We'd be pretty expensive too.

I was also very pleased to find at least some of the Future Force Warrior gear I thought I'd never see again hidden in one of the containers. While we all still had our eyepieces and computer systems, the only other gear we brought with us was on our backs. While the traditional BDUs we found were nice, the other clothing item we discovered inside was a godsend.

There was no official name for what they were, as far as I knew, but I liked to call them combat assault fatigues. Both pants and jacket sets had numerous pockets festooned over them, and were camouflaged in multicam, useful in almost any terrain environment. We also found duplicate pairs, colored and patterned in dark gray and black, meant for night operations. Because its defensive abilities required tight contact with the skin, each set seemed specifically sized for each of us, with a left over set for McDougal.

Along the shins, calves, thighs, hamstrings, groin, outer forearms and upper arms were thin pads that jutted out an inch from the clothing. Inside the pads was a polyethylene type gel that had a most unique property. In its normal state, the gel felt soft and squishy, like a stress ball, but when struck by a sudden and forceful impact, it instantaneously became as hard as titanium. The gel then liquidized a heartbeat later, ready for another impact, and it could take the repeated hardening and softening transition over and over again. Additional protective measures the outfit provided were small thin strips of a very light and flexible Kevlar-like material that ran vertically down the pants and horizontally along the jacket. For creature comfort, they were water resistant and additionally equipped with an internal A/C and heating system to keep the body comfortable in any weather condition

During the war in Iraq, the polyethylene substance was hoped to be the next evolution of the bullet proof vest, but early testing indicated it wasn't effective enough to risk the lives of troops. It wasn't until 2016, when advancements were made in its base properties, that the gel finally lived up to its potential. It had been a groundbreaking development for soldiers, having saved thousands of lives since its implementation.

I only had one problem with it. If it was so soft and flexible, I never understood why the entire pants and jacket set wasn't completely smothered in the stuff. Leave it to the military brass to cut corners. Even the helmets supplied in the containers were the old school versions that were notorious for being anything but bullet proof. At least they had the decency to cover the groin, but any impact to that region wouldn't end well anyway.

Sometimes I really wondered who was running the military.

Other than the combat fatigues, there was little other advanced equipment within the containers. We were still supplied with electronic equipment like night vision, flashlights, and the means to charge their batteries, but I guess the papacy didn't want to make its new soldiers too reliant on technology, something I was completely at ease with. A soldier was only as good as his training, instincts and determination. To rely on technology was a recipe for disaster.

So the days went.

Thankfully, two weeks to the day after Caligula set his time table, he sent us a message, indicating his three assassins were required. That morning, the six of us spent two hours prepping the team assigned on the mission.

Bordeaux gathered a large amount of C-4, at least thirty bricks, enough to bring down the Colosseum, had it been built already. Vincent borrowed Santino's UAV for aerial recon, and Helena grabbed the "Light Fifty" from storage. All three packed their night ops combat fatigues, tents and survival gear.

As they completed their preparations, Helena pulled me aside, a frustrated look on her face.

"Jacob, there's something I really need to tell you."

I groaned. Usually, when women "really" needed to tell me something, I ended up spending a long night cleaning up tissues.

Holding my hands in the air, I feigned innocence. "You know, if this is one of those, 'I may die tomorrow, so we should be together tonight' speeches, you really should know that tomorrow is now, and we kinda missed our chance last night. I mean, I could try and get it over within the two minutes we have, but I think that would kinda ruin the moment."

Surprisingly, Helena's look wasn't the one of annoyed anger I expected, but instead, she wore a smile that could make even the most womanizing of men's hearts think twice about her. I was ready for any reaction except that one. To make matters worse, she took a step closer, bringing her mouth just to the side of my ear and dropped her voice to a seductive whisper

"My, my, Lieutenant, aren't you the naughty one. Maybe you had better hope I don't make it back, or I may make you put your money where your mouth is."

I sighed, surprised at how easily I shrugged off my embarrassment. I really was getting used to her. "So, what is it you wanted to talk to me about?"

Backing away and ignoring her little performance, she cut right to the point. "I've never killed anyone with the fifty. I've never even fired it in the field."

"What!?" I practically yelled the word, enticing the rest of the team to turn in our direction. Throwing them a smile, I grabbed Helena by the arm and pulled her away from the group. "But your record said you had confirmed kills with it. Dozens."

She sighed. "My government tweaked my record a bit. They just wanted one of their own on the team and they knew the Pope wanted a female, and the team was looking for snipers. I was the only obvious choice. Don't worry. I'm not a spy or anything. Everything else you know is true.

I gave her a skeptical look, but I had to believe her when she said she had nothing to do with changing her record. It's hard to trust the Germans. Opting to focus on the problem instead, I put my hands on my hips, and looked at her sternly. "So what's the problem?"

She looked confused. "What do you mean, 'what's the problem'? I've never had to do this before. I was nervous in the training room with you backing me up for Christ's sakes."

"So the fuck what? You're a trained professional. Just do the math and don't forget to breathe. You don't need me."

"Are you sure? You said you'd always be…"

I reached my arms out and gently grabbed her shoulders, staring at her reassuringly.

"Helena. I understand your confidence has taken a hit since your late fiancé, but you know you're a great shot. Just focus. You'll do fine."

I gave her shoulders a squeeze, and smiled. She couldn't afford distraction on the mission, especially with two of her teammates' lives on the line.

She looked at the floor, sighed, and set her shoulders before straightening her posture, the confident demeanor I saw in the training room returning.

She looked up at me. "Thanks. I'm not sure where I'd be without you."

"Probably not in ancient Rome, for one."

She hit me on the arm, but it was playful. "Very funny. Anyway…" She said, glancing toward the rest of the team, none of whom were paying us any attention. "…thank you. Your confidence means a lot."

Nervously, she leaned up on her toes, and kissed me lightly on the cheek. Her kiss lingered just long enough to seem suggestive, more than the peck a mother would offer her son. As she pulled away, she looked sheepishly at the floor, before heading back toward the rest of the team looking over her shoulder briefly to smile at me.

I reached up and rubbed my cheek, ironically, on the same side of my face she had punched weeks ago. I wasn't exactly sure how to respond.

What was that for? She can't actually like me. I'm not that lucky. I'm just some guy that resembled some other guy, who she probably didn't want to think about. Still rubbing my cheek, my head shaking involuntarily, I turned to follow her. Vincent was giving some last minute orders when he noticed me.

"Hunter. Nice of you to join us. We're ready to head out, but there are a few points I need to go over first." He turned back toward the group. "First off, while we're gone, Hunter's in charge. Wang," Vincent looked over at the man who had been brimming with confidence and cockiness just a few weeks ago, but no longer, "I'm sorry, but you're in no shape to take over."

Wang had been steadily improving since McDougal's funeral. His sense of humor had returned, and considering how many goofballs were already in the group, he had slowly started fitting in again. He and Santino had formed an allied front against me and my music tastes, and their taunting made me miss my temporally lost mp3 player more and more.

But Wang knew he wasn't fully there yet, so he accepted Vincent's decision with a small nod.

"And Santino," Vincent said, directing his attention to the biggest goofball of them all, "sorry, but placing you in command..."

Helena interrupted. "...would be about as responsible as giving America's nuclear launch codes to a toddler."

Vincent's shoulders slumped. "Basically."

Santino was shocked, but not out of embarrassment. "Strauss? Was that a joke? A real, honest to God joke? I can't believe it. There may be hope for you, yet."

She looked him square in the eyes, pausing dramatically. "It wasn't a joke."

Santino hesitated. A look of genuine hurt creeping onto his face this time.

Helena smiled. "Just kidding."

Santino's own smile returned, although slower than normal, realizing he had just been played. He offered a mock bow. "How quickly the grasshopper becomes the master."

I laughed alongside everyone else, secretly happy because I knew Helena's jokes were a good sign. She'd taken my advice to heart and her confidence had reappeared.

Vincent cut off the laughter quickly. "All right people. Before we move out, there's one last thing. Hunter, apparently one of Caligula's closest advisers has some information regarding how we got here. I informed the emperor that I would send someone over to talk to him and try and figure this out. God knows, if anyone can, it's you. Work on it while we're gone. We should be back in about three weeks."

"Yes, sir. We'll hold down the fort," I said, before giving our modest accommodations a sour look. I shrugged. "Good luck."

***

Three weeks later, I was still waiting for Caligula to send for me. Within that time I had learned a very important fact of life: Santino was much more boring to be around when he didn't have any material to work with, and a depressed squad member and his equally sarcastic best friend don't offer much material. So I spent most of my time exploring the city on my own.

I couldn't believe how much I missed Helena.

Now, that would have sounded sappy and pathetic had we been dating, but we weren't, so it wasn't, thus making me feel only partially pathetic. I just hoped my friends in the field were all right, particularly her.

I thought I was about to go insane from boredom when I was finally summoned by Caligula. I was escorted by two of the original Praetorians who'd led us to the *Curia* the day we arrived. Gaius and Marcus were their names, but I had to constantly remind myself which was which because they were practically carbon copies of one another. Even so, with Vincent's help, I'd gotten to know them fairly well over the past month. We'd taken to each other like any group of professional military men would.

Nice fellas.

The Praetorians took me within the bounds of the *pomerium* to one of Rome's numerous libraries. The exterior facade looked magnificent, but once inside I found myself in a dimly lit, dust covered room, overcrowded with information decaying from mold.

It was a far cry from the snazzy library I'd worked in on my college campus, but the musty facility made my inner historian feel like a kid on Christmas morning. The place was a gold mine. Besides the hundreds of scrolls lying on what looked like modern day wine cellar shelves and tables with documents sprawled everywhere, I spotted the slinky man from the cavern I had seen almost a month ago.

Finally. Time to get some answers.

Noticing our approach, he nodded to the guards. They replied by performing an about face and marched out of the room, leaving the two of us alone. For the longest time, we just stood there measuring one another up before he started things off.

"My name is Marcus Varus. And you do not belong here."

I stepped closer to the man, hoping my size would intimidate him to the point where he'd be too scared to screw with to me. Barely a forearm's length away, the man held his ground and didn't so much as blink, as he waited patiently for me to speak up.

I ground my teeth in annoyance. "You can call me Hunter, and what do you mean?"

"Just what I said. Your presence here is a mistake and you must go home."

I just stared at him, my patience already wearing thin. That sentence was confusing enough without the added stress of what I thought he said. Too many ablatives. Or were those datives? I always got hung up on the grammar.

Taking a deep breath, I slowly straightened my back, raised my chin up, and pulled my shoulders back. I didn't have to do it too often these days, but pulling myself into perfect military posture gave me a sense of purpose, not to mention a few extra inches which demanded respect, something this little man did not show much of toward me.

I loomed over him with my additional inches, effectively enhancing the image that I was far larger than I really was. "I don't have time for twenty questions," I said grimly. "Now, how do I get home?"

The man was finally intimidated. Taking a step back, his throat visibly gulped. "Well, I'm not sure," he said, his words stammering indecisively. "What I do know is that those who opened the doorway thought they would find vast amounts of treasure. Not human beings. Especially not ones like you."

"What do you mean, 'the doorway?' Did it have anything to do with that sphere?" I couldn't think of the Latin word for sphere or ball, so I just mimicked its shape with my hands. The doorway he was referring to must have meant the portal that sucked us through time. My limited vocabulary was going to make this hard enough without Vincent, and trying to determine archaic terms, and convert them into colloquialisms I could understand would be another, much harder task.

The man just nodded at my question, wandering aimlessly around the room before he settled into a chair behind a table. His eyes moved toward the floor, and he seemed lost in thought. Maybe he was just trying to bullshit his way out of this so I didn't kill him, but then why bring me here at all?

"Look," I said holding out my hands. "Just calm down. Start at the beginning and don't leave anything out. We'll work this out together and maybe I can help you get me out of your life."

The man perked up at that. We'd only known each other five minutes, but it was clear he wanted nothing to do with me. Hopefully, the potential for me leaving was enough incentive to get him to work that much harder, and get me home.

So he talked.

And talked.

Unlike Vincent, who spent as few words as necessary to get his points across, Varus had a knack for allegory and long winded descriptions, for which he provided no context. Of course, that was probably the language barrier's fault, but it still took him fifteen minutes to get to the part about documents found with the sphere, finally getting to something useful.

Helena would have killed him.

"So, when I was presented with the sphere and documents, I immediately got to work translating them," Varus continued. "They are written in an old dialect of Etruscan. I am one of very few people who can still read it."

"Can you date them?" I asked.

"I can only extrapolate its origin from the context of the writings themselves. From that context, I have surmised that this document may have been written by Remus himself, or someone working closely with him. Are you aware of who Remus was?"

Remus? Co-founder of Rome? Of course I knew him. If what Varus said was true, the sphere would be one Rome's oldest relics. I had to make sure I played it off cool.

"I have heard of him in passing. What else did they say?"

"Not very much, unfortunately. It spoke of how he knew of his brother's plot to murder him, and that he had known about the plot for many weeks. Fearful that he would be unable to thwart his brother's attempt on his life, he sought help from some sort of adviser. Apparently, this friend was a druid from the north, a very powerful one, who, as the document indicates, possessed great power and abilities over nature. The result of which, appears to be the blue sphere."

"Magic?" I asked. Even though I had suggested it myself a month ago, I never really believed it. "You're joking, right??

"I, too, find the subject distasteful and hard to believe. And yet, here you are."

True. At least we agreed on something, and he did make a good point.

"So what does it do?" I asked. "Exactly."

"Besides bring annoying plebeians to my door in search of my aid?"

As we had moved our conversation to chairs, seated across from a table, I couldn't impose my height over the man. Instead, I leaned back in my chair, and put my hands behind my head. Wearing a tight, short sleeved t-shirt, I flexed my biceps, which, I had to give myself credit for, were in pretty darn good shape. He looked at my arms, and then at my face, before continuing.

"Does everything come down to physical violence with you? Are you just like those thousands of legionnaires who have nothing better to do than kill each other and fight in the dirt like children?"

I gave him a smile. "Of course. But I can make a swell turn-over cake as well."

He looked at me, obviously not understanding the reference. Frustration and annoyance obvious on his face, he picked up where he left off. "Apparently, the sphere was meant as a gateway to a vast treasure and the downfall of those who uphold the legacy of Remus' brother, Romulus. The Senate, I believe, felt that by treasure Remus meant money, and of course, with enough money anything can be accomplished. I can only imagine their surprise when you and your friends arrived instead."

"But why is it that we came here at all? Nothing happened until I touched the sphere, but I wasn't the first to do so."

"There was an obscure mantra at the bottom of the document, nearly indecipherable. What I could make out of it said something along following, 'the gateway shall bring treasure of unfathomable power. Once the relic has felt the touch from my loins, all the power of our descendants shall become theirs.' There is more, of course, but from what I gather, it would seem that perhaps those who are blood kin to Remus have the ability to utilize the sphere. But I do not understand what roll you play, as it would seem it was only the two of us who came in contact with the sphere. I know the Senate's lackeys kept it wrapped in a cloth. Yet, the two of us cannot be related. My family has always been very small. "

I barely heard anything past, "Senate's lackeys..." my mind completely focused on the table, deep in thought. Everything was starting to fall into place. I only needed one last piece of evidence to prove my train of thought.

I looked up and began a thorough inspection of Varus' face.

After two thousand years I had little hope of finding any similarities between the two of us. The differences alone were enough to dissuade any further inspection, but I was persistent. The man was short, whereas I was tall. He had black hair, instead of my brown, his face was round, mine was lean and hard. We didn't share a single similarity.

Except for one.

There it was. Staring right back at me. His eyes were nearly identical to mine. Inquisitive, just as Pope Gregory had said, with the same shade of ambiguous gray that could look either blue or green depending on our surroundings.

I got them from my mom.

It wasn't much, but it was enough to confirm the definite *possibility* that he may be some long lost ancestor of mine. It wouldn't be enough in a court of law, but it was something. I was astonished. But then something else hit me. One would think meeting a two thousand year old ancestor would be enough fun for one night, but if Varus was reading the document correctly, not only was he a ancestor of mine, but we were both direct descendants of Remus.

Now that fact definitely struck a chord. A direct descendent of Remus?

Awesome.

I suppose I shouldn't be surprised. The sheer amount of family trees that spider webbed down the millennia was amazing. It made the possibility that everyone in the 21st century was descended from somebody famous very likely. If you truly took your Bible to heart, one would argue that we were all cousins, descended from Adam and Eve.

I hadn't even known Remus had any children. It was always my impression that he and his brother were barely out of their teenage years before Remus was killed, but I couldn't be sure. Maybe Vincent can fill me in on the details later. What I did know was that their mother, Rhea, bore them not by any human father, but by the god, Mars. That was just a myth, of course, but it would certainly explain my own absolute awesomeness, not to mention my gray eyes. Mar's sister was Minerva, or Athena in Greek, and was regularly referred to as "Gray-eyed Athena" in mythology.

I'm going to choose to believe the god/eye color similarity had to be a coincidence.

Yah. A coincidence. I wasn't even going to touch on that one.

I continued to stare into the eyes of my great times a thousand grandfather or uncle, and frowned. I had always hoped to be descended from a Roman, but I had always wanted him to have been a bad ass centurion, leading men into combat and dying for glory, not some bookish nerd. Granted, as Santino so astutely pointed out, I was pretty much a big nerd at heart as well.

"Any of your family in the army?" I asked him.

"No. Why?"

Damn.

I was about to ask him what he made of all of this when his eyes widened, and he quickly stood up, his head bowing reverently. Surprised at his sudden change in attitude, I glanced over my shoulder to see another man enter the room. He was tall, blond, handsome, and had the same short, curly haired hair cut Julius Caesar had made so popular. It was the man I'd seen at the *Circus maximus*. The one I'd skeptically deduced as Claudius.

I rose as well, and bowed my head just to fit in.

The man smiled a smile I determined lacked any kind of warmth or genuine happiness. The sinister kind. He held out his hands, a failed attempt at friendliness. There was something about him that immediately made him unlikable.

"Varus," the man said, stepping forward to embrace him in a bear hug. "My friend. How good to see you. It has been awhile since I have seen you in the library."

"Yes, well, my duties to your nephew have kept me fairly occupied these past few months."

His nephew? This had to be Claudius. I couldn't believe it. I had never, not once, read an account of the man that didn't claim he was weak, feeble, and prone to stutters and twitches. He was a lame ugly duckling, not a stud quarter back! Who was this man?

He continued to smile. "And I see you have made a new friend. Please, no need to get up," he said cheerily, even though I was already standing. "Any friend of Varus is a friend of mine. I am Caligula's uncle, Claudius"

"He is no friend of mine," rumbled Varus.

Claudius ignored him. "Besides, I know you are one of the strangers who came through Remus' gateway. Now, that is reason enough to get to know you."

His smile was beginning to irritate me. Unlike Santino's, whose smile was always filled with good cheer and fun, annoyingly so, Claudius' merely disturbed me. He also knew about Remus' message, which only made me more suspicious, because it was quite well known back home that Claudius was one of those few people Varus mentioned who could read Etruscan as well.

I decided to play dumb. "Yes, I am one of the few who came through the gateway. It is a pleasure to meet you, sir." I opened my arms in a mirror gesture of his own. "Is there anything we can do for you?"

"Oh, no. I just wanted to meet you. Your potential is limitless. I want you to know that you can come to me for anything, and to ask that perhaps you may do some things for me, as your friends have done for my nephew?"

This was getting weirder by the second. The guy was coming off as heartwarming as even the most black hearted and malevolent of bad guys. They always start off all warm and fuzzy until they stick a shiv in your back, and you end up having to wait until the last ten minutes of the movie to save the day – only having already lost your family, girlfriend, best friend, and dog along the way.

I wasn't about to let that happen.

"I'll certainly keep that in mind," I replied, trying to sound sincere. "My schedule is wide open."

Claudius frowned for a brief moment before smiling again, finally understanding my joke.

"Humorous. Now, if you will excuse me. I have matters to attend to."

As the man turned, his traveling cloak swirled behind him in that bad-guy kind of way. He was gone a few seconds later.

I snorted. "Quite the character, isn't he?"

Varus smiled. "I've never liked him. He spends much of his time here reading history and spending many hours wasting my time. The man loves to listen to himself speak. It was through him that I learned the Senate had plans to utilize Remus' orb, which is why I ended up there when you arrived. I can't be sure, but it seemed as though he had something to do with it, and that his knowledge of the plot was not because he had simply overheard another's conversation."

Somehow, that didn't surprise me, but I didn't let my suspicion show. I couldn't understand why the man wasn't the sharp minded, but weak bodied man he was supposed to be. My mind kept wandering to the old BBC production of *I, Claudius* that I loved so much, and how well I thought the actor who played Claudius had done in mimicking his mannerisms.

Suddenly my suspicions started to grow. History, after all, was written by the victors, and it was none other than Claudius himself who succeeded Caligula after his assassination.

* * *

I spent the next few hours chatting with Varus and comparing notes on the situation, but I kept my theories to myself. By the time I left, Varus had learned little more about Remus' message, but at least we had ended on good terms, and I found myself starting to like the little man. He was sharp and curious. He asked if I would teach him English, and in return, he would help me with my Latin. I told him I would enjoy that, and that I looked forward to the opportunity. When my escorts arrived to take me back home, I excused myself and left with them.

Arriving at the house, I tossed Gaius and Marcus a quick salute, which they respectfully returned before opening the door and gesturing for me to head inside where I found a full house.

The away team had returned.

The team was sitting on the floor in a circle with a spot left for me. Noticing my arrival, Santino threw his arms in the air in a childlike greeting. "The prodigal son arrives," he squealed.

I looked at him squarely. "You realize the word, 'prodigal,' really only means that someone is bad with money, right?"

Everyone looked at Santino, smiles on their faces. He glanced at his squad mates, wearing an embarrassed expression of his own.

He looked at me. "I fucking hate you."

I smiled. "Love you too, buddy."

"If you two are done," Vincent interrupted, trying not to grin, "we were just about to begin our after action report. Maybe you can fill us in on where you've been when we're done."

"I'd be delighted, sir," I said, sitting between him and Bordeaux.

I noticed Helena sitting across from me, a downtrodden expression on her face. I made eye contact with her, and gave her a welcoming smile. Her expression brightened at my attention, but her face remained dour.

Shifting my attention, I started things off. "So, you guys are back early."

Vincent nodded. "Our guide was very proficient. Thanks to his direction and the location of the camp residing well inland of where we expected it to be, we made much better time than planned. Upon arrival, we scouted the camp from a distance, identified the high value target and his tent, and located key points to lay our explosives. Early the following morning, we made our way to the camp, and rigged it to blow. Our goal was to create more confusion than casualties as well as direct their attention away from us. We had to eliminate two guards during our insertion, whom we hid in a tent. When first light hit, we synchronized the assassination with the triggering of our explosives. At 0535, Lieutenant Strauss fired upon the HVT, the bullet penetrating the target's cranium. Lieutenant Bordeaux simultaneously triggered the explosive charges set around the camp, programmed on a timed sequence to detonate at random intervals." He paused, taking a sip of water from his CamelBak. "We lingered only long enough to confirm the HVT was down and that hysteria had erupted in camp. Satisfied, we left at 0545, encountered zero resistance, and made our way back."

I nodded. A perfectly successful mission. The only negative outcome I could think of was some random archaeologist in two thousand years discovering what looks like a manufactured rifle bullet in a skull that was dated to have existed during the Roman Empire. I can only imagine the book he'd write trying to prove that time travel existed by theorizing that modern soldiers were sent back in time to fight history's wars for them.

I was sure he'd be considered a crack pot.

"So, Hunter," Vincent continued, "did you discover an answer to our problem with Caligula's man?"

I looked around the room again, meeting each of their gazes in turn. Each was expectant, hoping I had somehow learned how to get us home.

"Well," I began, "I'm pretty sure I've confirmed my theory on how we got here."

"Maybe you should start at the beginning," ordered Vincent.

So I started with Varus, and how he had contacted me to discuss our arrival in the city. I told them about the document, Remus, the she-wolf and Mars, how Varus and I were related, and how we were both descended from Remus. I ended with how my rubber band sphere theory still seemed the most likely cause of our arrival.

Santino quickly spoke up. Wait, wait, wait," he said, rubbing his head in confusion. "So, if what you're saying is true, you're…part… she-wolf? Or are you part god? It's so hard to keep up with your stories sometimes, Jacob."

Everyone just stared at him.

Bordeaux rested his head in a hand. "*Merde*," was all he said

"Santino, you really can't be that stupid," Wang ridiculed.

Santino simply smiled.

"He's kidding," I said. "But there's more. As always. I also met Claudius, Caligula's uncle and next emperor of Rome. It know that sounds backward, but that's how it turns out. The important thing is that he is nothing like history paints him. History remembers him as sharp mentally, but weak, feeble, and physically twitchy, but he's nothing of the sort. Tall, blond, good looking, but mentally deranged at best. He's basically the Lex Luthor of the Roman Empire. Just with hair. I don't trust him. The guy's evil."

"Who's Lex Luthor?" Helena asked.

Santino rolled his eyes. "He's Superman's arch nemesis: billionaire, evil, scheming, plotting, bald. He's the ultimate bad guy." He sighed. "Women…"

She shifted her attention back to me. "Why didn't you just say that?"

I tossed my hands in the air.

"Whatever," Vincent interrupted before I could say anything else. "We'll keep him on our short list, but until we see him do something that contradicts what we know about history, we respect him like the rest of our benefactors."

"I like evil bad guys," Santino offered. "Their inflated egos make for big targets."

"They'd need to be, considering how you shoot," Wang quipped, another sign he was feeling better. Santino pushed him playfully, and laughed at his own expense.

"An interesting day, then," Vincent commented, "but we'll worry about Roman politics later. Bordeaux, break out the MREs."

The Frenchman smiled, his look indicating he was famished as well. "Yes, sir."

I wasn't hungry. Varus had some cheese, bread, and wine for us to snack on during our talk, so I headed to the small room I had been sharing with Helena. Finding my way to my bunk, I glanced around the room. Even though it was small, it had enough room for a few amenities, but I couldn't help from smiling. While my uniforms were folded neatly, the rest of my stuff was disheveled and unorganized, whereas Helena's gear and personal effects were neatly stacked, arranged, folded and organized. I guess it was a universal fact that no matter where you lived on Earth, or when, women were neater.

I heard Helena's voice from the doorway.

"Isn't it time you cleaned the house, dear?"

I continued smiling. "Sorry, honey, but there's a game on the TV and I can't be bothered. Why don't you go do the dishes?"

She laughed. "Men. You're all such lazy pigs."

"Can't fault that logic," I declared

Helena moved into the room and sat on the edge of her bunk. She placed her meal in between our beds and waited as it cooked in its self-heating pouch. Like the flickering of a fire, the magnesium ignited water boiling within generally had a hypnotic property to it, but I ignored it, and turned toward Helena.

"So how did the mission go? Really?"

She shifted uneasily. "Do you always know when something's wrong with people?"

I shrugged. "I've had a lot of insecure girlfriends."

"I bet you have," she said, retrieving her cooked meal. It smelled like the chicken with salsa entree, my favorite. She ate quietly, but quickly. What she had to say must have been important, but she needed her nourishment. I could understand why she didn't want to be distracted. Finished, she placed the rest of the MRE's contents in a pack, took a sip of water from her CamelBak, folded her hands in her lap, and looked me square in the eyes.

"I'm... sorry I didn't tell you this before, and please try to forgive me, but I think there's something else you should know."

"Oh, this should be good," I said, sitting on my bed, propping myself up with my hands behind me.

"Adminius was my first and only confirmed kill. In fact, he was the first man I've ever shot in cold blood..." she paused, "and up until that day in Syria, I had never even killed another human being before. I'm sorry."

She had to be joking. She was too good a shot to not have had years of practice. Every sniper knew shooting immaterial targets was completely different from shooting real people. It's not just something you can pick up in a day. I had to call her bluff.

"Yah right, Strauss. Next thing you're going to tell me is that you were never even in the military."

She just looked at me, her expression completely deadpan. There was nothing amusing in her eyes.

"You're kidding, right?" I asked tentatively. "There's no way... you couldn't...you've been in for years. Killed dozens of targets."

Her eyes continued to stare right through me.

I reclined onto my back, and started laughing. There was no other reaction I could think of. We'd gone into combat with a completely green rookie covering our backs, and still managed to survive. The situation was nothing, if not funny. I thought I was going to start crying from the laughter when my inappropriate reaction must have struck a cord with her.

"This isn't funny, Jacob. I was given my commission eight months before I came to Rome, and thrown into an accelerated basic and then KSK training program. My government knew they wouldn't be able to get one of their own on the team, unless they could offer something no one else could. The Pope was only taking the most select people. That's where I came in, a female who was also a good enough shot that they could mold me into a sniper, something no one else wanted to offer. They even shipped me off to the States to participate in one of your sniper schools. I don't know why they did it all, since our identities will never be leaked to the public, but that's what the Pope wanted, and that's what he got.

"When the GS9 agents came to my home and offered me the opportunity, I leapt at it. Like I told you, it was the first chance I had to get away from my life. I'm so sorry. I was forced to secrecy, but considering where we are, I felt the need to come clean. Everything else we've talked about is completely true. My father, hunting, Oxford, the Olympics, my fiancé. Everything."

Her speech left me with little else to do except stare at the ceiling, unsure how to respond. How could I trust her now when she had been so blatantly lying to me for so long? She was a stranger now, someone who'd broke the bonds of brotherhood and was someone I couldn't trust or rely on. I rolled onto my side and faced away from her.

"What do you want me to say?" I asked. "I forgive you? You didn't do anything wrong? How can I do that? Any reason I may have had to trust you is gone."

It's been my experience with women that they generally do things in unexpected and unpredictable ways. Many a time in a conversation, a woman will do something crazy. One comment will lead to reaction A, while a seemingly identical comment will result in reaction B, and at the end of the talk a completely different comment ends up eliciting reaction A again. It was completely insane and was pretty much the main reason I'd given up trying to understand women long ago. It was why, with my back turned away from Helena, I was completely unprepared for her unwarranted attack.

Her body check rolled me off the bunk, throwing me against the wall and forcing me onto my back once again. She followed it up by leaping over my body and situating herself in the door frame, straddling me as she sat on my stomach. She then grabbed my head in both hands and pulled me close, as she in turn leaned in, her face inches away from mine.

She stared at me, her eyes glistening like a cool beverage on a warm summer day. I tried to look away, but she pulled me even closer. With nothing else to do, I stared up at her and waited for what she had to say. I saw sadness there in her eyes, real sadness, the kind I had never seen there before, and my heart sank. It wasn't fair of me to tell her I couldn't trust her. Accelerated training or not, she'd still taken an oath. An oath she was now breaking. To make matters worse, her breaking of orders was nothing when compared to her emotionally sheltered life. To learn to trust me the way she did, only to have me turn my back on her now, must have been devastating. I was already regretting my flippant words.

A minute passed, every second of silence devastating.

"Jacob," she whispered. "You have to trust me, because you..." she paused, choking back tears, "...because you're the only person I trust. There's no one else left."

She lowered my head back toward the floor, but the pain in her voice was more than enough to keep my eyes connected with hers. Her words were a plea for help from a girl, no, a person who'd lost control of her life. It sounded more familiar than I cared to admit, but it was true. She was lost here in ancient Rome and needed to hang on to whatever felt familiar. I felt the same way, only I was too proud to admit it.

She hadn't done anything wrong. She'd been under orders and it wasn't fair of me to ridicule and berate her for it. She was right. I needed her more than I thought, and I wasn't about to throw that away now.

"Helena, I'm sorry. I shouldn't have been so flippant. I..." I tried to find the right words, "... I want to trust you, or at least try to for now. I hope you can forgive me."

Her green eyes continued to stare, but I felt her entire demeanor change as she let more of her weight sit on me.

"I can," she assured in a whisper. "Thank you."

With those words she brought her face closer to mine, hesitating only slightly at first, her wonderfully full lips puckering ever so slightly.

This was it.

The moment in all the movies where the hero finally scored and got the girl.

It had to be.

Boy, it was my lucky day.

As our heads came together, my mouth centimeters from hers, so close I could feel her breath on my lips and the heat radiating off her cheeks, I heard the most annoyingly ill-timed commotion I had ever heard. It sounded like someone had broken down our front door and was pillaging our home.

I looked up at Helena as she strained her head toward the door, trying to see what was happening. Gently, I placed my left hand alongside her cheek, shifting her face back toward mine.

She smiled as she looked down at me and my mind went blank. I could only think of one thing to say. It was the most cliché line I had ever heard.

"Rain check?"

***

We recovered from the moment and rushed to the adjoining room to see numerous Roman Praetorians crowding our building, with plenty more outside. Helena and I had our side arms at the ready, but lowered them when we saw the recognizable faces of our new friends. I noticed Gaius near the door, and offered him a friendly nod. He returned it imperceptibly, but I saw a look of worry on his stone hard face.

Vincent was standing between us and them, his arms upraised between us to ward off any aggressive action before it started. Wang and Santino were kneeling in the doorway opposite the entrance, their rifles directed at our guests. Both men were shirtless and looked as though they had been preparing to get some sleep.

"Stand down," Vincent ordered, motioning for all of us to put our weapons down.

He turned to face them, offering them a look of annoyed expectancy. The Romans waited patiently for us to put our weapons away. Once satisfied we wouldn't shoot them, the centurion, Quintilius, stepped forward.

"There has been an incident on the Palatine which requires your attention," he said, pointedly. "Earlier today, prior to your return from Gaul, Caligula became very ill, and is now bed ridden."

Vincent and I exchanged glances. This was it. The pivotal point in Caligula's reign, the catalyst for his legacy, but the timing was off. Caligula wasn't even in Rome when he got sick. I now knew it was no longer a question of whether or not we were changing things.

We were.

"We are unsure of the cause," Quintilius said, "but up until this morning, Caligula was in perfect health. We suspect poison. We…" he trailed off, glancing at his comrades before continuing, "we're here of our own accord. No one sent us. We were hoping maybe you could help him."

Vincent looked thoughtful, but Quintilius continued before he could say anything.

"There's more. We also have information of an armed mob congregating on the far side of the city, led by members of the Senate. Rumors of an uprising have been circulating for weeks now, and it looks like dissenters plan to take advantage of Caligula's weakened position. If you are truly here to help us, you must commit to our cause now. We may need to flee Rome at any time, and you won't be able to come back." He took a step forward and stared coldly at Vincent. "Are you with us?"

Vincent's eyes met the floor before he glanced over at me. I shrugged. We were well beyond the point of no return in regards to maintaining the status quo, and the alternative to helping seemed like a death sentence, anyway.

He nodded. "We're with you."

The centurion nodded as well. "We thank you. Please, make your way to the Palatine as quickly as possible. I believe the need for you to stay under guard is at an end, so please leave at your discretion, but do hurry. My men and I will attempt to quell the uprising before it ignites, but we cannot make any guarantees. Take what you can with you and we will arrange to have your extra supplies moved. Gaius will remain here with you, just in case. He'll follow whatever order you give him."

Vincent nodded, and tapped his closed fist against his chest. "We'll do what we can, Centurion."

The man returned the gesture before rounding up his men and leaving as quickly as he could, Gaius remaining with us.

Vincent started moving toward his room.

"All right, people. I want you ready in ten minutes. Get your three day assault packs ready. I want you heavy with ammunition. Looks we'll be saying goodbye to our little home away from home."

"Damn," Santino said, "and I was just about ready to plant a garden out front. I was thinking tulips."

***

Helena and I rushed into our room, despite the fact that most of our gear was already ready to go, and donned our night ops combat fatigues. The past month had given all of us plenty of free time, so even though our weapons had been sitting idle, they were clean, loaded, and ready for use. Vincent's order for a three day assault pack was basically code for bringing as much food and ammo as you can muster. Finding my small-go bag, I crammed in as many fully loaded magazines as I could. Thanks to the bag's versatility, I was able to tighten the shoulder strap to the point where I could fit it around my waist for use as a butt pack. It would allow for quick access to as much ammo as I hoped I'd need, without needing to hassle with a cumbersome bag.

That thought in mind, I made sure to attach a dump pouch to my belt as well. Normally in the field, a soldier's empty mag could simply be discarded on the ground and forgotten about. When they returned home, the military would provide them with replacements. Here, in ancient Rome, we no longer had that luxury, and while we had more than enough ammunition to supply the entire Normandy Beach invasion, we couldn't afford to frivolously waste the magazines.

Finding my assault bag, I gestured for Helena to toss me her own. When she did, I ran to our supply room. I stuffed both of our bags with a half a dozen MREs, enough food to last a month if rationed very, very closely, as well as extra empty magazines, and a few boxes of additional ammo. To round out our supplies, I added an entrenching shovel, a few hundred feet of paracord, a survival gear, E&E kit, some bottled water, and plenty of extra batteries with a solar panel charger into my bag. Besides the food and ammo, I added two sets of night vision goggles to Helena's pack, as well as a two man tent, which when packed was no larger than three pairs of jeans stacked on top of each other, and not much heavier. She had to travel light in case she needed to run off and play sniper. Plus she had to carry two weapons.

Just as I was about to head run back to my room, Bordeaux rushed in behind me, almost running me down with his bulky frame.

"*Excusez-moi*," he mumbled mockingly. "Rush, rush, rush."

Smiling at his own silliness, he shoved me into my room.

I stumbling through the doorway and shot him an ugly stare, which he, of course, completely ignored.

Helena noticed my clumsiness, and laughed. "Boy, you are quite the klutz, and not just around 'attractive women'," she said, batting her eyelashes at me. "I'm amazed you made it through puberty."

Offering her a sarcastic smile, I threw her assault bag at her a little harder than I should have. She caught it with a "whoof."

"And a temper too," she said, pressing the back of her palm to her forehead. "Hold me back." She continued smiling as she pulled on her vest, snapping it together before doing the same with her thigh platforms. She had her pistol on her right leg and magazine pouches for her DSR-1 on her left. She pulled on her bag, slung her DSR-1 over her shoulder, somewhat awkwardly with the large bag, and shouldered her P90. "I'll meet you outside, Jacob."

She tried to squeeze around me to get through the door but just before she could, instinct took over. I lashed out and grabbed her arm, swinging her around into my own arms. Before she could protest, which I was mostly sure she wouldn't, I leaned her back, pressed my lips against hers, and waited for her to punch me again.

I felt her stiffen ever so slightly, not out of apprehension or protest, or even fear, but perhaps just from the novelty of the experience. Her lips were soft and tender, and I felt her resolve tighten quickly. Almost immediately I felt her arms snaking around my neck and I knew I'd avoided another excruciating black eye. Pulling her even closer, I drank in as many details as I could. The sweet scent of her hair, the subtle yet equally pleasing odor of her skin, and the texture of her delicate lips. The stimulation was so intoxicating that I didn't want to let go; only doing so when I thought she might run out of air.

Backing away, I saw her eyes were closed and her lips still puckered. It was an expression as innocent as a young woman could wear after her first kiss with a new guy. Cupping her chin in a hand, I waited for her eyes to open.

When they did, I gave her a smile. "Just in case something happens."

She looked at me, her mouth moving but with no words coming out.

I heard someone clear their throat, and for a second I thought the moment would be ruined by a horrible joke from Santino. Instead, I looked over to see Bordeaux, still standing there, smiling in our direction. Catching my eye, he just shook his head with a smile and left the room.

Helena smiled as well and gave me a playful shove away from her. "Just don't get yourself killed, Lieutenant. I've decided I like you after all."

"Knowing there's someone to come home to makes surviving that much more important. Don't forget that."

"I won't." She said as she left. I watched her go for a half second wondering if I'd just won something. Like an *Awesome Contest* or something. Helena's affection was a prize any man would die for, but it wasn't that. It wasn't that kissing her was some grand victory, but it made me remember I had something to fight for again. Like I said. Someone to come home to. Trapped in Rome kind of took away that luxury, and I nearly kicked myself for almost depriving myself of it. Grabbing my own gear and snapping everything together on the run, I rushed out of my room, a grin worthy of Santino himself on my face.

Upon arrival, I noticed the front door was still open where Gaius stood guard, and the rest of the team had just started to file into the room. Helena was standing near the door and gave me a smile. Santino seemed to notice her joyful expression and arched an eyebrow in my direction. I gave him a shrug, and left it at that. Let him figure it out for himself.

Vincent was last out of his room, clipping his belt together as he rounded the corner. Not one to waste time on endless speeches, he moved toward the door. "Here we go. Remember, we don't know what's going on out there, so don't get trigger happy. We don't need to be the cause of an uprising that would never have happened had we not gotten involved."

I had to laugh at the hypocrisy of that statement. We'd already caused more than our share of problems that wouldn't have happened had we not been here. The riot most probably included.

Following Vincent, we made our way to the Palatine, with Gaius in the lead. Night had fallen, and we immediately noticed the glow of numerous fires popping up near the outskirts of the city. It looked as though Quintilius couldn't do much to stop the rioters after all.

With the riot in mind, I was having trouble understanding why this was happening now. Caligula had ruled for a number of years before he was finally deposed by his own Praetorians, and that was well after he had gone insane. So, why was this happening now? The only theory I could come up with is that our presence sped up someone's timetables, and instead of letting Caligula's insanity do the hard work of turning his own people against him, they were going to force the issue.

It didn't matter. We were on our way to the *Domus Augusti*, and I didn't have time to think about it. We double timed it and made the trip in less than fifteen minutes. Greeting us was a small unit of Caligula's bodyguards, fifty strong, guarding the front door. Seeing Gaius, they waved us through.

The home was sparsely furnished but majestic, inherited from Tiberius, and before him, Augustus. Moving through the atrium and main foyer, complete with a simple, but elegant fountain, we made our way into Caligula's bedroom, which, like the rest of the house, was nearly empty. His bed dominated the room, taking up almost half of the space, but leaving enough room to hold a hundred men. Moving inside, we immediately took up defensive positions. Bordeaux posted up on the main doorway we had just entered, and Helena moved to a balcony opposite his position, overlooking the city, pulling out her DSR-1. Santino and I moved to cover an adjacent hallway, the only other way into the room. Each of us pulled off our assault bags and tossed them in a corner.

Vincent and Wang moved toward Caligula with Gaius.

The *could be* great emperor of Rome lay in the center of his bed, with a light sheet covering his body. He was sweating profusely and his skin was gray and clammy. His closed eyes were fluttering rapidly.

Vincent stepped to the left side of the bed while Wang went to the right, both looking down at the seemingly dying man. Wang placed his hand on Caligula's forehead, as a mother would do her sick toddler. Shaking his head, he pulled out a stethoscope and a thermometer, while simultaneously checking his pulse. After using both tools and consulting his watch, his expression only seemed bleaker.

"What's the diagnosis?" Vincent asked.

Wang shook his head again. "People don't go from perfectly healthy to a bedridden fever in a matter of a few hours. If I had to guess, I would have to agree that poison is the primary suspect."

Vincent nodded, understanding the Romans' penchant for poison. "What can you do for him?"

"Well, I don't have the equipment to perform a full spectrum analysis of his blood, so there is no way to determine exactly what's wrong with him. However, I suspect that the poison isn't what's killing him."

"Then what is?"

"The fever," he said instantly. "A high grade one. I'm not the history buff you or Hunter are, but I know enough about medicine to know that poor sanitation is, and always has been, the leading cause of disease. As we've experienced, clean water is scarce here and people aren't aware of proper dietary habits either. I suspect the poison is very simple, because it doesn't need to work itself around the wonders of modern medicine. Instead, it attacks the immune system, shutting it down to the point where you easily contract the first disease you come across. It's like cancer. It doesn't kill you, but something as benign as a bloody cold that you contract and can't fight because your immune system is destroyed does."

"So what can you do for him?"

Wang sighed. "Well, treating a fever is not hard. Hunter said that when this happened the last time, or this time, or…" he looked confused, "…or whatever, when he recovered he went crazy. That's because they had no way to treat it, and the fever lasted long enough to cause brain damage. It can even cause you to go blind, or lose your hearing, or both."

"That means you can treat him?"

"I can, but it's going to take some time." Wang faltered for half a second.

He had just spoken more words in the past five minutes than he had over the past two months. Interestingly, combat medics go through some of the most intense training the military can throw at them. They sometimes end up more combat qualified than even some of the most elite operators. It was with that training, and every medics' ingrained primary instincts as a healer, that Wang was hopefully able to finally find something worth focusing on.

"Even in our own time," he continued, "kids who have a fever have to stay home from school for a few days depending on how tough they are. I can give him an IV drip of liquids, provide him with painkillers, give him some of our water to drink, keep him cool with ice packs, and place a damp, cool cloth over his forehead. Very basic stuff. We probably shouldn't move him until I have everything set up and give him at least a few hours to react to the treatment but after that, we can load him in my mobile stretcher platform and take him wherever we need to go."

"Good. Get to work. Hopefully, we'll just stay here and leave when he's better, but make preparations for immediate evac."

"Aye, sir."

Pulling off his bag, he extracted his stretcher, which he expertly unfolded next to Caligula's inert form. Attached to it was a pole, so that IV drips could be used during transport. Just as Wang pulled an IV pouch from his bag, I heard the clacking sound of hobnailed Roman boots running along the marble flooring.

It was the centurion, Quintilius.

Sweating only slightly, the man was breathing easily. He had his legion training to thank for that, as long marches and years of training transformed those men into triathletes. Stopping short near Vincent, he laid out the situation in an overly melodramatic fashion.

"We are undone. The mob is on the move, and will be here within the hour. They're marching with most of the Senate's approval."

"Damn it, Quintilius," Vincent growled. "How did this happen?"

"I am not certain" he said, shock evident on his face. "Even before your arrival, there had been grumblings in the Senate about Caligula's ascension, but never to the point where open rebellion would result. Many favored Claudius over Caligula, and while he has stirred up trouble during Senatorial sessions, I cannot believe he is involved."

"Excuse me," I said, approaching the two commanders, "but did you say many wanted Claudius as Tiberius' successor, and because he didn't get the job, he's been causing trouble?"

"Basically, yes."

"What are you thinking, Hunter," Vincent asked, no longer skeptical about my reasoning abilities.

"Two things." I said, holding up two fingers. "First, I wouldn't be at all surprised if we not only went back in time, but also jumped into a parallel universe. The theory of…"

"Hunter!" Vincent put some force behind the name.

"Sir?"

"Do *not* start!"

"Sorry, sir. Anyway, number two. What if Claudius was behind this, or was even the mastermind? I got nothing but a bad vibe from him earlier, and if what Quintilius says is true, he's got the means and the motive to perform a coup."

"Maybe," Vincent agreed reluctantly, "but even though things have changed slightly, that theory really isn't in sync with our own knowledge of history."

"Right. But like you said, things have changed. Maybe Claudius really ordered the assassination of Caligula in our history, and made up the story of hiding in the curtains to throw off historians. Hell, from what I've seen, he's done a fantastic job of rewriting history already. Nothing seems right. I think that when Caligula originally got sick, Claudius was behind the poisoning, just as he is this time. Except this time, since we're here, Caligula is here too. Not out of the city. Also, since we're here, we can stop him from getting so sick he never fully recovers."

"Doesn't that go against your policy of interference?"

"We've already fucked things up as it is. If we don't do something, who knows what will happen. We need to work on putting things right," I paused, another thought growing in the back of my head. "By the way, we're going to have a conversation about this when we get out of here, because I'm starting to formulate another theory, and it has nothing to do with Roman politicking."

Vincent stared at me.

He was hiding something from me. I knew it and he knew it. Something had been nagging me from the very beginning, ever since we were told about an equipment cache. Vincent's look was almost daring me to confront him, to create some kind of altercation, but this wasn't the place. I would have to deal with it later. Our other legion friend, Marcus, appeared out of nowhere and approached the three of us hastily.

"Sir," he said, likewise glistening but not breathing heavily. "We couldn't hold them back. The mob will be here in minutes."

"Gods..." Quintilius muttered.

"There's more, sir," Marcus continued. "Claudius is at the head of the formation, and he's somehow enlisted the aid of Praetorians."

"How is that possible?" Quintilius asked sharply. "There has been no talk of dissension. Our loyalty has been unquestionable."

I snorted. Yeah right.

Praetorians were notorious for their direct involvement in the ascension of nearly every emperor, save Augustus and a few later ones, but Augustus was the only emperor to maintain complete control over his bodyguards. Even Tiberius had to pay a tribute to them just to keep their loyalty, which later became a tradition for all newly appointed emperors. They would soon become political juggernauts with immense power over who might become emperor. They were known to have done away with numerous emperors they didn't agree with. That said, from what I knew at this point in history, they should have been devoutly loyal to Caligula. Their current prefect, Macro, had been essential to Caligula upon his rise to power, and even though Caligula should soon have him executed while spending time in the East, for now, he was loyal.

If the Senate and Praetorians did have plans to overthrow Caligula, they'd need a considerable amount of firepower just to get past us, so what better to use than an entire city? I suppose it made sense. Armor, training, and Roman stubbornness wouldn't to be enough for Praetorians to stop us. Twenty Roman Praetorians would be no more effective against us than twenty civilians, unless they got close, and then things would even up very quickly, but there would be a lot of bodies on the ground before they got that close.

Marcus didn't respond to Quintilius' question right away. Instead he tried looking around, maybe in the vain hope that

Quintilius would find someone else to question. But Quintilius was not in the mood for tentative subordinates.

"Marcus!? How has this happened? Where is Macro?"

Marcus' head snapped around and he looked at his centurion squarely. "He's dead. He was stabbed in his sleep in the *Castra Praetoria*."

Vincent and I shared knowing nods once again. Macro had played an essential role in the ascension of Caligula to the position of Imperator. But years later, as the emperor's obsession and paranoia grew, he'd had Macro banished, where he and his wife took their own lives. But now, he was a staunch ally of Caligula. He was an important puzzle piece to remove if any potential coup was to succeed.

Quintilius didn't appear saddened by the loss of his boss, but he knew the implications involved in his death. He shook his head in disbelief.

"Just how many of your Praetorians have gone rogue," I asked.

Marcus paused, not even trying to hide his fear. "Of the two cohorts in the city, only the three centuries here are still loyal. We're outnumbered seven to one."

VIII
Betrayal

Rome, Italy
November, 37 A.D.

"Three hundred men!? Against two thousand?!" I shouted. "Have you people no sense of loyalty? There's no way we can hold out against that many, especially when they're aided by a mob of…"

Vincent motioned for me to calm down. "Settle down, Hunter. You're not helping. Centurion, give me your strategic appraisal of the situation. Where are the remaining cohorts?"

"Two are on a training detail in the south, three are occupied on courier missions, and the remaining two are split up protecting various imperial family members, scattered throughout Italy."

"Shouldn't there be three cohorts in Rome?" Vincent asked.

Quintilius shrugged. "There were, but we have been busy and we didn't plan our training schedule properly. We're stretched thin."

I scoffed, completely flabbergasted at the entire situation.

Vincent's look told me to shut up. "What about your tactical assessment, Centurion?"

Quintilius wasted no time thinking it over. "We can hold out here for a while. I've called for the rest of my century to get here as soon as they can. I am unaware as to the situation of the other cohorts outside the city, but we cannot count on their help tonight. I will post a maniple of men in the courtyard, with a century in reserve. Our reinforcements will take up positions in the halls."

That would put just under two hundred men outside, with another eighty behind them, and the remaining century in the house.

"With your permission," he continued, "I would ask you to remain here, and provide support for my men. Hopefully, we will be able to inflict enough casualties to make them rethink their position, and have them disperse. Even two thousand men will have trouble taking this position, especially with your help." He paused, a look of uncertainty crossing his face. "I know of your abilities, but am uncertain of your tactics. What exactly can you do for us?"

"First of all, tell your men not to attack mine, they will be leaving the house for a few minutes."

He nodded, sending Marcus to inform the men outside.

"Santino, Bordeaux, get over here."

The two men complied, stopping before Vincent at attention.

"Santino, gather up all the remaining claymores we have, and plant them along the streets the mob will most likely be using. Set them up at intervals so that they don't all go off at once."

The man saluted, and went off to collect his charges.

"Bordeaux, do I even need to ask if you brought plenty of explosives?"

"*Non.*"

"Good. Line the hallways with C-4. Not a lot, we don't want to collapse the house, but enough to put some serious dents in the enemy's lines should they make it inside. Place additional charges outside along the interior of the courtyard."

Bordeaux nodded, and went to work.

"What are you having them do?" Quintilius asked.

"You were at our demonstration. Remember the column?"

Quintilius' face immediately brightened, a shred of hope emerging.

"Tell your men to not wander far from the house, and make sure you redirect your remaining ones to arrive from the rear."

That would be difficult. The back of the house was a steep hill, perfect for Helena's sniper perch, but not for a reinforcing army.

"The rest of us will provide fire support. When they reach the house, stay low, and we'll fire over you. If things get really bad, fall back and shield us while we put them down with sustained weapons fire. Remember the armor sets?"

Apparently the man did. Practically laughing, he struggled to salute before running off to inform his soldiers of our plans.

By the time Santino and Bordeaux returned, Wang had completed his setup and began a cursory inspection of Caligula's vitals at regular intervals, looking for signs of improvement. I looked at him and he shook his head. We'd have to wait awhile before he found any.

"So, what now?" Santino asked.

"Okay. Here's the plan." Vincent laid out his thoughts as clearly as he could. "Bordeaux, I want you upfront with the Romans. Provide as much support as you can from your position, but for the love of God, don't get yourself killed. When things get bad, fall back. Santino and I will take up positions here, at the main doorway, and wait for you to fall back. Hunter, hang back with Strauss and provide additional sniper support from her position. From the looks of it, you two will have a decent angle on the mob's flank. Try and make your shots count. If things start to get really bad, we'll pack up Caligula, and move him out the back as quickly as possible. Make no mistake, we are now outlaws, and even if we get Caligula out of here and healthy again, we'll be doing nothing but setting up a splinter government. If that happens, our best bet is to get in contact with the legions."

"Sir!" Helena called from her balcony. "We've got friendlies incoming. Six o'clock."

"Good. Direct them to the front." He turned back to us. "Any questions?"

We shook our heads, and made our way to our assigned positions. Eighty Praetorians shuffled past me, and I had to push through them just to get to the balcony. Still shaking my head, I fought my way through and made my way to Helena's position, thinking about how this wasn't going to be a fight, but a slaughter.

I'd had to kill civilians before, but never unarmed ones and each time I did, it was because I had a legitimate reason. Either I was going to die, or they were, and I never hesitated. The men coming for us were armed with pitch forks and torches, something out of an old black and white movie – a mob of villagers storming the steps of Nosferatu's castle.

They didn't have a chance, and I wasn't going to shoot them unless I felt threatened.

Reaching the balcony, I unslung Penelope, and released the spring keeping her bipod's legs parallel to the barrel. They snapped into a V formation, and I rested them on the banister, giving me a platform to peer through my Version II Modular Advanced Combat Optical Gunsight. The VerII ACOG was a top of the line combat sight. It had a modular zoom from 1-power to 8-power, perfect for close range fighting and distance shooting. It was slightly longer and thicker than an ACOG from ten years ago, but it was no more cumbersome. A simple touch interface along the side allowed for a single finger to slide along the exterior of the sight to determine the magnification. It was more a camera than a magnifier. It was a major step forward in weapon optics versatility, and its night vision capabilities made it an all-in-one purpose scope. It had been damn pricy, but I loved it.

"So what's the plan?" Helena asked. "And what's wrong?"

I had to smile a bit, despite the situation. It was nice to know she cared. "We're going to slaughter them. All of them. And for what? To save a man who will probably turn out all right anyway? I don't understand what Vincent's doing. We've already fucked up so much." I sighed, knowing I had to clear my head before others had to start relying on me. It wouldn't be fair to them. "Sorry. I guess none of that matters."

She continued to look through her scope. "It's nice to know you're not just going to fold up and let us get killed, especially me. Now, what does Vincent want us to do?"

"About what you'd expect," I answered. "Protect our flanks by keeping them from wanting to come this way. If any of them stray in our direction, we take them out. I don't know about you, but I'm not going to sit up here and pick off civilians. I'm targeting officers first, soldiers second, and only those civilians I deem an immediate threat last. If we can thin out the soldiers, our buddies out front can probably hold against the civilians all night."

She looked at me with concern in her eyes, and I couldn't help but notice her hands were shaking. "As simple as that?" She asked.

I tried to put on a sympathetic face. "It's never that simple, Helena. It's damn complicated actually, but if we don't do what we can here, we may not make it home to regret it later."

She nodded a few moments later, turning her attention back to her rifle to fidget with her scope.

***

Five minutes later, we saw the tip of the mob, led by rebel Praetorians, still clad in their ceremonial white togas. As I guessed, the plebeians were armed with pitchforks and torches, but some had clubs, axes, old swords, and other simple tools. They wouldn't be an issue, but the Praetorians, as powerful as any military group, were another matter.

"Sir," I called to Vincent. "Tangos inbound. ETA two minutes. Permission to engage?"

"Granted."

And with that, Helena and I rained fire down upon the unsuspecting Romans.

At first, they took little notice of the fact that many of their co-conspirators were dying around them. I let Helena do most of the work in the beginning, her DSR-1 and 10x scope far more accurate than I was with my ACOG. With it, she was able to surgically pick off men marching along the exposed flank of the column. She never shot two men standing next to each other, and so far, was only targeting soldiers.

After a few dozen Praetorians had fallen over the stretch of a few blocks, the rebels seemed to catch on to what was happening around them and started to panic. Most had no idea that we, and not the gods, were to blame for the deaths, and many civilians fled out of fear.

But not too many.

The vanguard's next step dissuaded far more, as they triggered the first of Santino's claymores. Each claymore was designed to explode in a hundred and forty degree arc, and was loaded with tiny pieces of shrapnel. Within seconds, dozens more were either dead or on their way toward the pearly gates. Crazily, the mob pushed on, still thousands strong despite the casualties and desertions. No longer hindered with the need to preserve the element of surprise, I opened fire in controlled bursts that sent maybe a hundred men to the grave. Combined with Helena's pinpoint strikes, we racked up an impressive kill count before they even reached the house's courtyard.

"What is it Americans say? Like shooting fish in a barrel?" Helena observed, disgust emanating from her voice.

"Yah, or like ancient Romans in the street. Real heroic."

Helena mumbled an agreement but didn't stop firing.

By the time the second claymore exploded, the mob had just reached the house's gated courtyard. Even so, their line still snaked around behind the house, offering Helena and me a few stragglers to pick off.

We left the civilians.

Without any more targets of opportunity remaining, I patted Helena on the shoulder, letting her know that I was falling back.

"Stay here and watch out for a flank. I'm going to see if I can help out front. If you need me give me a shout on the radio."

She turned and gave me a smile and a nod, but quickly focused in on her sights again, one hand on the trigger, the other reaching for a bag of ammunition.

I turned and headed back toward Vincent, checking my ammo as I went, and hearing a third claymore go off in the background. I had carried ten loaded magazines in my vest, but found each lying empty in my dump pouch. As smoothly as I could, I replenished my empty magazine pouches with fresh mags from my go-bag. Hopefully, I'd have time to reload my empty ones before the main assault.

Vincent and Santino were still standing in the doorway, waiting for the action to come their way. Since the area was still calm, I made a quick detour to the assault bag I had thrown in the corner, and retrieved a small box of ammo. Walking over to the swim pair, I started reloading empty mags.

"What's the situation on your front, Hunter?" Vincent asked.

"Between our sniper fire and claymores, I'd estimate around three hundred dead or injured," I reported, securing one of my freshly reloaded mags back in my go-bag, and retrieving another empty one from my dump pouch. "Maybe another hundred have fled. Most of the casualties are Praetorians, and the deserters, civilians."

"Anyone trying to sneak in?"

"No, sir. I think we've effectively scared the shit out of them."

"So far, so good then," he said offhandedly. "Wang says we still need to hold out for an hour or so before we can move Caligula. He's breathing easier, but little else has changed."

I nodded, apathetic.

Santino spoke up next. "When I was out planting claymores, only three by the way, I managed to send up my drone. We should be receiving aerial footage any second now."

My eyepiece flashed indicating new intel.

"Bingo," Santino said.

Sighing at my friend, I tapped my sleeve, and called up the information. Displayed on my eyepiece was a thermal video of the street below. It showed a huge mass of whites, oranges, and reds, indicating live bodies, but trailing behind it was an intermittent string of cooling corpses colored green, blue, and black. We had done more damage than I thought, but I also saw there were many more bad guys than we had originally estimated as well.

"Shit," I said. "I didn't think the road was that wide. There may be twice as many men out there than we originally thought."

Santino and Vincent were likewise looking through their eyepieces, their faces grim.

"We'll deal with it," Vincent said. "When Bordeaux reports contact we'll..."

The radio crackled to life. "Sir," Bordeaux's voice came in strained and distant. "Enemy contact at the gate. The mob has a ram, but many are attempting to scale the walls. We could use Strauss and Hunter up here."

I looked at Vincent.

"Go," he said. "Strauss..."

"I'm on my way," she called as she passed by, having already heard the transmission.

We passed through the atrium together, which we found packed with loyalist Praetorians. Most had worried expressions on their faces, looks of defeat and an utter lack of hope, but as we walked by, many perked up at the sight of us. While some of it could have been attributed to Helena's presence alone, I would bet many found us to be more than just symbols of hope, but agents of the gods themselves, sent to protect them in a time of crisis.

Sadly, the truth wasn't that we were sent to help stop the crisis, but that through our own blunderings, really just mine, we were one of the primary causes of it. No sense telling them that.

Near the entrance, I noticed Gaius and Marcus watching the ever-growing mob of protestors outside the gate. Unlike many of the Romans inside, these two were stoic and confident. Their eyes still showed they were willing to fight to the death if need be. They saw us approach and turned to speak.

"Lieutenant Hunter. Lieutenant Strauss," Gaius greeted, as the slightly senior ranking of the two.

I smiled at their use of our ranks. Over the past few months, my friends and I had spent lots of time chatting with our Praetorian guards, mostly about each other's cultures and peoples. One of the few things we did speak openly about was our military, along with our ranking system. Romans, no strangers to the chain of command, used a very similar hierarchy of command ranks. During our discussions, we managed to lay out the foundation that a lieutenant was of equal rank to a centurion, a captain was about equal to the highest ranking centurion in each legion, a colonel would be a tribune, and a general was known as a legate. Having synced up our chain of commands, the Romans insisted on treating us as though we were their own officers.

Flattering, to say the least.

Stopping a few feet from them both, I tapped a fist against my chest. Helena did nothing. A part of her still found this whole situation ridiculous, and scoffed at how the rest of us tried to fit in. Besides, it was even *more* of a boy's world here than it was back home. Needless to say, she was finding it difficult to fit in.

"Marcus. Gaius," I greeted them. "You two look like you've lost something. Forget your swords at home?"

The men chuckled, as they pulled their *gladii* half way out of their scabbards, proving they had in fact remembered them.

"No, sir," Gaius answered. "We merely wished to speak with you before you went outside."

"Battle's not getting any younger."

"With your permission, we would like to assist you in any way during the coming battle. Your weapons are indeed far superior to our own, but you cannot hold the enemy back forever. We would ask to serve as your sword arm when the battle gets too close."

I looked at them. Any man willing to place themselves in one of the most dangerous parts of a battlefield, just to protect a superior, or a friend, was someone impressive indeed. I'd be a fool to turn them down, especially since the only sword handling I'd ever done was when my friends and I would hit each other with sticks back when we were kids.

It would be nice having someone cover our backs.

"Of course," I answered. "Marcus, you're with me. Gaius, don't let anything," I emphasized my point by jabbing a finger at him threateningly, "happen to Lieutenant Strauss."

Marcus frowned ever so slightly, while Gaius smiled, nodded his head, and looked at my partner. She scowled at me.

It was only fair that I rewarded the guy who stepped up by letting him guard the prettier one, but I had more selfish reasons. Gaius was older, and a slightly better soldier. He'd be able to offer more protection, and I wasn't going to take any chances with Helena.

Our bodyguards in tow, we made our way to the palace grounds to come face to face with the invading horde.

Bordeaux's announcement of Romans scaling the walls became immediately obvious. Four had already reached the ground, while more were in the process of descending their rope ladders. The first man I targeted was the quickest on his feet and was already approaching our lines. Taking a step forward, I sighted him through my ACOG, and shot him in the head. Another step, and two more men went down with three round bursts to their chests. The last man went down with a head shot from Helena. The immediate threat taken care of, we picked off the rest of the unlucky souls descending into the courtyard or waiting on the ledges. Ten seconds later, the ropes were cleared of about twenty intruders. Smacking home a fresh magazine, I scouted the area for a good spot to post myself.

The large house boasted an equally large courtyard. Large, of course, being a relative term. It wasn't large by the opulent standards of many celebutantes back home, but it was still big enough to easily accommodate two hundred Romans, three time travelers, and enough room for a bloodbath between twice that many.

The front façade of the home looked like a miniature version of the Pantheon, with columns, Ionic in style, with a triangular centerpiece resting above. The entrance was wide, and opened on to a patio where the columns extended to the ceiling. Six steps then lead down to a path through the courtyard. The gate acted as a natural funnel into the courtyard, easily the best place to bottleneck the enemy. The walls were made of concrete, a dozen feet high and a foot thick, so unless the mob wanted to continue being shot off them, it's best bet was to come through the gate. Once the gate was down, the mob might reattempt to scale the walls while we were distracted.

With no concealment in sight, and not wanting to use Romans as meatshields, I made my way toward the nearest column, signaling Helena to follow me. Taking position behind the center-right column, I indicated Helena should stand behind the opposite one. Bordeaux came and calmly stood between us, ready to lay down suppressing fire while Helena and I chose our targets more carefully.

Even before we arrived in the courtyard, we'd heard the steady beat of a battering ram hammering against the gate. Made out of thick, wooden beams, it had started to splinter at about the same time we had killed the last of the climbers. By the time we took cover behind the columns, the gate gave way completely.

What took place before me was one of the most amazing sights I had ever seen.

Roman versus Roman.

It had happened more times than one would think. After the fall of the Julio-Claudian family, in about thirty or so years from now, very few emperors would elevate to the position of Caesar without the use of their legions. It was fascinating how willing Romans were to fight each other, their sense of honor and duty leaving little room for moral sensibilities or even peaceful negotiations. They were barbaric and warmongering, no matter how many roads, aqueducts, poets, laws, and countless other wonders of the world they created.

I loved these guys; their contradictions being so overwhelmingly ironic.

As the gate buckled and fell, dozens of plebeians poured through the gap, a smart tactic on the part of the rogue Praetorians. Send in the cannon fodder first. The shock troops. It forced our Praetorians to expend their supply of spears on them, thinning their ranks much as possible. When the two factions met, the rebels would be fresh, and able to just waltz up to the lines, literally on the coattails of their human shields. Or so they hoped.

As I predicted, the maniple of Praetorians arrayed before me unleashed a volley of *pila*, a Roman legionnaire's choice spear, immediately followed by a second. The air filled with spears, and row upon row of civilians fell to the ground, bleeding and dying from numerous wounds.

I had never seen such bloodshed in all my time as a SEAL. War was so distant and impersonal back home, but not here. I watched, not fifty yards before me as men were staked to the ground by falling spears, pierced through eye sockets, abdomens, necks, and everywhere else. Some were stuck together due to the powerful force of the heavy Roman spear.

My thoughts immediately went to Homer's, *The Iliad* and the gore and bloodshed he described there. Homer, who had no issue describing war as the despicable and inhuman event it was, never left a man to die without explaining how it happened, whether he be a king or common foot soldier. He described men being impaled through their groin and genitals, ears being stripped from their heads, limbs amputated, eye balls plucked from their skulls, and sword thrusts that ran straight through men's mouths. Unlike those Homeric men, at least these retained some of their dignity after they had fallen. Homer's heroes would carry away their kills in an attempt to maximize the spoils and riches they obtained while on campaign by stripping the fallen of their arms and armor.

None of those men even cared about Helen, the so-called face that launched a thousand ships. Not even Menelaus, her husband, or least of all her so-called "lover", Paris, who was cavorting with Trojan handmaidens soon after Helen's arrival. King of kings, Agamemnon, couldn't care less, nor did god-like Achilles, and even crafty Odysseus, my favorite Homeric character, was there for the wrong reasons. Although, in Odysseus' defense, he was tricked into going when he was forced to choose between going to war or killing Telemachus, his baby son.

All they cared for was money, spoils, and land, and even their so called desires for *areté*, or personal perfection in life, specifically on the battlefield, paled before their greed. At least the Romans were honest with each other about why they were fighting.

When the lines finally clashed, the slaughter ensued.

Our Praetorians stabbed with their short swords, adhering to their training of thrusting with the tip, as opposed to slashing wildly and cutting with its edge. The tactic worked well. Praetorians would cower behind their large shields, or *scuti*, before emerging to impale a nearby foe. Slowly, despite the mass of weight arrayed against them, our loyal Praetorians pushed the enemy back toward the gate, step by gradual step.

Like the three hundred Spartans at Thermopylae, the narrow gate and the short distances forced the advancing enemy into a narrow corridor, minimizing their numerical advantage. When they realized their tactical deficiency, small groups of men took to scaling the walls in an attempt to flank our position. Gunfire from inside the house indicated that some men were indeed trying to work their way in through the rear of our position. All those who attempted to come over the walls were summarily put down like those who had tried earlier.

So far we weren't running through too much ammo, only taking pot shots at the climbers, not wasting our time on low priority targets presenting themselves at the gate. Only a few times did I need to fire into the crowd when I saw a Praetorian in desperate need for aid.

So far the battle was going well. The enemy's tactic of sending in the civilians first had backfired. Our soldiers had practically pushed them back to the gates, and now the rebel Praetorians would not have the opportunity to push into the courtyard and form their lines before charging at us, a full complement of *pila* at their disposal. Now, they had to push through the gates on an equal footing. If only they didn't outnumber us by so much, we might have had a chance of standing our ground, instead of just fighting a delaying effort.

Then, a dozen feet or so from the gate, I saw the first major snag in our plan.

Smack dab in the middle of both sets of Roman Praetorians, the enemy ones just beginning to show their faces outside, stood Marcus Varus, poorly attempting to blend in with the angry mob around him.

I saw him and he saw me, and I knew he was only trying to reach his friend, Caligula.

The ballsy bastard was going to get himself killed.

I mumbled in frustration as I turned to Marcus. "Get ready, my friend. It's time for a rescue operation." Unsure as to what I meant exactly, his eyes narrowed in confusion, but he made ready to follow me all the same.

Waving my hand, I grabbed Helena's attention. "Cover me. I forgot my smiley face boxers back in our room."

"Wait, what are you…" Helena began as I took off down the stairs. I heard her call out behind me, but her words were drowned out in a roar of voices.

Running along the flank of my allies, I was doing my best to think of a plan on the move. I had grenades on me, but knowing Varus was in there, I couldn't just toss them in. In close quarters, my pistol was my best bet, but against sword and shield, I had little to protect myself.

As I made my way to the front line, I got an idea.

Grabbing Marcus and four other Praetorians, I started issuing orders. "About six rows into the enemy is a friend of mine. We need to get him. He's Caligula's friend as well." That was all they needed to know. "I need you to form a loose semicircle in front of me and just push through the enemy's line, a little left of center. You're going to have to trust me, but do not stop to engage unless someone gets in your way. When I give the word, duck behind your shields and wait. You'll know when to fall back."

The men looked at me bravely, only partly understanding their orders.

"You hear that, Strauss?" I radioed Helena.

"Are you fucking nuts? You're going to get yourself killed."

"You know, you sound really cute when you swear."

"Jacob…"

"Just shoot the guys behind me. I'll be fine."

Pissed off, the only response I received from her was a double click. At least she wouldn't let me die. At least not on purpose.

"Okay, Praetorians. Form up."

The five men, Marcus at the tip of the formation, pulled in front of me and waited for my order.

"Go!"

My escorts took off, not running, but quicker than anyone else on the battlefield. Our front line opened just enough to let us through and we systematically pushed the mob aside. The insanity of our attack worked well enough to both confuse and distract the mob as we pushed through. I heard the familiar cracking noise of shattered skulls coming from behind me, as well as the touch of warm liquid splashing against my neck, hapless men who, by paying me too much attention had caught Helena's. Three-fourths of the way there I took a sword blow to my right shoulder, luckily protected by my shoulder armor. It would bruise, but I wasn't cut. My attacker was rewarded with two rounds through his chest, compliments of my Sig. After another blunted sword blow across my lower back, and one of my guardians being beaten down, Varus was in arms reach. Hauling his ass beside me, I grabbed a grenade with my free hand, pulled the pin with my teeth, counted to three, and tossed it over my human shield's heads in the direction of the enemy Praetorians, mere arm lengths away.

Pulling Varus to the ground, I shouted, "Down!"

My men went to their knees, and locked their shields, their backs to mine. Within the few seconds that followed, I took a club to my side and a slash against my forearm, that one drawing blood.

The first man I shot in the head, but the second was taken off his feet by the force of the grenade that had just gone off.

In such close proximity, the grenade did maximum damage. Men in a ten yard radius were either on the ground dead, or dying. I took full advantage and shouted for my men to run. Before I could flee as well, I had one more job to do. Twisting at my waist, I took careful aim with one of the last bullets in my pistol, and shot the lead centurion in the head.

Thankfully, my Praetorians, while disoriented by the explosion, still had sense enough to run. Most of the civilian mob, however, were either still on the ground, shaking their heads clear, or fleeing in panic. Running on pure adrenaline, losing more blood than I thought from my arm, I quickly grabbed Varus, and rolled another grenade in the direction of the enemy soldiers. I was well within my lines by the time it detonated within theirs, taking out at least twenty more soldiers.

Frightened and temporarily leaderless, the Praetorians outside the gates fell back, just enough to allow their fleeing civilian allies to run, leaving only the professional soldiers.

Dragging Varus up the steps, I pushed him in the doorway.

"Go! Caligula's in his room. We're trying to buy some time before we can move him out of here."

"Th-thank you. I..."

"Just go! You can thank me later."

He nodded and ran inside.

I watched him flee inside before stumbling against a column behind me, but I managed to slowly slide myself to the floor as I clutched my arm in pain. I pulled back my sleeve, revealing a nasty laceration that ran from mid forearm to my elbow. Looking over my shoulder at the battle, I didn't see Helena crouch down next to me.

I was rewarded with a slap to my face.

"Ow!" I yelled, clutching my stung cheek. "That was the only thing that didn't hurt!"

"Don't you ever do something stupid like that again!" Her tone was angry but her expression relieved. "What were you thinking?"

"I had to save Varus. He's... important."

I guessed he was. For all I knew, he may be a direct ancestor of mine and I couldn't let him get killed now. Who knew what kind of paradox I'd create then. A "great, great, great times one hundred grandfather paradox," or maybe I'd just wink out of existence. The universe might just implode for all I knew. Or maybe I'd prove that grandfather paradoxes are nothing but shit science.

"Well, he'd better be," she said, grabbing my arm roughly. "This is bad. It needs to be treated."

I turned to look out over the battlefield again, seeing that both sides of Praetorians had not yet engaged. One was scared, while the other was just stalling for time. Once the enemy found another centurion to rally his troops, the fighting would reach a whole new level of bloodiness.

"Don't worry about it," I said. "It's just a scra…"

I didn't notice her pull out a package of QuikClot and pour it on my arm. I almost screamed, grinding my teeth together, settling for a painful moan to help maintain my dignity.

"Quit being a baby. It's just a scratch. Besides, I owed you one." She pulled out a bandage and wrapped it around my arm, pulling it tight, forcing me to bit my lip again. "I'd recommend you take it easy, but *that's* clearly not going to happen. Let Wang check it out ASAP."

"Yes, ma'am."

I popped a few pain killers, enough to hopefully dull the pain but not cause me to lose focus. Helena offered her hand. I took it and let her help me up, wincing as I felt my back, shoulder, and the entire left flank of my upper body beginning to bruise.

"So, now what?" She asked.

"We wait," I replied, shrugging off the pain.

We didn't have to wait for long. A replacement centurion was quickly brought to the front, and after a little pep talk, ordered his men to charge. Casting *pila* as they came, and receiving a single volley in return, the men sprinted toward our position as though the forces of Olympus were urging them on.

Their first volley incoming, I grabbed Helena and held her close. We squeezed ourselves behind her original column while Bordeaux hid behind my old one. As soon as the missiles fell to the ground, many flying through the air we had just vacated, we stepped around the corner, and started firing.

Helena's first target was the replacement centurion, while I went for the standard bearer, the soul of every legion. While another man would pick it up after it fell, the continuous falling of it would quickly dishearten those who noticed. After that, I went back to my practice of only shooting those who were immediate threats to my allies below. Helena did the same, while Bordeaux used his elevation to pour fire into the middle of the crowd, thinning it from within.

Despite our help, our line started to horseshoe inwards almost immediately, with the center of the enemy's line extending well through our own. I still saw no end to the enemy's forces, while ours were wavering. They would never break, but their fatigue was starting to show. Many of our people were hacked to pieces because of it. The reserve century tried to move around the left to get along the enemy's flank, but while a good idea, they just didn't have enough room to maneuver in the ways that made the Roman legions so effective. It would do little except stall the enemy a little longer.

I decided to abandon my selective targeting policy, and flicked my rifle's selector switch over to fully automatic, taking a moment to spray the most densely populated areas I could see. I mowed down dozens of men before my magazine finally ran out of ammo. I glanced over at Helena, who was likewise digging for loaded magazines that didn't exist.

I threw a rock at her to get her attention. The rear of our formation had backed itself up the stairs at this point, blocking clean shots, and making it hard to hear each other. When she turned to look, I pointed inside, and waggled my middle and pointer fingers, communicating my decision to fall back.

She nodded, and ran for the door. Bordeaux noticed her retreat, looked at me and nodded. He backed into the doorway, ready to fall back at moment's notice, but sticking around to provide as much support as he could.

Passing him, I thumped his shoulder to get his attention, before yelling into his ear, "hold the line. I'll report to Vincent. Don't forget to fall back."

He gave me a wide grin, and turned back toward the fighting while I ran as fast as I could toward the back of the house. When I arrived, I discovered that Caligula's room had completely changed. It was littered with bodies, Caligula was now on the floor, and Santino had his combat knife implanted through a man's chin, extending it into his skull. Pulling the blade free, he wiped it clean on the dead man's toga just before he slumped to the ground, and placed it back in a sheath. He started to whistle as he left the balcony, waltzing into the room as though nothing had happened, tiptoeing and skipping over maybe thirty men. I observed that most of the bodies in the room had died from similar knife wounds to the face, neck, and chest. Noticing my appearance back in the room, he pulled up short, as if surprised to see me. He appeared as carefree as a father tucking in his kids.

"Jacob! Nice to see you. How are things?" He asked as nonchalantly as a gossiping golden girl. He pointed at my arm.

"Oh, you know… had to play the hero and all that."

"Ah. Slayed the dragon, rescued the damsel in distress and saved the world did you?"

"Something like that."

Helena rolled her eyes, before offering her own sit rep. "The situation is rapidly deteriorating outside. We're going to need to hold in the hallways soon before falling back completely."

I nodded. "She's right. How's our patient?"

Each of us turned to Wang. He had his fingers around Caligula's feverish wrist, checking his pulse. I glanced at my watch, surprised to see that only forty five minutes had elapsed since the fight had begun. Wang said we'd need at least an hour.

When he looked up, his face seemed satisfied. "He's surprisingly well. His temperature has dropped and his pulse is steadying. I think it's safe to assume that he's made it through the worst of it. He should make a full recovery, but he could easily relapse. Let's give him another twenty minutes before we move him."

"Twenty minutes it is," Vincent replied. "Prepare to defend the room."

As if to capitalize on his words, Bordeaux came rushing in with Gaius and Marcus, who had lost track of Helena and I in the battle.

"They're breaking through," Gaius reported. "We have five minutes before our troops must retreat to the atrium."

Vincent nodded, turning to Bordeaux. "When I asked you to line the halls with demo, tell me you placed more than you were ordered to."

Bordeaux gave Vincent a look that suggested he'd be crazy to think anything but. "Of course. I have a backup detonator which should bring down the front structure of this house, but preserving this room." He paused as he surveyed the room. "Hopefully."

I sighed. Demo-guys.

"Great. Detonate the small charges at your discretion, but bring down the house only on my order."

"Sir," I spoke up. "I'm not all that fond of blowing up Augustus' house."

"Deal with it," he replied, moving to the doorway. "They'll rebuild it."

Around the time I said the word "house," loyal Praetorians began streaming into the hallway outside the room, clogging the space and creating a perimeter. They were a distraction. Out of the corner of my eye, I saw a shadowy figure emerge from the balcony, and sneak up behind Santino. I couldn't tell if he was a Praetorian or a civilian, but the knife he held told me enough. I shouted a warning to my friend as I brought my rifle to my shoulder only to realize I was too late.

Before I could bring my barrel to bare and enact some facet of revenge on the interloper, I felt a whoosh of air over my shoulder and I saw a spear fly toward Santino's head. Not enough time to move, Santino froze as the spear flew straight and true, right past his own shoulder and into the skull of the sneaking intruder.

I turned to see Gaius hold out a clenched fist, which was summarily punched by Marcus' own.

Well there's one for the history books. Roman soldiers showed signs of appreciation and congratulations by pounding fists, just as we did in our own time.

And me without my camera.

Santino had a look of complete shock on his face as he twisted at the waist to see the dead man behind him, *pila* protruding through the man's skull. The would-be assassin was so close to Santino that the spear vibrated over my friend's shoulder. Santino pressed his finger against the spear and gave it a nudge, watching as the man dropped to his knees and fell to the ground. Returning to his original position, he looked over my shoulder at the Romans.

"I love you guys," he said to them in English.

Marcus smiled and waved, clearly the one who threw the spear.

Breathing a collective sigh of relief, everyone in the room save Wang and Caligula made their way to the quickly collecting force of loyal Praetorians outside in the atrium. We had them line up, about twenty wide, and as many rows as we could deep. In these enclosed spaces we could hold out for a while, but not forever. I'd hoped to stall longer outside, but there were just too many, and I estimated we only had about a third of our original strength left. I was happy to see Quintilius had survived, although he was bleeding from a head wound. At least the men would have the benefit of a centurion to coordinate them.

Minor skirmishes were still being waged near the courtyard where loyal Praetorians had been separated from the rest of the group. Their sacrifices gave us the time we needed to set up a defensive wall of interlocking shields.

I saw the last of our men, cut off from our position, butchered by three rebel Praetorians. When he fell, the rebels stopped and looked in our direction. They looked tired and out of breath, but their faces revealed only the bloodlust that consumed them. Even if we could somehow lay out the situation peacefully, I knew they would continue fighting without pause. A minute went by as each side stared the other down, before the rebels roared in challenge and rushed us.

The two sides collided in a clamor of swords and armor and blood. Each side, professional to the core, began the long, arduous process of outlasting the other. This kind of warfare only lasted as long as one side could continue fighting. Not through a loss of men, but the loss of energy. Ancient battles could take days, and while this one wouldn't last that nearly that long, I did everything I could to even up the sides.

I tossed my last grenade ten rows deep into the enemy's position, but they learned quickly. Even though they hadn't figured out they could just throw it back, they did turn their shields to help block the explosion. Most weren't quick or smart enough to so, but some were. When the grenade exploded, a sizable hole opened up in their formation. Following my example, those of my friends who still had them threw their own grenades, each with similar results. Chipping, chipping, chipping away.

Five minutes elapsed.

Our lines started to buckle under the sheer weight of the rebel mass. Quintilius tried to rotate fresh troops to the front line regularly, but in the cramped and confused atrium, he was having trouble coordinating the effort. The enemy had no such problem, and were steadily streaming into our flanks and driving right through the middle of our lines. On the right, Bordeaux mowed down an entire line of the enemy with a hail of gunfire from his SAW. On the left, a Praetorian swung his sword toward Helena's head, but she managed to bat it aside with her P90. She pulled out her side arm, and shot the man in the stomach. Somewhere in the middle, Santino swung his rifle like a club and shattered a man's face.

We were getting desperate.

I noticed a pair of enemies attempting to engage Quintilius. I sighted one through my scope and sent a burst of fire toward him. The trio of rounds ripped through the man's neck and sent a stream of blood and gore toward his buddy. Distracted by the arterial spray, the other man went down with a sword thrust to the chest by Quintilius' steady hand.

By now, I couldn't tell the two groups of Romans apart. Both loyalist and rebel looked the same. They only fought each other based on who they didn't know, which would be very few people outside their own cohorts. The only Romans I could identify were Quintilius, fighting bravely while trying to maintain order for his few remaining soldiers, and Marcus and Gaius, fighting back to back.

"Fall back!" Vincent ordered his squad in English. He didn't have to tell me twice, and I began to strategically withdraw from the battle, making sure not to grow complacent on the way out and take a *gladius* to my back. I thought I was the last one out when I noticed Helena still blazing away with her P90, oblivious to our retreat.

I ran over and grabbed her arm. "Let's go!" I yelled over the noise. "We are leaving!"

Without protest, she let me drag her away, still firing when she found an opening. For a woman who had never seen war before, she was certainly taking to it like a tamed lion who'd finally found its wild side. I guess war was actually a pretty good way to release an entire life's worth of frustration and anger, and she had plenty to burn. Kind of like a giant stress ball, only it was too slippery to squeeze because of all the blood.

Running into the room, Santino and Vincent took up positions near the entrance, while the rest of us fanned out into the room. Vincent also signaled for Quintilius to order his own men to fall back, which they did in as orderly a fashion as they could manage. When the last line reached the doorway, Vincent gave the signal, and Bordeaux triggered his detonator.

The first explosion sent debris flying from the walls, hurling toward the enemy. Everyone in the room was hit with chunks of the house, and not one man escaped completely unscathed. It provided the window of time the one hundred-odd loyal Praetorians and my team needed to get the hell out.

"Marcus. Gaius," Quintilius bellowed shakily. "Pick up the Caesar and move him over the balcony."

The two men, still disoriented from the explosion, made their way toward Caligula and Wang. Each man grabbed an edge of the stretcher, interested by its superior design over their own versions, picked him up and moved toward the balcony. Quintilius ordered his surviving men to follow, while Vincent, Bordeaux, and Wang were the last ones out. Vincent, the very last over the balcony, ordered Bordeaux to destroy the home. Not even turning to admire his handiwork, he triggered the explosion, burying hundreds of rebel Praetorians in rubble.

Two managed to squeeze through the explosion, leaping over the balcony in an attempt to follow us. Wang spotted them first and put them down with a few bursts of fire from his UMP.

"Feel better?" I asked him.

He cracked his neck. "Playing doctor can be so boring…"

I smiled and patted him on the shoulder while we followed our allies through the dark streets of Rome. The city was unusually quiet for the early hour, only a few before midnight, and while usually the streets were bustling with nocturnal activity, a battle taking place in the home of the emperor would be more than enough to keep me inside as well.

Reaching the walls of Rome, we found a small, unguarded postern gate, and fled the Eternal City under cover of darkness.

***

Our first stop along the way was Caere, a small town four hours' march north. Stationed there were the two cohorts of the emperor's Praetorians on training duty, as Quintilius had mentioned earlier. We only stayed long enough for them to realize the predicament we were all in, and gather up their gear. A half hour later we were on our way, headed north along the *via aurelia*. The ancient road followed the coast, where we hoped to hook up with the nearest legion we could find. Caligula woke up just long enough to mention he had received word that one of his legions was on a training march around the Alps, and had chosen their winter camp in Cisalpine Gaul. With no other options available, we headed there.

The only problem I had working with a legionary force was their pace. On a normal day, a legion could march for five hours and cover around twenty miles of ground. On a forced march, it was closer to thirty miles, and that was with sixty pound packs on their backs. We, on the other hand, unsure as to who might be tailing us and not burdened by heavy packs, did not take any chances. We marched straight through the night, taking an hour long break early the next morning, and covered another fifty miles, with intermittent breaks, before resting to make camp.

By the time we were done digging the square trench around the camp, posting defensive stakes and sprawling out on the open ground, I was beat. Normally, legions traveled with the materials needed to create small cities each and every night, but rushed as we were, we barely had anything. I slept in my gear, and woke up the next morning too tired to even feel my wounds. We broke down what little of the camp we had, pushed on, and finally reached our destination outside of Lucca, just north of the Arnus River, sometime that afternoon.

Everyone was exhausted by the time we reached the legion camp, all except the Praetorians, that is. Had I been fresh out of BUD/S, I would have been fine, but I hadn't been forced to perform anywhere near this level of continuous activity for a long time. I legitimately felt like a lazy fat-ass. As for the Praetorians, they still possessed enough energy to set up defenses and seemed prepared for a lengthy engagement if need be. Approaching the gate, we called for the sentries to allow us access to the camp. They quickly obliged once Caligula had something to say about it.

He'd recovered well from his ordeals, and was the only person on the march lucky enough to enjoy the luxury of being drawn in a cart pulled by horses. He sat up in his stretcher and demanded entry by the power of Julius Caesar himself.

I couldn't help but be awestruck at the Romans' camp. I'd read about them in dozens of books over the years and knew just how efficient camp life was for a legion, but to witness it in person was a sight to see.

In both function and aesthetics, this fort was no different than the camp we had just left; simple in design, but strong in defensive capabilities. However, this one was made for long-term operation. There was a deep ditch, with the dug up dirt piled beyond it to make up the palisade, which had long wooden stakes protruding from it. Then came a large wood and stone wall, complete with thick gates, and as a last line of defense, enough room between the wall and the tents to keep the camp's inhabitants out of arrow range. The camp also boasted gravel-lined roads, armories, a hospital, an altar of worship, and seemed... homier, more lived in, with men bustling about as though it were a city.

It struck me as an odd thing that this camp wasn't built along the Roman frontier, but in Northern Italy, well away from any enemy force, and yet still boasted the same defensive parameters of any frontline bastion. Romans never missed an opportunity to continue their training, and were never caught with their pants down.

Well, almost never.

Each fort was constructed in exactly the same way. They were square, with four gates, one on each side. Cutting horizontally through the camp was the *via principalis*, or principal street. Situated smack dab at the center of that particular road was the *praetorium*, the legion commander's tent. South of his tent came officer's quarters, cavalry and auxiliary tents, tents for the legion's administrators and bureaucrats, men almost as important as the legionnaires themselves, and a miniature forum. North of the *praetorium* came eight blocks of tents, four across and two deep, with small roads dividing them. These were tents meant for the legionnaires, and local allied forces. Entering through the northern gate, the *porta praetoria*, it was a straight shot to the *praetorium*. As we walked, we had the eyes of the legion all over us. They'd all seen Praetorians before, some maybe had attempted to join, but the sight of the rest of us got their attention. Especially Helena.

What really got them riled up, however, was the sight of their emperor laid out on a stretcher, looking healthier than he did a day ago, but still weak.

News of our arrival traveled fast, and even before we reached the *via principalis*, the legion's commander emerged from his tent. A legate by rank, he was easily the highest ranking person in the camp, save Caligula himself.

The legate did not leave the immediate area of his tent, but waited, as any good commander would for us to approach his position instead. But when he noticed Caligula, he ran to meet him. Reaching the emperor's side, the man looked down at his weakened form.

"Caesar," he said. "What has happened? What has befallen you that requires your arrival here?"

Caligula managed to prop himself up on an elbow and offered the man a strong look. "There has been a coup. My uncle, the dog, Claudius," he spat on the ground as he said the name, "has seized power by swaying many of my Praetorians to his cause. I should have put him out to pasture as soon as I became emperor."

That was more interesting information to consider. Clearly there was bad blood between the two, but I couldn't say why.

"Gather your advisors, Legate. We have much to discuss."

"Indeed, Caesar," he said, before looking up at me, having already noticed and ignored our presence, only now indicating in our direction. "Who are these people?"

Caligula smiled. "Pay them no ill will. They are allies, and you would do well to call them friends. We will need them in the days ahead."

***

The *praetorium*, no bigger than a small classroom, was crammed with people. Its sole resident, Legate Lucius Livius Ocella Sulpicius Galba, had not only the longest name I'd ever heard, but was also one of the ugliest men I'd ever seen. He had a bumped nose, a double chin, busy eyebrows, and a receding hairline. Ugly wasn't even the worst adjective one could use to describe him, but his eyes contained an intelligence and determination that demanded respect.

His looks weren't the most intriguing thing about the man, however, and were the last thing on my mind when I realized he was actually Servius Sulpicius Galba, *the* Galba, the one who became the first emperor during the year of four emperors in 69 A.D. after the fall of Nero. I tried to remember what little I had learned about the man from my Intro to Roman History course at Dartmouth.

Born Servius Sulpicius Galba, he took the name Lucius Livius Ocella from his step mother who had raised, cared, and loved him. He didn't officially reclaim his birth name until after he became emperor, as short lived as that had been. He'd been a praetor once before, and had served as consul, and I assumed was taking on another command position now. He was known for his excellent generalship in Gaul, Germany, Africa, and Spain, and I thought I recalled he had become governor of the entire Iberian peninsula later in his life, prior to becoming emperor. I didn't know why he was in northern Italy now, or why there was even a legion stationed in northern Italy for that matter, but I assumed he had a reason.

The only other fact I knew about the man was that when Caligula died, he had been called upon by his friends to make a bid to take over. He declined and had served loyally during Claudius' reign. He seemed well at ease around Caligula now, and it wouldn't surprise me to learn that Caligula had observed him on campaign as a child.

To either side of Caligula, who now rested comfortably in Galba's bed, stood Marcus and Gaius, his dutiful caregivers for the past few days. Continuing clockwise around the room came Marcus Varus, Centurion Quintilius, myself and the rest of the team, and standing near the entrance was a tribune from one of the two Praetorian cohorts from Caere, Marcellus Pullo. Continuing along the other wall from the entrance came Galba's retinue. First came two slave scribes, a junior magistrate, the legion's *primus pilus*, or "first file", who was the first and foremost centurion in the legion and served as the prestigious 1st cohort's 1st century's centurion.

Interestingly, I had always thought *primus pilus* translated as "first spear." I always thought that *pilus* was another derivation of *pilum*, or spear. It wasn't until today that I learned it was a common mistake even in the Roman world.

Who knew?

To round out the group were the *praefectus castrorum*, the camp prefect, and five tribunes, some of whom were used for military use, others as administrators, and one who was appointed directly by the Senate, their eyes and ears in the legion. Lastly, standing by his desk next to the bed in which Caligula rested, was Galba himself, looking very angry, and rightfully so. The story we had just told him was not one that inspired confidence in the loyalty of mankind.

"That diseased rat of a man!" He screamed, pounding his fist on the table. "He isn't fit to lick the shit from Pluto's boots, and to think I once called him a friend. And you!" He continued, pointing an accusing finger in Quintilius' direction. "I suppose none of this is *your* fault. You damned high and lofty Praetorians, with your fancy togas and leisurely detail, with less loyalty than a rabid dog! How is it that you let this happen??"

Caligula answered for him. "Do not blame Centurion Quintilius, my friend. Without his loyal Praetorians, most of whom lie dead at this moment, I would not be here. It is obvious that Claudius has been planning this for months, maybe even before it was decided that I would succeed Tiberius. We are quite lucky. I had planned a trip to my family's island estate on Capri. Had I been there, it would have been far easier for him to seize power, but the unexpected arrival of these individuals delayed that trip," he finished, pointing toward me and my squad mates.

And another piece of the puzzle falls into place. Had we not shown up, Caligula would have gone to Capri and been poisoned there. That would match up with history's record of where and when he got sick. Claudius wouldn't have tried a grand assassination attempt, because all he would have needed to do was let nature take its course, and be appointed emperor himself once news arrived that Caligula had died from a mysterious illness. He never thought that Caligula would actually survive the poisoning, only to return as a total nutjob.

Instead, Caligula had gained newfound allies. Us. Allies who were far more powerful than anything Claudius could ever imagine, and he went ahead with his poisoning plans anyway, this time with a backup plan. He had recruited a small army to do his dirty work for him should the poison plot fail. The mob itself must have been formed around those who felt Claudius was overlooked and slighted when Caligula took over. Its size was probably augmented with people distrustful of us time travelers. There wasn't a soul in the city who didn't know of us, or what we could do. During those runs Helena and I took, we didn't just run into adoring fans, but also shady groups of men who would have stabbed us right then and there if they'd had the chance.

"Ah, yes. These curious looking people," Galba remarked dismissively, sounding just as Caligula had during our first few encounters. "You have explained their exploits, and I have no reason to doubt you, but I find it hard to believe you so easily trust those who won't even tell you the place of their birth."

Caligula chuckled. "You can trust them, Legate. We'll need them. Now, how are we to reclaim my empire?"

Galba sighed. "Claudius couldn't have picked a better time to start a civil war. Africa and the East are quiet, although Jewish rumblings may bring trouble in the future. Germany is quiet as well and I've just received word that an expeditionary force of Britons have run back to their island. I've had word of lightning strikes and a man's head spontaneously exploding as though the gods were involved. Very odd, but it allows us the freedom to focus on Claudius. Now, as for this legion, it was to go north to Germany, to help alleviate the loss of Quinctilius' three legions thirty years ago."

"But why are you here? *Training* a fresh legion?" Caligula asked, dumbfounded. "I recall commissioning the inception of this legion, but you were not assigned its commander. You have lead veteran men in battle throughout Germany and Spain. This is a demotion, and I never would have authorized it had you been ordered."

"I volunteered," Galba replied with a shrug, "and the Senate approved. After the incident in the Teutoburg Forest, I knew I couldn't let the fate of a legion rest on their commander alone. Rome's legions are the finest military forces the world will ever see, but I felt I could make them better. That's why I volunteered to train this legion, to make them the best. I've seen my share of combat, and I'm sure I will see more, but for now I've decided to turn my attention to training."

From what I knew, Galba had been a notorious disciplinarian, and a strict drill master. He would train good legions to replace those lost in the north.

When Publius Quinctilius Varus, no relation to my ancestor, Marcus Varus, at least as far as I knew, had been stationed in Germany in 9 A.D. he was taken by surprise and ambushed by Germanic tribes during what was later known as the Battle of the

Teutoburg Forest. He had been killed and his three legions annihilated. Only a handful of men survived, literally only enough to count on a hand or two, and their trio of standards were stolen, a very embarrassing moment in Roman military history. I'd read theories claiming the loss of those three legions was one of the earliest precursors to Rome's downfall centuries later. An audacious claim, but definitely one worth considering.

"Unfortunately," Galba continued, "I am not finished, and this legion, the *XV Primigenia*, hasn't completed its training yet. It was scheduled to be pressed into service next year, but in my opinion, can be rushed into deployment now. We have a full complement of legionnaires, as well as auxilia, and my command staff is well seasoned. My first file, Maximus Nisus," he pointed toward a stern looking man who nodded in greeting, "served under Tiberius and started his career under Agrippa. We are not lacking experience from them, but the boys are untried. With your two Praetorian cohorts, we can muster around twelve thousand fighting men. If Claudius manages to contact your remaining Praetorian cohorts, he can field around six thousand, along with gods only know how many auxilia and levied troops from Rome itself. It is difficult to say, but we would be hard pressed to take the city even if we had multiple legions under our control. We must plan carefully."

Galba looked around the room to make sure everyone was paying attention before turning to Caligula. "There is also the question of whether or not to involve other legions. I would recommend against it. Should word of a coup spread, a series of civil wars may erupt, and that could end very badly for all of Rome. I suspect Claudius understands this as well and will do nothing until he has eliminated you."

"I approve of your thoughts, Legate," Caligula assured. "What do you suggest we do?"

"Well, sir, as you know, we are nearing the end of the campaigning season. My suggestion is to wait until spring. We train the boys as hard as we can during the winter, and then lay siege to Rome, and hope for the best. That would be our best strategy."

Ah, the armies of the past. Not a war was fought between November and March and any war in progress practically called for an armistice until spring rolled around again.

"I concur, Legate. Make your preparations. We'll try to sneak some information out of Rome in the meantime. But for now, if you will, please make accommodations for my friends here," he said, again, pointing in our direction.

Galba grunted. "Very well. We have a few understaffed officers' tents they can use."

Vincent held up a hand. "We appreciate the offer, sir, but we have our own shelters. Just give us a spot."

Galba grunted. "So they speak Latin. Interesting. Fine. Take some room behind the *praetorium*, next to the forum."

"Thank you."

Caligula laughed. "Galba, old friend, you may want to watch them. If they make camp like they do war, I'm sure you will be most interested."

***

Making our way behind the *praetorium*, Santino, Bordeaux, and I unpacked the small, two man tents we'd added to our assault packs. Night had fallen, and we set up a portable battery powered lantern that lit up the small area where we intended to make camp. Combined with the glow sticks we had hanging from our vests, we had plenty of illumination.

Not to mention a crowd.

The tents were extremely simple in design. The frame was folded in on itself, and was made out of an extremely thin, flexible, and lightweight material, but also extremely durable and water proof. Laying it out, right side up, I pulled on a tab, and immediately backed away. No longer pinned in place, springs connecting the poles together shot out in a choreographed sequence, and within five seconds, a small, black tent materialized out of thin air. Those watching were stunned. I heard snorting coming from the *praetorium*, and looked to see Galba shaking his head before returning inside.

The three of us pounded a few stakes in the ground to secure our tents, before backing away to admire our handiwork. Hands on his hips, rifle still hanging in front of him, Santino shook his head.

"You know, sir," he said, speaking to Vincent, "I've been thinking."

"That would be a first," I jibed.

He ignored me. "Since we're going to be cooped up in these small tents for the entire winter, I was thinking maybe we switch up our swim team pairs. Just to shake things up." He made this last comment while looking at Helena, flicking his eyebrows and nodding toward his tent suggestively.

I punched him in his shoulder with more than just playful force.

"Never mind," he said, rubbing his arm.

"So, sir?" I asked Vincent. "Do you know anything about this particular legion?"

"Actually, I do, but not much." He looked around to make sure there weren't any legionaries around, even though he spoke in English. "Unfortunately, despite it's being named for the goddess Fortuna, this legion's luck doesn't last very long. It spent time on the Rhine and fighting the Britons, but was eventually destroyed in 70 A.D. along with a sister legion."

"Just out of curiosity," I continued. "Since Galba apparently trained this legion, who does it fight for during the 'war of four emperors'?"

"Ironically it sides with Vittelius, and fights directly against Otho *and* Galba. You have to remember that most of these men won't be serving in the legion thirty years from now during that civil war, so even though Galba first raised the legion, there would be little loyalty left to him."

I nodded. That made sense.

"Sir?" Santino queried. "How could you possibly know all of this?"

Vincent looked at Santino blankly. "I've been studying the classics since you were in diapers, son."

Santino shook his head. "And I thought Jacob was a dork."

"Anyway," Vincent said, moving on. "I don't know about the rest of you, but I'm taking a nap." He spoke with the first hint of lightheartedness I'd heard from him since taking command. Santino sighed, realizing he'd have to share the tent with the much older man for the winter.

Knowing my roommate smelled much better than Vincent did, I didn't have any such problems, so I went inside my own tent without comment. It was roomier than it looked from the outside, and I estimated it could fit at least three men about my size comfortably. I figured Helena and I, along with our gear, would fit snugly. Taking off my pack, I placed everything against the left wall, and unraveled my bed roll. It was thin and light, and while warm, I suspected I'd still need to borrow some Roman blankets for the winter.

After laying everything out neatly, I removed my shirt very gently, quickly becoming aware of the extremely large bruises spreading from the left side of my abdomen to my right shoulder, and all along my back. They hadn't hurt during the march and our first night because I'd been too tired to notice them, but I now was beginning to feel them. Combined with my arm, which still hadn't been properly tended to, I was quite a mess.

Helena came in and zipped the tent closed behind her.

Similarly unarming herself, she laid her bedroll down next to mine while I tried to redress my wound. I covered it with a new bandage, and tried to tie it off using my free hand and teeth. Helena noticed my clumsy or inelegant effort and moved close, taking the bandage in her own hands.

"Here," she said softly, "let me do that."

"Sure."

The wound wasn't that deep, but it traversed nearly my entire forearm. The scar would probably last my entire life, but I didn't mind. It would join all the rest.

Helena removed my sloppily arranged bandage and cleaned the wound as best she could. She took meticulous care of my arm, tending to it like a seasoned nurse and worried mother both. After cleaning it, she sprayed it with an antibacterial ointment, smiling at me sweetly when I flinched from the sting, and finally replaced the bandage, wrapping it tightly and securing it firmly.

She seemed satisfied the bandage wouldn't easily come off, so she moved her eyes to the extremely large bruise on my side. She frowned and probed it with a gentle touch. She must have thought it would be soothing, or something, but it was anything but. I winced at the pain and had to jerk myself away from her.

"Sorry," she said gently, moving her hand to my unharmed, but bare chest. "It looks bad."

"Really? Can't be any worse than the last bruise I had," I said sarcastically. In fact I couldn't have been farther from the truth. My entire body felt like it was on fire.

Helena opened her mouth to speak but shut it with exaggerated slowness. It didn't take a genius to know what was on her mind. I laid there in silence as well, trying to figure out how best to broach the subject of our earlier kiss. It would have been far easier had it been as innocent as it seemed, but it wasn't. Emotions had been high, adrenaline and endorphins pumped by our frantic rush to reach Caligula, and while the feelings had felt real enough – the question was how much they meant.

Helena leaned away from me suddenly and crouched on the balls of her feet, her forearms resting on her thighs. "Jacob, about earlier…"

I leaned myself up and waved a hand to cut her off. "It was what it was, Helena."

Her eyebrows narrowed. "I'm not sure how to respond to that."

"I care for you, Helena, I do, and that kiss…" I shuddered in comic relief and she smiled, "but there was a lot of emotions bandying about, brought on by a very stressful argument. I'm not so sure that's the best way to start something more intimate. I don't want to risk our friendship because of our impulsiveness."

She stared at me and sighed, falling backward onto her butt to sit more comfortably. "I understand, Jacob. I suppose I feel the same."

"You do?"

"Don't sound so relieved. I'm sorry I came off so strong, but I meant what I said back there." She paused and reached out to grab my hand. "And I do need you, but I don't want our insecurities to jeopardize what we already have. You're my friend, and that's enough."

I raised an eyebrow at her. "For now?"

She smirked and gazed at me intently. "Perhaps."

I didn't smile, but inwardly I felt good. Here was one of the first mature conversations I'd had in a long time and it was relieving. Our bond of trust had been rebuilt and it felt stronger now, more real. I squeezed her hand reassuringly and let go before lowering myself gently onto my bedroll, my head feeling only slightly better than it had a few minutes ago. While my emotions had been soothed, the physical ailments certainly had not.

Helena laid herself beside me and started to unbutton her pants. She stopped and looked at me. "Close your eyes, Lieutenant."

I smiled and did as I was told, clapping my hands over my eyes for good measure.

"If we're going to be living together, I think we'll have to come up with a few rules."

"Cohabitation rules?" I asked.

"Call it what you like, just keep your hands and eyes to yourself. Okay, you can look now."

I turned, half expecting her to be laying there naked, having just played me a minute ago, but I found her bundled up in her sleeping bag, nothing but her head and arms exposed. It was for the best I suppose.

She looked at me with dreary eyes. "We're going to be okay, right?"

I took a deep breath and looked toward the ceiling. "I really don't know, Helena. We may have changed history by keeping Caligula healthy and sane, but I don't know how much it will change. He may never reclaim the throne, and we'll be targets right alongside him." I took a second to think. "And if we can't get back to Rome, I don't know how we'll be able to find the sphere. I don't even know where to start even if we do find it and I…"

The sounds of soft snores coming from Helena interrupted me. I glanced over to find her completely asleep. It was probably just as well. She didn't need to hear my useless musings on if and how we could get home. I had no idea about anything really, and it wasn't worth speculating at this point. It was best to stay positive. Lord knows life wasn't about to get any easier, and we had to focus on the present. I had no idea when our last day in ancient Rome would come, but it wasn't impossible to foresee it coming soon.

One way or another.

Part Three

IX
Legion

Cisalpine Gaul, Italy
April, 38 A.D.

Life in a Roman legion camp was hardly one of leisure and comfort, or even restful slothfulness for that matter. In fact, life amongst the legions, even during non-campaigning months, was in fact nothing less than Hell on Earth. It was one of hardship, pain, suffering, and plenty of fun things to do. Roman drill masters and tacticians put me through tests and training scenarios that may have even driven my drill instructors back in BUD/S to tears.

Every day it was the same old grind over and over again. The repetition was enough to drive one insane, but of all of us, Helena had it the worst. She was the only woman in the entire camp, and under normal circumstances, wouldn't even have been allowed to enter the gates. Families or other confidants were rarely allowed to travel with the legions while on campaign, and as a result, many men became very lonely, very fast, and Helena had to deal with being an extremely attractive woman surrounded by, basically, very horny men.

There were three incidents before the boys let her into their little club, the first of which occurred the very next morning after we had arrived in camp. One of Galba's junior officers had been giving us a tour of the camp when a legionnaire seated outside his tent cooking breakfast stood up, and spanked Helena on her supple tush. I suppose she could have been asking for it. She'd borrowed a pair of Wang's BDU pants, which because he was just a little guy, were a few sizes too small, and scandalously tight on her. It wasn't until later that I learned she had done this on purpose. She'd anticipated her need to establish dominance over the unruly men, and hoped to incite a reaction exactly like the one she received so she could deal with it quickly.

She wasn't very thrilled when I stepped in and defended her before she could do it herself.

As soon as I witnessed the harassment, I snatched the legionnaires wrist in a quick motion and turned it in a direction it wasn't designed to rotate in. The move forced the man's body to instinctively lean back on his knees. I followed up the hold by kicking the back of his leg, dropping him to the ground. Following him to the ground, I landed on my back, and simultaneously pulled his arm so that his elbow rested against my knee. I could have ended it right there by applying enough pressure and wait for him to tap out, but his action had infuriated me.

So, pausing for only a moment, just long enough to make sure the man knew he had made a very stupid mistake, I pulled on his arm as hard as I could. His elbow bent in the wrong direction, and I heard a loud pop followed by a crack as I nearly broke his elbow in half. The crowd reacted with an understandable gasp of disgust at my results, if not my actions. The man was punished for assaulting a guest of the camp commander, and spent two weeks in the stockade after receiving twenty lashes from his centurion's olive branch, a ceremonial tool meant for inflicting pain and punishment in lackluster or disobedient legionnaires.

Later that night, Helena explained her plan, and though grateful for my help, asked that I let her handle herself next time.

I agreed.

She didn't have to wait long.

Two days later, after Galba was satisfied we had settled into the arduous routine of the camp, he had us perform a demonstration similar to the one we had showed Caligula back in the *Circus Maximus*. The emperor showed nothing but amusement at the general's unwillingness to accept his word, and approved the demonstration.

We shot some armor, blew some holes in the ground, and Helena shot an apple off the rampart near the *porta praetoria* from the gate opposite it. Additionally, since we had plenty of time to spare, Wang demonstrated his self-defense and hand to hand combat techniques. Wang borrowed from Asian forms he had known as a boy, and the Special Forces training he had obtained later to show the Romans many kinds of throws, takedowns, holds, pressure points, and submission moves, the last of which gave me the impression he watched just a bit too much professional wrestling as well.

We all had self-defense training, even Helena despite her accelerated basic training program, and we had also trained with

Wang during our month long lull period after arriving in ancient Rome. When Galba invited our entire squad, Helena included, to help demonstrate and teach these moves to his centurions and decurions, men just below the rank of centurion, one of them decided to get a little frisky.

The maneuver was simple. The decurion Helena was assigned to held a wooden training *pugio*, or dagger, in an inverted grip, and was instructed to jab it downwards toward her chest. Helena began her defensive move by grasping his wrist which held the knife, and followed by ducking under the dagger, putting her body up against his. This was followed by her final move, using her hips to toss him over her. It was martial arts 101, but the decurion had more than the self-defense class on his mind.

Helena was wearing boots, her BDU pants, and a white tank-top, the same as the rest of us. The difference between us and her, of course, was her curvy waistline and large breasts, and just before Helena tossed the decurion, he reached around with his free hand to fondle them. Successful though he was, his fun didn't last long.

To Helena's credit, she was unfazed by her attacker and followed through with her throw as planned. Instead of ending it there, she held onto his wrist, twisting it hard, stunning the man long enough for her to step around his arm, lock her ankles near his neck, and fall next to him, positioning him in a textbook arm bar maneuver. However, unlike in a cage match, she broke his arm, just above the elbow.

The man wailed in pain, clutching his crippled appendage. As he squirmed on the ground, I saw that the break was compound, and part of his radius bone pierced his skin. Helena, calm and collected, got to her feet, stepped around the decurion, reared her right leg back, and kicked him with the force of a freight train right in his groin. Unable to determine which body part hurt more, he continued wailing, but kept switching between straddling his arm and clutching his balls. Satisfied, Helena kicked some dirt on the man and turned to leave.

The decurion couldn't let it go though, and between cries of pain, managed to call Helena a whore, a bitch, and words I hadn't even learned yet. She stopped and returned to the man, who had now given up swearing and was fearfully trying to crawl away. Grabbing him by his broken arm, the pain almost driving him to unconsciousness, Helena pulled his back off the ground, and jabbed her middle three fingers into his throat.

She didn't break his neck, but it took him at least a minute before he could breathe again, and he never uttered another word, or even a pained sound, for a very long time after that.

Finished with her attacker, she turned and came to stand by Santino and me. The gathered crowd was stunned. Legionnaires, auxilia, centurions, tribunes, and even Galba himself stood with mouths agape, having witnessed everything. Passing by the general's position without a word, since her Latin at that point was still rather horrible, she gave him a look which transcended the language barrier, saying little more than, "you'd better hope this never happens again." Nodding in disbelief, Galba turned, and left the area. Afterward, no man in the camp dared even touch Helena, and those who had to spar with her were laughably nervous.

Except for one stubborn dumbass.

By the end of the second week, most of the legionnaires looked at her with nothing but respect and friendliness, and offered her the same jibes, jokes, and taunts they would any other man in the camp. The third incident, however, happened at the beginning of the third week. Helena and I made our way to visit Gaius and Marcus when along the way, a nearby legionnaire offered Helena a wolf whistle. Without pausing, she thrust her palm upwards into the man's nose, breaking it. The man got off the easiest of the three, and he proved to be the last who treated Helena like an object of interest. She was a legionnaire now, and while she still received jokes for being a female over the months, her sharp wit and evil eye always made sure she had the last laugh.

She slowly became a kind of mascot for the legion. The combination of her fighting prowess and physical beauty was very rare in the Roman world, and many legionnaires claimed she was Minerva personified in human form. Minerva was, among many things, the beautiful goddess of war and warriors, so the stretch didn't seem that unbelievable, even to my modern eyes. As the weeks went on, the men quickly realized they would not get far lusting over her, but they fell in love with her all the same, bestowing her with the title *Mater Legionis*, Mother of the Legion.

They even crafted a special suit of legionary armor specifically for her. Tailored to fit her frame, impressive, since no measurements were taken, she'd slipped into a red linen skirt and wool shirt, and draped the tight fitting and battle ready *lorica segmentata* armor over her head, which was custom molded to fit her comfortably around her chest. She attached a standard legionnaire belt, a scarlet cape, and pulled on her likewise newly fashioned *caligae*.

Boots laced and legs flashing, Helena took a stroll through the camp.

This time, many wolf whistles were offered, but Helena laughed off each of them, knowing they were offered only in jest, and directed more toward the armor than herself. She happily thanked the trio of men who had taken the time to remold the armor to fit her feminine curves, and even offered the lead designer and forger a kiss on the cheek in gratitude. The designer rubbed his face, and had the long, lost look of a man who had just fallen in love. His fellow men playfully shoved him, unhappy they weren't equally thanked, shaking him from his fantasy. Other men, who had observed the event, offered her swords, daggers, helmets, and other knickknacks. Helena joyfully ignored them.

As for the rest of us, fitting in was as simple as making sure we didn't do anything too stupid. We'd spent the time recounting war stories – our own of particular interest to the legionnaires, and theirs to me – gambling, and training.

Training defined the Roman military, as did more training, and even more training after that. While the Roman's benefited from our personal defense lessons, they didn't spend the rest of their days lounging either, and neither did we. We learned enough to hold our own in combat, but we'd never cut it as front line soldiers in the legions. After two months of hard training, other duties took us elsewhere. We spent much of that time analyzing our strategy for the upcoming campaign to retake Rome.

Normal legionnaire training took around six months, and every day of it started off with a run. Afterward came sword training, where centurions taught us the ins and outs of Roman swordsmanship. Romans fought with the tips of their swords, always stabbing, and never slashing. A legion fought like a machine, blocking and stabbing in choreographed sequence. It wasn't flashy or destined for accuracy in Hollywood, but it was effective, as many defeated barbarians could attest to. I knew the basics, and understood why they were so effective, but the others did not. One time, when Santino tried to slash down at his training partner with his wooden training sword, a centurion smacked him with his olive branch, just as he would have with any of his other trainees. Santino had not been happy, but had learned his lesson.

We also learned the fine art of spear casting, and even though I had no intention of trading in my rifle for a *pilum*, I figured it was still a good skill to learn. More intense training came in swordplay, how to hide behind our shields and rely on the person next to us for additional protection, as well as how to snap quick attacks with as little risk as possible. Legions fought as units, and any individual heroics were frowned up. Their strength relied on their discipline, maneuverability, and coordination, all philosophies drilled into us harder than pretty much anything I'd ever experienced before.

The modern military could take a page out of the Roman army's training playbook. As a result of the constant pace of physical and weapons drills, along with long distance runs, those of us who needed to shed a few pounds did so easily. Another thing we learned quickly was how to dig a mean ditch. Along with the digging came knowledge about Roman camp fortifications, how they were erected, and what we needed to do to contribute. If we had to move and build a new camp, the Romans made sure everybody could pitch in and lend a hand.

As for the rest of our wayward companions who had accompanied us the night we fled Rome, Caligula took to running a legion camp very efficiently, and Galba happily relinquished full control to his emperor. Fully recovered within a week, Caligula was seen walking amongst the troops, and training daily with the camp's officers.

The surviving Praetorians from the bloody battle in his home were commended, and as a group, were elevated to a newly created position within the Praetorian rank. The one hundred and five survivors, including Quintilius, who was promoted to the rank *primus pilus*, formed a new sect known as the Praetorian Sacred Band. The name was an homage to the Sacred Band of Thebes, a personal bodyguard unit to Theban kings that contained one hundred and fifty pairs of lovers. During one battle against the hoplites of Sparta, they defeated a foe which greatly outnumbered them, but were eventually slaughtered by Philip II of Macedon, whose victory removed the Greek city-states authority over the land.

Unlike their Greek counterpart, the Praetorians were not required to partake in homosexual activity and create sexual pairs, but the number of men was set permanently at three hundred.

Many of the survivors were promoted a rank or two, and they recruited the remaining men needed from the two Praetorian cohorts that had joined us in Caere, choosing only those they deemed feverously loyal. Once merged, the Sacred Band became Caligula's flagship unit, and newly promoted Quintilius became the highest ranking centurion in the camp, even higher than Maximus Nisus, the legion's own *primus pilus*. Nisus took Quintilius' promotion in stride, aware that Praetorians were rewarded with special privileges and honors. Quintilius took the promotion graciously and professionally, and even though I knew he was booming with pride and happiness, he never let on that he wasn't doing anything but his duty.

Gaius and Marcus were also promoted. Originally holding the rank of optio, a centurion's second in command, they were not only promoted to the centurion ranks, but also accelerated to the rank of *pilus prior*, or "superior file," the second highest ranking centurion in a legion.

A Roman legion was simplistic in design, but could become frustratingly confusing when it came to the specifics of the chain of command, and the finer details of its construction. A legion, comprised of around six thousand men, was broken into ten cohorts, containing slightly less than six hundred men each, which were broken into centuries. Six thousand was a rounded up number, most legions containing only slightly more than fifty two hundred front line soldiers, but when combined with officers, administrators, and other staff, the number was closer to six.

The breakdown of centuries got pretty confusing, but each cohort had six centuries, of about eighty fighting men each. Things got even more confusing, as the first centuries of each cohort was doubled in size, and depending on what cohort you were in granted you superiority, and certain centurions of equal rank still had more power than others...

It didn't really matter. The system confused even me.

The end result was Quintilius was in complete command of the Sacred Band, his orders coming directly from Caligula, and Gaius and Marcus each commanded one half of the three hundred man unit. It was a large honor for the two young men I had come to call friends, but they took their new posts like any seasoned soldier would. Caligula had no patience for tribunes in his Sacred Band, knowing that centurions were the real leaders on the battlefield.

And so things went.

Training and teaching and training and learning and training, we were quickly becoming well versed in military history, legion tactics and strategy, sword handling, horse riding, spear casting, and ditch digging. While not officially folded into the legion's command structure, we were treated as mercenaries may have been, albeit ones who weren't paid, and Vincent was invited to attend all command staff meetings. He ordered me to attend as well, unofficially promoting me as his second in command, which likewise garnered me no additional pay. Flattered, I accepted, and spent another large chunk of my time engaged in strategizing for the upcoming campaign against Claudius.

To keep me even busier, it was about the time when the first snow started to fall, in mid-December, that the Romans assigned us watch shifts to participate in during the course of the day. Each of us was assigned a different shift, which were rotated biweekly. My first shift landed me patrolling the ramparts between midnight and six in the morning. By the grace of God, our gear had managed to find its way to our camp a few weeks after our arrival, carried by a few loyal slaves of Caligula's, and was greatly appreciated by us all.

We found cold weather gear in the supplies, which made those long windy nights much more bearable. I didn't know how the Romans didn't freeze to death, but they endured, and somehow remained healthy. It honestly seemed like a miracle.

My watch shift rarely synced up with Helena's so we rarely had time to speak with one another. I missed her during that time. The sparks we'd felt months earlier had yet to rekindle, but we cherished the time we spent together nonetheless. It wasn't until late January that we were lucky enough to land watch shifts that kept both of our nights free, and while many of them were spent talking about our pasts, most revolved around current affairs and our lives in the Roman world.

We always had plenty to talk about. Over the past four months, I had started a process of lumping more and more responsibility for our predicament on my shoulders. My actual responsibility notwithstanding, I took it upon myself, and only myself, to try to understand our situation and find a way to get home. And even though it was difficult with little reference, I wracked my brain over the topic day and night. Neither Varus nor Caligula had thought to bring the orb or manuscripts with them, so all I could do was to think on the subject, something I did in excess.

The problem was that there wasn't anyone for me to talk to. Vincent knew the classics, but time travel was a mystery to him. Varus knew about the orb, but not how it was related to time travel. Santino had watched a lot of movies in his day, but was hardly the guy to go to for an existential debate about anything. Everyone else fell into one category or another, and it forced a sense of ownership of the problem onto no one but me. This was compounded by my new leadership position within the group when Vincent ordered me to attend Galba's meetings. Even there, he took a backseat during the proceedings to let my more – eclectic – mind cogitate on the issues. Vincent himself had even become a major internal debate because of those actions. I'd yet to understand a single decision he'd made in the half year we'd been stuck here. It all culminated in making my life extremely stressful, and Helena knew it.

"What's wrong?" She asked quietly one night, feeling something was amiss from across the tent.

"Hmm? Oh. It's nothing," I replied, likewise keeping my voice to a whisper.

She shifted onto her side to see me more clearly. "Come on, Jacob. I know you better than that by now. You have that far off look again. The one that says you're trying to wrap your head around something so complex that no matter how hard you try, you know you'll never figure it out. You know, like Santino when he's trying to figure out which boot goes on which foot."

I chuckled. "You always know what to say to cheer a guy up."

"I know," she said playfully. "So what's wrong?"

I sighed. "I don't know. I hate to sound like a broken record here, but I just can't shake the feeling that somehow we're here for a reason, and I don't mean just in this camp, but in Rome, in 38 A.D. Based on the decisions Vincent's made since we arrived here I can't help but think this whole thing is a setup. Somehow he knew we'd get sent here, and he knew that sphere would do something crazy, and now he's on some kind of mission he hasn't filled the rest of us in on. Except, everything we've done since we've been here has been a mistake, and as a result, we've totally fucked everything up."

"Are you sure you even deserve an answer?"

My eyebrows furrowed. "Of course I do. It's my fault we're here to begin with and I deserve to know everything I can to try and figure out a way home."

"Maybe that's not really you're responsibility either," Helena insisted.

"Not my… How can you say that? If not me, then who?"

She sighed and looked away. "If you want my advice, then I say you should forget about it, but if it means that much to you, talk to Vincent. Get him to talk to you."

"I guess. To be honest, I've been hoping to avoid that conversation, or to have him come out to us on his own." I took a breath and thought. She had a point that the longer I let this fester, the worse it was going to get. I had to clear my own conscience and there was only one way to do that.

"I'll talk to him."

***

If Helena had been right about one thing, it wasn't that talking to Vincent would make me feel better, but that by talking to him I would at least find the truth. I wished I'd never even tried.

A few mornings after we had talked, I went looking for Vincent. I found him eating breakfast with a number of centurions, talking and laughing with his fellow career military men. I loitered around the area while I waited for him to finish his breakfast, before approaching and asking politely if we could talk. He excused himself from his buddies, and took a walk around the camp with me.

We spent the first two laps discussing camp gossip, which believe it or not, was extensive, the weeks itinerary, and the weather, everything but what I had intended to confront him with. He noticed I was keeping something back, and demanded I just come out with what was bothering me.

So I did.

"Sir. Prior to our arrival here in Rome, did you, or any of your superiors, have any preconceived notions or intelligence regarding the methods, means, or motives behind how we got here?" I'd practiced the line over and over in my head for months, but I'd never had the guts to ask. I wasn't sure if I feared a reprimand or the truth more.

Vincent continued walking around the camp, thinking deeply before answering my question. "Yes."

I snorted out a laugh. Of course he did. There were too many plot holes in this story for him not to have.

"So, are you going to tell me, or am I going to end up with a horse's head in my bedroll tomorrow morning?"

"I'm not going to kill you, Jacob. You have a right to know." He sighed, and I felt frustration flowing off of him. "It wasn't supposed to happen the way it did. We had no idea things would turn out like this."

"Maybe you should start at the beginning."

He took a deep breath before continuing. "Six years ago, in 2015, papal historians were conducting routine research in the Vatican archives when they came across a document which spoke of a means to change the past. From what I was told, and from what I've learned here, I assume the document was the very same one you and Varus had discussed, or at least a copy. I assume so because the historians indicated it was written in a very old language, Etruscan they guessed, which proved nearly impossible to translate. However, it had numerous notes, scribblings and translation attempts scrawled all over it, as well as on attached notes. I assume the document you saw had no such writing?"

"No, sir. It didn't."

"You see? I've been learning from your little lectures. The notes must have been written sometime between now and when we found the sphere, as more and more people attempted to unlock its secrets, before it somehow wound up in our archives, lost and forgotten. Anyway, the few discernible facts historians pulled from the notes were about a blue sphere. At first, we thought nothing of it, until a news report surfaced in 2016 concerning the Museum of Egyptian Antiquities break-in. The one in Cairo."

"I remember reading about that," I replied, vaguely recalling the morning I read about it on my news feed. "Apparently nothing of value was stolen, except for two items, neither related in any way to the other. They never released what those artifacts were."

"That's probably because they thought their importance wasn't significant. However, we quickly learned that one of those artifacts was actually our lost blue sphere."

"Really?" I asked. "The plot thickens."

Vincent ignored my sarcasm. "From the security footage we knew the robbery was committed by known terrorists. Most were unrecognizable nobodies, but there was one the CIA identified for us. Abdullah."

Now things were getting interesting. "So, let me get this straight," I said, hoping I hadn't missed anything. "Your researchers recovered evidence of an ancient time machine, which just happened to be residing, inconspicuously, in an Egyptian museum, only to have said museum broken into by Islamic extremists and the sphere stolen? Then, in your infinite wisdom, you sent out a team to recover the sphere, hoping to utilize its abilities for yourself, and somehow magically make the world a better place?"

"You make it sound almost... wrong, but to answer your question, no, that was not actually the plan. Did you or Varus understand the part about how the sphere affects those who spend too much time around it?"

I thought about it. "Actually... no, that didn't come up."

Vincent huffed. "Well, our historians learned that there were some who, when in direct and constant contact with the sphere, developed interesting symptoms revolving around intense paranoia, Tourette Syndrome, dementia. These people were borderline insane, and prone to random acts of physical violence. Others who came into contact with it showed no affects at all. Sound familiar?"

I didn't flinch at his paternal tone. "No."

"I thought so. That information was in the notes. Now, think for a second. Intelligence agencies reported Abdullah as a rational man prior to the attack on the Vatican, a man low on their priority list because he was never pegged as one who would actually do anything crazy. But what does he do a year later after the museum robbery? He causes one of the most atrocious acts of terrorism the world has ever seen. And remember the condition we found him in? He was crazy. By the way, I want to add something to your ever-expanding theory on time travel."

I nodded, feeling excited, rather than annoyed.

"In our history, when nothing happened, you said the ball was packed up and lost to history, right?"

"It's a possibility, yes," I answered.

"'A possibility'?" He repeated with a smirk. "Well, here's my theory: what if it sat on Caligula's nightstand for months, or even years, *before* it was lost?"

I stopped dead in my tracks. I couldn't believe what he was saying, because it made perfect sense. The sphere *is* a part of our history, and may have indeed become a trinket of Caligula's when it seemed to serve no purpose. If its negative side effects were true, it would definitely explain how Caligula really slipped toward madness, as well as how it became worse and worse over his short reign.

"I must say, sir, your theory is compelling. If you're right, then I think it's especially important to find out where the sphere is now. Actually," I corrected, "we need to find out where both of them are."

"I know. I've been thinking about that as well, but I have no idea where they could be. Hopefully, they're locked away in a vault somewhere back in Rome."

I considered that for a moment. I knew it wouldn't be that easy. When we found them, we needed to destroy them. Even if we could find a way for them to return us to our original place on the timeline, home might not be how we remembered it anymore. We'd need to fix that first, too.

"You still haven't answered my question as to your motives behind us arriving here," I reminded him, not letting him off that easy.

Vincent stopped, and sat down on a large stone near the *porta decumana*, while I continued to stand near him. I looked up at the rampart and saw Helena standing on the platform, performing her guard duties. She noticed us beneath her and raised a questioning hand. I waved her off and turned back to Vincent who, meanwhile, had picked up a stick and started drawing lines in the dirt like an eight year old.

He took another long breath before continuing. "We weren't supposed to end up in ancient Rome," he said shaking his head distractedly as he admired his sand drawings. "The Pope hoped to bring the sphere back and study it, and maybe utilize it to help, but only if it could have been done safely, in a controlled way. The

Pope's first team was commissioned to look for the sphere. It had been unsuccessful so far, which is why our second team was created, to help in that search, while simultaneously eliminating terrorist threats."

I frowned. "Was McDougal in on it?"

"Of course. He was the one who came up with the plan to provide additional supplies for teams who had a direct lead on the sphere. He knew that anything could happen when dealing with something unknown, and he wanted us ready for anything. That's why we were given the supply cache. Just in case."

I looked at him suspiciously. "What about me?"

Vincent must have known I'd ask about that because he didn't hesitate. "We had no idea you would be the key to getting us here. Honestly, we didn't, but you were chosen for reasons other than the ones you were told. We knew the document was written in Etruscan, so chances were it had something to do with antiquity. We knew you were studying the classics before enlisting in the military, and thought it would be a good idea to recruit you. You'd be surprised to learn there aren't very many military men with the eclectic educational background that you have. I guess we got lucky, but I was just as surprised as you were when we ended up beneath that temple." He paused for a second. "There's... more."

I waited expectantly, folding my arms across my chest.

Vincent continued. "We're under orders to do all that we can to aid the regime in power, to help maintain peace and stability in whatever region we find ourselves in, for as long as possible." He paused again. "I was ordered to get involved. To... tweak things. Make them better. When we arrived here, I thought our luck couldn't have been better. Caligula showed such promise."

I threw my hands in the air, anger brewing deep inside my chest, and started walking in a small circle. "You can't be fucking serious! What about the church? Christianity? The Pope, for God's sakes?! What about our goddamned timeline?! Didn't you think about Charlemagne, Muhammad, Genghis Khan, King Henry VIII, Admiral Yamamoto... I dunno... Mary Fucking Steenburgen!?! Didn't you for one second think you might change all that?"

"Think about it, Jacob," he replied calmly, glancing around at the suspicious looks legionnaires had turned after my outburst. "Jesus has already died and risen. Most of our institution's background is just starting to establish itself as we speak, but in the East. No matter what we do here, things won't slow down over there. And think about Caligula. Does he seem like the kind of man who would persecute and destroy a population based on their faith like Nero?"

I thought about that. Caligula seemed far from that kind of man. He had the confidence and arrogance of any Caesar, but he was compassionate, caring, intelligent, and furthermore, a leader. He would have no problem with Christians.

I still couldn't believe what I was hearing. How could one so willingly try to change the past? The ramifications were unfathomable. Just because we thought we were doing the right thing didn't mean things would turn out for the better. Things could turn out worse. We had no idea which.

I turned my back on Vincent, put my hands on my hips, and looked at the ground. This was stupid. We were messing with shit no man had the right to mess with. We had no right to screw with the lives of all those who lived between 37 and 2021 A.D. I looked up at the rampart to see Helena leaning over the rail, her eyebrows furrowed in concern.

I turned back to Vincent. "I can't believe this. I really can't. So what do you suggest we do now?"

"Now? We continue what we're doing. We help Caligula retain his throne, and protect him as long as we can. Maybe help push him in the right direction. I understand Claudius was a far better emperor than Caligula had been in our original time, but it's obvious something has gone wrong with him, so we need to preserve Caligula. Here's another question I want you to think about. What else did Praetorians do besides protect their emperor, at least after Augustus?"

What else did they do? Was that a trick question? The only other thing I could think of was that they actually assassinated their emperors when they weren't protecting them. What did that have to do with –

Ah.

"They had a very influential say in who became the next emperor," I answered.

"Right. Damage to their loyalty has already been done during Tiberius' reign, but we know that the Praetorians were completely loyal to Augustus. What if they became the stalwart protectors they were designed to be once again? We may be dealing with a Praetorian rebellion here, but if Caligula is able to reestablish control, I have to assume there will be a cleansing of the guard."

"So, your plan is to stop the precedent of Praetorians controlling the ascendancy of the emperors? Make them into a dedicated bodyguard unit who merely comply, do their duty, and follow orders?"

"I think that would have an interesting effect on history. We're already seeing evidence that it could be possible with Caligula's Sacred Band. Three hundred loyal men can go a long way for an emperor."

That they could. The historian inside me was screaming right now. One side told me to preserve our history, and that if we interfered with it, we'd be no better than those men who tweaked what they recorded just because no one could stop them. That voice was too little too late, though, because the other voice was enthusiastically interested in how things could now turn out. Maybe I'd even have great epics written, devoted to my life's endeavors. They might even make me a god. It worked for Julius Caesar after all.

"So?" Vincent asked, interrupting my thoughts. "What do you think we should do now?"

What would I do?

I knew we couldn't change what we'd already done. As far as I knew, there wasn't any way I could change the past, as stupidly ironic as that sounds, so I might as well make the best of it.

I sighed. "I really wish you would have come to me earlier. We need to work on setting things straight, not changing things for what we perceive may be for the better."

Vincent stood up, and placed both hands on my shoulders, a gesture a father would offer his son. "You're a good officer, Hunter. Like McDougal said, you are quite the Renaissance man, intelligent, moral, and not unable to step back and make rational decisions, not unlike our friend, Caligula. I'm proud to have had this opportunity to serve with you."

He held out his hand, which I very slowly grasped.

"Thanks, I guess. I still can't believe this and I'm sure as shit not happy about it, but it is what it is." A cluster fuck, basically. "So, what should I tell the others?"

"Tell them what you will, if you feel they truly want to know. I leave it in your hands now. I know you'll make the right decision.

Later that night, after my watch was up, I slipped into the tent I shared with Helena, who was already in her sleeping bag. She was fast asleep, so I made every effort not to wake her, but when my head hit the pillow, her eyes fluttered open.

"I saw you talking with Vincent today," she said, her head facing away from me. "Seemed pretty intense. Did you find the answers you were looking for?"

"Yes." I couldn't think of anything else to say.

"Anything I should know about?"

I thought about that for a second. She deserved to know, as did the rest of the guys, but would their knowing really change anything? They'd just have the same problem I did, with the worst case scenario being it would undermine Vincent's authority. Even though I hardly felt it would come to that, we needed to stick together, no matter what.

"If I told you, would it change how you felt about anything?"

"No," she whispered, half asleep. "Like I said when we first arrived here, we have to worry about the here and the now. There's no way to change what was done, and even if there was the chance things might have turned out differently, there's no point dwelling on it. We just have to make the best of it."

"You're a woman after my own heart," I joked, but I wasn't sure if she cracked a smile or not. "I'll tell you one thing though: you are right. There is no way to change what happened, but I don't think making the best of it is what we need to do."

"Then what?"

I turned away from her and closed my eyes. "I don't know, but I'm going to find out."

***

Having spoken with Vincent, there was nothing else to look forward to but the upcoming months, which just about brought me up to the here and now: freezing my ass off on yet another morning watch.

Since that night after my talk with Vincent, Helena and I hadn't again had a free night together, as our watch schedules had kept us separated during that time. These days, by the time my shift was finished, it was time to go to sleep, and when I woke up, she was just finishing her shift, and was ready for bed herself. It got pretty lonely at times, but at least as I sat here on the *porta decumana* rampart, freezing my ass off at three in the morning, I had Santino to keep me company.

"Come on, Jacob. Don't lie to me. I know what's going on in that tent of yours."

"Santino, you of all people should know that I'd never tell you anything even if we were doing what say we're doing."

"That's not an answer, my friend."

"What makes you think you deserve one?"

"Come on!" He said insistently. "I'm freezing my balls off here. Give me something. Anything."

I shook my head. "You're helpless. And an asshole. We need to find you a woman when we get back to Rome."

"We'd better!" He exclaimed with a shake of his head. "A man can only go so long before going crazy. I don't know how you've done it since the nurse."

I frowned. It was still a bad memory.

"Sorry. Didn't mean to reopen old wounds."

"Don't worry about it," I assured.

Santino turned and leaned against the railing to face the wilderness. "It's hard not to."

I moved to stand against the railing as well, but leaned so that I could face my friend. "Why do you say that?"

He smacked the railing. "Jacob, you have a wonderful and beautiful woman sitting in your tent every night! And then the two of you prance about the camp all day like you hardly know each other, but we can all see it." He paused. "We can see a lot of things."

"We're just friends, John."

He huffed. "You're wasting your time if you ask me."

"Well no one asked you."

He snapped his head around and stared at me intently. "You shouldn't have to. Guys like us don't find a girl like her every day. You've been lucky enough to meet two that I know of, and you fucked up the first one. All I'm saying is that you'd better not let it happen again."

I turned away from my friend and looked out over our wall, past the ditch and wooden stakes, and into the clearing, the tree line far off in the distance. He was right. I'd never find another one like her. I didn't know why, but somehow that thought didn't comfort me.

***

Days later, I leaned up off my bedroll after a sleepless night, resting my arms on my knees, and hanging my head between them. I felt horrible, and I had no idea why, but I suspected it had something to do with that beef patty MRE I'd had for dinner last night. Lifting my head, and rubbing my hand over my face and through my hair, which was getting much longer than I'd ever grown it, I looked over at the empty spot where Helena normally slept.

I sighed. Maybe I was just getting lonely since I never seemed to see her these days.

"Ah, get up, Jacob," I said to no one in particular. "Today's too big a day for this shit."

I got to my feet, pulled off my shirt and looked around for a fresh one. Once I found one I thought was mostly clean, I snatched up my web belt, which held my tactical thigh holster holding my pistol and a few extra mags, and strapped it around my waist. My morning ritual completed, I unzipped the tent, stepped out into the frigid weather, and headed toward a trough of water. Normally used as the legion horses' drinking water, I dunked my head as deep as I could into the freezing liquid, a scene I'd seen a dozen times in Wild West movies. Whipping my head out of the icy cold bath just as quickly as I had dunked it, I sent a stream of water flying behind me, accidentally splashing Bordeaux as he walked toward his tent.

I stood and dried myself off as well as I could before I turned to see Bordeaux still standing there, a wet scowl on his face.

"Oh, sorry, Jeanne. Didn't see you there."

He walked up to me angrily, and snatched my dry shirt from my shoulder to dry his face with, then he shoved a loaf of Roman bread into my hand, fresh off the fire. It was tough and chewy, thanks to the gluten-rich wheat they used, but it offered enough sustenance to be the backbone of a legionnaire's diet, which was good enough for me.

"You all right, Jacob?" He asked with a mouthful of bread. "Today's a big day."

"I'm fine," I said, taking a bite of my own and mumbling around the food, "jus dinnt sweep swell."

He looked at me pathetically. "Well, get yourself cleaned up. We're expected in Galba's tent in a few minutes."

"Okay," I finished after gulping down my meal.

With that, I turned and headed back to my tent. I found the zipper and gave it a pull, only to find it stuck and refusing to budge. Gripping it with both hands, I tugged harder, only to have it stubbornly remain jammed. I started yanking furiously on the zipper. Never a morning person, my annoyance quickly turned to rage, and I couldn't stop myself from kicking the tent, unplanting one of the stakes in my tirade. Wang, emerging from his own tent, noticed my predicament, and came over to help, a steaming cup of tea in his hand.

"Here, Hunter. Let me try."

I conceded the zipper, throwing my hands up in frustration, and backed away.

Wang gripped the zipper lightly, gave it a yank to further close it before sending it on its way to open the flap, which it did easily.

He turned to look at me, taking a sip from the steaming mug. "You all right, Jacob? Today's…"

"…a big day. Right. I got it." I tried to breathe through my nose, hold it, and exhale through my mouth, an old Zen calming technique. "Thanks for your help. I'll see you in the *praetorium*."

He pulled his cup from his mouth to speak, but just as quickly replaced it to take another sip. The look on his face indicated he wanted to say more, but he knew how I was in the mornings. Shrugging, he turned toward the *praetorium* without another word.

Entering my tent, I threw off my web belt in anger, and tried to find a shirt to wear.

Could this day get any worse?

Finding a shirt that I assumed was clean, I slipped it on, replaced my web belt, and retrieved a fleece jacket I had found in our supplies. It was festooned with pockets, and could be worn in freezing temperatures, as well as in moderately cool days. It was even colored in olive drab. My favorite color, a good choice for any military man. Good camouflage.

As I left my tent, I closed the zipper with excessive carefulness, hoping to avoid any further complications. Checking my watch, I realized I only had a minute before I was late. Luckily, the *praetorium* was only a twenty step jog away. When I entered I was annoyingly rewarded with the fact I was the last to arrive.

My always punctual mother would have been disappointed.

At the center of the tent were two large tables, with two large maps displayed on top. The first was a rudimentary topographical map of the Italian peninsula, and rudimentary was putting it nicely. It was a far cry from the satellite imagery we used in our own time, but it would do. The map was only mostly identifiable, with the general shape of the country present, along with Sicily, Corsica, Sardinia, and plenty of landmarks, rivers, mountain ranges, and cities, most of which were close enough to where they were supposed to be.

The second map was a simple diagram of the city of Rome. It wasn't as detailed as the one I had framed and hanging on my wall back home, a diagram I'd hoped to use in my classroom once upon a time, but even so, it showed the city's largest buildings, walls, and gates accurately.

Arrayed around the tables were the usual suspects: Caligula, Galba, his *primus pilus* Maximus Nisus, Quintilius, Gaius, Marcus, Varus, three of the legion's tribunes, and a few slaves and freedmen administrators.

Santino and Wang stood next to each other, mugs of steaming liquid in their hands, probably debating their preferences for either coffee or tea again. By yet another grace of God, MREs included ground coffee, and we also found tea bags in the cargo as well. Teas weren't new in Rome, but coffee beans were indigenous to the Americas, resulting in some very jealous Romans. Centurion Nisus, in fact, had grown addicted to the stuff after his first taste, enamored by its caffeine content like so many college students. He and I had worked out a deal that sent my MRE coffee bean packages his way, for a portion of his salted pork rations. I had to side with the Brits on this one, as I had never really enjoyed coffee, and the idea of fire roasted bacon made me very happy.

Bordeaux and Vincent were next to the two debaters, while Helena stood around the corner, quietly chatting with Varus. She'd struck up a friendship with him just as I had, and had learned that the scholar was in fact married and expecting his first child. When she told me the news, I immediately wondered if that child was another link in the possible genetic chain that connected the two of us.

Hoping to glide in under the radar, I quietly took an open spot around the table, between Santino and Vincent, opposite Galba and Caligula, and waited for the briefing to begin. Caligula and Galba had been conversing quietly prior to my arrival, and continued after I had taken my place at the table, completely ignoring my entrance.

Score.

I glanced at Helena and she gave me a concerned look, which I answered with a slight shake of my head.

Focusing on the maps, I only had to wait a few seconds before Caligula asked for attention.

"As you all know," he started, raising his hand for silence, "we have received very little intelligence over the winter concerning Claudius and his hold on Rome. What we have learned, as Galba so astutely predicted, is that Claudius has not contacted any other legion to support his cause. We have to assume that he realizes his hold on power is only as strong as his ability to keep me from reclaiming it. Once I'm eliminated, no one will ask any questions as to his legitimacy, but until then, he's vulnerable."

He paused, looking each of us in the eye in turn.

"That said, I also face a problem. We, as well, cannot seek help. If we did, my own hold on power may slip, and we could see a series of attempted coups and power struggles for years to come. That would not be in the best interest of my empire. No. The best thing we can do is end this smoothly, quickly, and as quietly as possible."

"Exactly what will happen when this rebellion comes to an end?" Varus asked, thinking beyond the immediate military situation. "Even after we retake Rome, the news of Claudius' betrayal will travel like a wild fire, and we may find recalcitrant members of the empire also wishing to play their own hands. The Germans are still beating their war drums since their victories thirty years ago and the Jews in the East, especially, have been grumbling for years. A power struggle in Rome may incite them to take up arms against our legions stationed in Judea."

Nisus made a dismissive noise. "You're point, Varus? Our Eastern legions would crush any insurrection in a matter of months."

Some of the military men pounded their fists on the table in agreement. It wasn't a surprise they didn't think much of their Jewish protectorates in the East, since they hadn't given much cause for concern in the past. I knew, however, that not too far in the future, a Jewish rebellion would take place and last for many bloody years.

"Both Varus and Nisus make valid points," Galba interjected, raising his hands for silence among his men. "Our legions would have no problem dealing with open rebellion anywhere in the empire, but Varus' point that we need to contain the news is valid as well. There is no way to stop those who have traveled from Rome since we left, but once we retake the city, we can control the spreading of any new."

Caligula nodded. "Galba is correct. God's willing, once we retake Rome and depose Claudius, we will quickly restore order and make it appear as though nothing happened. Remember, news travels slowly during the winter months. Any persons returning to Rome, or traveling to Rome solely on the basis of determining whether or not Claudius staged a coup, will arrive to find nothing of the sort." Caligula paused, and looked as serious as I had ever seen him. "A seamless restoration of power is required. We can ill afford any doubt in the minds of patricians, equestrians, or plebeians alike. I am Caesar, not Claudius, and any who wish to challenge that claim will be dealt with."

The men, and one woman, around the room nodded, myself included. Even if I hadn't already known he was Rome's true emperor, I wouldn't have doubted it now. He spoke with such conviction and purpose, it was easy to see him as the leader of the known world, and not some mere mortal like the rest of us.

He looked around the tent again, seeing the hardened but confident expressions each person present had on their faces, and nodded. "With that, I turn this briefing over to the legate."

Galba cleared his throat.

"The problem we face is that of besieging a city with minimal forces." He indicated to the map of Rome with his hands. "The last few incidents of Roman military expeditions conquering Rome were the result of those in power fleeing and leaving the gates open behind them. We will not have that luxury. Additionally, a lasting artillery barrage is out of the question. We are not going to destroy half of Rome to simply knock down a few walls. That said, while our advantages are few, I believe they may be enough to retake the city.

"What we lack in experienced troops, we make up for in numbers. My legion and auxilia are at full strength, and alone consists of more men than the Praetorian contingent loyal to Claudius. Additionally, our auxilia are of German stock, men always itching for a fight. In my career I've never seen fiercer or wilder men. They will be very useful. Furthermore, Caligula's Sacred Band, along with two thousand additional Praetorians, all seasoned veterans, will form the heart of our lines. Lastly, we have five men, and one resourceful woman, each with abilities far superior to our own, and perhaps worth a cohort of men, each."

Well, that was a nice thing to say. During our months in the camp, I'd always gotten the feeling Galba never liked us much.

"Unfortunately," he finished, "their use in the battle will be limited at best."

Never mind.

"I've been going over their tactics and strategies with Vincent and his lieutenant for months, and I see little use for them. Their strengths lay in small unit skirmishes, stealth, and ambush, not in a large scale battle between thousands of men. However, that is not to say they won't have an important place in the upcoming battle." He sighed. "Vincent has voiced a concern over the amount of ammunition they can carry to the field, so they will be used for another purpose.

"Instead," Galba said, pointing at the walls of Rome, "they will be used as our gateway to the city before any fighting even begins. While the army is still a day's march out, Vincent and his men," he paused, glancing at Helena who gave him a cold look, "his people, will place their explosives at key junctions around the walls.

"As we have all experienced this winter," he continued, a hint of anger and annoyance in his voice, "these people are extremely efficient at reconnaissance, stealth, infiltration, and..." he hesitated, trying to find the appropriate wording, "... causing trouble, and should have no problem bringing down the walls without ever having to enter the city."

Standing before Galba, I forced myself to suppress a smile.

During our winter vacation in the camp, we had spent time playing the ancient equivalent of war games against the legion. Galba would allow Vincent and the rest of us to leave camp and spend time observing his defenses, before trying to capture a flag placed on a tent pole of the *praetorium*. It was a basic game of capture of the flag, something the Romans never played during their training, but one most militaries of the 21st century used regularly. The last time I checked, the score was 8-0 in favor of the troops from the future.

To be fair, the Romans never stood much of a chance. In one of our gear containers, we found a dozen air pistols and rifles. Also provided were hundreds of tranquillizer darts filled with a knockout agent capable of rendering a man unconscious for hours. Combined with Santino, as well as his UAV, sneaking in and getting out was as easy as boiling water.

The Romans were smart, and their defenses top notch, but they were no match for a modern Special Forces unit. Most incursions followed a simple step by step series of procedures. Helena and I would crawl forward under cover of darkness until we were within range of the air rifles, around fifty yards, and easily take out the guards on the ramparts.

Even though I had no desire to compete with Helena when it came to shooting, our war games inevitably proved who was the better shot, and it most definitely wasn't me. In my defense, she had picked up her first high powered rifle when she was a kid, whereas I had to wait until I joined the military. Even so, I held my own, and I tried to not let those cocky smirks of hers bother me, even though all I wanted to do was smack them right off her face every time.

Once the guards on the rampart were down, the rest of the squad would rush forward through the palisade and ditch, and scale the walls. Helena and I participated in the actual infiltration only once, so our AARs filled us in on how every other mission played itself out the rest of the time.

Bordeaux and Wang would stay stationed on the rampart, ready to provide cover fire, while Vincent and Santino would descend into the camp. Once on the ground, Vincent would hang back by the rope, while Santino would sneak through the camp and capture the flag, undetected each time, except for on one occasion.

For the most part, Galba arranged his defenses as strong as they would be on any regular night, not adding sentries or guards just because he knew we were coming. We wanted these games to accurately reflect the combat effectiveness each side could muster. Something we'd never actually determined of ourselves since we became a team.

It came as a surprise one day when we realized that we'd only been a team for a few months, and that we'd never actually had a chance to perform any team training together. At first we were worried the professional Romans would actually beat us, but as it turned out, we had little to worry about. We performed fantastically, meshing together like a unit that had seen combat for years.

So, on the one occasion that Santino *was* detected, it wasn't because someone fouled up, but because Galba had stacked the deck that night. I suspected it was probably because he was a sore loser, but Santino didn't seem to mind. It only made him change his style.

Galba had left the rampart security the way it always was, his first mistake, but had added two dozen guards outside his tent. He tried to rationalize these guards by saying there were always roaming legionnaires in the camp, and these had simply decided to station themselves outside the *praetorium* that night. Galba would soon realize that we still had a few tricks up our sleeves, and sheer manpower wasn't going to get him a quick victory.

Other than the tranq darts, which the Romans quickly learned to hate, another weapon of the future we had plenty of were flashbangs. Flashbangs were non-lethal grenades, meant to blind, deafen, and disorient anyone who came into contact with them. Many a morning at BUD/S, they were used as alarm clocks, the most efficient ones I ever had. Santino had brought along two nine-bangers with him, basically flashbangs that went off nine times in quick succession, bouncing around with each bang, each concussive blast overwhelming and disorienting those near them.

After sneaking to the edge of the *via principalis*, tranqing one legionnaire along the way, he quickly assessed the situation, determining he'd have to forfeit his perfect score of remaining unseen. Over the radio he asked Helena and Bordeaux to get ready, and once they announced they were, he transmitted a double click.

Receiving his all clear, Helena launched a red flare. The bright red flare lit up the night sky, slowly drifting to the Earth on its small parachute, achieving its desired effect. Every man in the camp looked up at the magical red light that had spontaneously erupted in the darkness, giving Santino the opportunity he needed to pull the pins on his nine bangers and toss them gently into the group of waiting guards.

The following explosions were louder and brighter than anything the Romans had ever experienced before, all eighteen of them. To the unaware Roman, the nine bangers would seem like lightning strikes and thunderclaps going off right at their feet, only worse. Santino was prepared and insulated from the explosions, and he bolted for the flag as soon as the first bang went off. It all went perfectly until in his hasty retreat, Santino managed to pull down one of the tent poles with the flag, collapsing the *praetorium*. Not wasting any time, he made a beeline for the *porta praetoria*, and didn't look back.

Those inhabitants of the camp who had been sleeping weren't any longer, but most were too afraid to leave their tents, not understanding the noises they heard, the flashes they'd seen, or the ominous red glare glowing through the thin linings of their tents.

As Santino ran, Bordeaux detonated the C-4 charge he had set against the *porta praetoria*, blowing the gate clean off. Waiting for Santino at the gaping hole in the Roman's wall, Bordeaux, along with Vincent and Wang fired blindly down the road toward the *praetorium* as fast as they could reload. When Santino reached the wall, each of them fled the camp. Only a few legionnaires tried to follow, but were quickly incapacitated by Helena and me, patiently waiting as snipers were trained to do. When the fugitives reached our position, Helena and I joined them in flight, made our way to the trees, and laid low for a few days.

We didn't want to return immediately, for fear of hurt feelings and angry legionnaires, so we spent the time celebrating our victory. We enjoyed some wine Santino had managed to pilfer during his short time in the camp and feasted on a deer hunted by yours truly.

When we returned a few days later, waltzing nonchalantly through the newly under construction *porta praetoria*, we received a few glares and angry expressions, but most were happy. Even those few we had actually shot were aware that the training exercise had been productive. We returned the flag to Galba, while Caligula stood next to him wearing an amused grin on his face. Galba on the other hand was not happy. One of the squad's errant tranquilizer darts managed to find its way into his thigh, and he had not awakened pleased.

In the end, every man in the camp, ourselves included, gained important knowledge, training, and insight into the ways of war. We had utilized our winter efficiently, and we all felt that much more confident about the upcoming campaign because of it.

Reminded of the night that five men and one woman had successfully defeated over twelve thousand men, I couldn't help but smile, despite my attempts not to. Galba must have noticed, because when I managed to snap myself from the day dream, I noticed he was glaring at me.

I gulped and shifted on my feet, turning my attention back to the maps sheepishly.

With a shake of his head, Galba continued. "Once night has fallen on the following day, they will bring down the walls and our army will rush through, hopefully catching the enemy asleep and disoriented. The auxilia will attack the *Castra Praetoria* directly, while the legion itself will head straight for the *Forum Romanum* and the *Domus Augusti*, subduing any opposition in their path and capturing the rebel leadership, especially Claudius."

Galba pointed to Vincent. "They will be our Trojan Horse, our key to the city, and like the Trojans, we will hit the enemy while they are at their most vulnerable. But," he said sternly, looking at each of us in turn, "once the walls come down, and my men enter the city, you will stand down and take a defensive stance only. Let us handle the suppression of the city. In fact, I'd prefer if you stayed out of the way completely."

Even after all this time, Galba still didn't trust us. Fight with us, use us, respect us, yes, but not rely on us. Galba was a tough man to please, but I couldn't fault him for how he felt. It was hard to trust that which you couldn't understand, and from a Roman's point of view, there was nothing that could explain us.

Galba was about to continue when we heard a commotion outside the tent. Caligula and Galba remained at the head of the table, waiting for a report to be made to them. When the tent opened, I expected to see one of the legion's junior centurions burst in with news. A woman entered instead, and every head in the tent turned to look, jaws dropping all around.

The woman was strikingly beautiful, dare I say, just as beautiful as Helena. Her slender neck connected to a face with full lips, high cheekbones, and an olive tanned complexion. Blond hair and royal blue eyes were an interesting contrast to her skin tone, but an alluring one. She was also tall, only a little shorter than Helena, and had a fullness to her slender frame that suggested a recent pregnancy. Adding to her beauty was her clothing, cut in a way which produced a slit along her left leg that ran nearly to her waist. It wasn't a style I'd seen amongst Rome's town women, but it definitely had an effect on all of us present, save probably Helena. It was also cut in a low fashion along her chest, revealing ample cleavage.

I thought I recognized her from somewhere, but I couldn't put my finger on where.

Santino rubbed his eyes, as though she was some figment of his perverted imagination.

I wasn't so easily fooled. There was something off about her. Her beauty was so unlike Helena's, which conveyed warmth and tenderness. Instead, she seemed devious, insistent, and cunning. Like so many bleach blonde, bimbo clones back in 2021, this woman knew she was beautiful, and used it only to achieve her own ambitions and goals.

The only man in the room not drawn to the woman's beauty was Caligula, who surprised us all by crying, "Sister Agrippina!" and rushing to her side.

"Sister?" Santino repeated, giving me a look.

The realization hit me like a truck. "Oh, no…"

Vincent understood. "Agrippina…"

X
Agrippina

Rome, Italy
April, 38 A.D.

I knew all about this beautiful, young, vile woman.

Agrippina, or Agrippina the Younger, as she is better known to history, was the oldest of Caligula's three sisters. In my undergraduate thesis about the Julio-Claudian family, I had spent ample time researching her in particular and, if I had learned anything about her, it was that she was trouble. If I remembered my dates correctly, she should be about twenty two, a very mature looking twenty two, if I were to judge. Pliny the Younger, a different Younger, recorded she had canine teeth, a sign of good fortune amongst Romans, and that physical detail allowed me to confirm this woman was indeed her.

Agrippina had been more than a mere seductress, but a very ambitious woman as well; perhaps one of the most ambitious throughout Roman history. After Caligula had gone insane, rumors started to circulate that an incestuous affair between him and all his sisters was taking place. In 39 A.D. she was involved in a plot to murder Caligula and replace him on the throne with someone she could control. When it failed, she was exiled, only to be recalled by her paternal uncle, Claudius, after he had become emperor.

In regard to Claudius, he went through three marriages, and Agrippina, two, before they wed each other. The incestuous marriage between Claudius and Agrippina was creepy enough, but then there was also the age difference, which seemed paltry by comparison. After they were married, she rose to an unprecedented level of power, becoming an empress of Rome, bestowed with the title Augustina, sharing power equally with Claudius on some levels. She became a force to be reckoned with. While not a policy maker herself, she held considerable influence with her husband-uncle, as well as those he ruled.

The kicker was that Agrippina had a son from her first marriage, which she manipulated Claudius into adopting and appointing as his own heir, superseding his biological son, Britannicus. A few years later, Claudius began to favor his own son again, and grew a pair by condemning Agrippina. Not long later, in 54 A.D., Claudius was poisoned by a plate of mushrooms and died. Many historians credit the assassination to none other than Agrippina herself, and her son, Nero Claudius Caesar Drusus Germanicus, better known simply as Nero, became emperor as a mere teenager.

I wondered where Drusilla was, another of Caligula's sisters. They had always been the closer ones. Granted if Agrippina was here, Drusilla was probably not far behind. Regardless, Agrippina had to have brought trouble with her, and if anything at all went right today it would be her leaving me out of it.

After quickly embracing his sister in a way any brother would, no sign of incest present, Caligula led her to his position at the head of the table. "My friends," he addressed to us all, making me actually feel important. "For those of you who do not know, this is my sister, Agrippina. Introductions can wait until later, dear sister, but these are my closest friends and advisors. Now, tell me, what brings you here?"

Since her arrival, Agrippina had been putting on a display of contained desperation, as though she were just barely containing a fit of sadness and rage. When Caligula finally asked her what was wrong, she released her emotions in a stunning performance that I should have expected from the woman.

"Caligula, brother! It is my son! Lucius!" She wailed the name, falling into Caligula's arms, weeping and pounding lightly on his chest. Her voice was high pitched, but despite the wailing, had a gentle purr to it that was easy on the ears. She was playing the part of the grieving mother well. Whether any emotion she was conveying was real or not was any man's guess.

"Lucius?" Caligula asked. "I was wondering whether you had given birth. I was horribly worried. Lucius." He repeated. "A good name. He will become a fine man."

Santino elbowed me in the ribs, whispering, "New mom, huh? I can tell." He emphasized his point by puffing out his chest subtly and shaking it from side to side. "Lost that baby weight quickly, too. Nice."

I turned toward him as inconspicuously as I could, a blank expression on my face. Smiling, he shrugged, and turned back to continue gawking at our guest.

Caligula kept his attention on his sister. "What has happened to him? Tell me."

"Claudius." She said the name with disdain in between bouts of tears. "Our uncle has murdered Gnaeus and taken my son hostage, saying that he will adopt him as his own to make him emperor one day. He plans to give him a new name. Nero he says. But he has forced me out of his home. I am not allowed to see my own son! Claudius has gone mad with power. Mad! He's always been a scoundrel, but something has changed him. Broken his mind. I'm afraid he may hurt my son!"

I looked at Vincent, and we both realized another piece of the puzzle had clicked into place, hopefully the last. Claudius must have the orb in his possession. That would explain his odd behavior.

Caligula tried to console her. "Sister. Do not worry. I will take care of it. Tell me. Are you expected back in Rome?"

"Yes. I told Claudius I was visiting Mother and our sisters in Arretium. I'm expected home in a few days."

"Did you come with anyone?"

"Yes. Two bodyguards."

Caligula looked at Vincent. "This seems like something well suited to your skills."

"Caesar," Nisus interrupted, raising a finger, "perhaps we should think about…"

Caligula snapped his head and glared at the senior centurion. Nisus lowered his hand, and glanced awkwardly around the table, shutting up.

Vincent nodded. "Indeed, Caesar. It would be the perfect cover to sneak us inside the walls of Rome. We can easily accomplish our task with only two of us, and it would prove far less dangerous to go in this way."

Galba huffed to himself, not really caring how much danger we had to deal with. He may have been a good general, but *definitely* a sore loser.

"Very good, Vincent," Caligula went on. "You have read my mind. Agrippina, we will discuss the plans tomorrow. For now…"

"No. Brother. I need to speak privately with the men accompanying me, at least one of them." She looked at each us in turn, pausing on Helena only to offer her a sneer, before stopping on me.

Aw, shit.

"That one," she said, pointing at me. "With the pretty face. I will talk to him before we go over anything."

Santino coughed and I couldn't help but glance at Helena before looking at the table. I hoped Agrippina would shift her attention elsewhere, but she must have noticed our exchange, and a smile crossed her face. A mean looking one. She walked over and put her hand on my arm.

"Fine," Caligula responded, giving me a look any good brother would give another man. "You may use my magistrate's tent, just to the right."

She gave him a smile, before looking up at me. "Come. Let us discuss things. It won't take long."

She yanked on my arm to lead me from the tent, but my right foot caught on the toe of my left boot when I tried to follow. Nearly tripping to the floor, I barely kept myself from falling.

This day just got worse.

***

I knew the magistrate was on duty elsewhere, so I expected the tent would be empty, but that thought didn't offer much comfort. Opening the flap for Agrippina, I followed her in. She took in her surroundings in a glance, before finding a chair and placing it near a table.

She patted it. "Sit. Please. Make yourself comfortable."

"Okay..." I said, dragging out the word.

I dusted off the chair before taking a seat, facing the table only a few feet away. Finding a piece of fruit, Agrippina began to eat it before sitting on the edge of the table. She folded her left leg over her right, forcing the slit of her dress to reveal more than just her leg, but also the side of her ample posterior. Leaning forward, exposing not just cleavage, but practically the whole show, she rested her elbows on her knees and continued to gnaw away. Slowly.

As she ate, she remained silent, but looked me up and down like a piece of meat. Her inspection made me feel only slightly more uncomfortable than I already was. I squirmed in my chair like a job applicant waiting for an interview. Apparently satisfied at what she saw, she hummed an approving noise, leaned back in a straighter posture, and shifted her clothing, exposing even more skin on her other leg.

"Did you enjoy my little performance back in the tent?" She asked nonchalantly.

I coughed. "Excuse me?"

"Oh, don't play coy with me," she said, tossing the piece of fruit over her shoulder. "I know you saw right through my act. I am very good at reading people, and I saw how you looked at me when I first walked in. You looked as though you knew me, but I never forget a face, especially not one so perfect as yours. I was at your little demonstration a few months ago, but that hardly means you know me."

I coughed again and shifted in my chair. She must have been that pregnant woman I noticed in the stands that I thought looked familiar. The one who winked at me.

"I'm sorry," I said, trying not to sound like a prepubescent boy, "but I'm not sure what you're talking about. I thought we were here to discuss your son."

"We are. I just wanted to make sure we understood one another. That performance was for my brother's clever, but unimaginative benefit, not to mention the lackeys he surrounds himself with, besides you, of course. In you, I saw trouble. Someone who might challenge me. That's why I felt the need to speak to you alone. To appeal to you in another way, besides that of a grieving mother. Something maybe a little more… personal?"

"What do you mean?" I asked cautiously.

"My son has indeed been kidnapped, and I am truly frightened for his safety," she said, her voice shifting into the grieving mother spectrum again. "I want you to know that if you save him, I will be yours to command. Anything and everything I am capable of doing, I will do for you."

She capitalized her last point by slipping off the table and straddling me. She had to pull her clothing well up over her hips, so as not to get caught in it, and to make matters worse, she also snatched my hands and placed them on her bare hips.

"Anything, and everything," she said, pumping her chest out so that her breasts nearly brushed against my face. "You will be the envy of all Rome. Trust me."

Stunned by her very forward actions, not to mention instinctually curious, I didn't immediately react when she grabbed my head and pressed her mouth to mine. There was nothing I could do. I was stuck in a seductive trap worthy of any black widow scenario. Two seconds later, as soon as she slid one of her hands along my groin, I quickly jumped to my feet, and pulled away from her.

Wiping my mouth out of shock, I backed up toward the exit in case I had to flee for my life.

"There is no need for that, Agrippina. I will gladly help you and your son if the emperor so wishes it. You have no need to do… that… again."

My leap from the chair had knocked her to the ground, and now she looked up at me as she propped herself up on her knees. Her look was pure sex and seduction. She wiped her mouth as well, finishing the motion by licking her fingers. I had to wince.

"Is it that Amazon in the tent? I saw the way she looked at you." She smiled. "She is very beautiful indeed. Perhaps I could arrange for the three of us, together, to…"

"That won't be necessary, thank you," I said quickly, although the thought stiffened more than just my resolve to get out of here.

"I could always have her… removed. If you so wish."

"What? No. No, of course not. Leave her out of this."

She looked at me coyly before jerking her head to the side innocently.

"As you wish," she said, rising to her feet, not wasting any effort to contain her dignity, not that she had much left anyway. "Now. We shall tell my brother the news."

I nodded, and held the tent flap open for her to exit. Wiping my mouth again, just in case, I followed behind her. Entering the *praetorium*, all heads turned to face us. Most wore neutral expressions, except for Helena. I hadn't seen her that angry since the day she had nearly beaten that legionnaire to death on the training ground.

I found my place next to Santino and Vincent, while Agrippina went to stand next to her brother. I glanced over at Santino, who was looking at me expectantly.

"What?" I asked.

He didn't say anything. Instead, he just turned and looked back at the maps.

I wasn't afraid of how Helena would take Agrippina's notice in me, but I decided to play it safe and ignore her. Instead, I looked at Caligula who was conversing quietly with his sister. She noticed my attention, and gave me a smile, flicking her eyes in Helena's direction, before returning her gaze to me, her smile widening.

And I thought this day couldn't get any worse.

Caligula turned back toward his staff after he finished his conversation with Agrippina. "Jacob Hunter. Are you ready to partake in this mission?"

It was the first time he had ever addressed me by name, and frankly, I was taken slightly aback by it. I'd spent months with him, accompanying Vincent numerous times during special briefings, but he'd never addressed me directly. I didn't even know he knew my name.

"I am, Caesar," I replied earnestly.

"Good. Who will accompany you?"

"I will," Santino answered quickly.

"Very good, John Santino. You will leave at dawn. Your mission is to retrieve my nephew first and plant your explosive material around the walls of Rome in preparation for our assault. My army will depart in two days. We will meet you outside of Rome upon your return. Do you understand?"

"Yes, Caesar," we responded in unison.

"Very good. Do not let me down. As for the rest of you, we will finish this briefing tomorrow afternoon."

There was a chorus of affirmatives as the men and women in the *praetorium* began to file out of the tent. As I left I looked over my shoulder at Agrippina, her expression one of overconfidence and victory. She was hiding something, only I didn't know what, but that hardly mattered at this point. What did matter was saving a child, and retaking Rome in the name of Caligula.

***

Later that evening, I was joined by the rest of my squad around a campfire Wang had built near our tent site. After the meeting, I had spent my time avoiding both Helena and Agrippina, an easy task since I had swapped watch duty with Bordeaux the other day and had to man the wall, while Agrippina spent her time in the *praetorium*. Even so, I'd spent the entire afternoon looking over my shoulder as I kept most of my attention on the tree line beyond the camp.

"We're going to keep this short and simple," Vincent began. "Some of us have an early day tomorrow. At 0430 tomorrow, Hunter and Santino will accompany Agrippina to Rome and rescue Nero, as well as place C4 around key areas along the walls and gates. There's no need to send six people when two will do. This way we can keep an eye on the legion during the invasion, whether Galba likes it or not." He paused and waggled his finger at Santino and me. "I expect you to rendezvous with the legion by the time we can see the city walls. Hunter, I hate to put you on the spot here, but what did you and Agrippina talk about? Don't leave anything out."

I shifted on the log stump I sat on, unsure what to say. We hadn't really talked about much of anything really.

"She tried to seduce me," I started, but was cut off by a collective utterance of annoyances. Wang threw his hands in the air in desperation while Bordeaux just shook his head.

"Of course she did!" Santino cried before kicking dirt at me.

"I said 'she tried to seduce me', not that she did. I got out of there before things got too crazy." I winced at my untactful wording. "She just wanted to assure me that her son really was captured, and that I had to do whatever I could to get him back," I said, leaving out the details of the whole seduction part.

"But why would she need to pull you aside, mate?" Wang asked. "We all saw her in the *praetorium*."

"Her tearful motherly routine was an act, or so she told me. A way to convince Caligula and everyone else since apparently she can't actually portray real emotions. She said she saw something in me that made her suspect I knew better, and she felt compelled to reassure me. It wasn't pretty."

"But why?" Bordeaux reiterated.

"Well, because she was right. I was immediately suspicious of her the minute I realized who she was. I take it none of you are familiar with her? Sir?" I asked Vincent particularly.

He shrugged. "I know who she is, but we've already established you're more familiar with Julio-Claudian history than I am."

"Out with it, professor," Santino ordered me impatiently.

"Well, to put it bluntly, she's an egotistical, ambitious, agenda-driven charlatan who will do whatever she can to get what she wants, including murder. She's very smart, very resourceful, and very persistent. Ancient writers credit her with poisoning Claudius, killing him, all to have her son Nero become emperor. She's extremely dangerous, and I didn't trust her. It's not surprising that she would pick me out of the crowd. She is extremely sharp."

"Why are we even trying to save Nero?" Wang asked. "I don't know much, but..."

Bordeaux cut him off. "*Excusez*, James, but I am confused. Why did she call him Lucius if his name is Nero?"

"Because his original name wasn't Nero," I explained. "He was born Lucius I Can't Remember The Rest, and wasn't named Nero until he was adopted by Claudius years from now. Gnaeus, by the way, was Agrippina's husband." I paused and turned to Vincent. "Interesting that Claudius chose Nero for his name even now, right?"

The older man nodded. "It truly is."

"Anyway," Wang put in before he question was completely derailed. "Wasn't Nero a loony? Like, really loony?"

"Maybe 'not even worth saving' loony?" Santino expanded suggestively.

"He was," I confirmed with a nod. He brought up a good point and the others seemed to concur.

"We can't let him die because we think we know what he may do in the future," Vincent responded. "At this point, he may never do those things."

Most of us nodded our heads in agreement.

"So what about Agrippina?" Santino asked.

"I don't know," I responded. "I guess we can trust her. For now, at least. Despite her affinity for tomfoolery and treachery, she did love her son, and I'd side with the fact that she does need our help."

"I'm not so sure," Vincent said. "Agrippina is not Nero. We know who she is and what she's capable of. Our intervention here won't change that like it may with Nero. I'm not so sure we can trust her."

"I think we can," I responded with a shrug. I noticed Wang and Bordeaux trade glances, and Helena continued to ignore the conversation, content to just stare into the fire. Vincent folded his arms and leveled his eyes at me, eyes that didn't seem very happy. I looked at each of my squad members in turn to realize none of them were looking at me. Not even Santino. "What?"

"You're wound up pretty tight, Jake," Santino offered. "We've all noticed it. I think Vincent just wants to make sure you know what you're doing."

"I know what I'm doing," I said sternly.

Santino nodded but didn't look satisfied. The uncomfortable silence continued until Vincent unfolded his arms and rested his hands on his knees. "It's your call, Hunter. If you and Santino are up for this then you have my approval. You're going to need to go in light, just enough to conceal beneath a toga."

"I'm ready," I said as confidently as I could.

Santino nodded.

"Well, good luck then," he stood and moved toward his tent before he finished his thoughts. "Get some sleep and we'll see you in a few days."

***

Lying on my bed roll that night, I couldn't help but think about what Santino said a few nights ago about never finding another woman like Helena. It couldn't have been a coincidence that someone like Agrippina, someone who could murder on a whim, would show up and basically threaten her. The idea had me more worried than the mission, but I couldn't write Agrippina off completely yet. History had already proved an unreliable source of information, so maybe she wasn't all that bad.

And maybe she really liked me…

As if on cue, Helena entered the tent, removed her duty gear, and slid into place beside me, but kept even more distance than normal. We laid there for a few minutes before I couldn't take the silence anymore. "Are you all right?"

She didn't turn to look. "There any reason I shouldn't be?"

"You seemed awfully quiet today, that's all."

"Maybe if you hadn't spent so much time with your new friend, you'd have seen just how talkative I really was."

I shot up to a sitting position. "You see? That's what I'm talking about. If I didn't know any better I'd say you were jealous."

She finally looked at me. "I'm not jealous."

"Then what's wrong?"

"I just don't trust her, and neither should you."

"I'm not."

"Then why go with her?"

"No, you tell me the truth first. Why are you so upset?" I tried to keep the frustration from infecting my tone, but I couldn't help it. "I hate games."

She sat up as well and barked a quick laugh. "Is that what this is to you? A game? I'll tell you now this most certainly isn't a game to me."

I shook my head. "I don't understand where you're going with this."

She looked surprised but laughed again as she shook her head. "You don't? After all these months, and you still don't understand where we're 'going with this'? After everything we've been through and everything we've shared?"

"Helena, what..."

"You really are a dense man, Lieutenant," she said, practically yelling. "Fine. Go get yourself killed. Don't expect any help from me."

I was suddenly very, very, angry. "I never asked for your help, Helena! I don't need it! I don't need anyone's!"

She looked at me with downtrodden eyes and nodded to no one but herself. I couldn't believe I said what I said when I said it. *I didn't need anyone's help?* Why would I say something like that?

"Helena... I..." I trailed off, not knowing what to say. Helena gave me one last sad look before she crawled under her sleeping bag and rolled away from me. I didn't understand how this conversation derailed the way it did and I didn't understand why, through all of the anger, I felt the first real connection with her in months. I wasn't an idiot. I thought I knew what she was implying and I was ready to go there as well, but everything had unraveled so quickly.

I stared at Helena's shapeless form within her sleeping bag and wondered about my own comments. They were so unlike me that even I had trouble even believing, but I'd said them – and I'd meant them.

I had to sleep, so I shifted onto my side to face away from Helena and closed my eyes. Sleep would not come easily tonight. I'd crossed a line I wasn't sure I realized I'd crossed until now and the thought frightened me. I didn't want to become the kind of person who couldn't or wouldn't rely on anyone. I needed my friends, and I especially needed Helena.

What had I done?

***

As we journeyed south toward Rome later the next day, Santino and I rode atop black Spanish stallions, a favorite amongst Rome's leading citizens. As a kid, my sister had taken horseback riding lessons for years and I would watch when it was time to pick her up. Every once in a while she would teach me a few pointers when she had time, so I had come to ancient Rome as a somewhat experienced equestrian. Santino, however, had a rougher time of it.

As he had learned how to ride over the winter, I'd had a hard time imagining the scrappy Italian from one of the seediest areas of New York ever riding a horse, and he proved my point by doing so like a drunken sailor. We had all gotten a good laugh out of it, and Helena, easily the most graceful of us all on a horse, took great pleasure in watching him fall time and time again.

As for Helena, I tried not to think about her, but my thoughts often drifted toward our last night together. When I tried to reconcile with her before I left, the only response I'd gotten was a sad and scared look from eyes that were bloodshot and puffy. She looked as though she hadn't slept all night, and had spent most of it crying. I couldn't stop thinking about that morning and how she looked. I didn't understand the tears at first, but I now realize she had to have been crying for me. Crying that I had become some kind of monster or that she somehow knew I was going to die in a place where she couldn't help me.

The thoughts plagued me, but at least I had Santino for company. We'd made good time on our first day, and I calculated we'd be in Rome within a few days. I had spent that time worried Agrippina might try something on me again, but I was happy to discover she had turned her attention elsewhere.

During our first night, she and Santino chatted quietly with one another as we sat in our rented rooms. People would be surprised to learn that Roman highways functioned much like modern day interstates, complete with Holiday Inn-type establishments dotted sporadically along the roadway, just without the turn down service and free continental breakfast. Our rooms were acceptable, and while the three of us were hanging out in Agrippina's room currently, we'd booked a second one for the boys. I sat aloof from them both, near the window, and cringed every time I heard giggles emanate from the treacherous woman as they joked and laughed freely. I was surprised that when I ordered lights out, Santino hadn't stayed the night. After we packed up the next morning, and continued our journey, I asked him why he hadn't.

"Big boobs, a firm ass, perfect skin, and a beautiful smile aren't everything I look for in a woman, you know," he answered.

I snorted. "Bullshit. What's the deal? She seemed willing and able, and if not willing, at least she wouldn't have said no." I paused. "Even if she is evil…"

"I know." He sighed. "Guess I'm getting soft in my old age. I just don't want to risk anything by jumping into bed with her. She seems like trouble."

"Oh, she is my friend, she is," I told him, an image of Agrippina's offer that involved Helena popping into my mind, "but I suspect it would be worth it."

"What are you two talking about?" Agrippina interrupted from behind us.

I looked back at her, noticing she still looked beautiful, but conservatively dressed for once. "Nothing, ma'am, just talking strategy."

She made a pouty sound and looked off into the distance. Maybe I was giving her too much credit, and she really was just some dopy teenager at heart.

I turned back to Santino and jabbed a finger toward his face. "Don't let your emotions get in the way of letting you do what you want. Doing so leads to all kinds of internal struggles and moral dilemmas. It can get ugly." I cocked my head, wondering where such hypocritical insight came from.

Santino glanced down at his horse's mane and shook his head with a big grin on his face. "You're not seriously lecturing me, are you? I mean, you do know who you're talking to, right? It's me."

I couldn't help but chuckle. "I know. I'm just saying."

He laughed again. "Well, you're just full of helpful information then, aren't you? Maybe you should have been a guidance counselor or something."

I snorted. "Yeah, right."

My poor sleeping habits continued that night, but not because of my own musings. Our new hotel was no cleaner than the last, but poor sanitation didn't stop Santino from acting on my helpful advice. Agrippina offered us some wine, which I indulged in lightly, but both of them had more than enough. As a result, Santino stayed behind while I went back to my lonely, cold room, and had to try and sleep through hours of sexual outbursts on more occasions than I cared to remember. They all started to blur together after the first one and gave me nightmares. They were fueled by weird outbursts from Santino, interestingly arousing cries of pleasure from Agrippina, and the insistent pounding of someone repeatedly smacking the wall that separated our two rooms.

As soon as the first wisps of dawn struck my face, I hauled myself out of bed as quickly as I could, nearly delirious from exhaustion. With a quick knock to wake up my travel companions, I rushed outside to ready my horse. As I pulled a strap to tighten my gear along his flank, a sudden shriek from the hotel drew my attention in its direction before I realized how horribly familiar the sound was. I sighed, and looked at a few other early risers who were outside and heard the noise as well. They laughed, knowing full well what was happening, and when Santino came waltzing out twenty minutes later with a radiant Agrippina on his arm, they whooped and hollered at him. He gripped his hands together and shook them alongside both sides of his head in a celebratory gesture in response. Whether the ne'er-do-wells outside understood what he was doing or not didn't matter. They loved it.

I looked over at him. "Quite the show of stamina last night you bastard."

He returned the look. "Yeah, it's my Italian blood."

"How appropriate. Feel any better?"

"Definitely, but I don't think I'll be doing that again. You were right. She's a freak."

I had to laugh and roll my eyes at the same time before mounting my horse and giving him a quick kick. "Don't worry. She has two sisters. Maybe one of them will be more to your liking."

He smiled at the idea, while I paused to let him think about it.

"However," I continued. "I hope you realize you may have just sired the next emperor of Rome."

"Yeah, I..." He paused after mounting his own horse. "Wait, what?"

"Seriously," I confirmed. "If something happens to Nero, and Agrippina has a child from your endless fornicating last night, he may become a Caesar. We can name him Julius Agrippa Augustus Germanicus Santino Caesar. I like that. Has a ring to it."

"You're kidding, right?"

"No, actually, I'm not. Plus, you may have just created your own great times a thousand grandfather since you've had relations with a woman from a time period you don't belong in."

"Wait. That can't really happen." He thought about it. "Can it?"

I let him stew for a few seconds before I started laughing. "No, from what I think I know, it can't. Just kidding."

"Oh, good," he said, looking laughably relieved.

***

A day and a thankfully quiet night later, the walls of Rome sprang into sight. Still a few miles out, I could see just how expansive the city really was, but its walls weren't what intimidated me right now, it was the two tiny little dots I saw flanking the small gateway. If we couldn't get through those guards, this mission would be scrubbed before it even began.

Santino and I had opted out of our HK416 rifles, which were long, somewhat cumbersome, and very hard to conceal. Instead, Santino had borrowed Wang's UMP, and I'd taken Helena's P90. These were easily concealed beneath our baggy togas, and billowing travel cloaks, securely tied down to our backs with their slings. Additionally, we packed night vision goggles, plenty of Bordeaux's C-4, a small but extensive medical kit put together by Wang, and enough ammo to take on a very small army. Most of this we kept hidden in locally made bags, which did well to conceal our gear, but weren't designed like our own to make what we needed easily accessible.

Hopefully, we wouldn't let things get confusing, but as Santino and I well knew, shit happens, and very quickly in our line of work. We'd stage the rescue while Agrippina distracted Claudius, grabbing the kid, and moving toward the walls of Rome to lay down our demo. Then we'd get the hell out of Dodge.

Easy.

By the time we reached the gate, I was only slightly nervous. I figured if everything went according to plan, this should technically be the hardest part.

I wasn't really expecting everything to go as planned.

Things never went as planned.

Luckily, the Praetorians we'd interacted with during our time in Rome were few, and all in the *Primigenia*'s camp, so there would be very few people who could easily recognize us. Santino could probably pass for a Roman, due to his height and dark features, and while I'd be a bit more suspicious, my physical characteristics weren't completely foreign in the Roman world. I'd also spent the past few weeks growing out my facial hair, so hopefully even the ladies who made time to watch me run wouldn't immediately recognize me.

The movement of traffic into the city was crowded and slow moving. The constant flow of traders, visitors, farmers, and other types of people made the road busy and bustling. My spirits were lifted when I observed that the guards seemed lackadaisical in their duty, and were just waving people through. When our turn came up, Agrippina flashed the guards a fantastic smile, and they wasted no time waving us through, unable to take their eyes off our female companion.

Through the gates, we made our way to the Palatine at a leisurely, and hopefully inconspicuous pace. Reaching the base of the hill, I noticed Claudius had not sat idle during the winter, and had spent the time rebuilding the home Bordeaux had destroyed with just a few pounds of plastic explosive. We abandoned our horses in a nearby stable owned by Agrippina, just outside the *pomerium*, and backtracked a bit to finish the trip on foot. Once inside the gated complex, Agrippina issued some last minute advice.

"My son is kept in a room near the back of the house, but you won't be familiar with the layout. Follow the main hallway. His room will be the first on the right once the hall meets a cross hallway. There will be guards. Now, there is an exit near my son's room. If you face his chamber, take the hallway to your left. The third door on your right leads to a small storage area. There is a doorway hidden behind a cabinet at the far end of the room. Claudius has installed many of these hidden exits in his home. His paranoia runs deep."

"Where will you be?" Santino asked.

"Claudius' room, where he may or may not be right now. I will head there to make sure he is not home. If he is, I will distract him while you retrieve my son. If he is not, I will join you as soon as I can."

As she spoke, I saw genuine pain and fear in her face, or at least as good as any impression I'd seen yet.

"Don't worry," I told her. "This will be a walk in the park."

"What does walking in parks have to do with anything?"

I sighed. "Never mind." These Romans needed to learn a few clichés.

"We'll get him," Santino comforted.

She nodded, before breaking away from us as we passed the threshold of the house.

As opposed to the sparse elegance the house had exuded the last time I was here, Claudius' new décor screamed crazed and opulent exuberance. The home was littered with statues, paintings and plants. It looked like an art museum had set up shop in a rain forest. The displays were random, and many were so obscene I had to look away.

Santino and I quietly made our way down the hall, our boots echoing softly on the hard marble. While our togas were an important part of the plan, we wore much of our combat gear beneath, save our vests. If we had to fight, we could ditch the togas, and be at near optimal fighting readiness in seconds.

Following Agrippina's directions, we made our way down the long, wide, main hallway. Along the way, we passed numerous rooms, and more artwork, the latter of which provided us some concealment as we kept moving. Santino, on point, started to slow as he approached the tee at the end of the hallway. If Agrippina's directions were right, Nero's room should just be around the corner. So far we hadn't seen any guards, which did little to ease my nervousness, but when Santino stopped, knelt, and looked around the corner using a small mirror, he indicated he saw two of them.

"You go first," he whispered. "Take out the far one."

I moved into position along the opposite wall, ready to hurl myself down the adjacent hallway. Securing one of my feet against the wall behind me, I nodded to Santino.

He held out three fingers, slowly counting them down to a clenched fist. When he did, I leapt into action. Using the wall as a springboard, I practically flew across our hallway, rounding the corner in as wide a turn as I could manage. Just as I caught sight of the guards, who were lazily resting their hands on the hilts of their swords, I fell into a roll, landing past the first guard, and right in front of the second. In one fluid motion I stepped up from the roll and swung my elbow upwards into the second guard's jaw. I heard teeth shatter, and felt my elbow bruise. I ignored the pain and wrapped my arm around the man's neck, and stepped behind him, placing him in an effective choke hold. Using his body as a shield, I turned to face the first guard while I choked the life from the man I held. My carefulness was unnecessary, however, as Santino used my distraction to simply walk up behind the first guard, and shove his knife upwards into the man's brain through the bottom of his jaw.

We dropped our fresh kills, opened the door into Nero's room, and dragged them inside.

"I thought they only did rolls in the movies," Santino wondered, dragging his kill.

"If you're going to do anything," I pointed out, "you might as well look good doing it."

He snickered. A few seconds later, we had the bodies in the room, and the door shut behind us. We only had one real test left, and that was making sure the boy didn't freak out when he saw us. He was only a baby after all, and I knew as much about them as I did women, which didn't inspire much confidence. I could only imagine Santino knew even less.

Moving further into the room, we took up positions on either side of the small Roman style crib that rested against the far wall. We peeked over the edge to see a baby boy, sound asleep and wrapped in a miniature version of a Roman toga. The toga even had a little purple seam.

"That him?" Santino whispered.

"Yup," I replied quietly. "There lies the soul of a man with the potential to kill untold thousands of men, women and children."

Santino regarded him closely. "Kinda cute, ain't he?"

"Yeah, a little bit."

The little guy did look kind of cute, especially with the mini toga on, but my mind refused to feel sympathetic toward him. Shuddering at the thought of what kind of man he could become, I bent down to pick him up, but just as I wrapped my hands around his small body I had to back off because he started to cry.

I looked at Santino. "I guess we probably should have thought this through, huh?"

"Here. Let me try," he offered, reaching into the crib. Picking the child up, Santino held him out in front of him, his elbows locked, keeping Nero as far away from his body as possible. The child didn't cry though, and both baby and Santino looked at each other curiously. Apparently satisfied at what he was seeing, young Nero started gurgling and even cooed at Santino.

"Aw," I said, "I think you made a friend."

"Yah," Santino said with a smile, cradling the child against his chest. "I guess I did."

Santino's motherly glow quickly evaporated once he patted Nero on the back, enticing the small child to spit up all over his toga. Santino wrinkled his face in disgust as young Nero gurgled and giggled at his expense.

I laughed with him. "Come on, mum. We need to get out of here."

Santino nodded and placed Nero in a small carrying cradle, little more than a piece of cloth wrapped and tied into a type of sling bag. The bag was in common use in ancient Rome as a baby carrier, and Agrippina had set it up for us before we arrived in the city.

With the baby secured against Santino's chest, we made for the exit. Since Santino was stuck playing babysitter, I took point this time, no need to place the child at any further risk. Back in the hall, we continued past the main hallway we had originally walked down, and counted three doors, entering the last one on the right. Finding the storage room, just as Agrippina had said, I located the cabinet and strained muscles to pull it aside.

And there was the door, again, just as she said.

Maybe she was on our side after all.

Reaching for the handle I gave it a yank, but it didn't budge. Frowning, I tried pushing against it, again with no effect. Frustrated, I threw my entire weight against it, but with no more success. I leaned closer to the door and analyzed the seam. I discovered that it had been cemented together, and no matter how hard I tried, the door wasn't going to budge.

I turned to face Santino. "We're burned."

"Figures," he replied, pulling out his knife.

I didn't waste any time replying. Instead, I moved toward the hallway we'd just come through, and gave it a quick glance. Still clear. Maybe the door was just another product of Claudius' growing paranoia. Quickly abandoning the storage room, I led Santino back to the main hall. Another quick glance showed the immediate area to be clear, but with all the flora and fauna in the area, I couldn't be sure. Knowing no other way out, I walked as calmly as I could down the hall.

We were about half way down the hall when doors started to open up all around us.

From the two rooms in front of us, a half dozen Praetorians emerged, and took up defensive positions to block our escape. From behind us, another door opened and only two Praetorians came out. The first of which was unlucky enough to walk into Santino's knife, which he held in a reverse grip, and had thrust behind him through the man's neck. The second man went down after I tore off my toga, pulled out my Sig, and put a round through his skull. No more Praetorians came from behind us, so we stood side by side, in defensive positions facing our remaining attackers. It didn't take long before I realized we had nowhere to retreat, so we held our ground, waiting for our foes to make the first move.

The Praetorians didn't budge though, at least not at first, appearing as if they were waiting for someone. Two minutes later, I realized who it was. Trailing behind another fifty or so Praetorians came Claudius, looking disheveled and unkempt, psychotic but alert, a devilish grin on his face.

As he approached, his Praetorians opened a lane for him to travel through. He was accompanied by a senior centurion I didn't know.

He stepped out in front of his men, which was nice of him, because it gave me a clear shot at his head. His men tensed, but no one moved, while he opened his arms wide, and frowned.

"Jacob Hunter," he said. "Is this how you treat friends from wherever it is you come from? I thought we had become instant ones the day we met."

I didn't dignify him with a response.

"Jacob, Jacob, Jacob," he taunted. "You pain me. First, you accept my invitation to come see me, but you don't visit, and now I find that you have kidnapped my son. Tsk, tsk." He waggled his finger at me. It was easy to see the man had lost all control over his faculties, and was quickly descending into a Jeffery Dahmer state of insanity, just as Caligula should have, perhaps proving Vincent's theory.

I was curious about one thing though. "What invitation?"

"What invitation?' Why, the one I sent you, of course. Didn't you get the message? I had to make sure it was you who came to see me after all, and not one of your other…" he waved dismissively at Santino, "whatever they are."

"You don't mean Agrippina?" I asked, confusion and anger swirling in my mind simultaneously.

"Agrippina? Did I send her? I do not know. Did I? It seems I've forgotten. What does it matter? She's served her purpose. What does matter is that you are here, and now, we can have some fun. Centurion, retrieve my son. When he's safe, the rest of you take them. Alive. No exceptions. Even the other one."

The nameless centurion moved toward us.

"Wait!" Santino called, carefully removing Nero from around his shoulder, and gently placing him on the floor.

The movement hid his true intention. As he placed the child on the floor, I saw him move his right hand, the one holding his knife, across his body, resting it near the left side of his waist. As he stood, he flung his arm upwards, releasing the knife, sending it flying toward Claudius. The knife missed, imbedding itself in the chest of the centurion instead, who had been standing just to the side and in front of him. The man looked down at the hilt of the combat knife for the briefest of seconds, before his head lulled backward and he collapsed.

True anger brewing in Claudius' eyes, he yelled, "Get them! Save my son first!"

We retreated as soon as he started issuing orders, utilizing the few seconds the Praetorians needed to avoid trampling Nero to our advantage.

"Move to the storage room!" I yelled at Santino. "Get the C-4 ready."

As we ran, I still had my pistol pointed in the general direction of the Praetorians, so I emptied my magazine into their formation, confirming at least four kills with the seven rounds I had remaining. Holstering my sidearm on the run, I pulled the P90 from my back, and pulled back the cocking lever, chambering a round.

We reached the storage room in seconds. I posted myself at the door, while Santino moved toward the smaller escape door, fiddling with a brick of C-4. He'd need to shave the brick into a much smaller portion, or the concussive blast from the detonation might kill us. He'd need a few minutes.

Seeing the first wave of Praetorians turning the corner, I unleashed a volley of gunfire in their direction. Helena's gun was perfect for this kind of work. Its small size allowed me to move it around easily in the cramped area with one arm, and its fifty round magazine was larger than any other rifle's we had, except Bordeaux's SAW, which I really wished I had right now.

For now, the P90 would do, and as I raked my fire left to right, mowing down man after man in a quick fluid motion, I started feeling like we might actually make it out of here. Each round struck a target in the narrow hall, and most men received more than just one wound. Claudius must have known this would happen, and yet he still sent these men to their graves. He really was nuts.

Unwilling to blindly sacrifice themselves, the Praetorians pulled back.

"How's that C-4 coming?" I asked Santino, who was still using a smaller knife on the stuff.

"I have no fucking clue how much of this I need so that it doesn't kill us. What the fuck are these walls even made out of?

Christ, I wish Bordeaux was here, and I never thought I'd be saying that about a Frenchy."

"Just hurry up," I yelled, slapping a fresh magazine in place. "They've pulled back for now, but they'll be back."

"Yeah, yeah. Don't rush me," he mumbled.

I ignored him, peaking around the corner. So far it was still clear.

"John..."

"I know. I know. I got it. Stand back."

Pulling back from the door, I joined him in the corner. Overturning a table to block the force of the blast, we crouched behind it. I saw Praetorians tentatively peak around the door just as we knelt behind our cover. Thinking our impromptu defenses were meant to counter their attack, they rushed us, confident a mere table wouldn't be enough to stop them.

"Now!" I yelled, almost pleadingly to Santino.

He didn't hesitate, triggering the charges before I could even finish the word. Shielded by the table and our protective ear pieces, the small charge didn't faze us much. The shock wave was just enough to knock us on our asses, but the rushing Praetorians took the full brunt of the blast. Those who rushed into the room sustained injuries from shrapnel and flying debris or died, while those in the hall were disoriented from the concussive blast. Even those still in the hall further back were stunned.

One step ahead of me, Santino rounded the table and made for the door. Hot on his heels, I bounded over the table, and followed. I saw that Santino had used a bit too much explosive and instead of just blowing the door off its hinges, he took out a large chunk of the wall as well.

Too interested in the wall, I didn't see Santino go down in front of me. Just as he left the room, a large wooden cudgel hit him right in the forehead dropping him like a rock. Only partially prepared, I was able to roll underneath the second swing which came at me from the other side of the blown wall.

Rolling to my feet, I shot my attacker, but was unable to shift my aim around to get the other man as well. His blow took me in the temple. My head swirling, I fell to my knees.

Gathered around me were dozens of blurry figures in white togas. As I knelt there, facing the hole we had just made, I saw

Claudius emerge. He walked straight up to me and back handed me across the face.

"I am not stupid!" He said, mad with rage. "I may be many things these days, but lacking in foresight is not one of them. As a god, how could I? I knew you would use your explosive devices to try and escape, and I posted guards accordingly."

I barely understood a word he said, as the world darkened around me. Falling on my side, I struggled to keep my eyes open.

The last thing I saw was a woman with light colored hair walk up to Claudius and kiss him intensely. I couldn't recognize who she was, or even determine who she might have been. Instead, all I could do was look at her menacingly familiar smile, just before a Praetorian slammed the hilt of his sword into my head, and watch as the world cut to black.

***

I woke to find myself suspended in the air. I had no idea how long I had been hanging like that, but I knew it wasn't long. The only thing I felt so far was pain. Hunger or thirst hadn't quite taken its hold on me yet. Craning my head to look around, the only things I saw were stars when another blow to my head knocked me out again.

***

Around the tenth time I was awakened and summarily knocked out again, I realized this must have been some form of torture. Just keep beating someone to the point of unconsciousness, let them sleep it off, and wake them up before starting all over again. I knew it was torture because each time it happened, it hurt more and more, and not only did the physical pain increase, but so did the pain in my stomach. I had to have been hanging for at least a day, but there was no real way of knowing.

After this latest beating, I was allowed to maintain consciousness. My head hurt so much I was having trouble remembering things, and I couldn't even picture my mother's face, or the empty platitudes my father would drill into my head. I couldn't remember where I was, or the name of the woman my mind kept drifting toward. All I knew were flashes and glimpses of a life I guessed were mine.

Finally able to keep my eyes open, a painful movement in and of itself, I forced myself to figure out where I was. The room was dark, gloomy, and had spider webs hanging all over the walls. I hated spiders. That much I remembered.

Of course, it might have just looked like spider webs because my eyes were practically swollen shut.

I looked to my left, and saw a man-like shape hanging in what I assumed was a similar fashion to how I was. His hands were tied to a cross beam, which was mounted on a wooden pole in the ground, forming a lower case t. His body was limp, and his head was hanging on his chest. The pose reminded me of something, but I couldn't quite place it. When I looked at my own hands, I confirmed that I was similarly hanging, and the only other support I received was from a small block under my feet that protruded slightly from the vertical pole.

Trying to shift my body, so that my legs took up some of the slack, I found I could barely move my arms. All the blood had drained from the veins, and my muscles refused to cooperate. To compensate, I used my legs to painfully push myself upwards, and immediately wished I hadn't. The act of taking pressure off of my arms forced all the pain toward that location, creating a whole new level of hurt to deal with.

Crying out, I woke my companion.

"Whe... where am I?" He said, likewise oblivious to our situation.

I tried to speak, but my mouth was too dry. I saw the man look over at me, a puzzled expression on his face.

"Who... who are you?" He said slowly, before recognition finally dawned on him. "Jacob? Is that you?"

Jacob?

Yes. Jacob. That was my name. Jacob Hunter. Service number... no, too many numbers. I was a US Navy SEAL, no former. I transferred to special service to the Pope. On a mission, we... and it all came flooding back to me.

Everything. Pope Gregory. McDougal. A blue sphere. Helena.

For some reason Helena's image burned brightest in my reclaimed memory. I remembered how much anger there'd been between us and how I'd left on such uneven terms. My first reaction was regret for how it turned out and how I had to make it right. I had to get back to set things right between us.

"Santino?" Yes. That was his name. "Do you remember anything?"

I looked over at my best friend. With that look my memory snapped into focus and I almost panicked when I realized what was happening to him. What must be happening to me as well.

We were being crucified.

Always considered one of the most drawn out, painful, and dehumanizing ways to die, I never really realized just how utterly horrendous it was. I remembered all those Sundays at Mass, looking up at Jesus of Nazareth hanging from his own cross, but his sculpture never seemed to reflect the sheer pain he must have been feeling, like the pain I was feeling now.

Santino must have regained his memory as well.

"We're being crucified?" He asked. "Crucified? Who fucking does that!?" At least his personality hadn't diminished, but as he finished his statement, he started coughing uncontrollably.

"Romans. That's who." I glanced around the room again. "Hang in there buddy. We'll get out of this."

Just as Santino was about to reply, another voice cut in.

"My, my, my, so eager to get down are we?" The demented voice I knew to be Claudius' said. "You've only been hanging there for a day or so, surely you aren't ready to leave yet? I have so many questions to ask you."

I watched as he stepped from the shadows in which he'd been hiding, holding something in his hands. I struggled in my restraints, not because I thought it would help, but because I was too stupid to realize it would hurt. The action alone nearly caused me to pass out again.

He stepped closer, a foot from my dangling body.

"What do you want?" The question came out resigned and defeated. I couldn't muster much else.

"Why, to expand Rome's power of course. And do you know how?"

Unable and unwilling to respond, I just hung there.

"So unexcited. How sad." He pulled his hands out in front of him, which were holding something covered with a piece of heavy cloth. "With this, of course." He pulled the cover away revealing the blue ball that started this mess. It shone dimly right now and I wondered if it was on.

"What does that have to do with me?"

"With you? Why, everything! You're the one who made it work. Don't play ignorant with me. That sniveling insect Varus said he saw you holding it when you first arrived. You are the fulcrum. The key. You can make it work."

"You don't understand what it does," I argued hoarsely. "It hurts people, makes them crazy. Don't you remember how you used to be just a few months ago? You were normal."

"Normal is such a relative term," he said, pulling the ball away and waving his hand in my face. "To you, it may seem like one thing, but to me, another. Who determines the normality of society if not those controlling it?" He paused, cocking his head to the side as he looked at me. "Why, me, of course! Now. Make it work," he said, thrusting the sphere in my face.

I looked wearily at him, feeling my life hanging by a thread. A thread I knew he could force me to dangle from for days to come.

"I... I don't know how."

Did the thing even have an on button?

Claudius slapped me. "You lie!" He slapped me again. For good measure I guess.

"Leave him alone, you fucking bastard," yelled Santino, coming to my defense. I would have smiled, if I wasn't doing everything I could just to remain conscious. Claudius was not amused, however, and signaled with his hand in Santino's direction.

Out of the corner of my eye, I saw two men rush forward, one man with two very large nails, the other with a large hammer. They didn't wait for further orders, and the first man placed a nail between the two bones connecting Santino's wrists, while the second man slammed the hammer against it.

Santino's scream was louder than my own after I had struggled against my restraints. Satisfied the first nail was secured, the two men moved on to his other wrist, likewise staking it to the cross in the manner science had proved was necessary for the body to not tear away from the nails. I saw my friend's head slump.

"You bastard! If you've killed him, I swear to God…"

"To which one?" Claudius barked, looking around the room, arms wide. "There are so many. Perhaps you swear to me? That would be ironic. Either way, you will unlock the true power within this orb."

"What do you actually expect to find?"

"Who cares?" He said, throwing his empty hand in the air. "As long as it's not more like you. I've seen who you are, and you've become so much less interesting than I'd hoped. What good are you, really? Now…" he shoved the sphere in my face again, "do it!"

The ball was so close, I couldn't help but look at it. I looked and looked, but had no idea what he wanted. He even pressed it against my cheek, but unlike last time, nothing happened. When he pulled it away, I continued to gaze into it and was just about ready to throw another insult at him when I thought I saw something, but as the image become clearer, a door slammed open and Claudius snapped the sphere away.

He moved over to the man, who was quickly and desperately saying something I couldn't hear. When the man finished, Claudius seemed even more furious and deranged. "It seems we have a bit of a problem," he said, looking in my direction. "No matter. I won't let you two get lonely."

He jerked a thumb in our direction, and twenty men piled into the room. These men weren't Praetorians, looking more like crooks, thieves, murderers and all the other nameless scum of the underworld, and they looked very happy.

"Don't kill them," was all Claudius said as he left.

The men joked and laughed, mumbling and grunting indecipherably to each other in a language I didn't understand. Once Claudius was gone, the men took the time to explore the room, looking for anything they could use to have a little fun. One man found an olive branch, similar to the ones I had been on the receiving end of a few times this past winter. Others found sticks, blunted knives, stones, and rope. Each of them circled around Santino and me threateningly. At least my friend was still unconscious.

The man with the olive branch walked up to me and spat in my face. Then he punched me in the gut, and started whipping my legs with the branches. His swats left large welts and cuts all over my calves and thighs. I was too weak to scream in agony, but my groans were plenty loud. It was at that point I realized I was completely naked, another blow to my dignity.

By the time the man started striking my back, and another man had begun cutting small lacerations into Santino's legs with a broken *gladius*, I heard something very familiar. It was the subtle clinging and clanking noise of something metal bouncing on a hard surface. Years of military training automatically kicked in, and I knew that sound could only be one thing.

A flashbang.

Squeezing my eyes tight, I tried to force myself to block out the inevitable bangs. I knew what was coming, but I was still unprepared for the actual detonation. The nine banger knocked me unconscious again, but only for a short while.

A minute later, I opened my eyes to see numerous blurry, black clad figures strolling through the room, policing the bodies of the now twenty dead torturers. One of them approached me, pulling off a balaclava, and stared up at my dangling form. Mask off, I saw the person release a mass of bunched up black hair, swinging it over her shoulders.

Helena tried to smile at me, but her façade of bravery faltered, revealing just how afraid she really was, even though her eyes looked as angry as ever.

"Miss me?" She asked.

XI
Siege

Rome, Italy
April-June, 38 A.D.

I looked away from my dark clad rescuer to figure out exactly what was happening. I saw three figures dressed similarly to Helena and looking more like ninjas than soldiers, move toward a still unconscious and naked Santino. I saw the largest of the three remove the nails from Santino's wrists, cut his bonds, and catch him as he fell onto him. The smallest figure pulled off a large bag, and tended to his wounds. I also noticed a number of Roman Praetorians moving through the room as well. I looked back at Helena, trying to form words, but my throat was too dry to utter a single one.

She looked at me expectantly. "Well? Nothing to say?"

A few seconds passed while I let my throat moisten.

"Please don't look down." I croaked.

She smiled and flicked her eyes downward anyway, glancing back up at me with a twinkle in her eye, but she wasted no time retrieving her knife from a sheath at her calf and cutting my bonds. Unable to bare my own weight, I collapsed into her arms, the pain threatening to knock me out again. She staggered only slightly under my weight, but refused to drop me. Gently, she lowered me to a sitting position and offered me the tube from her CamelBak. I accepted it and drank eagerly as she placed a large blanket over my shoulders. Choking on my last gulp, I spit water all over her, but immediately felt my head start to clear.

Frowning at her wet pants, she looked back at me. "So this is the thanks I get?"

"Sorry," I sputtered. "Couldn't help it." I wiped my mouth on her sleeve, and she gave me another look. "I hate to sound ungracious here, but what's the plan?"

In answer, another figure moved over to where we sat and pulled off his mask, revealing Vincent's weathered face.

"The plan is to get you two out of here," he said. "Unfortunately, getting in was the easy part, because the city is under siege now. Caligula has ordered an artillery strike. We'll have to dodge incoming fire as well as angry rebels. Can you walk? Can you fight?"

I shook my head. "I can walk, but not without help. My head feels like it's about to explode, and I can't see very well. If I look worse than I feel, I can only imagine how hard you guys must be working to keep your lunch down."

Helena angled her head to inspect my face. "It's not... that bad," she said, clearly lying.

"Santino is unconscious," Vincent continued, "and needs to be carried. We have fifty Praetorians with us, so that shouldn't be a problem, but we could still use all the help we can get."

I nodded. "Just give me a gun."

Helena placed a familiar object in my hand. "Here's Penelope."

I tried to look at her. "Umm... who?"

She shrugged. "You talk in your sleep."

I felt my cheeks get warm. It was only a little embarrassing that she knew I gave my rifle a name, and only slightly more that she knew I uttered it in my sleep.

"Don't worry," she whispered. "I'm not jealous."

I gave her a quick smile, at least what I thought might have been a smile had I been able to feel my face.

Wang came rushing over with an outreached hand. "Here, Hunter, take these." He held what I assumed were pain killers.

I swallowed them quickly with some more water. "Thanks, doc."

"Let's go," Helena said, pulling me to my feet with a strength I knew most women couldn't equal. She cradled me in a similar fashion to the way I had helped her the very first day we arrived in ancient Rome, and dragged me out of the room.

"Man, this is kinda nice," I commented. "You're not allowed to get hurt anymore. Only me."

"Deal, but lay off the desserts next time."

"Har har. Don't quit your day job."

I couldn't even remember the last time I had a non-MRE style dessert. Her struggles keeping me upright had nothing to do with my weight, but because I was offering far less help than she had been when I carried her months ago. I could barely limp, and it didn't take long before I realized she was mostly dragging me, as opposed to just supporting me. Just like the days carrying my drunken friends home back in college, their dead, fish-like state made them impossible to carry easily. I had to give her credit though because she was keeping up with the group well enough.

Vincent hung back with Helena and me, but Wang and Bordeaux were up in front with the vanguard of Praetorians breaking us out. I saw that we were rushing through the streets of an unfamiliar portion of Rome. Although, again, it probably only looked unfamiliar because I couldn't see shit. A part of me was thankful for that, but the other part wished I could see what was happening. It looked like an interesting fight.

"What's going on?" I asked Helena, blindly trying to get my bearings.

Before answering, I saw her tilt her head to look at the sky. Following her look, I tracked a dozen blurry and glowing red balls flying through the air.

"You're missing quite a show," she answered. "People are panicking and running through the streets. The city is in chaos. We're meeting only scarce resistance so far, easy kills for Wang and Bordeaux. Oh, Caligula's artillery is also lobbing balls of fire over the walls. I had no idea they could do that."

"You'd be surprised. They're pretty crafty," I told her as I stumbled on a rock, nearly falling to the ground.

I felt my head swim again.

"Jesus, you're a klutz, Hunter. You should have stuck to being a teacher," she said, trying to keep my spirits up as I found myself fighting harder and harder to stay conscious. After another dozen steps or so, I felt my eyes close and I started losing control over my legs. After another few steps, they gave out altogether, and I felt my hold on reality slip away.

The last thing I remembered before blacking out completely was Helena screaming my name.

***

I opened my eyes.

Flicking them left and right, the first thing I noticed was that I could in fact see. After a few minutes of blinking, my surroundings began to focus, but what continued to worry me was that I couldn't see much at all, just a bright white light.

Was I dead?

The only thing I remembered since being hung up in Claudius' torture chamber was a dream about two strikingly beautiful women, one dressed in a white, loose garment, the other in a black, tight fitting body suit. The two women had battled one another in vicious hand to hand combat for what seemed like days, neither one of them ever gaining the upper hand. They didn't fight in the comic, cliché cat fighting and bitch slapping style normally associated with two women duking it out, but with intense punches, kicks, eye gouges, and hair ripping, but with absolutely *no* fondling.

This was my dream, damn it! At least *some* clothing should have come off.

But I wasn't sure a lack of clothing would have saved me from the end because when both women finally noticed me, their duel ended and they shifted their attention toward me. Literal fire burning in their eyes, one set blue and the other green, both women turned to rush me, fists at the ready.

Hallucinations were a bitch.

I tried to put the disturbing dream out of my mind, and attempted to get a better look around. For all I knew, I may have been reacquired by Claudius. Maybe he was waiting for me to wake up before he tortured me again. I craned my neck to the right and noticed that I was in a tent, but the only objects I could see were a few empty tables and a desk.

I was distracted from my observation by a dark shape that positioned itself over my head. It took me a second to focus on the shape, but I didn't need my eyes to know that it was Helena. I could recognize her scent from across the room. It was that pleasant.

She smiled down at me, her smile more gorgeous than I'd ever seen it, and placed a hand on my cheek, stroking my brow with a thumb. "Nice to see you up, sleepy head."

"What happened?" I choked. "Where am I now?"

"You collapsed unconscious and Vincent had to carry you. We fought our way out of the city and made our way to the legion camp. We lost six men getting you out. You're in a hospital tent, and you've been out for two days."

That seemed like a good enough summary to me.

"Santino?"

She pulled back so that I could see past her. Behind her lay the figure of my friend, still unconscious, but breathing. I saw numerous bandages over his bare chest, arms and legs, and an IV drip poked into his forearm. In particular, I saw a bandage around his right wrist, renewing the image of his crucifixion in my mind.

"He's fine," she informed. "He's in worse shape than you are, but he'll make it. He lost a lot of blood, but Wang took good care of him. He says he'll make a full recovery."

"Good."

Satisfied he was all right, I straightened my head to rest my neck, and Helena loomed over me again.

"Can you sit up?" She asked.

I strained my back, but I didn't budge.

"Nope."

She frowned and I saw her glance away. She obviously had something on her mind.

No surprise there.

I looked up at her. "You saw me naked."

She looked back at me and a slight smile formed on her lips. "Yes. Yes I did."

"Well this is awkward…"

Her smile evaporated and she pulled away as she looked at her hands in her lap. I turned my head to look at her, but didn't say anything.

"Jacob, I… I just wanted to say I'm sorry for how I acted that night. I overreacted."

My back was starting to hurt from idleness so I tried to shift my position on the table again. The slight movement shot pain through every inch of my body and I felt my body fighting against the inevitable blackout I knew was coming. I thought the combination was going to kill me, but the pain slowly went away and my senses sharpened. I looked at Helena, whose concern was very clearly evident.

"Are you sure you're all right?" She asked. "I could come back if you want to rest."

"No," I said quickly. "Don't leave. I… I need you right now."

She leaned back. "Need?"

I closed my eyes. Maybe if I couldn't see her, this would be easier. "I fucked up, Helena. All this time I thought I had all the answers and knew what was best for me, you, the team, everyone. But I don't." I opened my eyes when Helena didn't say anything, but all she did was lean in closer to hover only a foot above me. "You didn't overreact. Not in the least. The past few months have changed a part me, and not for the better. I don't like it, and it's…"

I trailed off when I noticed how intently Helena was staring at me. Her eyes were sad and distant but their intensity threw me. I couldn't interpret what the expression meant. I was about to continue when Helena thrust herself at me and pressed her lips against mine, much as I did to her all those months ago. The shock wore off quickly and I found myself struggling to move my hand into her hair as she continued to work her lips lovingly against mine. I failed and the sound of my arm slapping against the table surprised Helena into pulling away.

"Oh, I'm sorry, did I hurt you?"

I gazed up at her lovely face and wonderful green eyes and smiled. "Of course not. I'm just a little surprised."

"I know," she said meekly. "Me too, but I couldn't help myself."

"You couldn't help yourself, *now*??" I asked with a weak smile. "When my face looks like I went twelve rounds with Rocky?"

She smiled. "I don't want to kiss you because of your face, Jacob, but because of what you said. I've felt you pulling away for months now, placing more and more burdens upon yourself and slowly pushing your friends, and me, away. What you said before you left about not needing me hurt." She looked at me almost angrily now as she relived the memory. "I didn't want to accept where that comment came from, but it had become difficult not to."

I glanced at Santino again to make sure he was still asleep. Our conversation was becoming increasingly personal and I didn't want him overhearing us. Luckily, he still seemed out cold. I turned back to Helena and frowned. "Helena I'm still the man I was before. Just…"

"No you're not. You're darker, more selfish, and more introspective, and not in a good way. It's become obsessive. I can understand not coming to me, but you've neglected even your best friend." She pointed at Santino. "I can count the number of conversations you've had with him over the past winter on one hand. You never go to him for help or advice, and you know damn well it's not always that bad. Why do you think he volunteered to go with you and Agrippina?"

I didn't have an answer.

"Because he's your brother!" She said. "The story you told me about what happened in North Korea forced it on you two, and you should be grateful for that shithole because of it. But he's just as worried about your recklessness as I am and wanted to keep an eye on you."

"How do you know that? Did he tell you?"

"He didn't have to, Jacob," she said softly. "I know."

"So why now?"

"Because I care for you, Jacob. I have for a very long time. I want to be with you and be there for you. When I saw you on that cross I was horrified. I couldn't believe how close I came to losing you."

I stared at the ceiling, the memory of my torture the only thing I could focus on despite Helena's loving words. "They were crucifying me, Helena. Crucifying."

"I know," she said, her tone shifting dourly. "When I came in and saw you and Santino hanging there, I couldn't believe it. Seeing it actually happen... it's hard to believe."

"Tell me about it."

"I'm sorry. I can only imagine how painful it must have been."

"I really doubt it." I took a deep breath. "I'm just glad it's over."

"So am I," another voice chimed in, interrupting us, "and I am extremely happy to see you awake."

As the voice came closer, I looked to my right to see Vincent approach and stand opposite Helena. He looked down. "How are you feeling, son?"

"Better," I answered. "Come to give me my last rites?"

He smiled. "No."

As I lay there, looking up at him, an epiphany sparked in my head. It was as though I had finally figured out this nagging feeling I'd had about him since we first arrived here. I didn't know why, maybe it was the drugs, but something in his expression and mannerism just screamed at me, triggered by how he had called me, "son."

I turned my head, and studied his face. "You're not a priest, are you?"

Vincent straightened while Helena shifted her look toward him, a confusion spreading across her face. He stood there for only a few seconds before he crossed his arms, and looked at me. His face suggested he was trying to find the best way to answer and he shifted his feet and looked at the floor.

"What gave me away?" He replied, raising his eyes.

I heard a sharp intake of breath from Helena, just slightly more surprised than I was. I met his eyes before responding.

"I've had my suspicions for a while, to be honest, but it wasn't until just now that I confirmed it. The way you called me "son" and not "my son" did it. You've done it before, but maybe my drugged up state has given me some advanced powers of observation, but the way you said it just clicked. The fact you've never insisted on presiding over Mass on Sundays didn't help much, either."

"There's just no fooling you, is there?"

I shrugged, immediately regretting it.

"Well... you're right. I am no priest. I've spent my entire life since leaving the Swiss military in the Pope's Swiss Guard, and I've spent more time in the Vatican than I have anywhere else. The Pope himself suggested the idea that we have a member of the clergy on the team, and he wanted me ordained, but I told him no." He sighed. "I've felt lots of things in my life, but never the calling to become a priest. Pope Gregory understood the sentiment, himself not having felt the call until somewhat later in his life. Instead, knowing I was the most experienced and willing man for the post, he gave me his blessing to assume the role, to act as a symbol and a reminder of who and what we were working for." He stopped himself, and looked at the floor again. "I guess there's no need to keep pretending then, is there? Ancient Rome has no need for Catholic priests. Especially phony ones."

"That doesn't exactly sound like something a pope would just allow," I said, skeptically.

"Desperate situations call for desperate answers, Jacob. Not many priests are fit for military duty."

"So, why didn't you go through with it?" Helena asked.

He looked thoughtful as he glanced at her, his look lingering ever so slightly. "I... have my reasons, but I think it's because I still want to have a family of my own one day. I'm not that old, you know."

"Why didn't you tell us?" I asked.

He sighed. "At eighteen our convictions are hills from which we look; at forty-five they are caves in which we hide."

I squinted. "Hemingway?"

"Fitzgerald," Helena answered for him with a smirk. "F. Scott."

I returned the look. "Smart ass."

Vincent smiled at us. "Were I a younger man, I may have come out with it, but time slows us down. Helps us think. Makes us patient. Hell," he paused, suddenly taking a moment to ponder his next thought. After an awkward moment, he continued, "Hell, were I a younger man, I may have taken my vows. Either way, it seemed best to keep my cover locked in a cave until you figured it out for yourself."

"Seems this outfit is full of surprises," I said. "What's next? Is Santino really a cross dresser?"

"I heard that," said a weak and raspy voice, "and could you keep it down? I'm trying to sleep."

The three of us turned to look over at Santino, who had his eyes open, but kept his head facing toward the roof of the tent. Helena pulled her chair next to him, and gripped his hand.

"How are you feeling?" She asked.

"Like I was just crucified. Oh, wait. Remind me not to let that happen again."

Helena smiled down at him. "Well, it's nice to see you haven't lost your charming personality."

I saw Santino's jaw working, and I assumed he was trying to keep his mouth from drying up, but then it looked like he was almost going to cry.

"I lost my knife," he said, as though it had been his mother.

"Don't worry," Helena told him, "we'll get you another one. A bigger one. I promise."

"Oh, that's nice…" he muttered, slowly drifting unconscious again.

"Get better, John," Helena told him, leaning down to give him a quick peck on the lips.

"I could get used to that," he mumbled as his small smile faded along with his consciousness.

"So are you upset with me?" Vincent asked as Helena returned to my side

"No." I answered firmly. "I'm a military man. I'm used to my commanders lying to me."

"And you?" He asked, looking at Helena.

She considered for a moment. "No, sir."

"Good. I was hoping you'd say that, the both of you. Honestly, I feel quite relieved. Maybe I can curse every once in a while now."

"That would be refreshing, sir, and since you're here, mind telling me how and why you came to rescue us?"

"It was Helena's idea," he answered immediately. "After you left, she came to me and voiced her dissent of the mission. She explained how you admitted to her that you didn't trust Agrippina, and that you knew something was off about the mission. However, since you couldn't refuse to help a grieving mother, you hoped to expose her plot by going through with it."

"I said all that, huh?" I asked, looking up at Helena. She gave me a look that suggested I shut the hell up and roll with it.

"So, once the legion arrived outside of Rome a few days later, and after you hadn't reported in, I asked Caligula if we could go in under cover of an artillery barrage, and get you out. He was reluctant to condone such an action, but in the end, decided it would send a strong message to the city's inhabitants. So he agreed, and even offered a contingent of his own troops to help."

"How did you find us?"

"After we snuck through one of the gates," Helena answered for him, "we asked some folks along the way for directions. They were very forthcoming. Besides, we had Santino's UAV."

"Ah, right." I took a deep breath, feeling the need for sleep wash over me. "Thanks."

Vincent smiled, and patted me on the shoulder. "Get some rest. We're going to need you one of these days." He nodded to Helena, and left the tent.

She watched him go. "Didn't see that coming."

"Yah," I replied. "Me neither, but I'm getting pretty good at reading people these days."

I thought about Agrippina, and how I was certain she was implicated in Santino and I getting our asses kicked and how she had so easily played us. I hadn't seen her clearly in that moment before I fell unconscious, but I knew it had to be her.

"Then again, maybe I'm not," I thought out loud.

Helena reached over and intertwined her fingers through my own. I looked over at her, and saw the same bloodshot and puffy eyes I had seen the day I left for Rome. I felt just as sleepy as she looked, but I finally found the strength to reach a hand up and grab her head. I stared at her for only a moment before I pulled her toward me. "Come here."

She didn't resist and I brought her into another kiss, this one sweeter and far more intoxicating than the last. Helena was right. We'd danced around our feelings and emotions for far too long. I've cared for her just as long as she has for me, probably longer. She pulled back after a few moments and kissed me lightly on the forehead.

"Like I said before Vincent arrived, you're heading in the right direction. The man I grew to care for is there again. For you to admit that you were wrong was a huge step. Your words and attitude are far more compelling than your face ever was, and I want to be there to help." She smirked. "Then again... I did see you naked."

I looked at her happily, more happy than I'd been in a long, long time. "Like what you saw, Miss Strauss?"

She shrugged. "I suppose so, but it's not like I have many references to compare it to."

"Ouch, Helena. Ouch. Maybe you'd care to return the favor? I'd love to offer you some constructive criticism. Trust me, it'd be my pleasure"

She reached down to cup the side of my cheek while unzipping her combat shirt, stopping the process just above her navel. "Don't get any ideas, Lieutenant. There'll be plenty of time for that..." she let go of the zipper just before things got interesting "...later."

"You're such a tease."

"Shut up, Jacob," she said as she tore the blanket covering my body away and slipped in next to me, pressing herself up against me gently. She kissed me again and laid her head against my shoulder as she wrapped an arm across my body carefully. "Don't worry. The hero always gets the girl. You'll just have to be more patient than most."

***

The nice thing about sieges was that there really wasn't much to do.

After I'd awakened for the second time, this time with Helena deep in sleep beside me, her head resting lovingly on my chest, I was still too weak to move. It left me with plenty of time to think, and one of the things that hit me hard was the fact that Santino and I had failed our mission. Not only had we been tricked by Agrippina into participating in her so- called humanitarian mission, an embarrassing defeat in and of itself, but we also failed to secure the demolition along the walls, which would have ended this mess a lot quicker. Instead, I woke up to find myself in the middle of a siege, a military blockade of an enemy city with the sole purpose of starving the city into fighting or surrendering. Sieges could last for a year, waste precious time, and never left the disgruntled innocent bystanders of the besieged city all that happy should there be a change in leadership. What made me feel worse was the fact I had failed a personal request from Caligula himself. I dreaded the day I had to get my ass out of that tent and face him.

I didn't have to wait long. Only a few hours after Helena joined me for her nap, Santino still unconscious on the bed next to me, Caligula had sought me out instead. I hadn't heard him enter the tent, and he had snuck up on me as quietly as Santino ever could. Caught unaware, my first instinct was to get up, only to find that I still couldn't move. I felt silly with Helena practically straddling me, but Caligula didn't question it.

To my surprise, his expression wasn't angry, nor did he seem upset. He hadn't stayed long, but he reassured me that while he was sorry we had failed in both missions, he wasn't upset. He was just happy we'd be available to fight for him whenever the siege lifted, but also pressured me for information on Claudius and his state of mind. I did my best to relay everything I could. He wasn't happy to learn of his turn toward insanity, but also didn't seem overly surprised. If I had to guess, I would assume he and Varus had done some more digging into the origins and meaning behind Remus' documents, and may have learned what Vincent and I already knew.

I also tried to apologize to him, as well as tell him about Agrippina's suspected role in my capture, but he left before I could. I wasn't sure how to feel as I watched his retreating back, but at least I wouldn't have to face him later. Suddenly feeling very tired, I fell back asleep.

Three days later, I finally gained the strength to get up and begin my rehabilitation. Wang had given me a clean bill of health, but also let me in on just how close I had come to death's door. I had been deprived of food and water for almost two days, had lost multiple pints of blood, and had my head beaten to the point where brain damage had only been a few more knocks on the cranium away. I was lucky to be alive, and as I sat on the table I had spent the past few days on, trying to knead feeling back into my muscles, he had pointed at Santino and practically proclaimed his survival an act of divine intervention. A man any less willing to survive wouldn't have, and Wang diagnosed that it was probably Santino's drive to annoy people that had kept him going.

With him still bed ridden, Helena and I started my rehab exactly the way we had done when she'd recovered from her injuries sustained in 2021. We started with stretches and light calisthenics, then onto walking and jogging, before I was finally able to start running again. Santino took a week to get out of bed, but was soon on his feet and getting stronger as well.

That was two months ago.

During that time, Santino and I pushed ourselves hard, and it wasn't too long until we were back at our peak physical readiness once again. Not that it mattered much. We didn't see any signs of the siege lifting any time soon.

Caligula's initial barrage of artillery had ended quickly after it had started. Its purpose was mainly to let the citizens of Rome know he was out there, but its cover for the rescue operation was still appreciated. As Caligula said before the operation even began, he had no intention of razing Rome to the ground, or destroying more property than he needed to. While the city had burned that night, little real estate was severely damaged, and the fires had quickly died out thanks in large part to the rainy spring months.

So, the siege would endure, either starving the people of Rome into surrendering, or sallying out in a counter attack.

Rome was many things, but self-sufficient it was not. It had grain supplies that could feed its citizens, but they wouldn't last forever. By the time Augustus took power seventy years ago, Rome had just finished fighting its third civil war in the past one hundred years, the last between Augustus himself and Marc Antony. The population of the empire, and the city itself, was at an all-time low. Now, however, more than a half century later, and another forty after Augustus enacted his legislation encouraging Romans to marry and have children, Rome was reaching a population level that it would soon find overwhelming.

Twenty five years from now, during Nero's reign, a fire would engulf the city, last nine days, and reduce entire sections of the city to rubble. Nero would later take advantage of the newly cleared land to build his golden house on top of the destroyed territory. During the fire, however, grain supplies were lost, and the very real revelation that Rome's citizens might starve occurred to many. While Nero had actually done a good job in rationing out the grain, and not dancing with his fiddle during the fire as Suetonius records, had Rome been ready for such a disaster, they may have been able to feed everyone, despite the loss of supplies during the fire.

As fate would have it, just as during the fire of 64 A.D., one of the few things hit during the initial artillery barrage was the city's grain supplies. It wasn't a major blow, but any loss to their food reserves brought the city that much closer to starvation.

Vincent and I determined that Rome's grain supplies probably wouldn't last the eight months Caligula's experts predicted. They just didn't have all the facts, let alone hindsight. Even so, we'd be here for a while.

To complete the siege, our legionnaires had spent days digging trenches and ditches three hundred yards or so away from the walls to encircle the entire city. The trench system was meant to contain the inhabitants as well as provide defense if the legion was attacked. Aiding our effort were two natural phenomena.

The first lucky break was the fact that Rome hadn't expanded to its largest point yet. The Aurelian walls hadn't been built, and its defensive line was still the city's original Servian Wall. The second blessing was the Tiber River, which worked as a natural barrier to the West. The legion merely took up residence in the *Campus Martius*, which also lay outside the walls, but between them and the

Tiber. Additional troops were also stationed on the opposite side of the river, effectively shutting down the city in the west.

Unfortunately, as the saying goes, "all roads lead to Rome", there were many points of entry for us to contain. The *via appia, aurelia, cassia, claudia valeria, flaminia, salaria,* and other smaller ones were all roads that passed through Rome, and each needed to be blocked. Therefore, each road received two centuries of legionnaires and a varied number of auxilia. Each century constructed a camp, much like the larger version they had wintered in on either side of the road. On the road, they placed wooden beams, attached together in a cross-bracing. These barriers reminded me of the anti-landing craft barricades the Nazis had placed along the shore of Normandy prior to D-day. The remainder of the legion was spread out along the trench network at set intervals in small camps, no bigger than a couple of tennis courts.

Most of these camps were provided with artillery pieces such as an *onager*. The word *onager* literally translated as "ass", a reference to how it kicked like a donkey when fired. It was basically a catapult, and while it was highly inaccurate, it was still able to throw heavy objects far distances. They scared the hell out of people, but weren't overly efficient.

Finally, scattered around the trenches were the legion's cavalry auxilia, who would be handy if the defenders decided to counter attack. Their quick response time would allow them to react to a breakout along the lines anywhere in a matter of minutes.

Caligula's command camp was the largest of all. It held us, his sacred band, his two loyal Praetorian cohorts, and the *Primigenia's* first cohort. It was located between *via cassia* and via *aurelia*, on the west bank of the Tiber, near where the Vatican would one day stand.

To help strengthen the defenses, Vincent had assigned us to patrol the trenches in our swim pairs occasionally throughout the day. The trenches, miles long, proved good exercise, as well as a warm up for what was to come.

On the tenth day of the siege, a supply train was intercepted trying to sneak supplies into the city. A ridiculous undertaking considering the blockade, but nonetheless, a caravan of some fifty wagons tried to breach our lines and move into the city. As it happened only two days after I had started limping my way around the camp again, I wasn't able to participate in the take down, but I did watch it from the ramparts.

The blockade runners were pressing their horses to full speed as they traveled down the street. Calmly and efficiently, a few dozen legionnaires posted themselves on the paved road, and planted stakes. Unable to dig them into the dirt, they positioned rocks to act as fulcrums, and planted a foot on the blunt side to keep them angled. The Romans managed to erect a barrier of overlapping sharp sticks, three rows deep, while they hunkered down behind their shields.

Horses were by no means stupid animals, and unlike in the movies where they would ride straight into their impending doom, these horses noticed the obstacles, and quickly veered out of the way. The turn forced them to slow just enough for more legionnaires to board the wagons and eliminate the passengers. The camp had gained additional supplies and horses, and the city of Rome continued to wane.

On the thirtieth day of the siege, Helena and I were on patrol, approaching one of the small picket stations placed sporadically along the trench system. We arrived to good cheer, as every legionnaire loved the sight of us. Well, at least the sight of Helena, but I tried to imagine they liked me too. Besides, it was always humorous to watch them scramble over one another just to seem more important in the eyes of the only woman they'd seen in months and had grown to adore.

Completing nearly half of our trip around the trenches, we took a break in the small outpost. In the center were temporary troop quarters and a small dining area, and along the perimeter of the trench was a small rampart that ran around the perimeter of the camp with another ditch system on the other side for added protection. Helena and I climbed one of the walls, and rested our rifles along the railing.

I'd lost Helena's P90 after failing to escape the *Domus Augusti*, and after Caligula came to see me that first day, I had feared that when she woke, she'd forget about our happy reunion and remember that I had lost her gun. Thankfully, Claudius had kept everything he'd confiscated from Santino and me in a room close by. It had been breached and cleared as well, and Helena and Wang had recovered their lost weapons. The only thing missing was Santino's knife. He was still lamenting its loss.

But thank God we'd found Helena's weapon. She might have hurt me.

She left her DSR-1 back in our tent, preferring the lighter weapon for our long patrols, so she pulled out a small monocular, and scouted the walls of Rome, looking for any sign or disturbance while I sighted through my scope. I frowned when I saw a small gate opening in the walls, and a small contingent of men rushing out in our direction, maybe four hundred or so in total. Some rode horses, but most were running on foot, and none of them wore armor, so I assumed they were civilians.

I flicked my safety off, and Helena and I opened fire on the oncoming men. They were close enough that I could have picked them off the walls had I the chance, but the defenders had learned that lesson early in the siege when Helena's kill count reached four tribunes and ten centurions, all from the city's Praetorian cohorts.

Just as we had done defending Caligula's home, Helena fired single and precise shots, even with her smaller gun, while I fired in controlled bursts. The enemy had to cross around three hundred yards of open ground before they reached the outer ditch, and we made them pay for it. We must have shot more than a quarter of their strength before they finally reached our outpost. Immediately, Helena and I abandoned the ramparts to let the more experienced legionnaires handle the initial onslaught. We lobbed a few grenades into the intruders' dense ranks just for good measure before jumping off the walls and into our trenches. When the grenades went off, twenty legionnaires cast their *pila* into the enemy ranks, impaling only a handful here and there before the enemy got their acts together and started scaling our wall.

Initially, the men on the rampart held them off easily. It was only a matter of knocking over their ladders, and sending them falling the short distance to the ground, but when there were too many to handle, the ramparts were abandoned, and men started spilling into the trenches.

The two centuries of legionnaires, plus Helena and I, were equally matched in numbers with our enemy by now, but we were all professional soldiers, whereas they were glorified peasants.

Organized, we stood shield to shield, waiting for them to waste themselves attacking us.

Wave after wave came at us, slashing, cutting, and stabbing, only to be repelled. These men were amateurs, men with no military training, nothing but a purpose driving their attacks, whatever that purpose may be.

By the time we cut the enemy's number in half again, I lost Helena somewhere in the confusion, and I could only pray that she was all right. Cut off from my swim buddy, I found myself in the middle of a line of three legionnaires. So far I had only been involved in small skirmishes and I'd seen many men cut down, but had yet to bloody my sword.

With only seven enemy combatants remaining, they had no time for heroics. Hitting our line, I blocked and stabbed, and blocked even more, before I saw a clear opening for my first kill. An enemy was engaged with the legionnaire to my right, and had over extended himself, falling onto his shield. I saw the enemy's exposed flank, and drove my sword up through the man's armpit, driving it into his neck. Freeing my sword, a stream of blood spewed all over my clothes and face. No time to react, I saw one of the last men swinging his sword with both hands downwards, in an attempt to split me in two.

I gave him no such chance. I caught the slice on my shield, blocking and sweeping his sword away, giving me an open shot at his entire front side. I looked right in his eyes and he looked back, immediately realizing his mistake. Gazes still locked, I thrust my sword right through the man's chest. I felt the blade slip through his ribs, and out his back. I'd hit him right in his heart, and he fell dead almost immediately, blood spurting from the wound and his mouth.

The last of the enemy slain, the surviving legionnaires bellowed a triumphant cry. They inspected the bodies, putting down any poor soul still left alive. It was a barbaric custom, but this was war, and definitely not one with any modern rules. Sanitation, food, medical supplies, guards – each of these things were at risk by harboring prisoners, and it would only hinder the siege. As immoral as it may have seemed, it was the only practical answer.

Only a few dozen of our men had died, while another twenty had sustained injuries. Our men would receive help, of course, and I did what I could with the limited medical kit I had on me. Tending to a legionnaire cut along his bicep, I applied a few butterfly bandages to the wound after wiping it with some anti-bacterial cream. Applying the last of the bandages, I was prematurely pulled away from the man by Helena, who grabbed my head and kissed me with a passion I hadn't experienced from her in days, well... hours really. My reunion with her incited most of the men watching to boo and throw dirt at us. The legionnaires had grown accustomed to seeing us together back in the winter camp, but now that we were clearly together, they let their humorous disapproval show whenever they could.

Poor jealous bastards.

That was the first of our mini engagements, and the only one I had participated in. Everyone else in the squad had received a small taste for sword combat during the siege as well, and each came away admitting they hated it, but happy they got some experience. These engagements had me worried though. If Claudius could afford to waste troops in these completely ineffective counter attacks, how many men did he really have? The enemy was losing far more than we were, and it led me to wonder if Claudius had recruited a larger army than Galba had estimated.

As for Nero and Agrippina, I had no idea where they were, and frankly, couldn't care less. A part of me wished the pair died in the initial artillery strike, but that seemed unfair. After all, young Nero was still technically innocent, and something as beautiful, albeit evilly beautiful, as Agrippina shouldn't be wasted.

On the thirty-seventh day of the siege, I awoke around four in the morning, and was not feeling well. I'd slept all right, but it must have been that damn beef patty MRE I had again the previous evening that woke me.

I've sworn off the stuff since.

With my upset stomach groaning, I got up slowly so I didn't disturb Helena. She was still fast asleep, the remnants of her clothing strewn about the tent after I'd aggressively removed them earlier. She looked perfect in the dim light from a dying glow stick that softly illuminated her body, so I retrieved my rifle as quietly as I could and left to wander through the trenches. It was still dark, and there were only a few sentries posted and awake. As I passed by them, they offered me friendly, but tired greetings, mostly paying me little attention. I continued on my morning walk until I found a nice spot to watch the sun rise in the East. Since high school, I had made it a point to just sit and watch the sun rise whenever I could. My time in the military, and in the Roman army, granted me many opportunities to be awake during the time, but never any to just sit and enjoy.

It had been a beautiful dawn, followed by an even more stunning sunrise. I didn't move until the entirety of the sun had cleared the horizon, and was floating just a few feet above the tree line, far in the distance. I could never figure out why I felt better after watching the daily event, I just knew that I did. It made me feel whole. I threw the sun a salute and continued on my trek.

Along the way, I stopped at each fort and used my rifle's scope to check out the walls in case trouble was abrewing. At the last fort before my camp, I set my sights just above a gate's entrance, and saw the last thing I thought I'd see. Agrippina was standing there, and oddly, she seemed to be looking right at me. There was no way she could have recognized me from that distance , but I could have sworn she'd smiled at me.

I lowered my rifle, rubbed my eyes with my hands and then the lenses of my scope with a rag. Raising my rifle again, I looked back at where I thought I had seen her only ten seconds earlier, but found nothing. Just an empty wall. I shuddered, finally realizing the odd contrasting similarities between Agrippina's smile, and Helena's eyes. Not a person in the world could either unnerve me or confuse me like those two women could. I went back to my tent thoroughly creeped out and wrapped myself around Helena. In seconds, I was back asleep with another hour to burn.

By the time the fiftieth day of the siege rolled around, I'd just about given up any thoughts of it lifting. Besides the few moments of excitement and action, there wasn't much to do. I spent my time running, practicing swordsmanship, cleaning and preparing my gear, spending some quality time with my reconciled lady friend, and working on my tan. I was a solid bronze, practically Helena standards, by the time Caligula called for a meeting of his senior staff. He told Vincent to bring the rest of us along.

All the usual suspects were present and accounted for, so Caligula began promptly.

"I am sure you are all aware of how the siege is progressing, so I'll get to the point." He paused, placed his fists on the table and leaned heavily on them. "We've just received reports indicating massive unrest in the city. Many of its citizens are calling for an end to the siege and demanding Claudius do something about it.

"Seven months ago, news of my apparent death didn't go over well with the public, and while Claudius' ascension was taken in stride, it was not overwhelming popular. Therefore, our arrival, and my apparent rise from the dead, has made the people question what actually happened the night we left. Thanks in part to Vincent and his people, many felt the gods themselves had fought against my Praetorians. Now, however, they are not so sure.

"This works in our favor. Claudius now has no choice but to face us in open combat, or risk the city rising against him. I do not care how unstable he may be, he is not stupid. He'll come out and face us."

He looked at each of us present and met each of our gazes. Most wore stone faced expressions, but some, mostly those of us who had never seen a military engagement of this kind, looked worried. He must have noticed our apprehension.

"Vincent. What can I expect from you and your people?"

Vincent shifted his feet, and looked at each of his operators. I gave him a reassuring nod.

"We'll fight for you, Caesar," he replied, confidently.

"Good."

"I think what the emperor meant is how can you help us?" Galba asked, still looking for a reason to keep us around.

"Three things," Vincent said, ignoring Galba. "First, we can lay a field of explosives on the battlefield the night before the engagement along a path where we expect our enemy to be. They will trigger when passed by. It should cause significant damage to small portions of the army."

"Wouldn't that require them to attack us? As it is we who are besieging them, it would seem that the orders of combat would be reversed," Galba said, continuing his skepticism and sarcasm.

"Not necessarily, sir. We can sneak close enough to the walls to lay them in the area the enemy will use to form their battle lines. We can hit them any time we want."

I groaned quietly. That would mean we, probably Helena and I, would have to spend hours crawling under the cover of ghilli suits just to get close enough to lay out a field of demo. It wouldn't be fun, but it would definitely work.

C-4 was very good at blowing up walls and bringing down buildings, but its blast radius and direction was very concentrated, so laying it on the ground to blow at the enemy's feet wouldn't work. We did have a few claymores left, provided in our supplies but what would really help were the few dozen antipersonnel mines we discovered. Nearly invisible to those not directly looking for them, the mines were equipped with laser trip wires. Once triggered, the mine would launch a device a few feet in the air, and explode outwards as it spun, tearing through skin and bone in a twenty yard radius. The few dozen of these we had would be very helpful, indeed.

"Second, we can provide rifle fire to help weed out the enemy at a much farther range than your *pila* volleys. Since we are within our range already, our sustained fire might force their hand, and cause them to charge us. Once both sides are within *pila* range, no matter who charges who, we will fall back through your lines and fire when targets of opportunity display themselves only."

"And the third?" Galba asked insistently.

Vincent looked around the room, maybe deciding if he wanted to continue or not. "Before the battle even begins, should Claudius be present on the battlefield, we, and by 'we,' I mean she," he said, pausing for emphasis as he pointed at Helena, "can eliminate him before he takes two steps onto the field."

Galba opened his mouth to speak, but just as quickly shut it. He had seen her shoot an apple off of a wall from a few hundred yards away, and must have known she could do what Vincent was offering. Whether he wanted to admit it or not, and since she was a better shot than even I was, Helena, not her rifle, was currently the single most effective weapon on the entire planet.

Caligula appeared more thoughtful than his general, as he too realized Helena could perhaps end the war before it even began. Still leaning on his fists, he looked up and for maybe the first time since both had known each other, looked her square in the eye, and spoke to her as a commander would any of his soldiers.

"Are you willing to do this?"

Helena looked at Vincent, who nodded, then at me. All I could do was offer a weak shrug. It wasn't my place to decide for her.

She looked down at her feet and thought it over before meeting Caligula's face.

"I am," she answered, mostly confident.

Caligula looked at Galba, whose face was unreadable. I knew what he was thinking, and it couldn't have been an easy decision. Just because you had the power to end a life on a whim, doesn't mean you should do so. Besides, enemy or not, crazy or not, Claudius was still Caligula's uncle, and I'm sure that fact had to weigh heavily on his mind. He turned his back on his staff, and rested his chin on an upraised fist.

Five minutes passed and he still hadn't made a decision.

"Caesar?" Galba queried tentatively.

Caligula's head dropped, but he soon turned back to face us.

"No," he said quietly. "No. Thank you, but I cannot condone that. He is my uncle, and both sides are aware of why they are fighting. Assassinating him at the onset of battle would do little to dissuade the troops. Whoever has more men standing at the end of the day will prevail, and will be able to maintain their hold on power through their own loyal troops. The less dissenters the better. This must be decided on the battlefield."

Bravo, Caligula. I had to imagine emperors both before, and definitely after, would have jumped at the opportunity to wield the kind of power Helena possessed. Sure, he'd used her before for the same exact reason, but it seemed as though the past few months had matured the man, his arrogant personality abandoned. If we could defeat Claudius, I saw a bright future for Rome.

As for Helena, she was obviously relieved. She'd gotten a taste of both combat and assassination lately, and had a definite knack for both, but I knew it didn't come easy for her. I knew she didn't like it. It had been the topic of many a late night conversation. I wondered if she would have cut it as a sniper back home. She had no choice here. Here it was kill or be killed, but it wasn't so black and white back home. She wasn't a bloodthirsty killer, and I had a renewed regret for bringing us here and causing all this shit.

"So, when the day comes," Caligula continued, "I expect your people to be at my side. They will have a place of honor, right beside me."

"It is indeed an honor, Caesar," Vincent answered, "but I believe we would be put to better use in a more active part of the field."

"Do not worry, I do not plan to loiter in the rear and stay safe in this battle. The troops will need their emperor guiding them, as much as their eagle. I leave it to you to keep me safe. Believe me when I say, I wouldn't be so quick to do battle myself if you were not there."

"We will do our best. Thank you, Caesar."

Caligula smiled, and looked over at his Praetorian *primus pilus*. "Don't look so glum, Quintilius. I would not be so eager to fight if you and your men weren't there as well."

Quintilius returned the smile, his dignity and pride restored.

"Let us talk strategy then," he said.

Finding his favorite map of the walled city, he started to lay out his preliminary battle plans. Before he could make any headway, a commotion from outside the tent forced us to stop.

"What now?" Santino asked.

I turned to Helena. "If it's Agrippina, just shoot her this time."

She flashed a toothy smile, but we breathed a collective sigh of relief when a simple messenger entered the tent instead, handing Caligula a sealed letter. The emperor thanked the man and started reading. I saw his eyes grow slightly before he crumpled up the letter and burned it with a candle.

"General, alert the troops," he ordered Galba. "Tomorrow we do battle. It seems Claudius has decided to come out and meet us in open combat. We'll continue this when you return."

Galba smiled, his expression itching for a fight. "With pleasure, Caesar."

XII
Endgame

Plains outside Rome, Italy
June, 38 A.D.

The following morning, I prepared for war.

It would be the kind of war I'd never seen before, and for the first time in my military career, I was truly afraid. Not just nervous like I had been many times before a mission, but genuinely scared shitless. This was the kind of random warfare that left almost no room to control your own fate. That worried me. A random spear here or a wayward sword thrust there. Each could end your life before you even knew it. Back home I was always on the offensive, choosing the time and place for battle and the how and why shit went down around me. Those would not be options available today.

I had slept well that night, capitalizing with Helena on the idea that we might not survive another day. It amounted to a good sleep, despite the predawn wake up time.

However, prior to our nocturnal activities, facing a completely novel way of waging war, we prepared our gear as well as we could for the unfamiliar battle ahead. The versatility of my combat vest really showed itself as I removed every single pouch, pocket or other modular item already applied, leaving it a bare canvas for me to work on.

The key to our effectiveness was the ability to maintain our weapons fire as long as possible. To help neutralize the fact that I had limited space on my vest to carry loaded magazines, I opted instead to carry a shoulder hoisted messenger bag. The bag allowed me to carry forty fully loaded magazines for my HK416, more than twelve hundred rounds of ammunition. On my vest, I attached dump pouches to catch my spent mags and a CamelBak on my back. Additionally, I set up my thigh mounted holster for my Sig on my right thigh, and prepared a similar thigh holster for my opposite leg that held pistol mags. Those added another forty eight rounds of ammunition.

I felt like Jesse Ventura wielding a minigun.

Last night had been productive, both emotionally and from a preparation standpoint, so I got up this morning feeling good. There were very few who could voluntarily face their own deaths and not feel even the slightest twinges of fear. Those of us who did took solace in good preparation and the companions we surrounded ourselves with. Between Helena, Santino, the rest of the guys, and an entire legion at my side, I felt confident, but not overly so. Overconfidence could be just as detrimental as ill preparation. Even so, I knew as the battle inched closer the fear would return with it.

Donning the rest of my gear, I kept myself light, but did all I could to offer my vulnerable spots as much protection as possible. My vest protected my chest, abdomen, sides, back, and shoulders, and would easily turn away thrown spears and most sword thrusts, but it still left vulnerable spots beneath my vest. The precision stabbing of a Roman with his *gladius* might be enough to find a way through my defenses, but I was still better protected than a legionnaire with his *lorica segmentata* armor.

The combat fatigues I wore would offer the most amount of protection. Its gel layers and Kevlar lining protected the majority of my body. Finally, I opted to forgo the optical lens and computer for the battle. I didn't expect to have much time to send E-mails today.

The last piece of equipment I retrieved was the only one I dreaded having to use. It was thirty inches long, double sided, and had a tip which could skewer a wild boar. It wasn't a *gladius*, like a standard legionnaire would use, but it would do the trick. During training, I'd found the smaller *gladius* simply too diminutive. It just didn't work very well with my tall frame and long reach. The instructing centurions had noticed my awkwardness, and ordered a longer sword furnished for me with all the other design features its smaller counterpart boasted. I had quickly learned to use it well, and soon Bordeaux had been given one as well.

Satisfied, I looked over at Helena, who was dressed nearly identically to myself, as she pulled her own ammo bag over her shoulder. I almost expected her to wear her breast-molded legionnaire armor, knowing what it would do for morale, but she chose the more protective route, something everyone, especially myself, understood.

"Ready?" I asked her.

In response, she slapped a magazine into her P90, leaned over, and gave me a kiss.

I smiled and jerked my head toward the tent's entrance. She left first, and I gave the tent one last look before I followed.

Outside, Vincent and Santino were already sitting on logs, warming their hands over a dying fire. Even though we were deeper in Italy than we had been during our time in the winter, and summer was quickly approaching, mornings were still chilly.

Each man was dressed similar to Helena and I, their swords strapped to their waists and their shields at their feet. We took a seat on a particularly long log lying on its side, and tried to warm up as well. A few minutes later, Bordeaux and Wang emerged from their tent. Bordeaux carried nothing on his chest rig, but had his three day assault bag in one hand, his SAW in the other. Sitting on another log, I noticed he was inserting the last few rounds of ammunition into one of his box magazines. The box magazines were large, about the size of a brick, and could carry two hundred rounds each. I estimated he had at least ten in his bag, with another already loaded into his weapon. He noticed my inspection and flicked his eyebrows in rapid succession.

The man loved his firepower.

Wang was geared up more traditionally, with most of his vest looking much the same as it always did. He had half a dozen magazine pouches with a few other miscellaneous ones, but he also had his large medical bag as well. It consisted of enough supplies and modern feats of medicine to provide more care for a century of men than a traditional Roman doctor could provide for an entire army. Even though he wasn't equipped to care for the entire legion, he'd still save more lives today than any other doctor. He'd hang back and do what he could from the rear.

They joined the rest of us as we warmed our bones.

It was an unusually chilly morning.

Quiet and contemplative, the squad sat and enjoyed our own personal calm before the storm, barely paying attention to the hustle and bustle of the active camp around us. Everyone had their eyes on the fire, their gazes glossed over, each of them running through the possible outcomes of the battle in their minds. They were nervous, but I had nothing but confidence in each of them.

Helena laid her head on my shoulder, her own gaze staring blindly into the fire. I wrapped an arm around her waist and looked over at Santino, who had broken his stare to offer me a supportive smile. I returned it, and tracked my attention over to Vincent, who had pulled his hands away from the flames, stuffing them into his pockets, and stood up.

"Everyone get something to eat?" He asked.

We nodded. Helena and I had shared the breakfast egg burrito MRE earlier, which had always surprised me as being exceptionally delicious.

Catching each of our nods, he nodded back. "Good. Today is going to be an interesting day." He sighed, and kicked a small amount of dirt into the fire. "That said, I have something important I need to say."

I straightened, feeling Helena take her head off my shoulder, interested as well.

"No matter how today's battle goes, afterwards, I am officially disbanding our unit. We will no longer be Praetorians. Considering our situation, I feel it is only appropriate. I will not become a mercenary captain and order you around in our new home. It hardly seems fair. I've spoken to Caligula, and he's agreed to retain each of you as centurions in his own Praetorian Guard, probably attached to his Sacred Band. Nobody is forcing this on you. I want each of you to choose for yourselves."

No one said anything, but it occurred to me that his decision was an acceptance of our fate in this world, and that he must have little faith in our ability to get home. I wasn't about to give up hope quite yet, but at least now we had a choice. He was giving us the freedom to make our own lives in the world fate had delivered us to. We couldn't change the fact that we were here, but at least now we weren't forced to live by the decisions made in another lifetime.

I stood. "Sir. I believe I speak for all of us when I say," I looked around for support, "that I think you made the right choice, and that we're very happy you did so."

Everyone else stood as well, offering their own agreements and positive sentiments. Vincent opened his mouth to speak, but he was cut off by the bellowing blast of a Roman trumpet blaring a call to arms. I looked over Wang's shoulder and saw hundreds of scampering men, each trying to find their place in the marching column that would lead them to the battlefield.

"Party time," Santino said.

***

Back when I was working on my Master's degree, I'd spent most of my time researching and writing about politics, legislation and social controversies. Needless to say, it was boring stuff, but my favorite professor always told me to write about the tedious stuff first and wait to write about my passion when it came time for my doctoral dissertation. It was a good idea, except I'd never gotten around to writing my paper on Gaius Marius, the man who'd been influential during the Jugurthian War, reformed the Roman army a generation before Julius Caesar came to power and had been drawn into two civil wars during his impressive seven consulships.

Military stratagem had always been a passion of mine, both modern and ancient. My knowledge of it had helped me receive my commission upon joining the Navy. I'd scored very well in intelligence tests, especially when it came to anything concerning tactics and strategy. The Navy had been disappointed when I chose not to pursue a career in its intelligence divisions, instead, deciding on a combat unit like the SEALs. It seemed like the right thing to do at the time. If I had to be in the military, I wasn't going to waste my time as a glorified pencil pusher.

I was going to fuck some shit up.

So, when I found myself arrayed on a battlefield, surrounded by a Roman legion with the walls of ancient Rome providing the backdrop, I was surprised to find that any fear I had felt was completely lost to feelings of curiosity, interest, and excitement.

Romans had always been good at warfare, from the rise of their monarchy to the fall of their empire more than a thousand years later. Very good. Their entire way of life was based upon it, and their conquests, because of it. What made them so proficient was their discipline, training, and most importantly their flexibility. Greek phalanx formations had been the epitome of modern warfare during the height of their power, but Roman manipular formations had changed that. What made maniples so versatile was their ability to work independently of the main body of the army. While the phalanx was distracted in a head to head battle, individual maniples could easily peel off and envelop the flatfooted phalanxes, crushing the soldiers who could not defend their flanks. Roman battle doctrine had evolved over the years, and now fought in much larger cohorts thanks to Marius, but the same idea still applied.

These tactics worked well when fighting barbarians and Greeks alike, but I imagined situations where both forces utilized these tactics would amount to nothing more than a prolonged bloodbath. While each side today would use these tactics, the makeup of each army couldn't be any more different.

Standing opposite Caligula's loyalist force was the rebel army of Claudius. His army was a mismatch of unit types, complementing each other very little, but making up for it in sheer numbers. The only thing these units shared were the purple cloaks they wore. Purple cloaks, reserved for the emperor alone, would never have been offered to troops whether they were Praetorians or not. It was just another indictment against Claudius.

Out in front were rows upon rows of what I assumed were Rome's *vigiles*. *Vigiles* were nothing more than firefighters, their goal not to extinguish flames, but to controllably destroy burning buildings to help quell the spread of the fire. They weren't soldiers, but they were still employed by the emperor, and were required to do what they were told. I couldn't see their armor, but they carried shields and spears. Not *scuti* or *pila*, but inferior equipment, and I had to assume their training was next to nil. They'd break easily, but there were seven thousand of them out there. More than our legionnaire force alone.

On Claudius' right flank stood the city's urban cohorts. Three in total, but totaling only fifteen hundred men, their training, arms, and armor were superior to that of the *vigiles*. These men were the police force of Rome, and were housed and trained with Praetorians, making them an opponent that could fight back.

On their left flank stood maybe another ten to twelve thousand men. These men wore little armor, if any at all, and were armed with small swords, daggers, sickles, hoes, pitchforks, clubs, and a plethora of other mob worthy items. These must have been whatever allies Claudius could muster that still supported his cause. Claudius didn't plan on beating us through generalship, but through force of numbers alone, and he still had the seven thousand rebel Praetorians, probably in formation behind the main body of the enemy who would be the real problem. Seasoned veterans, each, they alone would be hard to break with even an entire legion and its auxilia.

Caligula was going to have a fight on his hands, and while generals like Hannibal had been outnumbered in nearly every battle he waged, and almost always come out on top, I wagered Caligula wasn't quite the general he was. Very few men were, but Caligula still had plenty of assets to work with.

The first of which was his general. Galba was a good man, and a good leader and tactician, despite his annoying disapproval of my friends and me. His fate during the year of four emperors couldn't be entirely blamed on him. He had been old, and in desperate need of allies, which were scarce considering the many sides to choose from. He'd been unlucky, but history still remembers him as an able general. Caligula had left overall command of the legion to him while the emperor would only worry about his Praetorians.

Galba had positioned his troops in a way he hoped would combat the enemy's superior numbers. Unfortunately, between his legionnaires, Praetorians and auxilia, Claudius' line still extended nearly twice as far as his own.

On our right flank, opposite the massive numbers of civilian militia, Galba had placed his entire contingent of German auxilia. His three thousand infantry were well trained and armed, and had a tenacity about them I'd never seen before. They'd cut a swath through the civilians, hopefully breaking them quick enough to flank the more superior troops from the rear. Galba left his two thousand cavalry in reserve, but on the right flank as well, ready to sweep around once the civilians were broken, or to aid in that effort if possible. The last of the auxilia, his one thousand strong archers, were spread thin and positioned behind the infantry to screen their advance.

Contrary to standard Roman practice of putting the best troops on the right flank, Galba had requested that Caligula and his Praetorians take up position on the left. Both thousand man cohorts were split in half, and lined up five men deep, and a hundred abreast, forming four blocks. Behind them was Caligula's Sacred Band, arranged in an inverted square U, with Caligula in the center, riding Incitatus, the infamous horse wildly believed to have been named a consul during Caligula's crazy years. He was dressed as any other

Praetorian would be, with a common trooper's *lorica segmentata* armor. It was adorned with a long, flowing, purple plume, and an equally purple cloak wrapped around his shoulders, similar to how Julius Caesar would wear his brilliant scarlet cape into battle

With him were a few dozen other horsemen, forming his officer corps, which could act as a small cavalry contingent if needed. High above his men, he had a good view of the battlefield and could use his vantage point to send messengers on horseback to help coordinate his orders. Galba was similarly on horseback, with his own squad of cavalrymen, also ready to issue orders as well as fight if need be. Galba wore a set of his own personal battle armor, molded to look like a muscle suit, common wear for Roman generals. He stood out as well, but wore a more typical red cape.

Placed before him was his legion. The legion he had trained since they were raw recruits, but wouldn't stay with once they were commissioned. They were deployed in a checkerboard formation, similar to how old manipular formations would be set up. Each cohort was split in half and arranged so that the troops represented the black spaces, while the white spaces were the area in between each cohort. Galba had placed four cohorts in the first two lines, while the 10th cohort was placed on the far right of our formation, but kept intact as one large body. The third line was made up of two cohorts, with the double sized 1st cohort between them, with the last cohort stretched out, making up a fourth line in reserve. This formation would keep some men out of the battle to help when needed.

The *XV Primigenia*'s first cohort, which carried the legion's standard, the gold *aquila*, or eagle, was situated in the exact center of the formation, so that the entire army was more or less equidistant from their symbolic eagle. The men of the legion would rather die than see that eagle fall, and should it be captured the entire Roman army would be shamed. I couldn't remember if the three lost in the Teutoburg Forest had been reclaimed yet, but I knew that most standards found their way home eventually.

Then of course there was me and the five other hapless souls stuck alongside me in a story I couldn't possibly dream, even up on my best day. Our orders were simple, but open to considerable amounts of interpretation. Split up by swim pairs, we were placed at three places along our lines. Helena and I were put in the middle of the legion formation, right in front of the first legion's standard.

It was Helena's idea. I knew she wasn't letting the whole "Mother of the Legion" deal go to her head, but most of the men would be inspired fighting alongside her. Vincent and Santino were stationed on our left flank to deal with Claudius' crack troops. And on the right were Bordeaux and Wang. Bordeaux could probably lay waste to a third of the militia by himself if he had the chance.

Our standing orders were to march with the advancing army until a halt was called. We would then unleash hell until the enemy was so fed up getting shot to pieces that they counter attacked. The auxilia would then charge with the enemy, hoping to meet that flank in the open area between the two armies, furthering their chances of effectively flanking the rebel Praetorians. The enemy's charge would also trigger the claymores and antipersonnel mines, and leave them vulnerable to three volleys of *pila*.

Of course, we hadn't counted on ten thousand militia being present, or seven thousand *vigiles*, and even if all Claudius had were his Praetorians and the urban cohorts to fight with we would still have a tough battle on our hands. This was going to be a battle of wills, and while there never were any guarantees, Caligula and Galba remained confident they'd win the day.

My mind in order, I cracked my neck and looked to my left as Caligula rode out to the front of our formation, ready to give the cliché but inspirational speech always recited before a battle. He kept it short and succinct, even though I only heard a small part of it. I'd always wondered how one man could deliver a rousing speech to an entire army and still have every man hear it. I quickly realized the answer was simple.

They didn't.

That's not to say that I missed out on any important part of the speech. Caligula simply rode back and forth along the line, making sure that he hit on important points, never repeated himself, and made sure everyone heard something inspirational. I heard him speak of honor and duty, and how Claudius had defied an institution that had existed long before their ancestors had overthrown the ancient kings of Rome. When he came back, he finished his speech by declaring that what occurred on the battlefield today would affect the outcome of history and that it would have ramifications hundreds of years from now.

I wasn't sure if I hoped he was right or not.

Finished with his speech, Caligula reared his horse on his hind legs, a difficult feat without stirrups, and he roused his troops with his upraised sword arm. Every man around me raised their spears in salute before pounding them against their shields, yelling at the top of their lungs. I found myself swept up in the moment and had to raise my rifle as well, yelling indecipherably. I was hard pressed to deny the urge to fire my rifle into the air. It was one of the most surreal moments of my life.

Caligula rode his horse down toward the right flank, receiving louder cheers from those he was passing, before turning back and heading toward his Praetorians. I watched him go, confidence swirling through me after his speech and gallop across the lines.

I looked over at Helena. "Not bad, huh?"

"He's got my vote."

"You know they don't vote, right?"

She rolled her eyes. "I have been paying attention to your little history lessons."

"Really? Then how do you explain the snoring?"

"I'm awake for most of it," she argued. "You just need to pick a better time to start lecturing than when I'm trying to fall asleep." She paused. "I don't snore."

"Yah. Sure you don't," I told her with a chuckle.

She attempted a response, but was cut off by a chorus of legionary horns sounding off in unison. Just before the march order was bellowed, I leaned in and gave her a quick kiss.

"Remember," I told her. "No getting hurt. I'm too lazy to carry you around all the time."

She looked up at me, a look that suggested she wanted to punch me again, but her expression betrayed her true feelings. She didn't want to offer the loving gesture she reserved only for me because she knew it could be the last. If she did it, she would go into battle with that thought in the back of her mind. She tried to force a smile instead, turning to face the awaiting horde.

***

As the marching order blared, we moved in step with the legion. Claudius' troops held their lines, content to watch us move against them. I remember reading Julius Caesar's *Commentarii de Bello Civili*, literally, *Commentaries on the Civil War*, as a high school sophomore, and his description of the Battle of Pharsalus. There, he had his men charge against Pompey the Great's numerically superior troops because he understood a soldier's impetuousness of spirit when it came to battle. His argument was that Pompey's stationary troops wouldn't have the same kind of anger, confidence and zeal his own troops had because of the adrenaline rush they received from the charge.

Caesar's reasoning couldn't be universally confirmed. It may have worked for him, but that didn't mean it would for us. Either way, we had no intention of rushing upon Claudius' *vigiles* anyway.

As we marched, Helena and I concealed any evidence of our weapons and tried our best to blend in with the legionnaires. We walked behind the 4th cohort's *signifer*, who held his century's personal standard, different from every other century's, with markings to identify which cohort, of which legion, it belonged to. It was adorned with an open palmed hand surround by an olive wreath.

We hadn't marched long when the officers called for a halt. Vincent had probably signaled from the left that we were ready. With no further prompting, Helena and I took a knee, steadied our aim, and opened fire.

We were only a hundred and fifty yards away, and at this range, even the lowliest of marksmen in basic training would have scored good numbers. Helena lay prone, firing her P90 precisely from the ground. I assumed she was still targeting officers first and I followed Helena's example of selective targeting and took my time with every shot.

As I went through one magazine, five, ten, twenty magazines, I saw the body count start to build. Fifteen minutes later, I had fired nearly six hundred rounds and I was just starting to see the line of *vigiles* start to shift and maneuver, and I knew they were getting ready to counter attack. I looked to my right and saw the bodies of the militia heaped into mounds and being used as cover from the hailstorm of lead Bordeaux must have been throwing at them. To my left, Vincent and Santino's kills seemed to mimic my position's, and I figured the urban cohort must have taken especially heavy losses.

Ten minutes later, I dropped my thirtieth magazine, which I had to stuff in a cargo pocket because my dump pouches were full, and saw the line of *vigiles* finally thunder forward. Their lines were so thin in places I could see the occasional Praetorian lined up behind them, walking forward at a more reserved pace. To my right, I saw the civilians charge, along with our auxilia. That was my cue to prepare for a strategic withdrawal.

As planned, the counter charge floundered slightly when they hit the mine field.

Helena and I had been exceptionally busy last night.

After securing our gear for today's battle, we'd retrieved the ghilli suits we had been working on for the past two months, and went to lay the field. Ghilli suits were the epitome of camouflage. Designed by its wearer to mimic the exact contours of the earth they were trying to replicate, a well-made ghilli suit could make its wearer look like nothing more than a bump on the ground.

So, under the cover of darkness, around 2300 hours, still rather early, we slowly crawled out of the perimeter of trenches our legion had created and spent an hour crawling inch by inch toward our target location. Claudius' note had indicated the battle was to be fought on the terrain next to the *via aurelia*, decent of him to give us the exact coordinates to set up our demo. Only a hundred feet from the walls, Helena and I laid down a zigzag pattern of the few claymores we had, and the mines. It took us an hour to accomplish the layout, and another to sneak back to the trenches.

The first claymore's explosion sent fifteen or so men flying backward toward the Praetorians. Each was probably dead within seconds. The antipersonnel mines took a few seconds to go off when tripped while they were launched in the air. Those did the most damage, killing dozens of men in all directions. I was beginning to see large holes opening up in their formation, but not as big as I had hoped.

Standing, I tapped Helena on the shoulder who was still focused on her sights. I looked toward the advancing lines to see the survivors getting closer, but I also saw an enemy Praetorian go down as well, shot through the lines of *vigiles*. She pulled her head away from her scope and smiled.

I shook my head.

Grabbing the carry handle for her MOLLE vest, I yanked her to her feet. She squealed in surprise but quickly recovered and continued firing her rifle as I pulled her into formation. The enemy were only about fifty yards away when I heard the nearest centurion yell for the first *pila* volley.

About ten feet in front of the legion, I looked up to see a cloud of spears dim the sky above me before they fell into the *vigiles*' ranks. The three thousand or so spears, only half of the first volley, did practically just as much damage in one effort as my squad had done in fifteen minutes. The only difference was they had three thousand guys, whereas we only had six, not exactly a fair comparison.

As I watched man after man impaled through head, chest, torso, or leg I couldn't imagine why these mere firefighters were so willing to needlessly throw their lives away. These men didn't seem confused or unhappy. They just seemed angry. And so did I.

That's what confused me.

As I pulled Helena back through our ranks, the last two lines from our legion released their volley of spears. By the time the inbound projectiles found their marks, I saw the reason for everyone's craziness. Riding a black horse easily as tall as Caligula's, I saw Claudius sporting a wonderfully purple cape and armor. In his right hand he held a long cavalryman's sword, but in his left, high above his head as though it were a standard itself, was the blue orb that had started this fucking mess.

I guess that shouldn't surprise me. Claudius' prolonged exposure seemed to be increasing his insanity exponentially, and its possible effect on the troops wasn't that farfetched. While they hadn't turned into mindless zombies yet, something had to be driving them and I suspected it wasn't Claudius' charming disposition.

Helena and I moved toward the extreme right flank of the legion, its auxilia now engaged in battle out in the middle of the field. The auxilia were acting as predicted, cutting through the militia like a hot knife through butter. They were outnumbered four to one, but were still making headway through superior skill and determination.

The orb was another snag in our plan that would cause more trouble than we wanted. I was certain the undisciplined and untrained militia would not be so easy to break with it so near. That meant Galba would have to commit his cavalry reserves to that side of the battle prematurely.

Bordeaux and Wang linked up with us near the rear of the legion's farthest cohort on the right. We exchanged quick greetings and made our way along the long line toward the extreme left, and Caligula's position. One of the legionnaires noticed our movement and yelled, asking us where we were going.

"Orders," Helena announced loudly. "But don't worry. I'll be back."

The men in earshot cheered at the idea of her coming to aid them in the upcoming battle. I couldn't help but laugh.

"I wouldn't be surprised if they tried to make you a god after this," I told her as we jogged.

"Would you finally listen to me for a change if I were?"

"Why, of course, oh goddess."

She laughed and kept running. Wang peel off and join the legion's medical cadre where he'd stay and offer more help than every other doctor combined. Wounded were already trickling in from the battle with the *vigiles*. It seemed they were fighting harder than expected, another bad sign.

We passed by Galba on the way. He ignored us and continued yelling for updates on the right flank. We saw a messenger on horseback ride toward the right to determine the situation and appraise Galba upon his return. Reaching Caligula, I noticed the left flank was completely silent, and all I could see were rebel Praetorians off in the distance, patiently waiting just out of *pila* range. Vincent and Santino were there too, standing eagerly near the emperor's side. Vincent nodded in greeting while Santino clapped me on the shoulder.

"What happened over here?" I asked them.

"We focused our fire on the urban cohorts," Vincent reported. "There were fewer of them than the *vigiles*, and we probably killed two thirds of their men ourselves. By the time they charged, we'd switched fire to the *vigiles* on our side of the field. They were slaughtered with just one volley of *pila* from our Praetorians."

What a waste. Fifteen hundred men dead in a matter of minutes. What made matters worse was that we were the ones doing most of the killing. Why didn't it affect me the way I knew it should?

"Anybody else not really care that we're slaughtering people on a Hitlerian scale today?" I asked the squad.

Everyone's look shifted toward the ground. They seemed ashamed that they, too, were unphased by the killing, and that they didn't know why.

"Want to know why?" Santino asked.

I looked at him, wondering if he really had any answers.

"By all means, enlighten us," I told him.

"It's because of that fucking thing," he said pointing toward Claudius as he rode atop his great stead, glowing blue orb in hand.

"How do you know that?" I asked.

"It doesn't take a rocket scientist to figure it out, Jacob. It's what got us here and you said it's what drove Caligula insane before, and now its affect has reached every single person on this battlefield. It's clearly touched us, because we don't care that we're killing these people. We're losing our minds!" He yelled for dramatic effect. "If you ask me, the quicker we end this the better."

I looked at him and opened my mouth to speak but quickly shut it. I couldn't believe how much sense that made, considering how usually dimwitted he was.

"Clearly it's affected you," Bordeaux said. "That actually made sense." He shook his head, trying to rationalize Santino's analysis. "Doesn't it?"

"I guess it does," Vincent said, "It doesn't matter. We're committed."

I was still trying to wrap my head around Santino's epiphany when Galba came riding up to Caligula.

The emperor noticed his general's approach, and turned his horse to meet him near where we stood. "How goes the battle, Legate?"

"Not well, I'm afraid," he updated. "The auxilia are completely tied up and cannot disengage. I've already sent my cavalry to support them for fear that the sheer weight of that militia will come crashing down on my legion. As for them, we've taken some losses, not many, but more than we hoped. These bastards have somehow found the will to fight." He looked to his right, at the enemy

Praetorians, practically all that was left of Claudius' army. "I don't think we can hold them. They're fresh and very experienced. If we can't get the support of the auxilia, we may falter here."

"What will you have me do, general?"

It was nice to see Caligula conceding control to a more experienced military man, instead of trying to micromanage. The man had *definitely* matured.

"Hold here on the left at any cost. The only advantage we have is that Claudius has his best troops aligned against you, and if you can hold out long enough, maybe we can punch through and swing around to engulf them."

"We'll hold, Legate. You have my word."

"Yours is one of the few I trust, Caesar. May Mars guide you this day," Galba said, turning his horse to return to his men.

"And you, Servius," Caligula said to the retreating man's back. He turned to face Vincent. "The empire needs you. Do not worry about me. Just do whatever you can to cause as much confusion as possible. The Praetorians won't be used to your kind of presence on the battlefield." He paused and looked out over the chaos. "When you see the sign, come to my aid."

"What sign, Caesar?"

"You'll know it when you see it," and with that, he rode back to his own advisors, already issuing commands and words of encouragement.

"Well?" Vincent asked, getting our attention. "You heard the man. Spread out. Pick your fights, and stay out of the way of the professionals."

I saluted, a growingly superfluous gesture these days, and reached out for Helena's arm, pulling her in the general direction of the *XV Primigenia*'s 1st cohort. A short run later, we found it right where we left it, in the exact center of the legion's formation, its eagle prominently displayed high above. We took positions near to the legion's *aquilifer*, who held the eagle, perhaps the most important position in the entire army. He was unarmed, but he was a veteran, probably taken from another legion's pool of experienced soldiers to hold this new legion's eagle. He had to be brave because he could not run. To run would be the single most detrimental thing that could happen to a legion.

He wouldn't run. They never ran.

In front of him stood another signifier, and behind both of them was an imaginifer, another standard bearer who carried the face of the emperor, a reminder of who the legion was fighting for. In front of all three was Centurion Maximus Nisus.

"Any predictions?" I asked him.

The man's expression remained neutral. "I try not to think about the outcome of a battle before it truly gets underway. There are too many unknowns."

I nodded. I could relate to that.

"But," he continued, "I do believe Galba will call for a shift in our formation in a few seconds. Claudius is taking advantage of his numbers. Their lines extend well past ours, so Galba will call for our formation to spread out. It will open up gaps in our lines. If I were you," he paused, looking around as though giving us any suggestions would be a betrayal to his skeptical general, "I would look for these gaps and do what you do there. If you have any more of those, what do you call them? Grenades? Use them there."

"I'll keep that in mind, Centurion. May the gods smile on you today." I wasn't turning into a pagan, but it was what he would want to hear.

"And with you," he replied, professional to the core. He turned back to the lines to continue his study of the enemy's formation. They were finishing their last maneuver, just out of spear range. I looked to the right, trying to determine how the auxilia were doing, but all I could see was a jumble of men and horses. Only twenty minutes had passed since the *vigiles* had started their suicide rush, and I knew the battle could continue for hours before it showed any signs of waning.

I looked over at Helena, a reassuring quip on my tongue, but was distracted by a messenger riding up to Nisus' position. As the seer had predicted, Galba's orders were to expand the grid formation. He also ordered the third cohort to split into three maniples, and spread out along the rear. They would be crucial in securing weak spots in our lines.

Interestingly, the tactic was eerily similar to the one that, again, Caesar had used at Pharsalus. Like Galba, he'd used a nontraditional formation of four lines, instead of three, and used part of his army to work specifically to counter cavalry, as Galba was using part of his to hold the right. Hopefully, Claudius wasn't seeing the similarities.

As the messenger rode off, Nisus issued his command briefly and efficiently, and I quickly found myself moving in step with the cohort. Putting maybe thirty yards between the corners of each cohort, I was only slightly embarrassed when everyone else stopped moving, but I'd kept going. Some of the men laughed at me, and even Helena joined in the fun, having stopped on her mark.

I gave her a betrayed look, which she returned with a shrug.

Ignoring their jeers, I looked out over the legion and saw how these gaps in the checkerboard formation could easily become a problem. Had the formation been tight, the corners touching as it had been, the enemy would have a rough time breaching the gaps for fear of being surrounded. Since the half-cohorts were now spread out, the enemy could enter these holes in the line with less fear. Help would have to come from farther away, and would leave the area they'd just left undefended. That was why Galba had created four lines in the checkerboard, so that holes could be plugged easily with reserves from the third, and the fourth could be called on as a last resort.

Nisus was also right in assuming we could do some serious damage there. We only had a third of our ammo left, but the men who accumulated between the gaps in our lines would be exposed and distracted. A well placed grenade would kill many, and leave the rest stunned. Our legionnaires would then be able to close the gaps. I only had three grenades and one flashbang stowed away in pouches along my belt, but they'd still make a wonderful mess.

And just like that, the battle commenced again.

The enemy was less than a football field away, thousands of bodies and spears littering the space between us. The carnage made me want to puke, but I didn't have time. When the legion's trumpeters blasted the marching order, I felt the automatic surge of troops around me, and I stepped into formation with them. We tiptoed over the obstacles on the ground, the enemy doing the same as they marched forward to meet us. Seventy five yards out, I saw that our battle lines were at least as long as their own now. Another thirty yards later, it became easy to distinguish faces, armor and standards in more detail. When only twenty yards separated the sides, everyone stopped.

Normally, this would be the moment when onrushing barbarians would run face first into a swarm of *pila*, but not today. Instead, I heard the forward lines' centurions yell, "*pila*," wait while their men readied their spears, before yelling, "loose!"

Fifteen hundred spears flew out in unison, falling against the Praetorians, now comfortably secured beneath their *testudo* formation, an overlapping wall and roof of shields. The *testudo* formation worked well against arrows, slings, and non-pila type spears, but today it only helped, not guaranteed, a soldier's safety. Just as the last spears were reaching their mark, the second line's volley of spears flew out as well, inflicting even more casualties.

It had long been theorized that when a *pilum* hit shield, man, or ground, its soft iron shank would bend at an angle and become next to useless. It could not be cast back, nor could be pulled from a shield, because the angle made it impossible to extract it. However, modern testing had proven that to create iron soft enough to bend but not break after it impacted a nine centimeter thick *scutum* was nearly impossible.

What really happened, thanks to my keen observational skills, was that the heavy *pila* drove deep into most things it impacted. It proved the theory that *pila* did make shields worthless, not because its shaft bent, but because they punched right through them, and staked them into the ground. Roman shields were probably of the best quality in all of Europe, and while they turned away many of the spears, plenty found their way through the protective layer, and easily through the sturdy *lorica segmentata* armor.

The rebel Praetorians quickly recovered from the barrage and cast their own *pila*. Nearly seven thousand spears flew toward both legionnaires and loyal Praetorians, and most flew farther than our own men's had, their casters being older and stronger. Since Helena and I were not protected by the legion's *testudo* formation, we ducked beneath our overlapping shields, hoping we were lucky enough to weather the storm unscathed.

It turned out I wasn't that lucky.

I was never that lucky.

I felt two or three *pila* ricochet off my shield, my heart skipping with each impact, but the fourth spear plowed its way through my shield like it was made of paper. The only thing that saved my life was my vest.

The spear hit me like a lightning bolt, penetrating two of my spent magazines before stopping at the protective Kevlar lined within. The force of the impact knocked the breath from my lungs and disoriented me enough to lower my defenses. Helena tried to pull me closer to her so that her shield protected us both, but we were both bigger than the average Roman. Her shield was nowhere near big enough to cover us, but I appreciated the gesture as I tried to coax air back into my lungs. My heart continued to jump as each spear grazed off her shield.

I massaged the spot where the spear impacted, but it didn't help. I would have a bruise the size of a soccer ball on my chest tomorrow, but I couldn't complain. Without my vest, I would have been skewered.

Our fourth line let loose a small barrage that caught some of the enemy off guard. Both sides continued to exchange spears, casting and cowering, causing casualties here or there. I'd always imagined this part of a battle to be more exciting, with waves of spears cutting down hundreds of onrushing barbarians. Instead, we had battle hardened and disciplined Praetorians to deal with. Once the enemy cast their final volley of *pila*, they followed hot on the heels of their final volley of charges, and rushed forward.

The legion's third and fourth lines still had one last *pila* volley left. While only the third line loosed their spears, it did the most amount of damage to the speeding Praetorians. Helena and I added our own fire power, concentrating it on only a small fraction of Claudius' horde. We aimed toward a group headed in the direction of a cohort we knew to be under strength.

That small fragment of the enemy faltered, forty or so men falling to our combined fire, while many behind them tripped and fell over their dying comrades. The 6th cohort was rewarded with the arrival of disorderly Praetorians. They held their ground and cut the first men to reach them to pieces. It was a minor victory, hopefully one of many that would help turn the tide of the battle.

The rest of the legion's first line of half-cohorts did not fare as well. Thousands of Praetorians smashed into them, immediately initiating a systematic advance that pushed the legion back. Within minutes, the weight of the enemy force had pushed the first line back enough that the checkerboard was collapsing.

It was rare that a plan actually worked on the first try, but Claudius took the bait. Galba wanted the checkerboard formation to fall in on itself. When the rebels smashed into the first line their momentum stopped. Our second line, now only ten yards from the enemy Praetorians, rushed into the small gaps, counter charging the now preoccupied enemy. It clogged the holes with bodies, and allowed Galba an easier time of sending reserve forces from the third and fourth lines to help where needed.

On our left flank, Caligula's men were still holding back the enemy along our original line. The forces engaged over there were more equally skilled, and would have to endure a slugging match, while over here, Galba and Nisus would feint, counter attack, and maneuver small units wherever they thought them needed, in the typical legion fashion.

Helena and I waited for no such orders, and we found ourselves weaving our way through the battle at random. Running back and forth across our lines, my feet burned and my bruised chest heaved, but we had to play little Dutch boy to the legion's leaks. So far we'd only taken pot shots at the occasional target, but many more targets of opportunity were beginning to present themselves.

Nisus' plan for us to use our grenades was fruitless at this point. The lines had collapsed much too quickly. There were only a select few areas where we could do some damage. The Praetorians were just better soldiers. They easily drove wedges between our cohort halves and thrust men continuously through our lines.

Had Helena and I not been there they would have succeeded in some instances. Communication was essential, and when I heard a shout that there was a breach in the 2nd cohort's formation on the legion's left flank, I made my way in that direction, Helena beside me. We passed the 6th and 4th cohort along the way, each holding their own well enough, but when I saw the 2nd, I quickly assessed that the breach was more like a flood Noah himself would have trouble handling.

Right down the center, between the two cohort halves were waves of Praetorians bubbling inward toward the third line. Nisus was just about to send in a reserve force when he noticed us, and held back his orders, waiting to see what we would do first.

I started the party off with a grenade that I tossed deep into enemy lines, far enough to keep our legionnaires unaffected. I set my weapon to fully automatic and started walking toward the Praetorians like a British red coat during the American Revolution. Helena was right beside me as we fired into their ranks, inching closer and closer with every slow step. We started with the edges, concentrating our fire on the Praetorians closest to our allies, before sweeping toward the center, overlapping our fire, and working again toward the outer edge again. When the grenade went off, we had effectively killed every man trying to push through the bulge, and the respite gained from the explosion was enough for the 2nd cohort to fuse their lines together again.

I saw a century from the 3rd cohort in reserve take up position behind the 2nd's last line, to help alleviate the tension there. I knew the key to a legion's success was their mobility and versatility, but seeing it in action was extraordinarily impressive. That century could have done what Helena and I had, but it would have taken far longer, and cost both cohorts more men. Now, they were in the perfect position to strengthen the position.

Our task fulfilled, I looked around for another breach, but couldn't find a one, so I made my way back to Nisus' position. We had to be careful because our lines were very slowly being pushed back. We didn't want to risk a random sword thrust in our direction. Casualties were streaming in at this point, but we were holding strong on the left, as was the 10th on the right. Our formation was actually enveloping the enemy bit by bit, just as Hannibal's had at the battle of Cannae. While he'd feigned his center's weakness to draw the Roman attackers inside his lines to surround them, our center was in fact weaker, and we wouldn't be able to turn the tables as easily as he had.

Nisus had a smile on his face as we jogged back to the 1st cohort's standard.

"It's good to see you can actually deliver in a fight," he said. "Honestly, I had my doubts, but no more."

"Join the club," I muttered in English, glancing back at Galba, who still sat on his horse doing his best to maintain tactical command of the entire legion, leaving the small stuff to his centurions.

Helena and I waited patiently. A few minutes passed. I was getting restless.

Finally, I heard my radio crackle to life in my ear.

"Hunter, this is Bordeaux."

I pressed the PTT button. "Go ahead, Jeanne. How goes the fight on your end?"

"It's going," he replied, strain evident in his voice even over the radio, "but I think you should know that I can see some serious enemy troop movement occurring on your right flank. I'd inform that asshole centurion that he might want to reinforce the right."

I smiled. "Thanks for the update. I'll let him know. Hunter, out."

Since the day we first arrived in camp, Nisus had treated us the same as his general had, with distant mistrust and apprehension. Bordeaux probably had more reason to be annoyed with him than the rest of us. During a training exercise, Nisus, more than a foot shorter than the hulking Frenchman, had knocked Bordeaux unconscious when he whacked him on the temple with the blunt side of his *gladius*. The big guy had been out for an hour. Bordeaux had not been happy and hadn't had a nice thing to say about the centurion since.

"Centurion," I said, directing my attention to Nisus. "I would send some troops to the right. Immediately. The enemy is maneuvering in that direction."

Nisus' look betrayed nothing as he stared at me. "And how could you possibly know that? If you will, please leave command of this army to me."

I was about to tell the smaller man off and inform him just how lucky he was to have our help, when I saw a runner approaching quickly from the right.

"Sir," the man panted. "The 5th has been breached and the 10th is floundering. The enemy is pushing hard on the right."

Nisus looked at me and I gave him a condescending smile, while Helena, who had overheard our interchange, shook her head and *tsked* him. To the man's credit, he looked me in the eye and grunted a brief acknowledgment before turning inwards, thinking over the strategic situation.

"Gods," Nisus mumbled. "Issue the command for the entire 9th cohort to support both positions. Also, detach a century from the 3rd to find out what in the name of Mercury is happening with the auxilia. Clear it with the Legate first."

"I obey, Centurion," the man replied, saluting.

So much for Hannibal, then. No wonder things had seemed so calm. The Praetorians had been feigning along the entirety of our line while they were simultaneously maneuvering the rest of their troops to the right.

I'd barely started inching my way in that direction when I felt Nisus' strong grip on my arm. "No, my friend. That is not your fight. My men can handle it. We'll need you soon enough elsewhere."

I nodded, bowing to his authority.

So far, the third and fourth line had remained unengaged, but the front was steadily approaching our position. They'd be on top of us very soon. Things were about to get very messy. Another messenger arrived as more and more bodies fell to the ground in front of me and the 9th moved into position on the right.

"Centurion," he panted, "the left has been hit hard and the men are rapidly falling back."

I looked to the left past the 1st cohort, and saw staggering lines and wavering troops. Things were definitely not going as well as we'd hoped, and I couldn't see past them to find out what was happening with Caligula's men. I couldn't help but think this whole thing might have been a big mistake, and that our plans had failed the day Santino and I failed to set the explosives along the walls of Rome.

I looked to Nisus, waiting impatiently for my orders.

He was keeping his calm, but he knew he had to pull this thing together before it fell apart completely. "Go," he said to me. "Find the breach on the left. I will take the 1st and 7th to assist.

I nodded, before glancing over at Helena. "Ready for this?"

She tilted her head to the side and met my eyes. "I am, but remember…"

"No dying… I know."

"Right. Let's go."

We peeled away from the 1st cohort, and ran behind their lines as fast we could. We passed through the 7th cohort, receiving cheers as we did so before we came face to face with the grim reality that was the 8th cohort's fate. Its line wasn't only breached but being annihilated, chopped down by a swarm of Praetorians, and I quickly knew why.

Behind them, high on his black horse rode Claudius, sword and orb in hand, shouting orders, his anger and charisma driving his men forward.

Even so, he wasn't the problem right now, and I focused my attention on the troops.

Just as with the 2nd cohort only ten minutes earlier, the Praetorians had crashed into the gap between the cohort segments. Unlike before, they exploited it far more effectively and had pushed aside the halved cohorts beyond the point where they could help each other. There might have been forty Praetorians standing within the gap, effectively surrounding the 2nd.

Placing myself thirty yards from them, I dropped to a knee and started pouring fire into the gap. I counted two dozen men go down, before I had to reload. A new magazine in place, I pulled out my second grenade and readied to throw it. Helena was still firing her P90's larger mag, while simultaneously readying a grenade of her own.

The Praetorians noticed our intervention in their small victory, as did Claudius. He immediately recognized me and pointed his sword in my direction and yelled. Many men turned away from the legionnaires they were fighting and started running toward Helena and me, completely exposed and alone. I primed the grenade and chucked it in their path, and Helena quickly followed suit with her own.

The grenades detonated just as the first men passed by them, obliterating another dozen or so from their ranks. There seemed to be an endless stream of them funneling through the breach and I knew it wouldn't be enough. I kept up my fire from my kneeling position, reloaded, and spent one of my last magazines as they came within ten yards of my position. Then I froze when I saw them nearly upon us, having no idea what to do.

The training drilled into my skull during the past winter completely abandoned me. Hesitation in the face of impending death was an interesting feeling. It wasn't something I was familiar with, and because of it, I couldn't even *attempt* to help myself. All I could do was wait for the inevitable as I squeezed my eyes shut.

When it didn't come, I felt my fear turn first into confusion, before it turned into fear again. When I peeked through my right eye, I saw hundreds of spears flying over my head. It took me a second to realize these spears hadn't come from the enemy, but from a maniple of the legion's 3rd cohort, who had been ordered to secure this position as well. I got my senses about me in time to see three

Praetorians running at me, survivors of the *pila* barrage. No time to pull my shield from my back, no time to think, no time to run, when the first Praetorian lunged at me, my Special Forces training finally kicked in, and I immediately reacted to the threat.

Still kneeling, I pivoted away from the man's sword thrust, grabbing his sword arm in one motion. Using his forward momentum against him, I stuck out a leg, tripping him to the ground, while using his fall to pull me to my feet. Mid maneuver, his sword brushed across my forearm and opened up a nasty gash there, right where the last one had healed after escaping Rome.

Helena was not going to be happy.

The motion that threw him to the ground, and brought me to my feet, had so much momentum behind it, I nearly stumbled alongside him. With a little luck, I kept my balance, and turned to face my opponent, who was still lying with his face in the grass. Just as he started to twitch, I put a bullet in the back of his head.

I looked frantically for Helena, and quickly found her standing over the remaining two opponents, her shield at the ready. The bodies had a cluster of neat bullet holes in their chests.

Apparently, she hadn't panicked.

How embarrassing.

I turned back toward the gap in our lines, only to find it still there, and another wave of Praetorians running at us. I sighed and pulled out my sword and shield, slinging Penelope behind my back, waiting for the onslaught. I was so distracted by my own doom and gloom that I barely noticed my saviors from the 3rd cohort rush past me. As they ran past, I knew I wouldn't have to fight this battle after all. The one hundred and sixty legionnaires met those few remaining Praetorians, and started pushing them back toward the hole.

I fell to my knees and dropped my equipment, gripping my forearm.

Helena calmly walked over, knelt beside me, and gently inspected my arm. Shaking her head, she pulled out yet another bandage, pressed it against my arm and wrapped the wound.

"You really need to stop getting hurt," she told me matter of factly.

"I know, I just…"

"You have a shield for a reason."

"Yeah, but…"

"They help stop swords."

"But…"

"No excuses," she said, tightening the bandage to punctuate her order.

I groaned slightly under the pressure. It always seemed to hurt more when she was fixing me up.

"You are relentless," I said, smiling up at her as the pain rescinded. "It must be why I…"

I was interrupted by even more commotion. I turned to see the legionnaires nearest me looking to the far left, pointing with expressions of shock on their faces. I followed their outstretched arms to see both loyal and rebel Praetorians still pounding against one another. I also saw Santino and Vincent, running randomly throughout the battle, sticking together and using their rifles only against immediate threats. I saw Wang near the rear, working on a man who already had his left leg amputated. I had no idea where Bordeaux was.

The only thing exceptional enough to draw the attention of the entire legion had to be Caligula. He and his cavalry bodyguard unit had crashed into the enemy's line, and were steadily and smoothly chopping away at the enemy Praetorians, who were in complete shock at his reckless bravado. Claudius noticed as well, and moved to meet the challenge.

This must have been the sign Caligula had told us to look for, and Helena's expression confirmed my theory. She pulled me to my feet, and we ran to join Vincent and Santino, who were trying to make their way to Caligula's side as well.

"How much ammo do you have left?" I asked her, as we pushed allies to the side and sidestepped corpses.

"Half a mag, but a full load for my pistol. You?"

"Pistol's fresh, but only one mag for my rifle, and I'm saving it." I had already shouldered Penelope and pulled out my Sig.

After Caligula had gallantly charged forward, his Sacred Band had kept its U-formation, trying to follow in his wake. Normally, it would have been fruitless, but with Santino and Vincent helping out, they were moving through. Once Helena and I joined only a minute later, our Praetorians had effectively pushed the enemy's left flank aside, and were wheeling around, trying to get behind the enemy Praetorians who were still systematically destroying the *XV*

Primigenia. The legion was probably a bit below half strength at this point and could use our help as soon as possible.

Santino and Vincent had been reduced to their pistols as well, but protected within the Sacred Band's cocoon; the four of us could pick our targets with ease. We ignored our training of aiming for a person's center mass, and went for head shots. Moving along the interior of our lines, I would pop a shot off at the first target of opportunity, spin out the way, and find another target. It was tedious and gruesome work, but with two opposing forces deadlocked in a clash of shields, it was the only offensive gesture I could perform.

We pushed our way through the throng of bad guys as a unit, and found ourselves witnessing a spectacle one only read about in rare histories or mythology. Seated on their horses, Caligula and Claudius had engaged themselves in a duel of emperors, the death of one enough to perhaps end the war. It reminded me of Homer again, who when recording the duel between Patroclus and Hector, amongst many other duels, indicated men on both sides simply stopped fighting, to form a protective circle around the duelists, and watched.

If only that were the case here.

Instead, a circle had indeed formed around the emperors, with a diameter of about thirty yards to fight in, but instead of the perimeter watching, it was being contested as well. As though on secret orders, the Sacred Band spread out to fortify the circle, letting no one in, or out. It would be tough to accomplish, with many enemy Praetorians from the battle with the legion turning to aid their traitorous emperor now fighting behind their lines.

Caligula had made a far bigger mess than any of us could have ever hoped to.

I settled into position along the circle, waiting to see a target pop into view, while trying to keep at least one eye on the battle. When this was all said and done, I was writing it down, and it was going to be accurate to the letter. I'd lost track of Helena once again, but she seemed to be handling the whole legionnaire thing better than I was anyway.

She'd be fine.

***

Claudius scored the first victory.

Resourcefully, he used the blue sphere as a type of shield, its round and seemingly impenetrable exterior an interesting device to turn away sword thrusts. Caligula began his attack with a downward slash of his sword toward Claudius' wrist, but was surprised when his sword ricocheted off the orb. Claudius barked a laugh and used his foot, not hindered by a stirrup, to kick Caligula from his horse.

On his knees, Caligula waited for Claudius to run him down. Just as the emperor hoped, Claudius galloped forward recklessly. His horse gave Claudius a clear advantage, but it also bred overconfidence. As he reached the downed emperor, Claudius could never have foreseen that Caligula would wield a broken *pilum* like a baseball bat. Sidestepping the horse, Caligula swung at Claudius' abdomen, dropping him to the ground as well.

As their two steeds chased each other off the battlefield, Caligula did not let up. With both men unhorsed, they were once again on an equal playing field, but Caligula's younger and more vibrant body gave him the edge, and while he had lost his sword, he was not defenseless. He must have been paying attention during our self-defense lessons, occasionally sparring with Vincent, because when Claudius tried to slam the sphere into the side of his head, Caligula easily blocked the swipe with his broken spear. He pressed his advantage by twirling in a circle as he moved forward, using his speed to hurl a spinning backfist into Claudius's jaw. He finished his attack by sweeping into Claudius' body and tossing him to the ground.

With Claudius on his back, Caligula started raining soccer kicks to the usurper's head, and bludgeoning him with his broken *pilum*. The melee had turned into a brawl. Hardly a limb went untouched, and when his uncle rolled over onto his back, propped up on an arm, Caligula held the spear tip at his throat.

I couldn't hear what they were saying.

I was distracted when I had to block an incoming sword myself, and run my attacker through the abdomen with my own. When I looked back, Caligula had already fallen for the oldest trick in the book. Claudius had thrown a fistful of dirt in his face, and Caligula dropped his spear as he staggered back, clawing at his eyes to clear his vision. Claudius struggled to his feet and came at Caligula like a drunken bare knuckled boxer, scoring a few easy punches to sternum and face. Caligula covered up like any good boxer would after taking a few more blows and countered a quick jab with an uppercut to Claudius' jaw. The blow knocked the crazed man back a few feet and Caligula wasted no more time fooling around. In a very non-dramatic and un-heroic manner, Caligula picked up the iron spear head he'd dropped earlier and hurled it with all his might. With no wooden shaft, the spear did exactly what every modern historian theorized it couldn't. It hit its target square in the chest, the tip extending inches out of Claudius' back.

Still clutching the sphere as he fell to his knees, he looked down at the *pilum* in his chest, randomly grabbing for the shaft. Too weak to get a grip on the spear, he looked at his nephew before falling over onto his side. He tried to offer one last sinister smile, but with death's hold overwhelming him, so did the orb's influence wan, and his face seemed at peace. Caligula caught him just before he fell to the ground.

Turning away another sword blow, I was distracted and could never be sure, but I thought I saw tears running down the true emperor's eyes as Claudius uttered his last few words, his arms falling limp at his sides, and the sphere rolling a few feet away from his body.

Caligula gently laid his uncle on the battlefield, but without a second thought, pulled off his imperial purple cloak and wrapped the sphere within. He then tossed it to the nearest allied horseman and screamed for him to ride to one of the legion's camps and deliver it to Varus, and no one else. Caligula must have known of the sphere's corruptive elements, and thought that by distancing it from the rogue troops, they'd come to their senses.

Time would tell, but we were still outnumbered, and the horseman had barely made it past the lines.

The two Praetorian factions continued their merciless battle. The once nine thousand strong Praetorian contingent that had been wholly loyal to Caligula mere months ago must have been reduced to barely four by this point, only one thousand loyal to Caligula.

I had no way of keeping track of how many kills I had over the next thirty minutes, or how many allies and foes had fallen to their deaths around me. I'd been nicked, cut and wounded an equally unfathomable amount of times and there was no end in sight. Caligula had joined the rest of us in defending this small spot of land after his fight with Claudius, but even his presence wouldn't be enough. I started feeling fatigue set in when I thought I saw hope arrive in the form of ugly Germans slogging their way tiredly but loyally toward their legion. Always the pessimist, I figured they were just lost individuals from the battle on the right flank who had blundered into our part of the fight.

Between Caligula's Sacred Band and his two loyal Praetorian cohorts, I had to guess no more than seven hundred were left, and our lines began to reflect that fact. Just as the illusory Germans had come into focus, our lines started to buckle, holes opened, and more men started to die all around me. I was losing both hope and energy and knew we needed a miracle to get us out of this.

Wavering, I saw an enemy sword come swinging down toward my head. My body was too fatigued to raise my shield fast enough, but I was saved by a strong hand on my shoulder that pulled me out of the way. My savior rushed in and stabbed the man through the throat. I saw a horizontally plumed helmet, and knew it was Centurion Quintilius before he could turn to face me.

"Don't die yet, Hunter," he said with a smile. "This may be our last stand, but help is on the way."

He pointed with his sword toward what had originally been our right flank, and the phantom Germans I thought I'd seen. It turned out they were real, and were indeed making their way back to the fight. At the vanguard of the formation I saw Bordeaux, still full of energy and leading the charge with his SAW blazing away.

God, I loved that Frenchman.

The enemy Praetorians realized they were being outflanked, and something in their eyes clicked, as though all of a sudden they were seeing the fight in a whole new light. All continued to fight, but many with far less vigor. Some still seemed fully affected by the orb's influence, but the evidence that it was diminishing was obviously displaying itself.

I turned to Quintilius, ready to thank him, when I saw he was looking off toward our left, a look of worry on his face. I tracked his eyes, only to see what couldn't possibly be happening.

Only thirty feet away, so close I could almost reach out and touch her, Helena and Marcus were engaged with three enemy Praetorians in close combat. Marcus dispatched one easily, only to be stabbed in the leg by a second. He clutched his wound, and fell to the ground, screaming in agony. The fear for my friend was surpassed only, when in an attempt to save his life, Helena, having lost her shield, killed his attacker but had unintentionally turned her back on the last.

The remaining enemy leapt at her, smashed her sword from her hand, grabbed her by the arm and spun her around. Helena found herself staring eye to eye with a short, ugly Roman Praetorian who wore a smile of pure evil. Whether it was some remnant of the orb's power, or just some sick fetish over knowing his foe was a woman, I'd never know. The Praetorian moved his hand to her throat, the other still gripping his sword, and he paused for a brief second, just long enough for my eyes to widen in terror.

Helena tried to struggle against his grip, fighting to pry loose his hand with her own, but as tough as she was, there was little she could do. I saw her try to kick the man in the groin, but missed, catching him on the leg instead. Maneuvering his body to make sure she didn't succeed on her second kick, he looked up at her and smiled. She struggled and fought, but exhausted and outmuscled, the Praetorian cocked his arm back, and ran her through the stomach with the tip of his *gladius*. The sword made contact with her skin an inch below the protection of her combat vest, and with nothing to impede its progress, pushed its way straight through her back. Her green eyes ballooned open in pain and surprise, and her struggling ended.

I was already running before she'd kicked him, uncontrollable sounds of rage spilling from my throat, all feelings of fatigue or pain forgotten, Quintilius yelling after me. Adrenaline kicked my muscles into overdrive, but despite all my training, all my conditioning, I couldn't make it, and I watched from five feet away, as the man moved to finish her.

He still held Helena on his sword, staring at her, looking as though he thought to further violate her in some way when, while still at a dead run, forgetting my legion training once again, I swung my sword with all my might and severed the man's head from his shoulders. I released my sword as I finished my cut, allowing both head and *gladius* to sail through the air, not caring who they hit.

Helena was already falling with the decapitated Praetorian.

I wheeled around and slid beneath Helena as she collapsed in my arms, the Praetorian's grip still on the sword handle and her throat. I tore both away and kicked the body out of my sight. Cradling Helena's limp body, I reached with a trembling hand to cup her cheek while I pulled a bandage out of a pouch with the other. Knowing not to try and remove the sword, I put as much pressure on the wound as possible, a fruitless gesture, as I was completely oblivious to the mirror wound at her back.

She moaned under the pressure, but at least she was still alive. I turned her head so she could face me, and I felt tears welling in my eyes at the sight of her graying skin. I smiled down at her, trying to put on a brave face as I gently rocked her in my arms.

"What did I say about getting hurt?" I asked her, my voice faltering. "Only me, remember?"

She was so weak that when she tried to raise a hand to my cheek, it barely brushed it before falling to her side. A spasm of pain wracked her entire body, and she clenched each limb in unison, before going limp in my arms again.

"I'm sorry, Jacob," she whispered. "So sorry."

"Don't be, you'll be fine. Wang will be here any second now, and you'll be fine. You'll be… fine." I looked up, frantically searching for Wang, but he was nowhere in sight. The only thing I saw was the battle coming to a close with Praetorians dying and surrendering all around us. If only Helena could have hung on a few more minutes. If only she hadn't been so stupid. So brave.

If only I hadn't left her side like I said I never would.

Santino wandered up to us a few seconds later, clutching a superficial leg wound. His eyes were glazed, the thousand yard stare so prevalent amongst battle worn veterans on his face. No smile in sight. When his mind caught up to what his eyes were seeing, a look of shock and confusion spread over his face as he stared down at the dying woman he'd come to call a friend.

"Find Wang," I told him quietly, but Santino didn't move. He just stood there transfixed, unable or unwilling to comprehend what was happening. "Find Wang, Goddamn it!" I yelled, my voice cracking.

Hearing the pain and anger in my voice, he snapped himself from his trance and ran off to find our medic.

I looked back down at Helena, brushing dirty black hair from her face. "See? Everything's going to be fine." My hand shook uncontrollably and my heart pounded like a drum as I wiped blood from her mouth. "Everything's going to be... going to be..."

I couldn't finish. I squeezed my eyes shut and held her as close as I could. I pulled her against my chest and tried to will life back into her, but all the fire in her eyes were gone. Eyes that had once been her most alluring and vibrant feature somehow seemed to be slowly dimming to a dull gray.

She tried to smile for me, but coughed violently as she did. "I...it's okay, Jacob. I..." she said, looking back up at me, the quickest of sparks firing in her eyes, before another spike of pain forced her body into another series of spasms. "...I..." but her voice trailed off, her body fell still, and her eyes closed.

I knew what she was going to say. I knew because I didn't need her to say it for me to know it. I wanted to say something back. Something funny. Something hopeful. Something redeeming. I wanted to tell her I loved her too, but I couldn't. I couldn't give up. I wouldn't. All I could do was hold her close, feel as the last traces of life left her body, and for the first time since I could remember...

Cry.

Epilogue

Rome, Italy
August, 38 A.D.

    Someone knocked on my door. It was a quiet sound, but the sudden and unexpected nature of it roused me from my thoughts. It startled me, and I pinched my nose and swore under my breath in response. I looked at my surroundings, trying to remember where I was.
    The suites we had been given once Caligula reclaimed his position were luxurious, spacious, and far more comfortable than the dingy shack we'd stayed in those first few months in ancient Rome. I had a bedroom, a sitting room, a dining room, a study, and even my own bathroom, complete with running water for both bathtub and toilet.
    Romans were so clever.
    Lounging on a sofa shaped like a half bowl, my feet hanging over the one end, I had been sitting in contemplative silence for nearly an hour, the past year of my life replaying steadily in my head. I'd sped through most of it, skipping the boring stuff and the painful memories, focusing on the events just after the Battle for Rome, as Caligula had dubbed it once he had retaken control of the Senate.
    Bordeaux had saved the day during those last few moments. He had spent the entire battle with the auxilia and their fight with the overwhelming plebeian army. The battle hadn't gone so poorly for the German auxiliaries as everyone had thought, but it had been an excruciatingly arduous affair. As history could confirm numerous times, an undisciplined and under-armed force of civilians simply could not stand against fewer men should they be better trained, armed, and focused.
    Almost eight thousand of the eleven thousand-strong militia had been wiped out, but of the infantry, cavalry, and archers of the *XV Primigenia*'s auxilia, only three and a half thousand were lost. Once Bordeaux showed up, and seven fully loaded ammo boxes later, many of the enemy started surrendering, or trying to flee back to the city. I knew it had something to do with the orb's disappearance, but

in the end, it hardly mattered. With that part of the battle neatly wrapped up, Bordeaux had led the auxilia in a flanking charge. Their arrival had quickly tipped the scales in our favor.

Like their civilian allies, many Praetorians surrendered in that moment as well, confused expressions on their faces, seemingly with no idea where they even were. Their surrender occurred not a second too early. They had almost broken us. The only thing that kept us going was the thought of failing Caligula, who had been so brave risking his own life and killing his own uncle in open combat.

The knock came again, more insistently this time.

"All right, all right," I yelled at the door as I swung my legs over the edge of the sofa, and rose to my feet. My head swam as I got up, dizziness almost dropping me to my knees. I'd been lying there for an hour, and had gotten up way to fast.

I shuffled across my marble floor, trying not to fall in the process when I finally reached the entranceway, and steadied myself. Giving my head one last shake, I cracked open the door to see Santino and his stupid grin waiting out in the hall.

"Ready to go?" He asked, pushing past me and letting himself in. He made his way to a bowl of fresh fruit in the dining room that was replaced every morning by loyal servants. Taking off one of his boots, he plopped himself down in a stiff backed chair and rested his bootless foot over his booted one as he propped them up on the table. He was wearing traditional Roman wear, a white toga, just as I was, but we still felt uncomfortable not wearing our boots and combat pants beneath.

After the battle, Caligula had granted each of us citizenship, and with it, the right to wear a toga. As Augustus had said, "Romans, lords of the world, the toga-wearing race," only Roman citizens could wear them. I was honored.

Shaking my head, I shut the door and moved over to my table. I sat on it near Santino's feet, and shoved them off, wiping away any mark he may have left with my sleeve, inciting him to give me a hurt look.

"Can't have anything nice when you're around, can I?" I asked rhetorically.

"No, probably not," he replied.

I sighed. "Just give me a second."

There had been many casualties in the battle, but of all the consequences resulting from it, at least Santino's attitude hadn't changed. After the past few months with him, I now knew that if there truly was one universal truth, it wasn't that everything freezes, but that Santino would never change.

As for the casualties, there were too many to recall.

Nisus had died, brought down protecting the *aquila* that was never dropped. It took three men to bring him down, but the centurion I had barely known, but had grown to respect during the battle, would not be returning to help retrain the *XV Primigenia*. His loss hit the legion hard, but he was just one of many.

Of the legion itself, it had been practically destroyed. Half of the auxilia were killed, and only two cohorts worth of legionnaires were left to walk off the field. Many of the experienced officers had been wounded or killed, and even Galba had sustained injury when he had tried to drive his cavalry squadron to aid Caligula during his duel with Claudius.

The survivors were to be sent back North in another month or so, after some much deserved rest and relaxation in Rome courtesy of Caligula. He had even offered each surviving legionnaire, none of whom were officially commissioned yet, full retirement packages, including discharge and retirement payments and a plot of land to any who desired it. Not a one had accepted the gracious offer, and all would remain with the army.

Of the eight Praetorian cohorts that had fought in the battle, only fifteen hundred men survived. Once the dust had settled, Caligula interviewed each surviving tribune to determine exactly what happened after his escape from the city. Each had passionately denied any knowledge of his survival and claimed that Claudius had told them he had been appointed emperor by the senate, through Caligula's own will. The deranged psychopath had even staged a phony funeral to cover his tracks.

When the tribunes were asked why they hadn't ceased hostilities when they saw him on the battlefield, they replied that they couldn't explain it. It was as though some unseen force had been moving them toward combat, and it wasn't until Claudius had been killed that they felt the effects slowly wear away.

Caligula had apparently accepted this explanation and hadn't pressed that line of questioning further.

They were dismissed, pardoned and reinstated into the guard. As for those who had fought the day we were forced from the city, the few who were left were lined up along the old siege trenches and crucified.

The Sacred Band had lost half its strength, but with the support and leadership of Quintilius, Gaius, and Marcus, whose wound had missed any vital arteries, it would be quickly reorganized and be as loyal as ever. From now on, the Sacred Band would never leave Caligula's side, and even remain housed with him. One half would be on duty at any given time while the other half would remain in the *Castra Praetoria*, and would be chosen from only the most loyal and able men available.

As for those of us formerly employed by the Vatican, many outcomes, decisions, and scars, both physical and emotional, were made and accumulated.

Just after Caligula's duel with Claudius, Vincent had been severely wounded. He had been stabbed through his forearm, doing massive damage to his left arm. Wang had been there to do what he could, but he couldn't save the arm. Roman surgeons had amputated it, just below the elbow, and Wang had done what he could to stave off infection and ease Vincent's pain. His recovery time lasted a month, only minus an arm, and I remembered sad times when I noticed him automatically reaching out with his severed arm, only to realize it was no longer there. Hopefully, over time, he'd get used to living a normal life without it.

Santino's wounded leg only needed a dozen stitches, while Bordeaux had fought a substantial part of the battle with an arrow sticking out of his back. It had found itself lodged in his trapezius muscle, near his neck, an errant missile from an archer. Bordeaux's overly muscled physique had probably saved his life, as the arrow hadn't made it past his dense muscle structure. Wang, not trained in arrow removal, had allowed a Roman doctor handle it, using ancient forceps, a tool developed in Greece specifically for arrow retrieval. Both had recovered easily.

I was fine for the most part. My arm needed stitching and would leave another scar that would bisect the last one that had just healed there. Add to that another dozen or so scrapes and gashes; I was a mess but had survived relatively unscathed.

As for our decisions, Vincent made his to leave Rome and Caligula's employ to tour the empire about two weeks ago. He voiced an interest in heading East to find the origins of Christendom. He'd sworn, his remaining hand raised in a promise gesture, that he would not do anything to affect its development, and I hoped he'd keep his word.

Wang had decided to leave as well, indicating he would go to Greece, and perhaps teach their doctors a thing or two about modern medicine. A month ago, as he prepared to leave, I'd clapped him on the shoulder and told him he'd have a fun time learning Greek, and that he'd sooner enjoy Duran Duran than the annoyingly complex language. He gave me a smile, said his goodbyes to everyone who had gathered to see him off, and left.

Bordeaux, another old timer, only a handful of years younger than Vincent, had lived many lives. He'd admitted that the only one where he had been truly happy was the short year he had spent with his wife. He hoped he could find that kind of companionship again, and with no more use for fighting, he too had set off, going North, with no real destination in mind.

They'd all taken plenty of supplies and gear, and despite retiring, brought their weapons and plenty of ammo. They'd be fine out in the wilderness of ancient Rome, and I hoped I crossed paths with them again someday.

"These olives are stale," Santino reported, his mouth half full.

"I thought you didn't like olives," I said, my hand on the door to my room.

"Eh," he muttered, inspecting one in the light, "they're growing on me."

I rolled my eyes. Unfortunately, or fortunately, I was still trying to decide which, Santino had chosen to stick around.

That left just one person.

I tried not to think about my own personal last moments on the battlefield. They had easily become some of the most horrific ones I've ever experienced. I had nearly given up myself, wondering if I could ever have been happy living while she didn't, but I endured.

I sighed.

I tried not to think about it.

Reaching for the door, I paused when it seemingly opened on its own accord. Curious, I quickly pressed my hand against it and shoved it open, hoping to catch any interloper off guard. I was still pretty jumpy considering the kind of reception we'd had in Rome over the past year.

I took a tentative step inside as my hand hovered near my Sig. I crept forward and was surprised to notice a figure step out from behind the door, surprising us both. I nearly dropped to a knee for a better firing position, before recognition dawned on me.

I looked across at a set of brilliant green eyes, the same set that had haunted and loved me for nearly a year. Her skin looked paler than normal, and she'd lost some weight during her lengthy recovery, but the lovely face of Helena stared back at me with the same angry expression I'd grown to love in return.

She leaned against the door and clutched her chest with a hand. "For Christ's sakes, Hunter! You nearly gave me a heart attack bursting in here like that," she told me, slightly out of breath.

"Me?!" I responded with a frown. "What the hell are you doing out of bed?"

I reached out to take her hands in my own and led her to our bed, the most comfortable thing I've slept on since my childhood one. She moved slowly, and I sat her down next to me before I rested a hand on her forehead.

"You know you're not supposed to exert yourself," I told her, my hand still pressed against her skin. "At least you don't seem to have a fever."

She brushed my hand away. "Hunter, will you please stop? You're worse than my mother. Wang said I could start walking around weeks ago, and I wasn't going to miss this for the world."

I frowned again.

In those last few moments after I had broken down, Helena had hung to life by a thread. Perhaps by divine intervention, a wandering Roman medic from the legion had spotted his fallen *Mater*, and rushed to her aid. The man had been efficient, quick and thorough. Recognizing that the sword had done little damage to her internal organs, he had gently removed the blade and gone to work cleaning and containing the wound.

I remembered the field doctor roughly pushing me aside as I tried to hold her. There had been so much blood. So much. It had driven me to the point of helplessness even with the Roman medic there.

I sat beside him for what seemed like ages, but my mind forced my body from the scene. I'd gotten up and wearily stumbled around until I found a rock to sit on. The battle was just starting to wrap itself up around me, and after a few seconds of rest, I started to weep. Just like Odysseus in his opening scene in *The Odyssey*, I sat on that rock, overlooked nothing in particular, and cried for the one I loved the most. Odysseus had sat there every day for years, and my suffering felt just as long. His salvation came in the form of the fleet-footed Hermes who told him the good news that Zeus had convinced his brother, Poseidon, to lift the ban that had forced him from seeing his beloved Penelope. All I got instead was Santino, who slowly approached my rock, and placed his hands on my shoulders.

Feeling his touch, I turned to see Wang. Santino had found him working on a fallen Praetorian who was too far gone to help. As soon as Wang had heard Helena's name, he'd dropped what he was doing and rushed to her side as fast as his legs could carry him. He'd ordered the Roman medic aside, and his fingers danced with graceful care, and his presence offered the briefest seconds of hope.

Then, she died.

At least, her heart had stopped beating, but with a few hits of his mobile defibrillator, Wang managed to revive her, repair her struck internal organs including her pancreas and large intestine, put her back together, sew her up, and save her life. It had taken him almost three hours kneeling in the mud and the blood on that battlefield, but he'd somehow managed to pull her from the jaws of death. Bordeaux had joined Santino, arrow still lodged in his back, kneeling around Wang as he worked, keeping vigil while I remained glued to my rock, too afraid to face the worst. Many other legionnaires came and kneeled with them. When Wang finally walked over and told me the good news, it took minutes for his words to sink in, but when they finally did, I rushed to her side to find her unconscious and as pale as a ghost.

But alive!

I tried to thank him with a bear hug that launched him a foot off the ground, but nothing I said could truly convey how I felt. He'd smiled and told me our happiness would be thanks enough. After that, I'd spent the next three weeks in a field hospital with her, surrounded by thousands of other wounded soldiers. I rarely left her side before she was allowed to leave and join me in the beautiful home we had been given near the Palatine, interestingly on the spot where the Colosseum should be standing in about forty years or so. When I passed that bit of information on to Helena, she had coughed out a laugh and said she couldn't make any promises she would survive if I kept lecturing.

Still too weak to move around much, she was trapped in bed, and even with modern antibiotics and Wang's direct care, her recovery hadn't been as graceful as it would have been in a modern hospital. She'd contracted a fever, and the wound on her back became infected, but she was resilient, and Wang was always there to help. A few weeks before he left for Greece, Wang finally gave her a clean bill of health and directions to start getting into shape. He never would have left Helena before making sure she would make a full recovery. And although it had been over two months, she was still far from one hundred percent.

Helena leaned forward slightly on the bed and looked up at me. "Are you all right, Jacob?"

I smiled at her. "Me? I'm fine. I'm just glad you're all right."

I patted her on the knee and leaned in for a kiss. She didn't pull away, and I found myself lying on the bed next to her a few seconds later.

"You know," she said in between breaths and lip locks, "I still haven't properly thanked you for taking care of me."

I smiled, and pushed her gently away. "Now, *that*, you definitely haven't been cleared for! Let's not push it."

She smiled back. "You're such a tease."

"I know. It's why you love me," I answered, getting to my feet. "Come on. We should probably make sure Santino hasn't choked on an olive or something."

"We should?" She asked.

I chuckled, gripped her hands again, and slowly pulled her to her feet. I handed her the cane fashioned for her, and held out my arm for her to rest against as well. We walked out of the room together to find Santino, feet back on the table, trying to toss olives into his mouth. Judging by the body count on the floor, he hadn't been very successful.

Putting his boot back on, he jumped to his feet when he saw us. "Finally! Let's go. I'm starving."

I shook my head. "Just so you know, I'm not going to let you crash on my couch much longer. You need to find your own place."

"I have one," he said, information that I unfortunately already knew, "but your place is cleaner."

I shook my head, and looked to Helena for support. Over the past few months, Santino hadn't just been freeloading, but helping care for Helena when I had to do things like sleep, eat or other daily necessities. Needless to say, she didn't hate him anymore, and with a heart of gold, could never force him to leave, even though he had a perfectly fine place right next door.

She shrugged at me and smiled.

My shoulders slumped. "You're lucky you're my best friend and my girlfriend actually happens to like you," I told Santino. "When does that ever happen?"

He smacked me on the shoulder. "Couldn't have happened to a better guy. Now. Can we please go?" He asked, moving to Helena's opposite side and taking her arm, tossing her cane on the couch.

"Seriously, Hunter," she said. "I'm starving!"

I sighed, completely defeated. "All right. At least this should be an interesting evening."

Interesting? Maybe, but I wasn't exactly looking forward to it.

Reclaiming an empire, even when you were the legitimate sovereign, wasn't an easy task. When we had marched into the city, there were small pockets of resistance of little consequence. Stubborn senators with delusions of grandeur and dreams of a seat on the throne defended their lives with hired servants and slaves. These were the men who had probably planted the seed of rebellion in Claudius' mind to begin with. Unaffected by the orb, their own egos fueled their quest for absolute power. Any remaining Senators who couldn't prove their loyalty were crucified next to their Praetorian allies. As for the orb, it was history. It was taken to an undisclosed position by Varus, and he hadn't told us where it was. No one knew where the second one was either.

The next step was a conscription, which was basically a list of names, and if yours was on it, you were a free target for any legionnaire, bounty hunter, or civilian alike willing to sell your ass to the State. Any and all assets were to be seized and your life forfeited. Dictators like Marius and Sulla had abused the process to eliminate those disloyal to them, but Caligula only targeted those directly involved in the plot. As a result, almost a fourth of the Senate was rounded up and crucified, order had been restored, and those who remained would think twice before ever crossing Caligula, especially with his devoutly loyal Sacred Band by his side.

Finally, where the patrician families of Rome suffered, its lower classes prospered. After the siege, Caligula ordered immense grain supplies to be imported to the city from neighboring towns, all of which were completely willing and happy to help. Some plebian families even found their way into new found wealth and power. Those who had rallied against Claudius during the siege were commended, and some were even offered vacant Senate seats, and with them, the honor of citizenship.

To further benefit the people of Rome, Caligula had proposed plans to erect a stadium of epic proportions, one that could hold immense gladiatorial fights, races, and naval battles, all for the viewing spectacle of the people. It had been an idea whispered in his ear by Vincent, along with a suggested location, right in the vicinity of my current home. Caligula thought it was a good idea, and promised those residents they would be moved to better homes, and recruited a young, upstart architect to begin planning its design, with a start construction date in a year. The original Colosseum's architect was lost to history, so for all I knew, Caligula's chosen man may very well have been the actual designer, recruited decades earlier.

Vincent would never learn.

So that was that.

Rome was under control and with its rightful ruler popularly and sanely in place. The rest of the empire's knowledge of the incident was reduced to mere rumors spread by traveling citizens. Santino and I had accepted Caligula's offer to remain as bodyguards for him, as did Helena, who would join us when she recovered. It wasn't so much a bodyguard position, but as agents he could call on for "special" assignments.

It was the best posting I'd ever had because Caligula hadn't asked us to do anything yet, except for the occasional appearance in the *Curia*, dressed in our full military gear. The rules of the *pomerium* were restricted to swords, spears, and shields, so our rifles fell through a loop hole that allowed us to carry them.

Caligula was also sympathetic to my desires to care for Helena, and knew that three would be better than two on any assignment he sent us on. With that in mind, he told Helena, on one of his occasional visits, to take her time healing. Other bonuses included our housing assignment, an income that easily put us in the equestrian class, those wealthy Roman businessmen who weren't part of the patrician senatorial class, and invitations to numerous dinner parties, most of which Caligula himself invited us to.

Which is where we were headed now, only this one wasn't hosted by Caligula, but by his sister.

Agrippina.

I hadn't told anyone about what I saw that day Santino and I were captured. About how she had possibly set us up, and how she had been present at the moment we were captured. The evidence was circumstantial, as Claudius could have been lying about sending her as a messenger just to get a rise out of me, and I still couldn't be sure it had actually been her smooching him after I had been hit over the head.

Besides. Who would I tell? Caligula wouldn't believe me. He seemed completely secure in the notion that Agrippina was a sweet little angel, and now a mother to boot. If I told Helena, she would have crawled out of bed, dragged herself to Agrippina's home, and ripped her throat out with her bare hands. While the latter outcome was somewhat appealing, I couldn't condemn someone on circumstantial evidence alone.

So, arm in arm, the three of us slowly made our way to the *Domus Augusti*, where Agrippina had taken up residence with her brother. Passing through the familiar gate, and two familiar Praetorians now back in their traditional white togas, we made our way into the house of Augustus.

While, it was no longer the same house Augustus had built after Bordeaux had destroyed much of it; Caligula kept its original name, a tribute to his great grandfather. While the exterior had been reconstructed beautifully by Claudius, Caligula removed every piece of callous art he had adorned it with. The end result was the same kind of austere, yet beautiful home it had originally been. Met at the door by a house slave, something I'd never get used to but could do little to change, we were escorted through the house and into the dining room.

The room was devoid of any modern semblance of formal dining accoutrements or ware. Instead of chairs, there were low couches arranged in a U, with tables laid out in front of them. Lying on couches while eating dinner was every lazy man's dream, and after experiencing it a few times, I never wanted to go back. All the Romans needed was a television with some Monday Night Football, and life would be complete.

We mingled with increasingly familiar people. I chatted with Varus while Helena and Santino struck up a conversation with an off duty Quintilius and his wife. We didn't have too much time for small talk as Caligula and Agrippina arrived only a few minutes later. Once they were announced, we made our way to the dining tables and got comfortable.

Agrippina seated herself at the head of the table with Caligula and her young son, Nero. Santino, Helena, and I were seated at their right, a place of honor, Varus and Quintilius directly across from us to their left, with the rest of the guests scattered throughout the couches. As soon as everyone was settled, house slaves were called to bring forth various dishes of steaming delectables.

The dinner had been delicious, and the evening fun. Chicken, beef, vegetables of all kinds, grains, and fruits for dessert, it was a feast fit for kings, and I wondered how these Romans stayed in such good shape eating so much all the time. I already felt my waistline beginning to tighten and I had to promise Helena that I'd hit up the *Campus Martius* next week for a workout.

With dinner completed, the evening slowed down to alcohol induced conversation. I found myself pretty drunk, lounging on my back, and munching on fruit Helena was playfully lowering into my mouth. She told me to close my eyes while she found something new to feed me, and as a result I felt a syrupy liquid spill down my chin. I opened my eyes to see Helena pouring honey from a cup. I laughed and knocked the cup away, gently pushing her into Santino. He was talking to a young, pretty, Roman woman and glared at me when Helena interrupted his conversation. I couldn't help but laugh again as I rolled onto my back and Helena moved to lie next to me, her head on my stomach.

I stared up at the ceiling feeling drunk, gluttonous and happy for the first time in years. The world I had left had been filled with nothing but war, one that had no end in sight. Albert Einstein once said, "I know not what weapons World War III will be fought with, but World War IV will be fought with sticks and stones". He was probably right, and I knew it was only a matter of time before someone started the chain reaction that would end it all. Ancient Rome, however, I knew had a future, and maybe with my help, a better one. We'd done too much to the timeline as it was, so there was no sense resting on our laurels now and not trying to help.

The future aside, it was also the first time since I was a kid I could honestly admit I had everything. With Helena at my side, my best friend Santino at my back, and the emperor of Rome as my employer, I couldn't find much to complain about. I sighed, lay back, and drank in the moment.

It wasn't until I heard the innocent giggle of a small child that I remembered life was never perfect. Out of the corner of my eye I saw young Nero on the ground in a corner. I also saw a dozen attendants playing with and spoiling him right in front of me. It gave me a bad feeling in the pit of my stomach.

"Friends and family," Caligula suddenly announced, struggling to sit up on his couch, arms spread at his sides to maintain his balance. "I am so very glad you could join my sister and I for dinner tonight, and a wonderful dinner it was, I might add."

Many of the guests offered their own positive sentiments to Agrippina, as though she had anything to do with the actual cooking of the meal.

"I, myself, am not quite finished," Caligula announced, slurring his words drunkenly, still munching on part of his entrée, "but I have an announcement, a very important one that will affect the continuation of my imperial reign."

I glanced over at Santino and Helena, the latter's expression looking confused, while the former was still trying to cop a feel. I gave her a shrug. I was beyond making predictions based on historical precedence at this point.

"My lovely sister and I have been discussing events at great length, and I have come to a decision. I hereby announce that due to my lack of children, as of this afternoon and recorded in my living will, Agrippina's son, Nero, will succeed me as Caesar in the circumstances of my death. Should that happen before he reaches the age of fourteen, Agrippina shall rule in regency till the day he is."

There was a chorus of applause and adulation from the guests present. As for me, my jaw practically hit the floor. I couldn't believe what I was hearing. After all we'd gone through and all we'd changed, establishing Caligula as potentially one of Rome's greatest emperors, Nero would still take over and ruin everything. I looked over at the young child, and even at six months of age, I saw the beginnings of the man he would become, the servants continuing to pamper and spoil the boy.

I looked over at my two companions, who were just as confused as I was, but obviously not truly grasping the implications. Even Varus, sitting across the table from my position looked as confused as the three of us. If he didn't know, this must have been a recent decision.

I looked back at Caligula, heartened by his vitality and youth, knowing it would be a long time before Nero could actually become Caesar. Caligula was so much more popular and protected than ever, it would take an act of the gods to bring him down. I laid my head back down against a couch cushion and continued to stare at the ceiling in comfort.

I felt myself falling asleep when I heard the clatter of a plate beside me. I peeked through my right eye and saw Caligula eating a small, dark brown mushroom from the plate that must have fallen to the floor in his drunken stupor. I sniveled at the sight as mushrooms were never my favorite. Something about eating fungus bugged me. They always seemed to...

My train of thought stopped as a word association sprang to mind. Something about Caligula and mushrooms should have been important to me, but I was too drunk to remember. Claudius. Mushrooms. Caligula. Agrippina.

Poison.

I tried to get up and warn him, but my mind and body were too slow. I watched as he took a bite, glancing at it curiously, but pleasingly, before his eyes tightened in confusion and concern. He dropped the mushroom and his hands grasped at his throat while a white, frothy substance foamed at his mouth. Most dinner guests were still elated and discussing Caligula's announcement but when he fell to the floor and convulsed from a seizure, every guest rushed to their feet, and ran to his side.

All except Agrippina.

She was still seated on her couch, looking down at the emperor's shaking form, but only for a moment before she turned her head to look right at me. A slow smile crept across her face, and I thought I saw her shaking slightly in laughter. I looked back at Nero, and back at her, whose smile broadened just slightly before she turned back to Caligula, now in horrified sister mode.

"What's happening to him?" Helena asked, bewilderment in her voice.

"We have to go," I said. "Now."

"What? Why?" Santino asked, looking from me to Caligula and back and forth.

"Come on!" I almost yelled, grabbing Helena and helping her off the couch. Pulling her close to make a quick getaway, I was about to start announcing politely that we were leaving, but realized everyone's attention was elsewhere. Only Varus, holding his friend and emperor's head in his arms, paid us any attention. He looked angry, but he knew as well as I did that fingers might soon be pointed in our direction. His look suggested he felt we were innocent, but I couldn't be sure. All I knew was that in a place like Rome it was better to avoid getting caught than to stick around with even the slightest bit of suspicion directed toward you.

I nodded to my friend and hauled Helena out of the room, Santino catching up to help me with her.

Not even to the house gate, realization seemed to dawn on her. "We didn't actually change anything, did we? What you said before, about fate finding a way to set things straight."

I thought about it.

It made sense. With Claudius out of the picture, the only logical thing for fate to do was to have Agrippina rule while she waited for Nero to turn fourteen. She had practically ruled alongside Claudius anyway.

I thought about it.

No, I couldn't buy that. I wouldn't. There was no way some natural force controlled the outcome of all living things. I had free will. I had a choice. I controlled my own fate and so did Agrippina. We had to stop the madman I knew Nero would become from ever taking the throne. For all I knew, the current situation would make things far worse than I could possibly imagine.

"No," I said, thinking hard about what to do. "We're fucking changing things."

I sifted through every shred of knowledge I had about ancient Rome. There had to be something we could do. Both Caligula and Claudius may be dead, and with it Rome's chances of a bright future, but there must be someone who can help. I cross referenced as many dates, names and events as I could in my mind to try and find someone.

I could only think of one man. Only one man in the entirety of the Roman Empire could have a positive effect on the course of history. He was the only one because he'd done it before. He'd taken an empire on the brink of collapse and realigned it back toward greatness.

Vespasian.

COMING SOON

Keep reading for a brief snippet from the next book in the ongoing Praetorian Series: *To Crown a Caesar*.

Sometime in the future…

It took us about a week and a dozen pointed fingers later, but we soon found our way to the enormous legionary barracks that was the army's camp.

To say it was huge was an understatement.

It sat on the west bank of the Rhine River and was called Vindonissa. It had been built around the birth of Christ and has since been called home by the *Legio XIII Gemina*, and if history was at all accurate, the *Legio XXI Rapax* should have just moved in. Along with Galba's *Legio XV Primigenia* and Vespasian's *Legio II Augusta*, that accounted for four of the six legions meant to embark on the campaign.

It would be a difficult nut to crack as all that firepower would make sneaking in a challenge. Santino's UAV would have been helpful for advanced recon, but it was no longer available so we'd have to reconnoiter the camp the old fashioned way.

Like all legion forts, it had been constructed far from the tree line, a defensive strategy that ensured an attacking force would have to abandon the natural cover provided by a tree line to enter missile fire range.

General George Washington, before he was a general and when he was still a Redcoat, had made the mistake of not clearing out the tree line around Ft. Necessity before a battle during the Seven Year's War. The blunder had left much of his force dead, and he and his remaining men were just barely able to hold the line.

No insult to George Washington, but Romans would never make that mistake. Their camps were so efficient and practical that no matter how many legionnaires were present, the fort would always be built around the same basic principles, just scaled up.

Camps worth keeping around, like this one, generally had far larger walls around their perimeters and were built with stone instead of wood. The higher walls would make our infiltration route more difficult, but once inside we'd instantly know our way around. The only possible snag was that we didn't know exactly where Galba's tent would be. Vespasian, as the overall commander of the entire army, would be staying in the *praetorium* this time, not him.

But the *praetorium* was always situated directly in the middle of the camp, set halfway along the *via principalis*, and it didn't take a huge leap in logic to assume Galba would be nearby. As one of Vespasian's legates, he was only one step below Vespasian in the chain of command, and the army's generals would be posted near each other. All it would take is a legionnaire who valued his life more than his pride to tell us where Galba was.

Simple.

We set up our own camp about two miles inside the tree line and camouflaged our tents as well as we could. We buried them beneath a rock outcropping that jutted out over the landscape, creating a nice little space for our tents beneath. We secured large bushes around the perimeter and draped a camouflage net over everything. The site was practically invisible, and I was confident a scouting party would never spot it.

Once our hideaway was concealed, we spent a few hours resting before using the cover of night to scout the Roman camp from the trees. Using a mixture of infrared and night vision optics, we were able to identify and chart the movement of guards upon the walls. We timed their patrol route and noted which directions they paid attention to at all points along their patrol.

At daybreak, Helena used a camera with a telephoto lens the size of a soda pop bottle to take panoramic shots of the camp and its surrounding. While she was taking her pictures, I retrieved my small journal from a cargo pocket and took some time to sketch the landscape with a few pencils. While using both sketches and photographs may seem redundant, utilizing them together was a practice indoctrinated in snipers, recon marines, and other units for decades.

We returned to camp in the early evening, having shifted our recon position a handful of times, arriving to a freshly cooked dinner delivered by Santino. He had shot, cleaned, and cooked a deer while

Helena and I were away, and by the time we joined him, he was already packing the leftovers in salt, preserving them for a lifetime.

As we ate, we pored over the images taken earlier, quickly remembering that we were no longer dealing with amateurs. Legionnaires were professionals. They weren't a peasant army roused by a belligerent warlord in a time of fickle bloodlust, but career soldiers. Warriors. This was their job. And they were very serious about their craft. It took us an hour before we even found a possible loophole in their defensive network.

We were able to note a single weak area – a blind spot along the north wall where patrolling guards left an opening, dead center of the wall. The segment of the wall in question was particularly dark and was left unguarded for about three and a half minutes – more than enough time to scale the wall and sneak inside.

Helena and I spent the rest of the evening preparing for the operation to come, while Santino complained about having to stay behind and play spotter. He wanted to see "Ol' Triple Chin," as he had dubbed Galba for his jowls and multiple chins, but we didn't have a ghilli suit for him. Helena and I were both trained snipers, and camouflage with the use of a ghilli suit was our stock in trade, not Santino's. While he may have been able to sneak up on God Himself, his kind of stealth was different from ours. He was a master at hiding in plain sight or in a crowd, but the art of camouflage was, as my trainers had said, less about avoiding detection and more about simply being undetectable at all.

Ghilli suits allowed us to be one with the environment. They were handcrafted and modular so that Helena and I could tailor them to mimic whatever environment we wanted. We'd spent most of the past few days doing just that, adding bits of grass and local fauna to them, crafting the perfect disguise.

By the time we finished them two days after finding Vindonissa, it was too late for Helena and I to delve into the conversation I knew we needed. We mostly kept to ourselves, but by 0200 on the third day, I tried to purge all thoughts plaguing my mind as we launched the operation by crawling our way through the low grass of the meadow toward the camp, back in sniper-mode.

Focused and meticulous.

We made the first leg of our journey smoothly and without incident in a little under an hour. We didn't have to worry about anything like random search lights since Roman torches could barely reach out past their palisade. Additionally, as luck would have it, tonight's moon was a waning crescent, about as far from full as it was going to get.

When I pushed my arm out again to inch myself forward, all it came into contact with was air. I looked out from under my hood and saw the ground fall away steeply. We'd made it to the trench. I tapped my toe twice in quick succession against the soft grass, letting Helena know we'd made it to the first major impediment. She gave my ankle a gentle squeeze to confirm she understood, and I slide forward.

Navigating the trench was easy, just down to the bottom for a few meters, then back up. We'd noted the previous night that the ditches appeared freshly dug, possibly as simple upkeep to ensure they were kept clear. But it also left the soil loose and littered with freshly dug grass, just enough for our grassy ghilli suits to blend right in.

The trip took about ten minutes. When I bumped my head against something hard after crawling up the other side of the trench, I knew we'd reached the palisade. Glancing up, I peeked through my hood of grass and took in my surroundings. The wall of the Roman fort stood immediately in front of me, at least thirty feet high.

I sent a double click to alert Santino that we had arrived by tapping my radio's push-to-talk button twice in rapid succession. We waited for what seemed like an hour before I heard Santino's faint voice in my ear.

"Clear. Four minutes on my mark…" he paused "…mark."

Helena was already rising to her feet, turning her back to me as she shrugged out of her ghilli suit. I pulled it off her shoulders and packed it into her backpack while she did the same with mine. We wore our night ops combat fatigues with our olive drab MOLLE vests over them. We were lightly armed, but Helena also had a small grappling hook dangling from her vest, which I dutifully retrieved and prepared to toss over the wall. I made a few quick circles in the air as I spun the hook, releasing it on the fourth. It went sailing over the wall and silently made contact with the rampart's floor thanks to its rubber tips. I pulled the rope until it was taut; giving it another tug just to be sure it was secure. Satisfied, I started my ascent, Helena right behind me.

A short climb later, I bounded over the lip of the wall, landing quietly onto the rampart. I sidestepped immediately to the left so Helena could land behind me. When she did, we gathered up the rope and I reattached everything to her rig.

I risked a quick look out over the camp, seeing for the first time an endless sea of torches illuminating an incalculable number of tents, all lined up in neat little rows. In that moment, I couldn't avoid a slight sense of unease tickle the back of my mind at the fact that I hadn't brought Santino instead of Helena, because this was when we could have really used him. I could see guards aplenty scattered through the interior of the camp and there were thousands of residents randomly going about one bit of business or another.

We'd anticipated as much, but the idea of sneaking through the forest of tents below us was unsettling. Santino could have walked down the *via principalis* stark naked and gone completely unnoticed, but I had to be here since I was the only one with enough facts to talk to Galba and Helena's ghilli suit didn't fit him. It hadn't been out of the question for us to craft his own ghilli suit out of locally made materials, even if it wouldn't have been up to the standards of our modern ones, but none of us had voiced any concerns during the planning stage about his absence. Four years ago, I probably wouldn't have considered bringing Helena on such a dangerous mission. She'd been a green rookie, chosen for the Pope's Praetorians because of a falsified record, but four years of operating with Santino and me had honed her into an effective military machine.

I tried to push it out of my mind as Helena placed her hand on my back, indicating she was ready to move. I reached behind me to tap the side of her leg to confirm I was ready as well. When we reached the first guard, I took aim with my air pistol fitted with tranquilizer darts, but didn't fire. I knew enough about Roman camps to know that if this guard didn't meet up with his partner, now at the other end of the wall, an alarm would go up almost immediately. Instead, we took advantage of our dark camouflage and quietly shifted positions to the inner edge of the rampart, and crawled our way behind him.

At one point, I thought I would have to shoot him when I saw his head snap around in our direction, but it turned out he was merely swatting at an insect. He turned towards the center of the wall to meet up with his buddy a few moments later, and I let out a slow breath through my balaclava. I glanced at Helena, only my eyes revealing my relief. She returned my look with a flick of her own green eyes and a gentle nudge to urge me forward.

When the guard was out of sight, I pulled Helena's grappling hook and rope from her MOLLE vest once again. I placed the hook on the rampart's wooden floor near the corner and tossed the rope out over the inner wall. The corner was pitch black so we had no insecurities about standing out against the lightly colored stone wall. I maneuvered myself out over the wall and fast roped to the bottom, taking stock of our surroundings after touching the ground, waiting for Helena to join me. Our corner of the camp seemed deserted at the moment, but that could change at any moment. When Helena's boots hit the grass behind me, I turned to see her jerk the rope to dislodge the hook, stepping aside to ensure it didn't fall on her. After it landed, I picked it up and secured it to her rig for the last time, and we moved off into the small city.

There might have been a thousand rows of tents before us, each containing eight sleeping men, and I had no idea how many tents there were per row. To find our way through, we simply picked a narrow avenue in one of the denser areas of the camp and slowly made our way toward the center, looking for a potential legionnaire to interrogate.

We didn't have to wait long before our first candidate appeared.

A man stumbled out of his tent nearly on top of us, muttering about how he really had to use the bathroom. Helena moved first and tackled him to the ground, covering his mouth in one quick motion. I knelt beside him and pushed my small boot knife against his throat.

"Galba," I whispered into his ear. "Where's his tent?"

The man's eyes were filled with shock, wide open and unbelieving, as though he were witnessing an apparition before him. He trembled and I heard the sound of running water beneath me. I glanced down to see that the man had urinated himself. Helena looked down as well, just in time to shift her knee out of the way. She looked back up at me and rolled her eyes.

"*Galba?*" I whispered with some force this time, driving my knife deep enough to draw a droplet of blood.

The legionnaire shook his head vigorously, his eyes wide with terror. Helena moved her hand just slightly. "Two tents behind the *praetorium*, three in the direction of the *porta decumana*."

I nodded. "Thanks. Your helpfulness won't go unrewarded."

Helena covered his mouth again and I shot him with a tranq dart before he could do something stupid. She looked at me with wide, annoyed eyes, not finding my parting words nearly as humorous as I did. We waited a few seconds for the affects to take hold and I removed the dart. I rolled him near the entrance to his tent with the shove of my boot. A random passerby wouldn't suspect any foul play, just another drunk passed out on the ground, and he'd probably be too out of it when he woke up to even remember us.

I flicked my fingers towards the *praetorium* and we carefully stalked our way through the camp. It took us about fifteen minutes, but we were eventually in position to cross the *via principalis*.

Luckily, traffic wasn't heavy, but there were guards posted sporadically. If not for a few parlor tricks Santino had taught us about creating diversions and dividing and conquering, this operation would have been over almost before it had begun.

But we were lucky, and our insertion seemed complete when we found ourselves in front of the tent the legionnaire had indicated was Galba's. I glanced at my watch. 0330. We had a few hours before the army started its daily hustle and bustle. I followed Helena as she reached the tent's entrance and gave the camp one last look. Nothing seemed out of the ordinary so I patted her on the shoulder and followed her inside.

I stepped into a large open space, littered with mobile furniture and storage containers scattered throughout in a haphazard manner. After a second to take in my surroundings, I went directly to the bed. Looking down, I saw the fat face of the ugly man I knew to be Galba. I never did figure out how his head always looked so fat while his body stayed in the tip top shape of any legionnaire.

Helena and I exchanged nods, and I bent over to clasp a gloved hand over his thick lips.

His eyes shot open, but he didn't flinch, try to escape or utter a noise. In his eyes I saw immediate recognition, even with our concealing facemasks. He was one of the few people who knew who we were. I held a finger vertically over my covered mouth and waited for him to nod in understanding. When he did, I slowly removed my hand.

"You," he growled. "I should have you arrested and crucified. I've recently received word from the empress that you have officially been charged with the murder of Caligula." He narrowed his eyes at me angrily.

I cocked my head to the side and looked at Helena. Her indecipherable figure shrugged. That was news to us. I'd always wondered why she hadn't pegged his murder on us years ago, but I guess it was better late than never for her.

Interesting timing, though.

I pulled off my mask, revealing a face I knew was familiar to him and stood up straight.

"Servius. I need you to listen to me."

"Listen to you?! Why should I do that, you traitorous murderer?"

I leaned down and whispered, "Servius, do you really think we killed Caligula?"

Galba looked at the foot of his bed before looking back at us, shifting positions so that he was sitting up and crossed his arms over his chest. It gave him the appearance of a chubby, stubborn two year old.

"No," he said. "I don't. You are many things, but I always considered you loyal, and since you didn't try to usurp power for yourself after his death, I see no motive."

Helena removed her own mask and pulled her very long hair from beneath the back of her vest.

"Listen to him, Galba," she said. "You may not want believe what he has to tell you, but you need to trust us."

I looked over at Helena, who had cleaned up since our time in the tavern, and was back to the ravishing green eyed beauty I'd always known her to be.

"So you brought your woman," Galba commented as he looked around. "Of course you did. Where is the funny one? I actually liked him."

I'm sure Santino will be ecstatic.

"Servius," I pressed, "what I'm about to tell you will sound ridiculous, outlandish, and frankly impossible, but I need you to keep an open mind."

"Why do you keep calling me that?" He asked nervously. "My name is Lucius, not Servius."

"No, it's not," I said sternly. "Your real name is Servius Sulpicius Galba. You only took the name Lucius Livius Ocella Sulpicius Galba from your step mother and her family, who loved you dearly and raised you as one of their own." I saw his eyes widen in surprise. "Now, let me tell you another story. One about you, me, Rome, its future, and how I need your help to ensure its very survival."

If you're interested in Edward Crichton's Sci-Fi epic *Starfarer: Rendezvous with Destiny*, keep reading for a sneak peek at the first few chapters.

INCOMING TRANSMISSION . . .

TO: John Paul Sterling, Admiral, Allied Space Navy (ASN)
FROM: Alexander Mosley, First High Admiral, Allied Space Navy (ASN)
ORIGINAL REPORT: Richard Alderman, Colonel, Office of Strategic Space Intelligence (OSSI) - Original Report Attached
SECURITY LEVEL: **CLASSIFIED**

XXXXX   -   XXXXXXXXXX   -   XXXXX

SUBJECT: Anomalous ISLAND Activity - Action Required
SENT: 11.13.2595 (11:20:11)
AUTHENTICATION CODE: **Echo Echo Bravo Zero Zero Seven Echo**

Admiral John Paul Sterling,

This could be big, J.P., so I'll dispense with the usual pleasantries. Word has been sent to OSSI that our Chinese friends have encountered an anomaly along ISLAND Transit Route AlphaCOL-BetaCOL. The spooks haven't been able to get anything specific out of the Chinese yet, but it has The Star Destiny Corporation, at least, very concerned.

They're going to lose contact with the ISLAND Liner *Sierra Madre* on the aforementioned course very soon, and while OSSI isn't saying much, we could be talking about another rumored contact with alien technology aboard an ISLAND. That or they may have simply experienced their first mishap with WeT Tech.

Consider this your unofficial readiness report. Prepare the Third Fleet for immediate redeployment back to Earth and launch the *Alcestis* as soon as possible. I don't think I need to remind you to keep your wits about you, John Paul. There's more at play here than even I'm aware of, and I can't offer you much more advice than that. This won't be some silly sim we mucked about with back at the Academy. Something big is about to happen and something about it stinks.

Regards,

First High Admiral Alexander Mosley, ASN
Admiralty Board, Chair
Washington Aerospace Naval Headquarters, Luna

P.S. Should we get through whatever this thing is, I'll get you a case of that ancient Jamison swill you love so much.

<<<<< **SEE ATTACHED FILE FOR ORIGINAL REPORT** >>>>>

SECTION 1
The ISLAND

High Earth Orbit /
ISLAND Liner *Sierra Madre* – Red Zone /
Power Conduction Shaft – Delta /

11.06.2595
07:35:08 Zulu

That which defines man is nothing more than what he leaves behind. In no other way will he be remembered when his presence in this universe becomes little more than dust to aid in the formation of new celestial bodies, and the onset of space travel centuries ago only added to this legacy. Later, the ability to travel to other planets cemented it. If every human in existence simply vanished from reality, the ISLAND Liner *Sierra Madre* would remain, drifting through the depths of space for time immemorial.

And whoever finds it will think it little more than a hulking piece of junk.

Senior Chief of Electronics Dhaval Jaheed knew that was unfair assessment of a large portion of the ISLAND, but the in the presence of so many undocumented, unbundled, ungrounded, and unfamiliar wires, connectors, cables, circuits, and other forms of electronic mayhem before him gave him pause to curse the wretched ship. It was a safety inspector's worst nightmare, and the Red Zone was already an extremely dangerous, almost mystical, place, quarantined from entrance by all ISLAND passengers and staff.

Senior Chiefs never sent technicians into the area, mostly because they never needed to, but the occasion had arisen today, much to the dread of every technician under Dhaval's supervision. His rank of ISLAND Senior Chief of Electronics gave him seniority over every electrician or technician aboard the *Sierra Madre*, and made him the only person he was willing to send into such a hazardous portion of the ship. The rest of them were all back in the Green Zone, the outer layer of the ship that surrounded the Red Zone like an egg encasing its yolk.

Despite knowing it was in his best interest to focus on his work, it was difficult for Dhaval not to wonder exactly what kind of genius would let something as important as an ISLAND Liner fall into such disarray. ISLANDs were the sole means of transportation to Earth's colonies, and the only way to keep humanity's presence amongst the stars connected. The mess he was in now was a disgrace to mechanics, technicians, electricians, and engineers alike, but he supposed that's what happened after hundreds of years of neglect.

"Find the breaker yet, Chief?" Asked an unwelcome voice that infiltrated every recess of his mind. It came so suddenly that Dhaval stumbled from his perch overlooking the exact breaker box he had in fact been searching for. He shot his hand out to seize the nearest stabilizing handle, only to have it break away from the shaft in his grip. His life was spared by a safety cable that secured his belt to a ladder rung – which amazingly held firm. Dhaval dangled there for a few moments, his forehead glistening with sweat as he stared down the conduction shaft, noticing the green safety lights fixed to the wall descend only about ten meters before becoming overwhelmed in darkness. The shaft descended for hundreds of kilometers, all the way to the Core, but few knew what was down there.

Dhaval touched a red button on his exo-suit, and a small object shot out from a mechanism on his back. The magnetic wafer attached itself to the metal wall and reeled him back into a standing position upon his perch. Once upright, he deactivated the magnetic anchor and took a deep breath as it recoiled.

"Chief?" Came the disjointed voice in his head again, somewhat more worried.

Dhaval gritted his teeth in frustration and keyed his com. "This is Senior Chief Jaheed. I've found the conduit. Initiating repairs now."

"Copy that, Chief. Be careful down there. Some of that equipment could be a hundred years old."

Dhaval paused for the briefest of seconds in frustration before returning to his work.

As far as he knew, he was the first person to visit this realm of the ISLAND since the last round of ship wide upgrades and renovations that had expanded the *Sierra Madre's* overall size and mass to its current level. There may have been the riff raff and Unwanteds who had inherited the bowls of the ship over the past few centuries, but even they were smart enough to stay out of the conduction shafts and rarely breached the Red Zone.

The only reason he was even down here was because the ISLAND's Senior Systems Officer had identified a small power drain that originated in the very spot Dhaval now occupied, one that threatened the ship's next WeT Jump. Such a problem hadn't arisen in the thirty five years since Dhaval had been conscripted to work aboard the *Sierra Madre*, but it wasn't Dhaval's position to question how such a problem had arisen. His job was simply to fix the broken conduit and bring the conduction shaft back to peak efficiency. All he cared about was that the one hundred year old power box he was currently manhandling seemed repairable. He pulled a data cable from his chest rig and jacked it into a port that seemed like it would accommodate the plug. Numbers and figures poured across the Lens in front of his left eye, most of which was meaningless gibberish even for someone as experienced as Dhaval, but he comprehended enough to tell him it was at least fixable.

Just as Dhaval thought he had enough information to begin, he heard a loud metallic bang above him that reverberated through the shaft. It was repeated a number of times before ending just as suddenly as it began. It sounded like someone carelessly knocking over machinery as they moved through the area.

"Hello?" Dhaval called into the darkness, knowing he was supposed to be alone. He hadn't been sure what he'd heard, but it sounded distinctly like moving people. "Hello?" He repeated. "Is anyone there?"

Only silence answered him.

Dhaval shrugged and eyed the darkness above him one last time before returning to his work.

You're getting paranoid in your old age, Dhaval.

He shifted in his seat and got comfortable on his perch, locking his exo-suit into a comfortable sitting position for a long repair job. The *Sierra Madre* wasn't due to depart on its two year voyage for another nine hours, and Dhaval had no idea how long this was going to take. The last thing he wanted to do was report a failure to Ship Master Na and risk delaying the ISLAND's departure time. This was the young woman's first voyage as ship master of an ISLAND Liner, and rumor had it that she was as ruthless as she was new to the position. Upsetting her would not bode well for even a veteran like Dhaval Jaheed, for no matter how good he was, he was still an Indian aboard an ISLAND – little more than a slave on a farm.

Earth /
Havana, Cuba /
ISLAND Departure Spaceport /

11.06.2595
08:00:00 Zulu

In a time of great prosperity, the most obvious course of action is toward progress.

Growth.

Modernization.

To build toward the future and create a utopia of high tech splendor.

It's what happened in the days following the end of Earth's population crisis and later economic boom that came with the advent of interstellar trade and colonization. Cities across the globe became shining, glimmering metropolises of glass and light, more beautiful than ever, but not Havana, Cuba. Its spaceport was the sole means of transportation to the High Earth Orbit ISLAND Docking Facility in the western hemisphere, and a prosperous city because of it, but it appeared little more than a dirty small town on the cusp of social annihilation.

At least that's how it seemed like to Carl Lawson as he sat in a local cantina, waiting for the departure time for his shuttle to arrive. The seedy bar was something out of a Western vid, an entertainment genre made famous once again after centuries in obscurity. It was a setting that belonged in a museum, like the one Lawson had in fact seen at the Cleveland Museum of Ancient American History when he was eight years old. The only difference being the lack of holographic personifications of living, breathing humans performing any number of mundane, yet clichéd tasks like bartending, piano and card playing, wenching, and the like. This bar was authentic, with real live people enjoying the relaxed, stress free setting in which Havana still exuded. On any other day, Lawson probably could have died content as he sat amongst fellow travelers in seek of a cold *cerveza*, but life was never completely stress free, especially not with his folks visiting to see him off.

"This isn't what you want to do," his father, John Lawson, said from across the table. "ISLANDs only come back to Earth every three years."

"About two actually," Carl Lawson replied, not understanding his parents sudden desire to dissuade him from leaving. He ignored his father and turned toward the bartender. "*Señor, una cerveza mas, por favor.*" The bartender nodded and tossed him a can of beer and Lawson couldn't help but smile.

Where has this place been all my life?

"But you won't know anybody," his mother, Eileen, chimed in with her ever chipper voice. "All your friends and family are on Earth, not to mention your friends in the military."

Outwardly, his mother was the sweet and caring type you'd find in any homestead across the galaxy, but Carl had known the truth behind it since he was a toddler. Underneath that façade of motherly kindness was the attitude of a woman who simply didn't give a shit, and only kept up her disguise to fit in with societal pressures. The fact that she still treated him like a child, instead of the forty five year old man that he was, said something about her. She was the kind of person who would shop for yet another needless product to sooth her own fickle desires on her Lens' Inter-Lens Service, while maintaining only the barest semblance of attention during what someone else would consider a very personal conversation.

"Mom," Carl said with a sigh. "Why do you think I'm even doing this? The only actual friend I have left is coming with me, so why stay."

The statement wasn't a question, and he didn't expect his mother to answer anyway. Not because she knew it hadn't been a question, but because he knew she didn't actually care.

John Lawson ignored his wife and pressed on. "You realize, son, that if you leave, you'll be doing little more than admitting your own guilt and running away in shame?"

Carl turned away from his mother, who no longer seemed interested, fixating her attention instead on the young Cuban bartender whose biceps were at risk of bursting through the sleeves of tropical style shirt. He fixed his father with a stern gaze and lowered his voice.

"Is that why you're here? To convince me to stay on a world that would rather see me hung by the gallows because the firing squad would be too quick? There's nothing left for me here. At least if I go, I can visit in a few years when things have quieted down. In time… who knows? Maybe I'll be able to return one day."

"No one is saying you should go on the Lens and draw attention to yourself, son, but if you stay and lead a quiet life, at least you can say you kept your honor intact and stood your ground."

"Whose honor exactly am I protecting? Yours or mine? Better be careful, Dad. You don't want to be taken off the list of all those holiday parties you're always invited to."

"Don't take that tone with me. I'm past caring about whether what happened was your fault or not, but our reputation has already been blemished by all this as it is, and the only thing you can do to repair it is to stare your accusers in the face and refuse to admit defeat."

"I already did that. Don't you remember when they stripped me of my rank and all my accomplishments and held me up as an example to save face with the Chinese? No, I did my part thank you much. I think I'm well and done with all that bullshit."

John Lawson folded his arms and glared at his son, watching as Carl swallowed that last of his beer.

"Don't do this, Carl. Don't expect a home to come back to if you do."

Carl smirked at his father and picked up his travel bag before getting to his feet and throwing some anachronistic monetary coins down on the table. Physical money may have been extinct on Earth for centuries now, but for those traveling to the outer colonies, it was a necessity, not to mention for those few who knew to stop at this lovely hole-in-the-wall before departure. "Don't worry, father. I haven't been coming back to one since the day you tried to save your *own* face in all this at no one's expense but my own."

With nothing left to say to his father, he reached out and grabbed his mother's arm before passing by her. He leaned down and gave her a kiss on the cheek, knowing he'll miss her despite all her faults. "Say goodbye to Lilly for me, mom."

Eileen flicked her eyes away from her beefcake pretty for just a second. "Oh, your sister will miss you terribly. Won't that help you cha…"

"Goodbye, mom."

"Oh, well, goodbye, dear." She turned back to her lustful desire and said nothing else.

Lawson looked back at his parents, now both ignoring him for completely different reasons. He couldn't believe it had come to this. His own parents had turned their backs on him in a time when he needed them the most. When the entire world was against him, he should have been able to turn to them and expect comfort and reassurance, but no such sentiment existed, and he was on his own.

Carl Lawson versus the universe.

He turned and headed toward the door, stopping only briefly to take in the surreal atmosphere of one of the most unique places he'd ever visited. With a nod of approval he walked out into the dusty streets and turned north toward the only sign of progress and hope as far as the eye could see: the spaceport.

And his future.

High Earth Orbit /
ISLAND Liner *Sierra Madre* – Green Zone /
Command Deck – Bridge /

11.06.2595
08:35:16 Zulu

"Ship's status?"

"All indicators save one show green, ma'am."

"What's the situation in Power Conduction Shaft – Delta? Are we on still on schedule?"

"Senior Chief of Electronics Jaheed is on it ma'am. His controller indicates he should have the problem locked down well before our time of departure."

"Good," Ship Master Mei-Xing Na replied behind a cool smile, pleased at her new crew's performance.

She abhorred incompetency – a cancer that had to be rooted out of as soon as it was discovered – and would not have been pleased with lackluster personnel. Whether her perfectionism was a byproduct of her Chinese ancestry or her own tenacity for perfection was anyone's guess, but she knew that her own personal level of expectation came from hard work and a selfless dedication to the fruition of her life's goals, and today would mark her first steps toward fulfilling her destiny. Today, she would take her first voyage as the ship master of an ISLAND Liner, and she wasn't about to let incompetency blemish such a step.

"Ship Master," another voice called out from her right. "Docking Control has indicated the first wave of shuttles are on approach. We should expect our first class passengers to arrive within the hour."

Mei-Xing nodded, but a sneer crossed her face at the continued use of the Common language amongst her crew. It was an excessively antiquated speech, an ugly speech, burdened and littered with the drivels of the old English language.

It may have been the language of international trade, commerce, and cooperation centuries ago, but the galaxy is so much bigger now! She thought. *With Chinese as the dominant language on more planets than any other, isn't it time for us to speak our own language, with our own people, on our own ships?*

She frowned. There was little hope to be found in such thoughts. The Americans were still too heavily involved in galactic affairs for Common to just go away, even if all they'd been reduced to was a security guard for planet Earth. There was also the problem that while all ISLANDs were crewed by Chinese, they were still staffed by their subservient Indians, creating yet another language barrier. Mei-Xing sighed to herself. Common was taught to every new born baby alongside their own native languages. There was no changing that now.

No matter how disgusting it felt on Mei-Xing's tongue.

"Ship Master?" The voice spoke again.

"Very good, Mister Chen," She said, glancing at the chronograph in the upper right hand corner of the oval Lens situated in front of her left eye.

08:36:02.

Only about a minute late. She supposed that was within even her standard of punctuality, especially considering how complex the last twenty four hours before an ISLAND launch was.

She blinked and sent a slight mental nudge toward her Lens, and a visual feed of the docking bay sprang into view. She saw the deck crew scurrying about with guidance lights in their hands, red carpets sprawled along the deck to help facilitate the boarding of travelers, and concierges, ready at the beck and call of any passenger to set foot aboard the *Sierra Madre*.

Good, good.

With another mental nudge, the Lens feed shifted back to her To-Do-List, which she kept as her default setting. She checked off the numbered event concerning the arrival of passengers and looked at the next thing on the list. She already knew what it was, but the internal comfort of continuously checking her lists gave her piece of mind. Item number five for the day was to rest until 14:00:00 when the next item on her list came about. It was barely nine o'clock in the morning, but she'd already been on the bridge for nine hours performing the ISLAND's pre-flight check lists with her bridge crew. Feeling weariness creeping in, she stood from her command chair and surveyed the bridge.

Built like the quarter of a sphere removed from the remainder, the ship master's chair was seated at the very center of the bridge, raised above all other stations by a semicircular platform about a meter above the deck. Arrayed around her from her two o'clock vantage point to her five o'clock and her ten o'clock to her seven o'clock were the duty stations of her crew. Everything from navigation to communication to ship's systems and a half dozen other flight sensitive tasks. Beyond these stations, wrapping around the entirety of the curved section of the bridge was the transparent viewport that connected the bridge to the emptiness of space. It wrapped above and behind and around Mei-Xing as she stood at the foot of her dais, and all she could see was space. It was something she had enjoyed immensely since her first moment on the bridge of her new command only one week ago.

Immaculate, the bridge was lit with bright lights and streamlined interfaces. It had red carpeting on the floor and wood paneling along the bulkheads, luxury items that simply screamed: civilian. It was nothing like the cold steel and colorless white Mei-Xing had seen aboard the Allied Space Navy's ships of war she had toured during her training.

Interestingly, she had to admit that she approved of the sterility of those ships more.

Finally, directly behind the ship master's chair was the lift, which she promptly started for.

"XO," she said as she stepped off her dais. A small man with a well-greased comb over straightened from his position overlooking the shoulder of the ship's Communication Officer.

"Ma'am?" He asked.

"The bridge is yours."

"Aye, ma'am," he replied with a slight nod. Mei-Xing did not return it but made sure her look lingered just enough to be obviously suggestive. Her executive officer didn't dare make mistakes while she was away, and her subtle look served as a reminder that he'd better not. It wasn't that she was unsure of his abilities, in fact, she couldn't ask for a more competent first officer, but that she never dropped her persona, not even for him.

She didn't want her crew to fear her, but she demanded their respect all the same.

She turned and entered the lift, but instead of indicating her intended destination with a simple thought through her Lens, a door whooshed open in front of her, opposite the one she'd just came through. Stepping through, she entered the atrium of her personal quarters, a space about the size of a small living room despite its sole purpose as a place to receive guests and store her footwear.

Once through the lift doors, which silently closed behind her, she immediately slouched her shoulders and rolled her neck. She wasn't a machine, despite what others may think, and she needed to relax as much as the next person. She slipped off her bulky duty boots and placed them in a small compartment that quickly retreated back into the bulkhead after she'd placed them within, and opened the large, ornate door to enter her new home.

Those who knew anything about space travel, especially those like the Chinese or Americans who dominated the practice, understood that space was always at a premium aboard a spacefaring vessel. The Americans would especially understand this, as their use for space travel revolved almost solely around combat, where every cubic inch of a spaceship was used to fit ammunition, life support, provisions, berths, or any number of mission critical essentials. The Chinese understood this as well, and abided by such a concept with most of their ship designs.

But not for ISLAND Liners.

Inter-System Luxury Aerospace Destination Liners had no need to worry about space constrictions. Each ISLAND was almost five hundred years old, beginning their lives as simple transport shuttles that ferried supplies from Earth to China's first colony on Mars in the late 20th century. But as time progressed, repairs and refits had been necessary, giving designers the unique opportunity to build on top of the existing infrastructure, creating larger and larger ships. Four hundred years later, those original ships had grown to immense sizes, each slightly different from the next. Each ISLAND was literally the size of Europe's largest countries, hundreds of kilometers long, and half as wide and tall. Shaped like an angular, blocky cone, the engine block was the wide base and the bridge its tip. They were space worthy countries capable of supporting millions of passengers.

Designed for comfort and leisure, Mei-Xing, as ship master, was entitled to the most extravagant suite on the ship. Two stories with five rooms, three baths, a solar to view the stars, a central atrium, dining room, and equipped with an emergency escape capsule, it was easily the most opulent accommodation available. Decorated in mainly Chinese motifs, Mei-Xing could almost pretend she was back on Earth in her ancestral home that had provided her with so much.

She looked at the vaulted ceilings, tassels, hangings, bronze sculptures, and gold inlaid furniture and sighed. Here was a place worthy of her accomplishments. It was a place where she could relax and enjoy the fruits of her labors. She glanced at the central fountain that flowed gracefully into its basin and touched the water. It rippled at her gesture and she smiled, continuing her way toward her room and up the port side staircase, having already chosen that she would only descend down the starboard side one.

It took her nearly thirty seconds to climb the stairs to the landing separating her quarters from the rest of her suite. Reaching out to grasp the intricate handle before her, she twisted and opened the wide double doors and entered her immaculately furnished room that gleamed in pristine opulence. She started the process of undressing herself as she strode across the room, removing each piece of her uniform carefully, meticulously folding each article of clothing and placing them on her dresser and throwing her undergarments down her hidden laundry chute.

Before stepping into bed, Mei-Xing moved toward her full body mirror she'd brought with her from her childhood home. It was an ovoid with gold designs twirling around the edges, coming together at the top to form two small cherubs blowing small horns at the other. It had been a gift from her grandmother for her eighth birthday and she had always treasured it.

What she really loved about the mirror, however, was how it presented her body. Of course, Mei-Xing knew it reflected her no differently than any other mirror, but something about the gold designs and cherubs framed her in a more perfect way.

She was tall for a Chinese woman, standing at 1.75 meters, with a strong body most women would be hard pressed to replicate. Her face was just as hard as her body, with small but full red lips and dark eyes that could look as intensely serious as they could sultry. Her skin was smooth and soft, but it was the angle of her cheeks that provided her with the prized sternness she was so proud of.

Assured that her face was clear of any blemishes she may need to take care of, she lifted a hand to cup her breasts. They were firm and well sized and Mei-Xing hummed in satisfaction. She then turned to the side to inspect her backside, likewise content at its shape and firmness, but then she frowned. Upon closer inspection, her abdominal muscles seemed less defined than normal, showing almost an imperceptible amount of paunch over her otherwise taut stomach.

We'll have to do something about that, wont we, Mei-Xing?

The last week hadn't left her much time for physical exercise, and she could now see the results of her sedentary lifestyle. It did not make her happy, but she knew once her ISLAND was successfully under way, she'd have time to work on it again. With one last squeeze of her behind, she nodded at her reflection and quietly padded her way toward her bed. Slipping in beneath her silk sheets, she nudged her Lens to deactivate the lights in the room and set her alarm to wake her in four hours.

She needed to be well rested. ISLAND departures were still a big deal for the citizens of each planet it visited, and even though the ship wouldn't be back for two years, and in that time any mistakes her crew may make well and forgotten; *she* would not forget them. She would take them to the grave – should such a day ever in fact arrive for Ship Master Mei-Xing Na.

ABOUT THE AUTHOR

Edward Crichton, a native Clevelander, lives in Chicago, Illinois with his wife, where he spends his time coming to grips with his newfound sports allegiances. A long time enthusiast of Science Fiction, Fantasy, History and everything in between, he spends his time reading, writing, and overusing his Xbox.

Until recently, Crichton had often hoped for a cat, but his wife decided to let him have a baby boy instead. Due in November of 2013, he and his wife could not be more excited.

His Sci-Fi epic *Starfarer: Rendezvous with Destiny*, was released in April of 2013, and the latest book in his *Praetorian* Series: *A Hunter and His Legion*, was released in September of 2013. Crichton hopes to spend a few months bonding with his wife and newborn child before getting back into writing, but he still hopes to release his next book by the summer of 2014.

Edward's website and blog can be found at:
sites.google.com/site/edcrichtonbooks

You can also Like/Comment on his Facebook page, follow him on Twitter @EdCrichton or Email him at EdCrichton85@gmail.com

Printed in Great Britain
by Amazon